THE LAST DAYS OF POMPEII

THE LAST DAYS OF POMPEII

An Historical Novel

Adapted by

S. FOWLER WRIGHT

FROM THE NOVEL BY
EDWARD BULWER-LYTTON

THE BORGO PRESS

MMXI

INTRODUCTION

EDWARD BULWER-LYTTON, by the general verdict of his contemporaries, was in the first rank of Victorian novelists, and *The Last Days of Pompeii* was considered to be his greatest work.

He had breadth and vigour of imagination, vivacity and originality of conception, and a fine sense of dramatic climax. He could construct a good story, and tell it well.

His defect, on which the critics of his own day were not silent, and which is more antipathetic to the literary standards of the succeeding century, was that his vocabulary was luxuriant as his imagination, and much less artistically controlled.

This defect, which was natural to the quality of his genius, was encouraged by the insistence of the libraries of his time that a novel must be of full three-volume length. Authors gave that which the trade required, and readers became expect in glancing rapidly over redundant matter, without resentment, and without prejudice to their appreciation of the quality of that which lay before and behind it.

It has been the aim of this redaction to adapt a great novel to the inclination of a later century, without detriment to its integrity. In this process, it has been considerably shortened, but to describe it as abridged would be to use a misleading term. No incident has been omitted: no angle of presentation has been obscured. Conversations are sometimes terser: diffuse reflections are sometimes curtailed, but only where mutilation of content was not involved.

Bulwer Lytton's strength was in the quality of his imagination: his weakness became most evident in the lyrics he wrote with such fatal facility. These have been retained, for they are pertinent to the narrative, and where excessive length has been reduced, they have not been mutilated by omission of stanzas, but reconstructed in such a way that the original thought and imagery remain entire.

It is hoped that this treatment will have adapted a great work of imagination to the fashion of a succeeding century, without obscuring—perhaps even more fully exposing—the genius which gave it birth.

It has been the redactor's aim that even one already familiar with the original should miss nothing, nor be aware of difference, either in manner or style.

BOOK ONE

1. Two Gentlemen of Pompeii

"Hallo, Diomed! Shall I see you at Glaucus' supper tonight?"

Diomed, a man of middle age and portly frame, paused at this greeting from one of shorter stature and fewer years, who wore his tunic in the loose effeminate folds which indicated the coxcomb as well as the gentleman of his time.

"Alas, no, dear Clodius! I am not invited. A scurvy trick from one whose table is said to be the best in Pompeii."

"Which is more than the truth. The meats may be good, but the wine is never enough for me."

"Well, there may be reason for that. Wine is dear, if it be of the quality which must be served by one of his wealth—or that which it is said to be. He may be poorer than you suppose."

"Then we must use our time while the sesterces last. With another year there will be another Glaucus to find."

"And besides, he is fond of the dice."

"He is fond of all pleasures. And while he is fond of giving suppers, we should be fond of him."

"So you should. But some evening you must sup with me, if you will. My reservoir has lampreys you might approve. And I would ask Pansa to meet you.

"I should be pleased. You need have no state for me! But the day wanes. I must hurry on to the baths. And you?"

"To the quæstor. I have business of state. And then to the Temple of Isis. *Vale!*"

Diomed bustled on, and Clodius strolled slowly in the opposite direction. "An ill-bred, ostentatious fellow," he thought. "Does he suppose we forget he is the son of a freedman, because we eat at his house? Were not wealthy plebeians sent from heaven for spendthrift nobles to win their money, and share their feasts?"

He strolled on to the Via Domitiana, now crowded with chariots and pedestrians, and exhibiting the gay and animated exuberance of life and motion which could still be seen in Naples in later days.

The bells of the cars, gliding rapidly past each other, jingled merrily in his ears, as he smiled and nodded to the occupants of those which were most elegant or fantastic, for in Pompeii no idler was better known.

"Hello, Clodius! How have you slept on your good fortune?" a young man in a chariot of most fastidious and graceful fashion cried in a pleasant musical voice.

His horses, driven by a charioteer at his side, were of the rarest Parthian breed, with slender limbs that seemed to disdain the ground, and yet became instantly motionless at a touch of their driver's hand. They stood as statue-still as though they were one of the breathing wonders of Praxiteles.

Their chariot's surface of bronze was wrought in the still exquisite workmanship of Greece, with reliefs of the Olympian Games.

Its owner wore no toga, for, at this period, the old patrician garment was ridiculed by the leaders of fashion, but his tunic glowed with the richest colour of Tyrian dye. Its buckles sparkled with emeralds. The chain of gold which fell from his neck was clasped by a serpent's head, from the mouth of which hung pendant a large signet ring of elaborate and most exquisite workmanship The loose sleeves of the tunic were fringed with gold, and its waist was confined in a girdle wrought in arabesque designs, which served in lieu of pockets for the reception of stylus and tablets, handkerchief and purse.

The young man himself was of that slender and beautiful symmetry from which the sculptors of Athens chose their models. His Grecian origin betrayed itself in his light but clustering locks, and the perfect harmony of his features.

"My dear Glaucus," Clodius replied, "I rejoice to see that your losses have affected you so lightly. Your face shines with happiness like a glory, as though inspired by Apollo. Anyone who observed us might think that you had been the winner, and I had lost."

"And shall we change our spirits because dull metal has left our hands? By Venus, no! While there are chaplets to crown our hair, and while the cithara sounds in unsated ears—while the blood in our veins is as lightsome as Lydia's smile, time itself is but the treasurer of our joys. You will remember that you are supping with me to-night?"

"Who will forget when Glaucus invites?"

"But where are you going now?"

"I should be for the baths, but I must wait for the opening hour."

"Well, I will go with you. The chariot can return." He stroked the nearer horse, which responded with a neigh of pleasure, and lifted ears. "So, my Phylias, it shall be a holiday for you today… Clodius, is he not beautiful?"

"Worthy of Phoebus…or of Glaucus," the noble parasite replied.

2. Of a Blind Flower Girl,
And of the Woman Whom Glaucus Loved

The two young men sauntered through the streets, talking idly of the matters that came to mind.

They were in the quarter which was bright with the gayest shops, having open interiors radiant with the gaudy yet harmonious colours of frescoes which varied continually in fancy and in design. They showed shelves of marble, bearing vases of wine and oil. They had purple awnings, covering seats which invited the weary to rest, and the indolent to lounge. Country girls were stationed at short intervals, offering baskets of blushing fruit and alluring flowers. Fountains cast up sparkling showers that moistened the dry heat of the summer air. The gay troupes that gathered round the more attractive shops were robed in bright colours, among which the Tyrian purple was most frequently seen. The slaves that passed at a quicker pace bore on their heads buckets of bronze, which had been cast in most graceful shapes. The whole scene was one of glowing and vivacious excitement, to which the Athenian spirit of Glaucus responded joyously.

"Talk no more of Rome," he said to Clodius. "Pleasure is too stately and ponderous in those mighty walls. Even in the Golden House of Nero—in the palace of Titus—there is a dullness of magnificence at which the eye aches and the spirit droops. But here we have brilliance of luxury without the lassitude of its pomp."

"That is why you make your summer retreat here?"

"Yes. I prefer it even to Baire. I grant its charm; but the pedants who resort there, and weigh out their pleasures by the drachm!"

"Yet you consort with the learned here, and your house is littered with Homer and Æschylus—with epic and drama."

"So I do. But these Romans mimic my Athenian ancestors in such a ponderous way. Even at the chase, there will be a slave carrying a Plato, so that they may not lose their time should the boar be lost; there will be some droning freedman reading Cicero's *De Offi-*

ciis even while the dancing girls sway before them with all the allurements of Persian art."

"Pleasure and study are matters which should not mix. Oh, my Clodius! It was only the other day that I paid a visit to Pliny. He was sitting writing in his summer house, while an unfortunate slave played on the tibia. And there was his nephew nodding his conceited little head in time to the music while he was reading Thucydides' account of the plague! The puppy saw nothing incongruous in mixing a love song with those loathsome details."

"Well, there isn't much difference."

"So I told him; but he was too much of a coxcomb to take the jest. He answered gravely that it was only the insensate ear that the music pleased, while the book elevated the heart! 'Ah!' wheezed the fat uncle, 'my boy is quite an Athenian, mixing the *utile* with the *dulce*.' O Minerva! How I laughed in my sleeve."

Though Clodius was secretly a little sore at these remarks on his countrymen, he affected to sympathize, partly because he was by nature a parasite, and partly because it was the fashion among the dissolute young Romans to affect contempt for the very birth which, in reality, made them so arrogant; it was the mode to imitate the Greeks, and yet to laugh at their own clumsy imitation...

Beneath the porticos of a light and peaceful temple where three streets met, a young girl stood, with a basket of flowers on her right arm, and a small three-stringed instrument of music in her left hand. The progress of the two friends would have been impeded by the crowd that had collected round her, even had their own inclination not been of the same kind.

"It is the blind Thessalian," Glaucus said. "She has a voice which it is always a pleasure to hear."

As he spoke, she began to sing, in a strain that was sweet and clear, and suited to the simplicity of the words she sang:

> "Buy, oh buy my flowers!
> For yours is a world of light,
> And nothing of these the blind girl sees
> Whose home is the House of Night.
> They are all for the night too gay.
> In your eyes they behold the day.
> Buy, oh buy my flowers!"

"A bunch of violets, sweet Nydia," said Glaucus, dropping a number of small coins into the basket, as he chose his flowers.

The blind girl started at the sound of the Athenian's voice. She blushed vividly, as she answered in a low voice: "So you are returned," and then, as though speaking to herself, and unconscious of those around who were also selecting flowers and dropping sesterces into the basket: "Glaucus has returned."

"Yes," he said. "I have been here no more than a few days. I shall want you for my garden again. I should have been sending for you. No one else shall arrange my flowers."

She smiled joyfully at the words, but did not answer, while he withdrew from the crowd.

"She is a client of yours, this child?"

"Yes. I like her voice. And she is from Thessaly."

"The witches' country."

"Oh, I find every woman a witch! And in Pompeii every beardless face—"

"And here is one of the fairest coming—old Diomed's daughter. The wealthy Julia!"

As Clodius spoke, a young lady, with a veil over her face, and followed by two female slaves, approached them, on her way to the baths.

"Fair Julia," Clodius said, "we salute thee"—but, as she half-raised her veil, exposing a bold Roman profile, cheeks over whose natural olive art had laid a fairer and softer rose, and the brightness of full dark eyes, it was upon Glaucus that they were turned.

"So you are back!" she said. "And has Glaucus forgotten his friends of a year ago?"

"Julia," he replied, in a tone as light as her own, "Zeus does not allow even Lethe to flow continuously, and Aphrodite knows no Lethe at all."

"Fair words you have never lacked."

"Who would, when the object is so fair?"

Julia turned to Clodius. "We shall hope to see you both before long at my father's villa."

"The day on which we visit you will be marked with a white stone."

The girl dropped her veil, and went on without further words, but her last glance had been for the Athenian, one of affected timidity, which had suggested both tenderness and reproach.

Glaucus said: "She is surely a handsome girl."

"You would have said that a year ago in a warmer tone."

"Yes. I was dazzled by what I took for a gem. I know better now."

"Nay, all women are alike at heart. Choose a fair face and a handsome dower, and what more can you hope to have?"

It was still somewhat too soon for the baths to open, and the two friends turned toward the nearby beach, and the sight of the open sea—a sea which, at that time of year, on that delicious coast, seemed to have renounced its prerogative of terror, as its quiet surface reflected the loveliness of the deep-blue sky.

Pompeii at this period was a miniature of the civilisation to which it belonged. Its shining bay was crowded with merchant vessels, gilded pleasure galleys, and the fishing-boats of the town.

In its minute but glittering shops, its tiny palaces, its baths, its forum, its theatre, its arena, its energy and corruption, its refinement and vice, it was a model of the great world-empire of its time, destined to be destroyed in a way which would avert destruction, and become a revelation to later ages.

The two friends seated themselves on a little rock that rose from the level sand. They were silent for a time, subdued to reverie by the sunlit scene.

Clodius shaded his eyes from the burning sun, while his mind wandered into calculations of the gains of the previous week, from which he was roused at last by the voice of Glaucus: "Tell me, Clodius, have you ever been in love?"

"Yes. Many times."

"It is said that those who have loved often have loved never. They have worshipped counterfeit gods."

"Well, there are worse things than they."

"I don't say you are wrong. I adore the shadow of Eros. But I adore himself more."

"Will you tell me you are really in love? Do you neglect your meals? Do you avoid the theatre? Do you write elegies? Certainly, if you are, you dissemble well!"

"Oh, I have not gone that far! Rather I say with Tibellus:

'He whom love rules, where'er his path may be,
Walks safe and sacred.'

"But I am not in love. Though I might be if its object were in my reach."

"Then I can guess who that object is. It is Diomed's daughter. But she adores you, and makes no effort to hide it. And I say again that she is handsome and rich. She will bind her husband's doorposts with golden fillets."

"But I am not for sale. She is handsome, I grant you that. I do not say, at one time—had she not been a freedman's daughter—but no—her manners are not those which a maid should have—and her mind has no culture but that of which pleasure will make pursuit."

"You are ungenerous. Who then is the virgin that you approve?"

"If I knew that! But I will tell you the tale. I was in Naples some months ago, and I entered the temple of Minerva to offer prayers—both for myself and for the city on which Pallas no longer smiles. It was silent and empty. I imagined myself to be quite alone; but I was startled in the midst of the darkness by a deep sigh."

"I looked round, and a girl was behind me. She had raised her veil, as her prayer required. Our eyes met. Never have I seen a more lovely face. It was sad, but with an expression that increased its beauty. I saw tears in her eyes, and I guessed that she was an Athenian also, and that grief for our fallen city was in her heart as it was in mine, as we had prayed together."

"I asked her gently: 'Are you not also of Athens?'"

"She half drew her veil as I spoke, but answered softly: 'I was born in Naples; but it was my parents' home.'"

"I felt as though I had known her long as we stood together in that temple of the goddess of our fallen city. I followed her as she went out, and was about to ask her where she dwelt, when a youth, who, from his appearance, may have been her brother, met her on the temple steps. She turned to me to say farewell, and, as she did so, we were separated by the crowd."

"She would not leave my mind, and I should have sought her on the next day, but that I had letters recalling me to Athens in haste, for a suit had been brought by my relatives which attacked my inheritance. When that litigation was happily ended, I returned to Naples, and had enquiries made through the whole city, but they were vain, and I came to Pompeii to distract my mind by its pleasures from vain regret."

Clodius did not reply, for there came a sound of steps which approached with the dignified slowness natural to him who made them, and they looked round upon a man, the Egyptian Arbaces, whom they both knew.

He was scarcely in his fortieth year, tall and thin, but of a nervous sinewy frame.

He had the dark skin of his race, and his features, which were otherwise somewhat of a Grecian cast, were distinguished by an aquiline nose, and hard, visible bones which denied the graceful contours that were often retained, even through years of manhood, by the ancient Greeks. His eyes were large and black, and a deep, thoughtful, half melancholy calm was in their commanding gaze.

Furtively, both the young men made with their fingers the sign which protects from the evil eye.

"It must indeed be a beautiful scene," the Egyptian said, "which draws the gay Clodius, or Glaucus the all-admired, from the crowded thoroughfares of the city."

"Are the attractions of Nature so much the less?" Glaucus asked.

"To the dissipated, yes."

"An austere reply, but scarcely a wise one. 'Pleasure delights in contrasts.'

"So say the young philosophers of the Garden, mistaking lassitude for meditation. They think, because they are sated with others, that they know the delights of loneliness. When Cynthia revealed herself to Endymion, it was after a day passed, not among the feverish haunts of man, but in the stillness of mountain ways."

"It is a beautiful simile," Glaucus answered, "but most unjust. You forget that youth is of a tireless vitality. As for myself, I have never experienced satiety for a single moment."

The Egyptian received this reply in silence, though with a smile of such blighting coldness that even the unimaginative Clodius felt an inward chill.

But after a pause, Arbaces added, in a softer and more melancholy voice than he had used before: "Yet, Glaucus, you may do well to enjoy the hour that is yours. We are both wanderers from our native lands and our fathers' ashes. What is there left for you but pleasures, or for me but regret?"

"He is a strange man," Glaucus said, as he passed on. "But cold though he may seem, there are other orgies than those of Osiris in his gloomy mansion, or scandal lies, as it often will."

3. An Evening Revel

Heaven had given to Glaucus every blessing but one: it had given him beauty, health, fortune, genius, illustrious descent, a heart of fire, a mind of poetry; but it had denied him the heritage of freedom. He was born in Athens, the subject of Rome. Succeeding early to an ample inheritance, he had indulged that inclination for travel so natural to the young, and had drunk deep of the intoxicating draught of pleasure amidst the gorgeous luxuries of the imperial court.

He was an Alcibiades without ambition. He was what a man of imagination, youth, fortune, and talents readily becomes when you deprive him of the incentive of ambition. His retreat in Pompeii—alas! the colours are faded now, the walls stripped of their paintings!—its main beauty, its elaborate finish of grace and ornament, is gone; yet when first given once more to the day, what eulogies, what wonder, did its minute and glowing decorations create—its paintings—its mosaics! Passionately enamoured of poetry and the drama, which recalled the wit and heroism of his race, that fairy mansion was adorned with representations of Æschylus and Homer. And antiquaries, who resolve taste to a trade, have turned the patron to the professor, and still (though the error is now acknowledged) they style in custom, as they first named in mistake, the disburied house of the Athenian Glaucus *"The House of the Dramatic Poet."*

The patrician residence of the period was usually entered by a small passage, to a hall sometimes with (but more frequently without) the ornament of columns; around three sides of this hall were doors communicating with several bedchambers, the best of these being usually appropriated to country visitors. At the extremity of the hall, on either side to the right and left, if the house were large, there were two small recesses, generally devoted to the ladies of the mansion; and in the centre of the tessellated pavement of the hall was invariably a square shallow reservoir for rainwater, which was admitted by an aperture in the roof above, which could be covered at will by an awning. Near this impluvium, which had a peculiar sanctity in ancient eyes, were sometimes (but at Pompeii more rarely than at Rome) placed images of the household gods—the hospitable hearth, often mentioned by the Roman poets, and consecrated to the Lares, was at Pompeii almost invariably formed by a movable brazier; while in some corner, often the most ostentatious place, was deposited a huge wooden chest, ornamented and strengthened by bands of bronze or iron, and secured by strong hooks upon a stone pedestal so firmly as to defy the attempts of any robber to detach it from its position.

In this atrium, clients and visitors of inferior rank were usually received. In the wealthier houses, a slave peculiarly devoted to the service of the hall was invariably retained, whose rank among his fellow-slaves was high and important. The reservoir in the centre must have been rather a dangerous ornament, but the centre of the hall was like the grass-plot of a college, and interdicted to the passers to and fro, who found ample space in the margin. Opposite the entrance, at the other end of the hall, was an apartment in which the pavement was usually adorned with rich mosaics, and the walls covered with elaborate paintings. Here were kept the records of the family, or those of any public office that had been filled by the owner; on one side was often a dining-room, or triclinium; on the other, a cabinet, containing whatever curiosities were deemed most rare and costly; and invariably there was a small passage for the slaves to cross to the further parts of the house without passing the apartments thus mentioned.

These rooms all opened on to a square or oblong colonnade. If the house were small, its boundary ceased with this colonnade; in which case its centre, however diminutive, was ordinarily appropriated to the purpose of a garden, and adorned with vases of flowers, placed upon pedestals, while under the colonnade, to the right and left, were doors, admitting to bedrooms, to a second triclinium, or eating-room (for the Romans generally appropriated two rooms at least to that purpose, one for summer, and one for winter—or perhaps, one for ordinary, the other for festive, occasions); and if the owner had literary proclivities, a cabinet, dignified by the name of library—for a very small room was sufficient to contain the few rolls of papyrus which would be deemed a notable collection of books.

At the end of the colonnade was generally the kitchen. Supposing the house were large, it did not end with the colonnade, and the centre thereof was not in that case a garden, but might be adorned with a fountain or basin for fish; and at its end was generally another eating room, on either side of which were bedrooms, and, perhaps, a picture-saloon. These apartments communicated again with a square or oblong space, usually adorned on three sides with a colonnade, though usually longer than the first. This was the proper vivarium, or garden, being commonly adorned with a fountain, or statues, and a profusion of gay flowers; at its extreme end was the gardener's house; on either side, beneath the colonnade, were sometimes, if the size of the family required it, additional rooms.

At Pompeii, a second or third story was rarely of importance, being built only above a small part of the house, and containing rooms for the slaves, differing in this respect from the more magnificent edifices of Rome, which generally contained the principal eating-room on the second floor. The rooms themselves were ordinarily of small size, but the suite seen at once from the entrance must have had a very imposing effect: the hall richly paved and painted, the graceful colonnade, and (if the house extended farther) the opposite banquet-room and the garden, which closed the view with some gushing fount or marble statue.

Where the garden was small, its wall was frequently tinted to deceive the eye as to its extent, imitating a far perspective—a metricious delusion which the graceful pedantry of Pliny himself adopted, with a complacent pride in its ingenuity.

The house of Glaucus was at once one of the smallest and one of the most adorned and finished, of all the private mansions of Pompeii. It was entered by a long and narrow vestibule, on the floor of which the image of a dog in mosaic, with the well-known *Cave canem*—"Beware the dog." On either side was a chamber of some size; for the interior part of the house not being large enough to contain the two great divisions of private and public apartments, these two rooms were set apart for the reception of visitors who neither by rank nor familiarity were entitled to admission to the penetralia of the mansion.

Beyond the vestibule was an atrium, that, when first discovered, was rich in paintings, which can now be seen in the Neapolitan Museum, depicting the partings of Achilles and Briseis. Who does not acknowledge the force, the vigour, and beauty, employed in delineating the forms and faces of Achilles and the immortal slave!

On one side of the atrium, a small staircase admitted to the apartment for the slaves on the second floor; there also were two or three small bedrooms, the walls of which portrayed the rape of Europa, the battle of the Amazons, and other subjects of traditional art.

Beyond was a reception room, across which, at either end, hung rich draperies of Tyrian purple. On the walls were depicted a poet reading his verses to his friends; and in the pavement was inserted a small and most exquisite mosaic, typical of the instructions given by the director of the stage to his comedians.

Beyond this saloon was the colonnade; and here the mansion ended. From each of the seven columns that adorned this court hung festoons of garlands; the centre, supplying the place of a garden, bloomed with the rarest flowers placed in vases of white marble, that were supported on pedestals. At the left hand of this small garden was a diminutive fane, resembling one of those small chapels placed at the side of roads in Catholic countries, and dedicated to the Penates; before it stood a bronze tripod: to the left of the colonnade were two small cubicula, or bedrooms; to the right was the triclinium, in which the guests were now assembled.

This charming apartment opened upon the fragrant garden. Round the table of citron wood, highly polished and delicately wrought with silver arabesques, were placed three couches, which were still more common at Pompeii than the semicircular seat that had grown lately into fashion at Rome; and on these couches of bronze, studded with richer metals, were laid thick quiltings covered with elaborate embroidery, and yielding luxuriously. It was here, on the evening of the day with which we are dealing, that Glaucus received his friends.

"Well, I must own," said the ædile Pansa, "that your house, though scarcely larger than a case for one's fibulæ, is a gem of its kind. How beautifully painted is that parting of Achilles and Briseis!—what a style!—what heads!"

"Praise from Pansa is indeed valuable on such subjects," said Clodius gravely. "Why, the paintings on *his* walls! Ah! There is, indeed, the hand of a Zeuxis!"

"You flatter me, my Clodius; indeed you do," replied the ædile, who was celebrated through Pompeii for having the worst paintings in the world; for he was patriotic, and patronized none but Pompeians. "You flatter me; but there is something pretty—Ædepol, yes—in the colours, to say nothing of the design;—and then for the kitchen, my friends—ah! That was all my fancy."

"What is the design?" said Glaucus. "I have not seen your kitchen, though I have often witnessed the excellence of its cheer."

"A cook, my Athenian—a cook sacrificing the trophies of his skill on the altar of Vesta, with a beautiful muræna (taken from the life) on a spit at a distance—there is some invention there!"

At that instant the slaves appeared, bearing a tray covered with the first preparative initia of the feast. Amidst delicious figs, fresh herbs strewed with snow, anchovies, and eggs, were ranged small cups of diluted wine sparingly mixed with honey. At these were placed on the table, young slaves bore round to each of the five guests the silver basin of perfumed water, and napkins edged with a purple fringe. But the ædile ostentatiously drew forth his own napkin, which was not, indeed, of so fine a linen, but in which the fringe was twice as broad, and wiped his hands with the parade of a man who felt he was calling for admiration.

A splendid *nappu* that of yours," said Clodius. "Why, the fringe is as broad as a girdle!"

"A trifle, my Clodius! A trifle! They tell me this stripe is the latest fashion at Rome; but Glaucus attends to these things more than I."

"Be propitious, O Bacchus!" said Glaucus, inclining reverentially to a beautiful image of the god placed in the centre of the table, at the corners of which stood the Lares and the salt-holders. The guests followed the prayer, and then, sprinkling the wine on the table, they performed the wonted libation.

This over, the convivialists reclined themselves on the couches, and the business of the hour commenced.

"May this cup be my last!" said the young Sallust, as the table, cleared of its first stimulants, was now loaded with the substantial part of the entertainment, and the ministering slave poured forth to him a brimming cyathus—"May this cup be my last, but it is the best wine I have drunk at Pompeii."

"Bring hither the amphora," said Glaucus, "and read its date and its character."

The slave hastened to inform the party that the scroll fastened to the cork betokened its birth from Chios, and its age a ripe fifty years.

"How deliciously the snow has cooled it!" said Pansa.

"It is just enough."

"It is like the experience of a man who has cooled his pleasures sufficiently to give them a double zest," exclaimed Sallust.

"It is like a woman's 'No'," added Glaucus: "it denies to increase desire."

"When is our next wild-beast fight?" said Clodius to Pansa.

"It stands fixed for the ninth Ides of August," answered Pansa: "on the day after the Vulcanalia—we must have a lovely young lion for the occasion."

"Whom shall we get for him to eat?" asked Clodius. "Alas! There is a great scarcity of criminals. You must positively find some innocent or other to condemn to the lion, Pansa!"

"Indeed I have thought very seriously about it of late," replied the ædile gravely. "It was a most infamous law which forbade us to send our own slaves to the beasts. Not to do what we like with our own! It is an infringement on the rights of property."

"It was different in republican days," sighed Sallust.

"And this pretended mercy to the slaves is a disappointment to the whole people. How they love to see a good tough battle between a man and a lion! And it may all be lost (if the gods don't send us a good criminal soon) through this cursed law!"

"What can be worse policy," said Clodius, sententiously, "than to interfere with the amusements of the people?"

"Well, thank Jupiter and the Fates! We have no Nero at present," said Sallust.

"He was a tyrant indeed; he shut up our amphitheatre for ten years."

"I wonder it did not create a rebellion," said Sallust.

"It very nearly did," returned Pansa, with his mouth full of wild boar.

Here the conversation was interrupted for a moment by a flourish of flutes, and two slaves entered with a single dish.

"Ah! What delicacy hast thou in store for us now, my Glaucus?" cried young Sallust, with sparkling eyes.

Sallust was only twenty-four, but he had no pleasure in life except eating—perhaps he had exhausted all the others, yet he had some talent and a disposition of some amiability.

"I know its face, by Pollux!" cried Pansa. "It is an Ambracian kid."

"I had hoped," said Glaucus, in a melancholy tone, "to have procured you some oysters from Britain; but the winds that were so cruel to Cæsar have forbid us those delicacies."

"Are they in truth so delicious?" asked Lepidus, loosening to a yet more luxurious ease his ungirdled tunic.

"Why, in truth, I suspect it is the distance that gives the flavour; they want the richness of the Brundusium oyster. But at some, no supper is complete without them."

"The poor Britons! There is some good in them after all," said Sallust. "They produce an oyster!"

"I wish they could produce us a gladiator," said the ædile, whose provident mind was musing over the wants of the amphitheatre.

"By Pallas!" cried Glaucus, as his favourite slave crowned his streaming locks with a new chaplet, "I love these wild spectacles well enough when beasts fight beasts; but when a man, one with bones and blood like ours, is coldly put on the arena, and torn limb from limb, the interest is too horrid. The yells of the populace seem to me more dire than the voices of the Furies chasing Orestes. I rejoice that there is so little chance of that bloody exhibition for our next show!"

The ædile shrugged his shoulders. The young Sallust, who was thought the best-natured man in Pompeii, stared in surprise. The graceful Lepidus, who rarely spoke for fear of disturbing his features, ejaculated "Hercule!" The parasite Clodius muttered "Ædepol!" and the sixth banqueter, who was the *umbra* of Clodius, and whose duty it was to echo his richer friend, when he could not praise him—the parasite of a parasite—muttered also "Ædepol!"

"Well, you are used to these spectacles; we Greeks are more merciful."

"The kid is excellent," said Sallust. The slave, whose duty it was to carve, and who valued himself on his science, had just performed that office on the kid to the sound of music, his knife keeping time, beginning with a low tenor and accomplishing the arduous feat amidst a magnificent diapason.

"Your cook is, of course, from Sicily?" Pansa asked.

"Yes, of Syracuse."

"I will play you for him," said Clodius. "We will have a game between the courses."

"Better that sort of game, certainly, than a beast fight; but I cannot stake my Sicilian—you have nothing so precious to stake me in return."

"My Phillida—my beautiful dancing-girl!"

"I never buy woman," said the Greek, carelessly rearranging his chaplet.

The musicians, stationed in the portico without, who had commenced their office with the kid, now directed the melody into a softer and gayer strain; they chanted that song of Horace beginning "*Persicos odi*," impossible to translate, which they imagined applicable, to a feast that, effeminate as it may seem, was simple enough for the gorgeous revelry of the time.

"Ah, good old Horace!" said Sallust, compassionately; "He sang well of feasts and girls, but not like our modern poets."

"The immortal Fulvius, for instance," said Clodius.

"Ah, Fulvius, the immortal!" said the umbra.

"And Spuræna; and Caius Mutius, who wrote three epics in a year—could Horace do that, or Virgil either?" said Lepidus. "Those old poets all fell into the mistake of copying sculpture instead of painting. Simplicity and repose—that was their notion; but we moderns have fire, and passion, and energy—we never sleep, we imitate the colours of painting, its life, and its action. Immortal Fulvius!"

"By the way," said Sallust, "have you seen the new ode by Spuræna, in honour of our Egyptian Isis? It is magnificent—the true religious fervour."

"Isis seems a favourite divinity at Pompeii," said Glaucus.

"Yes!" said Pansa, "she is exceedingly in repute just at this moment; her statue has been uttering the most remarkable oracles. I am not superstitious, but I must confess that she has more than once assisted me materially in my magistracy with her advice. Her priests are so pious, too! None of your gay proud ministers of Jupiter and Fortune; they walk barefoot, eat no meat, and pass the greater part of the night in solitary devotion!"

"An example to our other priesthoods, indeed!—Jupiter's temple wants reforming sadly," said Lepidus, who was a great reformer for all but himself.

"They say that Arbaces the Egyptian has imparted some most solemn mysteries to the priests of Isis," observed Sallust.

"He boasts his descent from the race of Rameses, and declares that in his family the secrets of remotest antiquity are preserved."

"He certainly possesses the gift of the evil eye," said Clodius. "If ever I come upon that Medusa front without the previous charm, I am sure to lose a favourite horse, or throw the canes nine times running."

"The last would be indeed a miracle!" said Sallust gravely.

"How mean you, Sallust?" returned the gamester, with a flushed brow.

"I mean, what you would leave me if I played often with you; and that is—nothing."

Clodius answered only by a smile of disdain.

"If Arbaces were not so rich," said Pansa, with a stately air, "I should stretch my authority a little, and inquire into the truth of the report which calls him an astrologer and a sorcerer. Agrippa, when ædile of Rome, banished all such terrible citizens. But it is the duty of an ædile to protect the rich!"

"What think you of this new sect, which I am told has even a few proselytes in Pompeii, these followers of the Hebrew God—Christus?"

"Oh, mere speculative visionaries," said Clodius: "they have not a single gentleman amongst them; their proselytes are poor, insignificant, ignorant people!"

"Who ought, however, to be crucified for their blasphemy," said Pansa, with vehemence: "They deny Venus and Jove! Nazarene is but another name for atheist. Let me catch them, that's all!"

The second course was gone—the feasters fell back on their couches—there was a pause while they listened to the soft voices of the South, and the music of the Arcadian reed. Glaucus was the most rapt and least inclined to break the silence, but Clodius began already to think that they had wasted time.

"*Bene vobis!* My Glaucus," said he, quaffing a draught to each letter of the Greek's name, with the ease of the practised drinker. "Will you not be avenged on your ill-fortune of yesterday?"

"As you will," said Glaucus.

"The dice in summer, and I an ædile!" said Pansa, magisterially; "it is against all law."

"Not in your presence, grave Pansa," returned Clodius, rattling the dice in a long box; "your presence restrains all license; it is not the thing, but the excess of the thing, that hurts."

"What wisdom!" muttered the umbra.

"Well, I will look another way," said the ædile.

"Not yet, good Pansa: let us wait till we have supped," said Glaucus.

Clodius reluctantly yielded, concealing his vexation with a yawn.

"He gapes to devour the gold," whispered Lepidus to Sallust, in a quotation from the *Aulularia* of Plautus.

"Ah! How well I know these polypi, who hold all they touch," answered Sallust, in the same tone, and out of the same play.

The third course, consisting of a variety of fruits, pistachio nuts, sweetmeats, tarts, and confectionary tortured into a thousand fantastic and airy shapes, was now placed upon the table; and the attendants also set there the wine (which had hitherto been handed round to the guests) in large jugs of glass, each bearing upon it the schedule of its age and quality.

"Taste this Lesbian, my Pansa," said Sallust; "it is excellent."

"It is not very old," said Glaucus, "but it has been made precocious, like ourselves, by being put to the fire—the wine to the flames of Vulcan—we to those of his wife—to whose honour I pour this cup."

"It is delicate," said Pansa, "but there is perhaps the least particle too much of rosin in its flavour."

"What a beautiful cup!" cried Clodius, taking up one of transparent crystal, the handles of which were wrought with gems, and twisted in the shape of serpents, the favourite fashion at Pompeii.

"This ring," said Glaucus, taking a costly jewel from the first joint of his finger, and hanging it on the handle, "gives it a richer show, and renders it less unworthy of thy acceptance, my Clodius, on whom may the gods bestow health and fortune, long and oft to crown it to the brim!"

"You are too generous, Glaucus," said the gamester, handing the cup to his slave; "but your love gives it a double value."

"This cup to the Graces!" said Pansa, and he thrice emptied his calix. The guests followed his example.

"We have appointed no director to the feast," cried Sallust.

"Let us throw for him, then," said Clodius, rattling the dice-box.

"Nay," cried Glaucus, "no cold and trite director for us, no dictator of the banquet, no *rex convivii*. Have not the Romans sworn never to obey a king? Shall we be less free than your ancestors? Ho! musicians, let us have the song I composed the other night: it has a verse on this subject, 'The Bacchic hymn of the Hours'."

The musicians struck their instruments to a wild Ionic air, while the youngest voices in the band chanted the song that Glaucus had composed to delight his guests.

They applauded loudly. When the poet is your host, his verses are sure to charm.

"Thoroughly Greek," said Lepidus; "the wildness, force, and energy of that tongue it is impossible to imitate in Roman poetry."

"It is, indeed, a great contrast," said Clodius, ironically at heart, though not in appearance, "to the old-fashioned and tame simplicity of that ode of Horace which we heard before. The air is beautifully Ionic; the words put me in mind of a toast. Companions, I give you the beautiful Ione."

"Ione!—the name is Greek," said Glaucus, in a soft voice. "I drink the health with delight. But who is Ione?"

"Ah! You have but just come to Pompeii, or you would deserve ostracism for your ignorance," said Lepidus; "not to know Ione, is not to know the chief charm of our city."

"She is of the most rare beauty," said Pansa; "and what a voice!"

"She can feed only on nightingales' tongues," said Clodius.

"Nightingales' tongues!—beautiful thought!" sighed the umbra.

"Enlighten me, I beseech you," said Glaucus.

"Know then—" began Lepidus.

"Let me speak," cried Clodius; "you drawl out your words as if you spoke tortoises."

"And you speak stones," muttered the coxcomb to himself as he fell back disdainfully on his couch.

"Know then, my Glaucus," said Clodius, "that Ione is a stranger who has but lately come to Pompeii. She sings like Sappho, and her songs are her own composing; and as for the tibia, and the cithara, and the lyre, I know not in which she most outdoes the Muses. Her beauty is most dazzling. Her house is perfect; such taste—such gems—such bronzes! She is rich, and generous as she is rich."

"Her lovers, of course," said Glaucus, "take care that she does not starve; and money lightly won is always lavishly spent."

"Her lovers—ah, there is the enigma! Ione has but one vice—she is chaste. She has all Pompeii at her feet, and she has no lovers: she will not even marry."

"No lovers!" echoed Glaucus.

"No; she has the soul of Vesta, with the girdle of Venus."

"What refined expressions!" said the umbra.

"A miracle!" cried Glaucus. "Can we not see her?"

"I will take you there this evening," said Clodius; "meantime—" added he, once more rattling the dice.

"I am yours!" said the complaisant Glaucus. "Pansa, turn your face!"

Lepidus and Sallust played at odd-and-even, and the umbra looked on, while Glaucus and Clodius became gradually absorbed in the chances of the dice.

"By Pollux!" cried Glaucus, "this is the second time I have thrown the caniculæ" (the lowest throw).

"Now Venus befriend me!" said Clodius, rattling the box for several moments. "O Alma Venus—it is Venus herself!" as he threw the highest cast, named from that goddess.

"Venus is ungrateful to me," said Glaucus, gaily; "I have always sacrificed on her altar."

"He who plays with Clodius," whispered Lepidus, "will soon, like Plautus's Curculio, put his pallium for the stakes."

"Poor Glaucus!—he is as blind as Fortune herself," replied Sallust, in the same tone.

"I will play no more," said Glaucus; "I have lost thirty sestertia."

"I am sorry—" began Clodius.

"Amiable man!" groaned the umbra.

"Not at all!" exclaimed Glaucus: "The pleasure I take in your gain compensates the pain of my loss."

The conversation now grew general and animated, the wine circulated more freely; and Ione once more became the subject of eulogy to the guests of Glaucus.

"Instead of outwatching the stars, let us visit one at whose beauty the stars grow pale," said Lepidus.

Clodius, who saw no chance of renewing the dice, seconded the proposal; and Glaucus, though he civilly pressed his guests to continue the banquet, could not but let them see that his curiosity had been excited by the praises of Ione: they therefore resolved to adjourn (all, at least, but Pansa and the umbra) to the house of the fair Greek. They drank, therefore, to the health of Glaucus and of Titus—they performed their last libation—they resumed their slippers—they descended the stairs—passed the illuminated atrium—and, walking unbitten over the fierce dog painted on the threshold, found themselves beneath the light of the moon just risen, in the lively and still crowded streets of Pompeii.

They passed the jewellers' quarter, sparkling with lights, caught and reflected by the gems displayed in the shops, and arrived at last at the door of Ione. The vestibule blazed with rows of lamps; curtains of embroidered purple hung on either aperture of the tablinum, whose walls and mosaic pavement glowed with the richest colours of the artist; and under the portico which surrounded the odorous voridarium they found Ione, already surrounded by adoring and applauding guests.

"Did you say she was Athenian?" whispered Glaucus, ere he passed into the peristyle.

"No, she is from Neapolis."

"Neapolis!" echoed Glaucus; and at that moment the group, dividing on either side, gave to his view that bright, that nymph-like beauty, which he had found impossible to forget.

4. A Priest of Isis

When Arbaces parted from Glaucus and his companion, and approached to the more crowded part of the bay, he paused and gazed upon that animated scene with folded arms, and a bitter smile upon his dark features.

"Gulls, dupes, fools, that ye are!" muttered he to himself; "in business or pleasure, trade or religion, cheated equally by the passions that you should rule! How could I loathe you, if I did not hate! Greek or Roman, it is from us, from the lore of Egypt, that you have stolen the fires that give you souls. Knowledge—poetry—laws— arts—even your barbarous science of war—filched from us as a slave may filch the fragments of an ended feast!

"And now the mushroom herd have entered their masters' land! The pyramids look down no more on the race of Rameses. The eagle exults over the serpent of the Nile. Our masters are you now? You are not mine! My wisdom controls you still, though with fetters that none can see. So long as craft masters force—so long as religion has but one cave from which oracles can delude mankind—the wise will possess the earth.

"Even from your vices Arbaces distils his pleasures—pleasures secret and inexhaustible, of which your enervated minds cannot conceive or dream. Fools of ambition and avarice! Your thirsts for vulgar office and all the mummeries of servile power provoke my laughter and my scorn. For my power extends as widely as the credulity of mankind. Thebes may fall and Egypt be a derided name, but the subjects of Arbaces are subjects still."

He went to the town, his tall figure always conspicuous in the crowd, and entered the small but graceful temple of Isis, whose worship was still popular and esteemed, in competition with Grecian gods.

The temple had only recently been built, to replace that which had been destroyed by earthquake sixteen years before, and its oracles, which, if not of divine origin, were of profound human wisdom, had become the popular fashion of the day. Clothed in mysterious language, they were not of a definite meaning, adroitly adapted to the circumstances of those who sought them, and contrasting notably with the generalities of the rival temples.

Arbaces passed through a varied crowd, in which the commercial element predominated, gathered before the numerous altars which rose in the open court. For in the walls of the cellar, elevated on seven steps of Parian marble, and ornamented by the sacred pomegranate of Isis, were niches containing statues of many deities which were admitted to grace the court of the Egyptian goddess. The many-titled Bacchus, the Cyprian Aphrodite, the dog-headed Anubis, the ox-god Apis, mingled with Egyptian idols of uncouth form and forgotten names; while on an oblong pedestal which occupied the interior building, the statue of Isis herself stood beside that of the silent and mystic Orus.

But the worship of the Egyptian goddess was no longer performed with the forms and ceremonies which were rightly hers. The mongrel nations of the Southern Europe of this modern time, with a mixture of arrogance and ignorance, confounded the religious ceremonies of all climes and ages. The temple of Isis in Pompeii was served by Greek and Roman priests who were ignorant of the language and customs of her ancient votaries.

Now a beast had been slaughtered upon her altar, and the crowd watched in anxious expectancy as two sacrificial priests, with naked shoulders and loose white garments girded around them, drew back from the sacrifice they had prepared, and the superior flamen bent to inspect the victim's entrails, and to read the auguries which they revealed.

Arbaces paused at the side of the merchant Diomed to make a whispered enquiry as to the purpose of the sacrifice.

"We are merchants," he replied, "who ask the fate of our vessels, which sail for Alexandria tomorrow."

"You do well. Isis is the goddess of agriculture, but she is the patron of commerce also."

He turned his head to the east, as though absorbed in silent prayer.

Meanwhile, at the foot of the steps, a priest began to play a solemn air on a long wind-instrument. Another priest, halfway up, held a white wand in one hand, and the votive wreath in the other. At the summit, two others stood, one holding a palm branch, and the other a slender sheaf of corn, while a stately ibis—the bird sacred to the Egyptian worship—looked mutely down from the wall upon the site, or stalked beside the altar at the foot of the steps.

The watchful crowd sank into a deathlike silence as another priest, naked save for a cincture round his waist, rushed forward and, dancing with wild gestures, implored the goddess to answer the merchant's prayer.

As he ceased, exhausted, there was a low murmur from the body of the statue: the head moved, the lips parted, in a hollow voice came these mystic words:

> "There are waves like chargers their manes that throw;
> There are graves that wait on the rocks below;
> The high winds rise, and the dark clouds lour,
> But blest are your barques in the fearful hour."

"That is good," Diomed commented. "There are often storms at this season, but our vessels will go safely through them."

"Lauded be the goddess!" his companions echoed. "Her predictions are never equivocal."

The chief priest, raising his hand for silence, which the worship of Isis enjoined beyond the capacity of the lively Pompeians, poured a libation upon the altar, and concluded the ceremony with a short prayer.

The crowd dispersed, but Arbaces remained by the railing, and, as the temple cleared, one of the priests approached and saluted him with an appearance of friendly familiarity.

The man had a countenance of repulsive ugliness, but his animal frame was well-fitted to execute whatever impulse might be born in an evil mind. The broad chest, the nervous hands, and the lean gaunt arms, bared to above the elbow, indicated a form capable alike of great active exertion or passive endurance. But the shaven skull was almost apelike in its low and narrow confirmations, the eyes, dark and small; rolled in a muddy and yellow orbit: the skin was puckered into many deep and intricate wrinkles: the nose, short and coarse, was distended at the nostrils like a satyr's, and the thick but pallid lips, the livid and motley hues of the parchment skin, completed a countenance which would cause terror to many, and distrust and repugnance to all who saw it.

"Calenus," Arbaces said, "you have improved the voice of the statue by following my suggestion, and the verses were excellent. It is always best to predict good fortune, unless it be absolutely impossible."

"I thought I had done well, for there are always storms at this time of year. And if they should go to the bottom, where can a mariner rest better than there?"

"Right, my Calenus. If only Apæcides would take a lesson from you! It was of him that I wished to speak. Can you admit me to one of your less sacred apartments?"

The priest led the way to one of a number of small chambers which surrounded the open gate. He seated his guest at a small table on which eggs and fruit, cold meats, and vases of excellent wine were spread. The entrance was closed by no more than a curtain drawn across it. Those who spoke there should speak low, or avoid secret matters. They spoke low.

"Thou knowest," Arbaces said, "that it has ever been my maxim to attach myself to the young. From their flexible unformed minds I carve out my best tools. Of the men I make disciples or servants; of the women—"

"Mistresses," Calenus concluded, a livid grin distorting his ungainly features.

"Yes. I do not disguise that woman is the great appetite of my soul. As you feed the victim that you will slaughter, I rear the votaries of my pleasure, which is in the soft unconscious progress from innocence to desire. It is thus that I defy satiety, from the young hearts of my victims sustaining the freshness of my own sensation. But to the subject on which I came. You know that, by the death of their parents before they left Athens, I became the legal guardian of Ione and Apæcides. I have not neglected my trust.

"To Apæcides, I taught the solemn faith of Isis. Docile and mild, he responded readily. I unfolded to him those divine allegories which expound her religion. I excited in one who is peculiarly alive to religious fervours the enthusiasm that imagination begets on faith. Finally, I placed him among you.

"So you did. But we find that, in teaching faith, you let wisdom go. He is horror-stricken now that he is no longer duped. Our secret and speaking statues dismay and revolt him.

"I have heard that he is frequenting the company of those of the new faith, who are hostile to all our gods."

"That is what I feared," Arbaces answered, "from some reproachful words which I had from him yesterday. I must continue my lessons. He must understand that there are two stages of sanctity. The first is Faith: the second Knowledge. The first is for the vulgar: the second for the sage."

"I have never experienced the first, nor I think have you," Calenus said.

"You mistake," Arbaces answered gravely. "I believe to this day Nature has a sanctity I cannot resist if I would. I believe—and from that belief has been revealed—but we wander. It is of Ione I would speak. I have told thee that, till I saw her, I knew not the love of which my nature is capable. She shall be more than mistress to me. She shall be bride and queen."

"I have heard that she is a second Helen."

"Yes. She has a beauty that Greece has not excelled. But she has more than that. She has a spirit worthy to match with mine. She has a genius beyond the nature of women. Keen—dazzling—bold. She can comprehend the most subtle argument. And she has freedom of mind. She can stand alone. She is all I have imagined—all I have sought in women. She must be mine. For her, I have a double passion. I wish to enjoy beauty of spirit as well as form."

"But, as yet, she is not yours?"

"Not entirely. She loves me, but as a friend—with her mind only. She fancies in me the paltry virtues which I have the profounder virtue to scorn. She is proud and ambitious. She gathers crowds to her feasts. Her voice enchants, and her poetry subdues them. She would be considered the successor of Erinna."

"Or, perhaps of Sappho?"

"But Sappho without love!"

"I have encouraged her in this bold attempt—in this indulgence of vanity, this pursuit of pleasure. I have sought to enervate her mind. To surround her with lovers—hollow, vain, frivolous, whom she must despise, so that she may become aware of the want of love.

"Then, in those soft intervals when lassitude succeeds excitement, I can interest her mind—attract her passion—possess her heart. It is not youth, nor gaiety, nor beauty, which will be sufficient to win her. Her imagination must be conquered, and the life of Arbaces has been a continuous triumph, over the imagination of others."

"And you have feared no rivals? The gallants of Italy are skilled in the art to please."

"No. Her Greek soul despises the barbarian Roman."

"But thou art not a Greek."

"Egypt is the mother of Athens. I have taught her this, and in my blood she venerates the older dynasties of the earth. But I will admit that I am not entirely at ease. She has been silent and melancholy. It may be the beginning of love—or its want. In either case, my operations should not delay. That is why I have come to you."

5. Progress of Love

The beautiful room in which Glaucus had received his guests on the previous evening was now bright with morning sunlight, which entered through a row of casements along the upper side of the wall, and through the door, which stood open, revealing the small garden, adapted for indolence rather than exercise, and fragrant with many blooms.

It shone on tessellated pavement and glowing walls, of which every panel held a painting of exquisite art. Eyes that wandered from the representation of Leda and Tyndarus (still in the museum of Naples) would be drawn to that of Eros leaning on Aphrodite's knee or to Ariadne sleeping unconscious of the perfidy of her lover.

But there was a joy in the heart of Glaucus which was more than the sunlight gave. "I have seen her!" he said aloud. "I have found her again! I have heard her sing—the songs of glory and Greece. I have spoken to her. Like the Cyprian sculptor, I have breathed life into what was no more than my own dream."

A shadow darkened the floor of the sunlit entrance, and a young girl entered. She was dressed simply, in a long white tunic. She carried a basket of flowers, and a bronze water vase. Her features were not exactly beautiful, and were set into an expression of melancholy unusual to one so young. But they were soft and gentle, and their look of tranquil endurance had banished the smiles, but not the sweetness from her lips. There was nothing visibly wrong with her eyes. Their expression was clear and serene, but the caution and timidity with which she moved was an indication of their defect. She had been blind from her birth.

"They tell me Glaucus is here. May I come in?"

"Ah, Nydia, so you have come? I felt sure you would."

"Glaucus knew how kind he has always been to me who am poor and blind."

"Who could be otherwise?" It was the tone of a compassionate brother.

She sighed. "You have not been long back?"

"It is the sixth day."

"And you are well? But who could be otherwise who can see the sun?"

"You are well also? But how you have grown! By next year you will be considering what answer to give your lovers."

She blushed at the remark, but she frowned also. "I have brought you flowers," she said. "They are poor, but fresh."

"I will wear no other garland but those you make."

"Are the flowers in the garden thriving?"

"They are wonderful—as though the Lares themselves had tended them while I was away."

"I am pleased at that, for I came to water them as often as I could."

"How can I thank you? I had no thought that I had left so watchful a memory."

"I have not been for the last nine days. I have been away."

Her voice was embarrassed, and the hand with which she raised the watering vase trembled, as she turned to attend to them again.

"Poor girl!" he thought, as his eyes followed her. "It is a hard doom to see neither earth, nor stars, nor your fellowmen."

His mind went back to Ione, and was interrupted again by the entrance of Clodius. It was significant that, while he had confided to him, on the previous day, the secret of his first meeting with her, he was now averse from even mentioning her name.

He had seen her, bright, unsullied, in the midst of the gayest and most profligate gallants of Pompeii, reversing, it seemed, their very nature, and the fable of Circe—converting animals into men. And she had become more than a beautiful girl, once seen, and passionately remembered. She was now the mistress—the divinity of his soul.

He felt only resentment when Clodius praised her, and answered so coldly that the Roman imagined that his fancy had been disappointed at this second interview. He was the more content to think it, because he hoped that Glaucus would wed the daughter of the wealthy Diomed, and so augment the store of gold which was now flowing so readily into his own coffers. Finding that conversation flagged, he soon left, and a few minutes later Glaucus went out, with a purpose of seeking Ione at her home.

He passed Nydia on the threshold, who knew his step easily. She said: "You go out early?"

"It is the invitation of Campania's skies."

"Oh, that I could see them," she murmured, so low that he passed on without hearing. When he had gone, she took the staff with which she had become dexterous to guide her steps, and went back to her home.

She soon turned from the more gaudy streets, and entered a quarter of the town but little loved by the decorous and the sober. But from the low and rude evidences of vice around her she was saved by her misfortune. And at that hour the streets were quiet and silent, nor was her youthful ear shocked by the sounds which too often broke along the obscene and obscure haunts she patiently and sadly traversed.

She knocked at the back-door of a tavern; it opened, and a rude voice bade her give an account of the sesterces. Ere she could reply, another voice, less vulgarly accented, said:

"Never mind that, Burbo. Her voice will be wanted again soon at our rich friend's revels; and he pays, as thou knowest, pretty high for his nightingales' tongues."

"Oh, I hope not—I trust not," cried Nydia, trembling; "I will beg from sunrise to sunset, but do not send me there."

"And why not?" asked the same voice.

"Because—because I am not—because it is hateful, because—"

"Because it is unfit for a slave in the house of Burbo?" returned the voice ironically, with a coarse laugh.

The Thessalian put down the flowers, and wept silently.

Meanwhile, Glaucus sought the house of the beautiful Neapolitan. He found Ione sitting amidst her attendants, who were at work around her. Her harp stood at her side, for Ione herself was unusually idle, perhaps unusually thoughtful, that day. He thought her even more beautiful by the morning light, and in her simple robe, than amidst the blazing lamps, and decorated with the costly jewels of the previous evening; and not the less so from the blush that greeted his approach.

Accustomed to flatter, flattery died upon his lips when he addressed her. They spoke of Greece; this was a theme on which Ione loved rather to listen than to converse; it was a theme on which the Greek could have been eloquent forever. He described to her the silver olive groves that yet clad the banks of Ilyssus, and the temples, already despoiled of half their glories—but how beautiful in decay! He looked back on the melancholy city of Harmodius the free, and Pericles the magnificent, from the height of that distant memory, which mellowed into one hazy light all the ruder and darker shades.

And Ione listened to him, absorbed and mute; dearer were those accents, and those descriptions, than all the prodigal adulation of her numberless adorers. Was it a sin to love her countryman? She loved Athens in him—the gods of her race, the land of her dreams, spoke to her in his voice.

From that time they saw each other daily. At the cool of the evening they made excursions on the placid sea. At night they met again in Ione's portico and hall. Their love was sudden, but it was strong; it filled all the sources of their life. Heart—brain—sense—imagination, all were its ministers and priests.

One evening, the fifth after their first meeting at Pompeii, they were returning, with a small party of chosen friends, from an excursion round the bay. As the rest of the party conversed with each other, Glaucus lay at the feet of Ione silently, until she broke the pause between them.

"My poor brother," said she, sighing, "how once he would have enjoyed this hour!"

"Your brother!" said Glaucus; "I have not seen him. Was it he for whose companionship you left me at our first meeting?"

"Yes."

"And is he here?"

"Yes."

"At Pompeii! But not constantly with you?"

"He has other duties," Ione answered sadly; "he is a priest of Isis."

"So young, too; and that priesthood, in its laws at least, so severe!" said the warm-hearted Greek, in surprise and pity. "What could have been his inducement?"

"He was always enthusiastic and fervent in religious devotion; and the eloquence of an Egyptian—our friend and guardian—kindled in him the pious desire to consecrate his life to the most mystic of our deities. Perhaps, in the intensity of his zeal, he found in the severity of that priesthood its peculiar attraction."

"And he does not repent his choice? He is happy?"

Ione sighed deeply, and lowered her veil over her eyes.

"I wish," said she, after a pause, "that he had not been so hasty. Perhaps, like all who expect too much, he is revolted too easily!"

"Then he is not happy in his new condition? And this Egyptian, was he a priest himself? Was he interested in recruits to the sacred band?"

"No. His main interest was in our happiness. He thought he promoted that of my brother. We were left orphans, and Arbaces sought to supply the place of our parent. You must know him. He loves genius."

"I know him already; at least, we speak when we meet. But for your praise I would not seek to know more than I do now."

"Yet he is kind, and wise, and gentle," answered Ione.

"He is happy to have thy praise!"

"His calm, his coldness,' she said, evasively pursuing the subject, "are perhaps but the exhaustion of past sufferings; as yonder mountain" (and she pointed to Vesuvius), "which we see dark and tranquil in the distance, once nursed the fires forever quenched."

They both gazed on the mountain as Ione said these words; the rest of the sky was bathed in rosy and tender hues, but over that grey summit, rising amidst the woods and vineyards that then climbed halfway up the ascent, there hung a black and ominous cloud, the single frown of the landscape. A sudden and unaccountable gloom came over each as they gazed; and in that sympathy which love had already taught them, and which bade them, in the slightest shadows of emotion, the faintest presentiment of evil, turn for refuge to each other, their gaze at the same moment left the mountain, and, full of unimaginable tenderness, met. What need had they of words to say they loved?

6. The Fowler Resets His Snares

During the early days of the meetings of the Grecian lovers, Arbaces had been little at the house of Ione, being preoccupied by her brother's attitude, both pride and selfishness being aroused and alarmed at the sudden change which had come over the spirit of the youth. He feared lest he himself should lose a docile pupil, and Isis an enthusiastic servant. Apæcides had ceased to seek or consult him. He was rarely to be found; he fled when he perceived him at a distance. Arbaces was one of those haughty and powerful spirits accustomed to master others; he chafed at the notion that one once his own should elude his grasp.

It was in this mood that he passed through a thick grove in the city, which lay between his house and that of Ione, in his way to the latter; and there, leaning against a tree, and gazing on the ground, he came unawares on the young priest of Isis.

"Apæcides!" said he, laying his hand affectionately on the young man's shoulder.

The priest started, and his first instinct seemed to be that of flight. "My son, what has chanced that you desire to shun me?"

Apæcides remained silent and sullen, looking down on the earth, as his lips quivered, and his breast heaved with emotion.

"Speak to me, my friend," continued the Egyptian. "Speak. Something burdens thy spirit. What hast thou to reveal?"

"To thee—nothing."

"And why is it to me thou art thus unconfidential?"

"Because thou hast been my enemy."

"Let us confer," said Arbaces, in a low voice; and drawing the reluctant arm of the priest in his own, he led him to one of the seats which were scattered within the grove. They sat down—and in their gloomy forms there was something congenial to the shade and solitude of the place.

Apæcides was in the spring of his years, yet he seemed to have exhausted even more of life than the Egyptian; his delicate and regular features were wan and colourless; his eyes were hollow, and shone with a brilliant and feverish glare; his frame bowed prematurely, and in his hands, which were small to effeminacy, the blue and swollen veins indicated the lassitude and weakness of the relaxed fibres. You saw in his face a strong resemblance to Ione, but the expression was altogether different. In her, enthusiasm was visible, but it seemed always suppressed and restrained. In Apæcides the whole aspect betokened the fervour and passion of his temperament, and the intellectual portion of his nature seemed, by the wild fire of the eyes, the great breadth of the temples when compared with the height of the brow, the trembling restlessness of the lips, to be swayed and tyrannized over by the imaginative and ideal. Fancy, with the sister, had stopped short at the golden goal of poetry; with the brother, less happy and restrained, it had wandered into visions more intangible and unembodied; and the faculties which gave genius to the one threatened madness to the other.

"You say I have been your enemy," said Arbaces. "I know the cause of that unjust accusation: I have placed you amidst the priests of Isis—you are revolted at their trickeries and imposture—you think that I too have deceived—the purity of your mind is offended—you imagine that I am one of the deceitful—"

"You knew the jugglings of that impious craft," answered Apæcides; "why did you disguise them from me? When you excited my desire to devote myself to the office whose garb I bear, you spoke to me of a holy life—you have given me for companions an ignorant and sensual herd, who have no knowledge but that of the grossest frauds—you spoke to me of men sacrificing the earthlier pleasures to the sublime cultivation of virtue—you place me amongst men reeking with all the filthiness of vice—you spoke to me of the friends, the enlighteners of our common kind—I see but cheats and deluders! Oh! It was basely done! Young as I was, the sunny pleasures of earth before me, I resigned all with happiness and exultation, in the thought that I resigned them for the abstruse mysteries of diviner wisdom, for the companionship of gods—for the revelations of Heaven—and now—now—"

Convulsive sobs checked the priest's voice; he covered his face with his hands, and large tears forced themselves through the wasted fingers.

"What I promised to thee, that will I give, my friend, my pupil: these have been but trials to thy virtue—it comes forth the brighter for thy novitiate—think no more of those dull cheats—assort no more with those menials of the goddess—you are worthy to enter into the penetralia. I henceforth will be your priest, your guide, and you who now curse my friendship shall live to bless it."

The young man lifted up his head and gazed with a vacant and wondering stare upon the Egyptian.

"Listen to me," continued Arbaces, in an earnest and solemn voice, casting first his searching eyes round to see that they were still alone. "From Egypt came all the knowledge of the world; from Egypt came those early and mysterious tribes which (long before the hordes of Romulus swept over the plains of Italy, and in the eternal cycle of events drove back civilisation into barbarism and darkness) possessed all the arts of wisdom and the graces of intellectual life. From Egypt came the rites and grandeur of that solemn Cære, whose inhabitants taught their iron vanquishers of Rome all that they yet know which is elevated in religion and sublime in worship. And how deemest thou, young man, that that dread Egypt, the mother of countless nations, achieved her greatness, and soared to her cloud-capped eminence of wisdom?—it was the result of a profound and holy policy. Your modern nations owe their greatness to Egypt—Egypt her greatness to her priests. Rapt in themselves, courting a sway over the nobler part of man, his soul and his belief, those ancient ministers of God were inspired with the grandest thought that ever exalted mortals. From the revolutions of the stars, from the seasons of the earth, from the round and unvarying circle of human destinies, they devised an august allegory; they made it gross and palpable to the vulgar by the signs of gods and goddesses, and that which in reality was government they named Religion. Isis is a fable—start not!—for that for which Isis is a type is a reality, an immortal being; Isis is nothing! Nature, which she represents, is the mother of all things—dark, ancient, inscrutable, save to the gifted few. 'None among mortals hath ever lifted up my veil', so saith the Isis that you adore; but to the wise that veil *hath* been removed, and we have stood face to face with the solemn loveliness of Nature. The priests then were the benefactors, the civilizers of mankind; true, they were also cheats, impostors if you will. But think you, young man, that if they had not deceived their kind they could have served them? The innocent and servile vulgar must be blinded to attain to their proper good; they would not believe a maxim—they revere an oracle. The Emperor of Rome sways the vast and various tribes of earth, and harmonizes its conflicting and disunited elements; thence comes peace, order, law, the blessings of life. Think you it is the man, the emperor, that thus sways?—no, it is the pomp, the awe, the majesty that surround him—*these* are his impostors, his delusions; our oracles and our divinations, our rites and our ceremonies, are the means of *our* sovereignty and the engines of our power. They are the same means to the same end, the welfare and harmony of mankind. You listen to me rapt and intent—the light begins to dawn upon you."

Apæcides remained silent, but the changes rapidly passing over his speaking countenance betrayed the effect produced upon him by the words of the Egyptian—words made tenfold more eloquent by the voice, the aspect, and the manner of the man.

"While, then," resumed Arbaces, "our fathers of the Nile thus achieved the first elements by which chaos is destroyed, namely, the obedience and reverence of the multitude for the few, they drew from their majestic and starred meditation that wisdom which was no delusion; they invented the codes and regularities of law—the arts and glories of existence. They asked belief; they returned the gift by civilisation. Were not their very cheats a virtue? Trust me, whosoever in yon far heavens of a diviner and more beneficent nature looks down upon our world, smiles approvingly on the wisdom which has worked such ends.

"But you wish me to apply these generalities to yourself; I hasten to obey the wish. The altars of the goddess of our ancient faith must be served, and served too by others than the stolid and soulless things that are but as pegs and hooks whereon to hang the fillet and the robe. Remember two sayings of Sextus the Pythagorean, sayings borrowed from the lore of Egypt. The first is 'Speak not of God to the multitude;' the second is: 'The man worthy of God is a god among men.' As Genius gave to the ministers of Egypt worship, that empire in later ages so fearfully decayed, thus by Genius only can its dominion be restored. I saw in you, Apæcides, a pupil worthy of my lessons—a minister worthy of the great ends which may yet be wrought: your energy, your talents, your purity of faith, your earnestness of enthusiasm, all fitted you for that calling which demands so imperiously high and ardent qualities: I fanned, therefore, your sacred desires; I stimulated you to the step you have taken. But you blame me that I did not reveal to you the little souls and the juggling tricks of your companions. Had I done so, Apæcides, I had defeated my own objects; your noble nature would have at once revolted, and Isis would have lost her priest.

"I placed you, therefore, without preparation, in the temple; I left you suddenly to discover and to be sickened by all those mummeries which dazzle the herd. I desired that you should perceive how those engines are moved by which the fountain that refreshes the world casts its waters in the air. It was the trial ordained of old to all our priests. They who accustom themselves to the impostures of the vulgar are left to practise them—for those, like you, whose higher natures demand higher pursuits religion opens more godlike secrets. I am pleased to find in you the character I had expected. You have taken the vows; you cannot recede. Advance—I will be your guide."

"And what wilt thou teach me, O singular and fearful man? New cheats—new—"

"No—I have thrown thee into the abyss of disbelief; I will lead thee now to the eminence of faith. Thou hast seen the false types: thou shalt learn now the realities they represent. There is no shadow, Apæcides, without its substance. Come to me this night. Your hand."

Impressed, excited, bewildered by the language of the Egyptian, Apæcides gave him his hand, and master and pupil parted.

It was true that for Apæcides there was no retreat. He had taken the vows of celibacy; he had devoted himself to a life that at present seemed to possess all the austerities of fanaticism, without any of the consolations of belief. It was natural that he should yet cling to a yearning desire to reconcile himself to an irrevocable career. The powerful and profound mind of the Egyptian still claimed an empire over his young imagination; excited him with vague conjecture, and kept him alternately vibrating between hope and fear.

Meanwhile, Arbaces pursued his slow and stately way to the house of Ione. As he entered the tablinum, he heard a voice from the porticoes of the peristyle beyond, which, musical as it was, sounded displeasingly on his ear—it was the voice of the young and beautiful Glaucus, and for the first time an involuntary thrill of jealousy shot through the breast of the Egyptian.

On entering the peristyle, he found Glaucus seated by the side of Ione. The fountain in the odorous garden cast up its silver spray, and kept a delicious coolness in the midst of the sultry noon. The handmaids, almost invariably attendant on Ione, sat at a little distance; by the feet of Glaucus lay the lyre on which he had been playing one of the Lesbian airs. The scene—the group before Arbaces, was stamped by that peculiar and refined ideality which we still, not erroneously, imagine to be the distinction of the ancients—the marble columns, the vases of flowers, the statue, white and tranquil, closing every vista; and above all, the two living forms, from which, a sculptor might have caught either inspiration or despair.

Arbaces, pausing for a moment, gazed on the pair with a brow from which all the usual stern serenity had fled; he recovered himself by an effort, and slowly approached them, but with a step so soft and echoless, that even the attendants heard him not, much less Ione and her lover.

"And yet," said Glaucus, "it is only before we love that we imagine that our poets have truly described the passion; the instant the sun rises, all the stars that had shone in his absence vanish into air. The poets exist only in the night of the heart; they are nothing to us when we feel the full glory of the god."

"A gentle and most glowing image, noble Glaucus."

Both started, and recognised behind the seat of Ione the cold and sarcastic face of the Egyptian.

"You are a sudden guest," said Glaucus, rising, with a forced smile.

"So ought all to be who know they are welcome," returned Arbaces, seating himself, and motioning to Glaucus to do the same.

"I am glad," said Ione, "to see you at length together; for you are suited to each other, and you are formed to be friends."

"Give me back some fifteen years of life," replied the Egyptian, "before you can place me on an equality with Glaucus. Happy should I be to receive his friendship, but what can I give him in return? Can I make to him the same confidences that he would repose in me—of banquets and garlands—of Parthian steeds, and the chances of the dice? These pleasures suit his age, his nature, his career; they are not for mine."

So saying, the artful Egyptian looked down and sighed; but he cast a glance towards Ione, to see how she received these insinuations of the pursuits of her visitor. Her countenance did not satisfy him. Glaucus, slightly colouring, hastened gaily to reply. Nor was he, perhaps, without the wish in his turn to disconcert and abash the Egyptian.

"You are right, wise Arbaces," said he; "we can esteem each other, but we cannot be friends. My banquets lack the secret salt, which, according to rumour, gives such zest to your own. And, by Hercules! When I have reached your age, if I, like you, may think it wise to pursue the pleasures of manhood, I shall be doubtless as sarcastic on the gallantries of youth."

The Egyptian raised his eyes to Glaucus with a sudden and piercing glance.

"I do not understand you," said he, coldly; "but it is the custom to consider that wit lies in obscurity." He turned from Glaucus as he spoke, with a scarcely perceptible sneer of contempt, and after a moment's pause addressed himself to Ione. "I have not, beautiful Ione," said he, "been fortunate enough to find you within doors the last two or three times that I have visited your vestibule."

"The smoothness of the sea has tempted me much from home," she replied, with a little embarrassment.

The embarrassment did not escape Arbaces; but, without seeming to heed it, he replied with a smile: "You know the old poet says that 'Women should keep within doors, and there converse'."

"The poet was a cynic," said Glaucus, "and hated women."

"He spake according to the custom of his country, and that country is your boasted Greece."

"To different periods, different customs. Had our forefathers known Ione, they had made a different law."

"Did you learn these pretty gallantries at Rome?" said Arbaces, with ill-suppressed emotion.

"One certainly would not go for gallantries to Egypt," retorted Glaucus, playing carelessly with his chain.

"Come, come," said Ione, hastening to interrupt a conversation which she saw, to her great distress, was so little likely to cement the intimacy she had desired to effect between her friends, "Arbaces must not be so hard upon his poor pupil. An orphan, and without a mother's care, I may be to blame for the independent and almost masculine liberty of life I have chosen; yet is it not greater than the Roman women are accustomed to—it is not greater than the Grecian ought to be. Is it only among men that freedom and virtue are to be deemed united? Why should the slavery that destroys you be considered the only method to preserve us?"

Arbaces was silent, for it was not his part to condemn the sentiment she expressed, and, after a short and embarrassed conversation, Glaucus took his leave.

When he was gone, Arbaces, drawing his seat nearer to the fair Neapolitan, said in those bland and subdued tones in which he knew so well how to veil the mingled art and fierceness of his character: "Think not, my sweet pupil, if so I may call you, that I wish to shackle the liberty you adorn while you assume; but which, if not greater, as you rightly observe, than that possessed by the Roman women, must at least be accompanied by great circumspection, when arrogated by one unmarried. Continue to draw the crowds of the gay, the brilliant, the wise themselves to your feet—continue to charm them with the conversation of an Apasia, the music of an Erinna—but reflect, at least, on those censorious tongues which can so easily blight the tender reputation of a maiden; and while you provoke admiration, give, I beseech you, no victory to envy."

"What mean you, Arbaces?" said Ione, in an alarmed and trembling voice. "I know you are my friend, that you desire only my honour and my welfare. What is it you would say?"

"Your friend—ah, how sincerely! May I speak then as a friend, without reserve and without offence?"

"I beseech you do so."

"This young profligate, this Glaucus, how didst thou know him? Has thou seen him often?" And, as Arbaces spoke, he fixed his gaze steadfastly upon her, as if he sought to penetrate into her soul.

Recoiling before that gaze, with a strange fear which she could not explain, the Neapolitan answered with confusion and hesitation: "He was brought to my house as a countryman of my father's, and I may say of mine. I have known him only recently; but why these questions?"

"Forgive me," said Arbaces, "I thought you might have known him longer. Base insinuator that he is!"

"Why that term?"

"It matters not: let me not rouse your indignation against one who does not deserve so grave an honour."

"I implore you to speak plainly."

"So I will. You know his pursuits, his companions, his habits: the revel and the dice make his occupations—and, amongst the associates of vice, how can he dream of virtue?"

"Still you speak riddles."

"Well, then, know, my Ione, that it was but yesterday that he boasted openly—yes, in the public baths, of your love to him. He said it amused him to take advantage of it. I will do him justice, he praised your beauty. Who could deny it? But he laughed scornfully when Clodius asked him if he loved you enough for marriage, and when he purposed to adorn his door-posts with flowers?"

"Impossible! How heard you this base slander?"

"Nay, would you have me relate to you all the comments of the insolent coxcombs with which the story has circled through the town? Be assured that I myself disbelieved at first, and that I have been painfully convinced by several ear-witnesses of the truth of what I have reluctantly told thee."

Ione sank back, and her face was whiter than the pillar against which she leaned for support.

"I own it vexed—it irritated me, to hear your name thus lightly pitched from lip to lip, like some mere dancing-girl's fame. I hastened this morning to seek and warn you. I found Glaucus here. I was stung from my self-possession. I could not conceal my feelings; nay, I was uncourteous in thy presence. Canst thou forgive thy friend?"

Ione placed her hand in his, but replied not.

"Think no more of this," said he, "but let it be a warning voice, to tell thee how much prudence thy lot requires. It cannot hurt thee, for a moment; for a gay thing like he is could never be honoured by even a serious thought from Ione. These insults only wound when they come from one we love."

So cunningly had the Egyptian appealed to Ione's ruling foible—so dexterously had be applied the poisoned dart to her pride, that he fancied he had arrested what he hoped, from the shortness of the time she had known Glaucus, was but an incipient fancy; and, hastening to change the subject, he now led her to talk of her brother. Their conversation did not last long. He left her, resolved not again to trust so much to absence, but to visit—to watch her—every day.

But no sooner had his shadow glided from her presence than woman's pride—her sex's dissimulation—deserted his intended victim, and she burst into passionate tears.

7. The Baths of Pompeii

When Glaucus left Ione, he felt as if he trod upon air. In the interview with which he had just been blessed, he had for the first time gathered from her distinctly that his love was not unwelcome to, and would not be unrewarded by her. This hope filled him with a rapture for which heaven and earth seemed too narrow to afford a vent. Unconscious of the enemy he had left behind, he passed through the gay streets, repeating to himself, in the wantonness of joy, the music of the soft air to which she had listened with such intentness; and now he entered the Street of Fortune, with its raised footpath—its houses painted without, and the doors admitting the view of the glowing frescoes within. Each end of the street was adorned with a triumphal arch: and as Glaucus now came before the Temple of Fortune, the jutting portico of that beautiful fane (which is supposed to have been built by one of the family of Cicero, perhaps by the orator himself) imparted a dignified and venerable feature to a scene otherwise more brilliant than lofty in its character.

That temple was one of the most graceful specimens of Roman architecture. It was raised on a somewhat lofty podium; and between two flights of steps ascending to a platform stood the altar of the goddess. From this platform another flight of broad stairs led to the portico, from the height of whose fluted columns hung festoons of the richest flowers. On either side the extremities of the temple were placed statues of Grecian workmanship; and at a little distance rose the triumphant arch crowned with an equestrian statue of Caligula, which was flanked by trophies of bronze. In the space before the temple a lively throng were assembled—some seated on benches and discussing the politics of the empire, some conversing on the approaching spectacle of the amphitheatre. One knot of young men were lauding a new beauty, another discussing the merits of the last play; a third group, more stricken in age, were speculating on the chance of the trade with Alexandria, and amidst these were many merchants in Eastern costume, whose loose and peculiar robes, painted and gemmed slippers, and composed and serious countenances, formed a striking contrast to the tuniced forms and animated gestures of the Italians.

Sauntering through the crowd, Glaucus soon found himself amidst a group of his merry, dissipated friends.

"Ah!" said Sallust, "it is a lustrum since I saw you."

"And how have you spent the lustrum? What new dishes have you discovered?"

"I have been scientific, and have made some experiments in the feeding of lampreys; I confess I despair of bringing them to the perfection which our Roman ancestors attained."

"Miserable man! And why?"

"Because, it is no longer lawful to give them a slave to eat. I am very often tempted to make away with a very fat butler whom I possess, and pop him slyly into a reservoir. He would give the fish a most oleaginous flavour! But slaves are not slaves nowadays, and have no sympathy with their masters' interest—or Davus would destroy himself to oblige me!"

"What news from Rome?" asked Lepidus as he languidly joined the group.

"The emperor has been giving a splendid supper to the senators," answered Sallust.

"He is a good creature," said Lepidus; "he never sends a man away without granting his request."

"Perhaps he would let me kill a slave for my reservoir?" returned Sallust, eagerly.

"Not unlikely," said Glaucus; "for he who grants a favour to one Roman, must always do it at the expense of another."

"Ah, Glaucus! How are you? Gay as ever!" said Clodius, joining the group.

"Are you come to sacrifice to Fortune?" asked Sallust.

"I sacrifice to her every night," returned the gamester. "I do not doubt it. No man has made more victims!"

"By Hercules, a biting speech!" cried Glaucus, laughing.

"The dog's letter is never out of your mouth, Sallust," said Clodius, angrily; "you are always snarling."

"I may well have the dog's letter in my mouth, since, whenever I play with you, I have the dog's throw in my hand," returned Sallust.

"Hist!" said Glaucus, taking a rose from the flower-girl, who stood beside.

"The rose is a token of silence," replied Sallust; "but I love only to see it at the supper-table."

"Talking of that, Diomed gives a grand feast next week," said Sallust: "are you invited, Glaucus?"

"Yes, I received an invitation this morning."

"And I, too," said Sallust, drawing a square piece of papyrus form his girdle: "I see that he asks us an hour earlier than usual: an earnest of something sumptuous."

"Oh! He is as rich as Crœsus," said Clodius, "and his bill of fare is as long as an epic."

"Well, let us to the baths," said Glaucus: "this is the time when all the world is there; and Fulvius, whom you admire so much, is going to read us his last ode."

The young men assented readily to the proposal, and they strolled to the baths.

Although the public baths were instituted rather for the poorer citizens than the wealthy (who had baths in their own houses), yet, to the crowds of all ranks who resorted to them, it was a favourite place for conversation, and for that indolent lounging so dear to a gay and thoughtless people.

Our party entered by the principal porch in the Street of Fortune. At the wing of the portico sat the keeper of the baths, with his two boxes before him, one for the money he received, the other for the tickets he dispensed. Round the walls of the portico were seats crowded with persons of all ranks; while others, as the regimen of the physicians prescribed, were walking briskly, stopping every now and then to gaze on the innumerable notices of shows, games, sales, exhibitions, which were painted or inscribed upon the walls. The general subject of conversation was, however, the spectacle announced in the amphitheatre; and each newcomer was fastened upon by a group eager to know if Pompeii had been so fortunate as to produce some monstrous criminal, some happy case of sacrilege or of murder, which would allow the ædiles to provide a man for the jaws of the lion: all other more common exhibitions seemed dull and tame, when compared with the possibility of this fortunate occurrence.

"For my part," said a jolly-looking goldsmith, "I think the Emperor, if he be as good as they say, might have sent us a Jew."

"Why not take one of the new sect of Nazarenes?" said a philosopher. "I am not cruel, but an atheist, one who denies Jupiter himself, deserves no mercy."

"I care not how many gods a man likes to believe in," said the goldsmith; "but to deny all is something monstrous."

"Yet I fancy," said Glaucus, "that these people are not absolutely atheists. I am told that they believe in a God—nay, in a future state."

"Quite a mistake, my dear Glaucus," said the philosopher. "I have conferred with them—they laughed in my face when I talked of Pluto and Hades."

"O ye gods!" exclaimed the goldsmith, in horror; "are there any of these wretches in Pompeii?"

"I know there are a few: but they meet so privately that it is impossible to discover who they are."

As Glaucus turned away, a sculptor, who was a great enthusiast in his art, looked after him admiringly.

"Ah!" said he, "if we could get *him* on the arena—there would be a model for you! What limbs! What a head! He ought to have been a gladiator! A subject—a subject—worthy of our art! Why don't they give him to the lion?"

Meanwhile Fulvius, the Roman poet whom his contemporaries declared immortal, came eagerly up to Glaucus: "Oh, my Athenian, you have come to hear my ode! That is indeed an honour; you, a Greek—to whom the very language of common life is poetry. How I thank you! It is but a trifle; but if I secure your approbation, perhaps I may get an introduction to Titus. Oh, Glaucus! A poet without a label; the wine may be good, but nobody will laud it! And what says Pythagoras?—'Frankincense to the gods, but praise to man.' A patron then, is the poet's priest; he procures the incense, and obtains him his believers."

"But all Pompeii is your patron, and every portico an altar in your praise."

"Ah, the poor Pompeians are very civil—they love to honour merit. But they are only the inhabitants of a petty town—*spero meliora!* Shall we within?"

"Certainly; we lose time till we hear your poem."

At this instant there was a rush of some twenty persons from the baths into the portico; and a slave stationed at the door of a small corridor now admitted the poet, Glaucus, Clodius, and a troop of the bard's other friends, into the passage.

They entered a somewhat spacious chamber, which served for the purpose of the apodyterium where the bathers prepared themselves for their luxurious ablutions. The vaulted ceiling was raised from a cornice, glowingly coloured with motley and grotesque paintings; the ceiling itself was panelled in white compartments bordered with rich crimson; the unsullied-and shining floor was paved with white mosaics, and along the walls were ranged benches for the accommodation of the loiterers. This chamber did not possess the numerous and spacious windows which Vitruvius attributes to his more magnificent *frigidarium*. The Pompeians, as all the Southern Italians, were fond of banishing the light of their sultry skies, and combined in their voluptuous associations the idea of luxury with darkness. Two windows of glass alone admitted the soft and shaded ray; and the compartment in which one of these casements was placed was adorned with a large relief of the destruction of the Titans.

In this apartment Fulvius seated himself with a magisterial air, and his audience, gathering round him, encouraged him to commence his recital.

The poet drew forth from his vest a roll of papyrus, and, after hemming three times, as much to command silence as to clear his voice, he began his ode.

By the plaudits he received, it was doubtless worthy of his fame; and Glaucus was the only listener who did not find it excel the best of Horace.

The poem concluded, those who took only the cold bath began to undress; they suspended their garments on hooks fastened in the wall, and receiving, according to their condition, either from their own slaves, or those of the thermæ, loose robes in exchange, withdrew into that graceful and circular building which yet exists, to shame the unlaving posterity of the south.

The more luxurious departed by another door to the tepidarium, a place which was heated to a voluptuous warmth, partly by a movable fireplace, principally by a suspended pavement, beneath which was conducted the caloric of the laconicum.

Here this portion of the intended bathers, after unrobing themselves, remained for some time enjoying the artificial warmth of the luxurious air. And this room, as befitted its important rank in the long process of ablution, was more richly and elaborately decorated than the rest; the arched roof was beautifully carved and painted; the windows above, of ground glass, admitted but wandering and uncertain rays; below the massive cornices were rows of figures in massive and bold relief; the walls glowed with crimson, the pavement was skilfully tessellated in white mosaics. Here the habituated bathers, men who bathed seven times a day, would remain in a state of enervate and speechless lassitude, either before or (mostly) after the water-bath; and many of these victims of the pursuit of health turned their listless eyes on the newcomers, recognizing their friends with a nod, but dreading the fatigue of conversation.

From this place the party again diverged, according to their several fancies, some to the auditorium, which answered the purpose of our vapour-baths, and thence to the warm bath itself; those more accustomed to exercise, and capable of dispensing with so cheap a purchase of fatigue, resorted at once to the calidarium, or water bath.

"Blessed be he who invented baths!" said Glaucus, stretching himself along one of those bronze seats (then covered with soft cushions) which the visitor to Pompeii sees at this day in the same tepidarium. "Whether he were Hercules or Bacchus, he deserved deification."

"But tell me," said a corpulent citizen, who was groaning and wheezing under the operation of being rubbed down, "tell me, O Glaucus!—evil chance to thy hands, O slave! Why so rough?—tell me—ugh—ugh!—are the baths at Rome really so magnificent?"

Glaucus turned, and recognized Diomed, though not without some difficulty, so red and so inflamed were the good man's cheeks by the sudatory and the scraping he had so lately undergone. "I fancy they must be a great deal finer than these. Eh?" Suppressing a smile, Glaucus replied:

"Imagine all Pompeii converted into baths, and you will then form a notion of the size of the imperial thermae of Rome. But a notion of the size only. Imagine every entertainment for mind and body—enumerate all the gymnastic games our fathers invented— repeat all the books Italy and Greece have produced—suppose places for all these games, admirers for all these works—add to this, baths of the vastest size, the most complicated construction— intersperse the whole with gardens, with theatres, with porticoes, with schools—suppose, in one word, a city of the gods, composed but of palaces and public edifices, and you may form some faint idea of the glories of the great baths of Rome."

"By Hercules!" said Diomed, opening his eyes, "why it would take a man's whole life to bathe!"

"At Rome, it often does so," replied Glaucus, gravely. "There are many who live only at the baths. They repair there the first hour at which the doors are opened, and remain till they are closed. They seem as if they knew nothing of the rest of Rome; as if they despised all other existence."

"By Pollux! You amaze me."

"Even those who bathe only thrice a day contrive to consume all their lives in this occupation. They take their exercise in the tennis-court or the porticoes, to prepare them for the first bath; they lounge into the theatre, to refresh themselves after it. They take their prandium under the trees, and think over their second bath. By the time it is prepared, the prandium is digested. From the second bath they stroll into one of the peristyles, to hear some new poet recite; or into the library, to sleep over an old one. Then comes the supper, which they still consider but a part of the bath; and then a third time they bathe again, as the best place to converse with their friends."

"*Per Hercule!* But we have their imitators at Pompeii."

"Yes, and without their excuse. The magnificent voluptuaries of the Roman baths are happy; they see nothing but gorgeousness and splendour; they visit not the squalid parts of the city; they know not that there is poverty in the world. All Nature smiles for them, and her only frown is the last one which sends them to bathe in Cocytus. Believe me, they are your only true philosophers."

8. Arbaces Cogs His Dice

The evening darkened over the restless city, as Apæcides took his way to the house of the Egyptian. Avoiding the more lighted and populous streets as he went on his way apparently sunk in thought, a man of sober and staid demeanour touched him on the shoulder.

"Apæcides!" said he, and he made a rapid sign with his hands: it was the sign of the cross.

"Well, Nazarene," replied the priest, and his face grew paler. "What wouldst thou?"

"Nay," returned the stranger, "I would not interrupt thy meditations; but, the last time we met, I seemed not to be so unwelcome."

"You are not unwelcome, Olinthus; but I am sad and weary; nor am I able this evening to discuss with you those themes which are most acceptable to you."

"O backward of heart!" said Olinthus, with bitter fervour; "and art thou sad and weary, and wilt thou turn from the very springs that refresh and heal?"

"O Earth!" cried the young priest, striking his breast passionately, "from what regions shall my eyes open to the true Olympus, where thy gods really dwell? Am I to believe, with this man, that none whom for so many centuries my fathers worshipped has a being or a name? Am I to break down, as something blasphemous and profane, the very altars which have deemed most sacred! Am I to think with Arbaces—what?"

He paused, and strode rapidly away in the impatience of a man who strives to get rid of himself. But the Nazarene was one of those hardy, vigorous, and enthusiastic men, by whom God in all times has worked the revolutions of earth; and those, above all, in the establishment and reformation of His own religion—men who were formed to convert, because formed to endure.

He did not suffer Apæcides thus easily to escape him. He overtook, and addressed him thus: "I do not wonder, Apæcides, that I distress you; that I shake all the elements of your mind; that you are lost in doubt; that you drift here and there in the vast ocean of uncertain and benighted thought. I wonder not at this, but bear with me a little; watch and pray—the darkness shall vanish, the storm sleep, and God himself as he came on the seas of Samaria, shall walk over the lulled billows, to the delivery of your soul. Ours is a religion jealous in its demands, but how prodigal in its gifts! It troubles you for an hour, it repays you by immortality."

"Such promises," said Apæcides sullenly, "are the tricks by which man is ever gulled. Oh, glorious were the promises which led me to the shrine of Isis!"

"But," answered the Nazarene, "ask thy reason, can that religion be sound which outrages all morality? You are told to worship your gods. What are those gods, even according to yourselves? What their actions, what their attributes? Are they not all represented to you as the blackest of criminals? Yet you are asked to serve them as the holiest of divinities. Jupiter himself is a parricide and an adulterer. What are the meaner deities but imitators of his vices? Turn now to the God, the one, the true God, to whose shrine I would lead you. If He seem too sublime to you, too shadowy, for those human associations, those touching connections between Creator and creature, to which the weak heart clings—contemplate Him in his Son, who put on mortality like ourselves. His mortality is not indeed declared, like that of your fabled gods, by the vices of our nature, but the practice of all its virtues. You are sad, you are weary. Listen, then, to the words of God—'Come to me,' saith He, 'all ye that are heavy laden, and I will give you rest!'"

"I cannot now," said Apæcides; "another time."

"Now—now!" exclaimed Olinthus earnestly, and clasping him by the arm.

But Apæcides, yet unprepared for the renunciation of that faith—that life, for which he had sacrificed so much, and still haunted by the promises of the Egyptian, extricated himself forcibly from the grasp; and feeling an effort necessary to conquer the irresolution which the eloquence of the Christian had begun to effect in his heated and feverish mind, he gathered up his robes, and fled away with a speed that defied pursuit.

Breathless and exhausted, he arrived at last in a remote and sequestered part of the city, and the lone house of the Egyptian stood before him. As he paused to recover himself, the moon emerged from a silver cloud, and shone full upon the walls of that mysterious habitation.

No other house was near—the dark vines clustered far and wide in front of the building, and behind rose a copse of lofty forest trees, sleeping in the melancholy moonlight; beyond stretched the dim outline of the distant hills, and amongst them the quiet crest of Vesuvius, not then so lofty as the traveller beholds it now.

Apæcides passed through the arching vines, and arrived at the broad and spacious portico. Before it, on either side of the steps, reposed the image of the Egyptian sphinx, and the moonlight gave an additional and yet more solemn calm to those large, harmonious, and passionless features, in which the sculptors of that type of wisdom united so much of loveliness with awe; halfway up the extremities of the steps darkened the green and massive foliage of the aloe, and the shadow of the eastern palm cast its long unwavering boughs partially over the marble surface of the Stairs.

Something there was in the stillness of the place, and the strange aspect of the sculptured sphinxes, which thrilled the blood of the priest with a nameless and ghostly fear, and he longed even for an echo to his noiseless steps as he ascended to the threshold.

He knocked at the door, over which was wrought an inscription in characters unfamiliar to his eyes; it opened without a sound, and a tall Ethiopian slave without question or salutation motioned to him to proceed.

The wide hall was lighted by lofty candelabra of elaborate bronze, and round the walls were wrought vast hieroglyphics, in dark and solemn colours, which contrasted strangely with the bright hues and graceful shapes with which the inhabitants of Italy decorated their abodes. At the extremity of the hall, a slave, whose countenance, though not African, was darker by many shades than the usual colour of the south, advanced to meet him.

"I seek Arbaces," said the priest; but his voice trembled even in his own ear. The slave bowed his head in silence, and leading Apæcides to a wing without the hall, conducted him up a narrow staircase, and then traversing several rooms in which the stern and thoughtful beauty of the sphinx still made the chief and most impressive object, Apæcides found himself in a dim and half-lighted chamber, in the presence of the Egyptian.

Arbaces was seated before a small table, on which lay unfolded several scrolls of papyrus, impressed with the same character as that on the threshold of the mansion. A small tripod stood at a little distance, containing incense from which the smoke slowly rose. Near this was a vast globe, depicting the signs of heaven; and upon another table lay several instruments of curious and quaint shape, whose uses were unknown to Apæcides. The farther extremity of the room was concealed by a curtain, and the oblong window in the roof admitted the rays of the moon, mingling sadly with the single lamp which burned in the apartment.

"Seat yourself, Apæcides," said the Egyptian, without rising.

The young man obeyed.

"You ask me," Arbaces continued, after a short pause, in which he seemed absorbed in thought. "You ask me, or would do so, the mightiest secrets which the soul of man is fitted to receive; it is the enigma of life itself that you desire me to solve. Placed like children in the dark, and but for a little while, in this dim and confined existence, we shape our spectres in the obscurity; our thoughts now sink back into ourselves in terror, now wildly plunge themselves into the guideless gloom. In this state, all wisdom consists necessarily in the solution of two questions: What are we to believe? And what are we to reject? These questions you desire me to decide?"

Apæcides bowed his head in assent.

"Man must have some belief," continued the Egyptian, in a tone of sadness. "He must fasten his hope to something; it is our common nature that you inherit when, aghast and terrified to see that in which you have been taught to place your faith swept away, you float over a dreary and shoreless sea of incertitude, you cry for help, you ask for some plank to cling to, some land, however dim and distant, to attain. Well, then, listen. You have not forgotten our conversation of today?"

"Forgotten!"

"I confessed to you that those deities for whom smoke so many altars were but inventions. I confessed to you that our rites and ceremonies were but mummeries, to delude and lure the herd to their proper good. I explained to you that from those delusions came the bonds of society, the harmony of the world, the power of the wise; that power is in the obedience of the vulgar. Continue we then these salutary decisions—if man must have some belief, continue to him that which his fathers have made dear to him, and which custom sanctifies and strengthens. In seeking a subtler faith for ourselves whose senses are too spiritual for the gross one, let us leave others that support which crumbles from us. This is wise—it is benevolent.

"Suppose the mind a blank, an unwritten scroll, fit to receive impressions for the first time. Look round the world—observe its order—its regularity—its design. Something must have created it—the design speaks a designer: in that certainly we first touch land. But of that which created the world, we know, we can know nothing, save these attributes—power and unvarying regularity—stern, crushing, relentless regularity—heeding no individual cases—rolling—sweeping—burning on; no matter what scattered hearts, severed from the general mass, fall ground and scorched beneath its wheels. I believe in two deities, Nature and Necessity; I worship the last by reverence, the first by investigation. What is the morality my religion teaches? This—all things are subject but to general rules; the sun shines for the joy of the many—it may bring sorrow to the few; the night sheds sleep on the multitude—but it harbours murder as well as rest; the forests adorn the earth—but shelter the serpent and the lion; the ocean supports a thousand barques—but it engulfs the one. It is only thus for the general, and not for the universal benefit, that Nature acts, and Necessity speeds on her awful course. This is the morality of the dread agents of the world—it is mine, who am their creature. I would preserve the delusions of priestcraft, for they are serviceable to the multitude; I would impart to man the arts I discover, the sciences I perfect; I would speed the vast career of civilised lore; in which I serve the mass, I fulfil the general law, I execute the great moral that Nature preaches. For myself I claim the individual exception; I claim it for the wise—satisfied that my individual actions are nothing in the great balance of good and evil; satisfied that the product of my knowledge can give greater blessings to the mass than my desires can operate evil on the few (for the first can extend to remotest regions and humanize nations yet unborn), I give to the world wisdom, to myself freedom. I enlighten the lives of others, and I enjoy my own. Yes, our wisdom is eternal, but our life is short; make the most of it while it lasts. Surrender thy youth to pleasure, and thy senses to delight. Soon comes the hour when the wine-cup is shattered, and the garlands shall cease to bloom. Enjoy while you may. Be still, O Apæcides, my pupil and my follower! I will teach thee the mechanism of Nature, her darkest and her wildest secrets—the lore which fools call magic—and the mighty mysteries of the stars. By this shalt thou discharge thy duty to the mass, by this shalt thou enlighten thy race. But I will lead thee also to pleasures of which the vulgar do not dream; and the day which thou givest to men shall be followed by the sweet night which thou surrenderest to thyself."

As the Egyptian ceased there rose about, around, beneath, the softest music that Lydia ever taught, or Ione ever perfected. It came like a stream of sound, bathing the senses unawares; enervating, subduing with delight. It seemed the melodies of invisible spirits, such as the shepherd might have heard in the golden age, floating through the vales of Thessaly, or in the noontide glades of Paphos. The words which had rushed to the lip of Apæcides, in answer to the sophistries of the Egyptian, died tremblingly away. He felt it a profanation to break upon that enchanted strain—the susceptibility of his excited nature, the Greek softness and ardour of his secret soul, were swayed and captured by surprise. He sank on the seat with parting lips and thirsting ear; while in a chorus of voices, bland and melting as those which waked Psyche in the halls of love, rose the following song:

THE HYMN OF EROS

"By the cool banks where soft Cephisus flows,
A voice sailed trembling down the waves of air;
The leaves blushed brighter in the Teian's rose,
The doves couched breathless in their summer lair.

While from their hands the purple flowerets fell,
The laughing Hours stood listening in the sky—
From Pan's green cave to Æglés haunted cell,
Heaved the charm'd earth in one delicious sigh.

'Love, sons of Earth! I am the Power of Love!
Eldest of all the gods, with Chaos born;
My smile sheds light along the courts above,

My kisses wake the eyelids of the Morn.

Mine are the stars—there, ever as ye gaze,
Ye meet the deep spell of my haunting eyes;
Mine is the moon—and, mournful if her rays,
'Tis that she lingers where her Carian lies.

The flowers are mine—the blushes of the rose,
The violet-charming Zephyr to the shade;
Mine the quick light that in the Maybeam glows,
And mine the day-dream in the lonely glade.

Love, sons of earth—for love is earth's soft lore,
Look where ye will—earth overflows with me;
Learn from the waves that ever kiss the shore,
And the wind's rapture of the heaving sea.

All teaches, love!—The sweet voice, like a dream
Melted in light; yet still the air above,
The waving sedges, and the whispering stream,
And the green forest rustling, murmured 'LOVE!'"

As the voices died away, the Egyptian seized the hand of
Apæcides, and led him, wondering, intoxicated, yet half reluctant,
across the chamber towards the curtain at the far end; and now, from
behind that curtain, there seemed to burst a thousand sparkling stars;
the veil itself, hitherto dark, was lighted by these fires behind into
the tenderest blue of heaven. It represented heaven itself—such a
heaven, as in the nights of June might have shone down over the
streams of Castaly. Here and there were painted rosy aerial clouds
from which smiled, by the limner's art, faces of divinest beauty, and
on which reposed the shapes of which Phidias and Apelles dreamed.
And the stars which studded the transparent azure rolled rapidly as
they shone, while the music, that again woke with a livelier and
lighter sound, seemed to imitate the melody of the joyous spheres.

"O! What miracle is this, Arbaces?" said Apæcides in faltering
accents. "After having denied the gods, art thou about to reveal to
me—"

"Their pleasures!" interrupted Arbaces, in a tone so different
from its usual cold and tranquil harmony that Apæcides started, and
thought the Egyptian himself transformed; and now, as they neared
the curtain, a wild—a loud—an exulting melody burst from behind
its concealment. With that sound the veil was rent—it parted—it

seemed to vanish into air: and a scene, which no Sybarite ever more than rivalled, broke upon the dazzled gaze of the youthful priest. A vast banquet room stretched beyond, blazing with countless lights, which filled the warm air with the scents of frankincense, of jasmine, of violets, of myrrh; all that the most odorous flowers, all that the most costly spices could distil, seemed gathered into one ineffable and ambrosial essence; from the light columns, that sprang upwards to the airy roof, hung draperies of white, studded with golden stars. At the extremities of the room two fountains cast up a spray, which, catching the rays of the roseate light, glittered like countless diamonds. In the centre of the room as they entered there rose slowly from the floor, to the sound of unseen minstrelsy, a table spread with all the viands which sense ever devoted to fancy, and vases of that lost Myrrhine fabric, so glowing in its colours, so transparent in its material, were crowned with the exotics of the East. The couches, to which this table was the centre, were covered with tapestries of azure and gold; and from invisible tubes in the vaulted roof descended showers of fragrant waters, that cooled the delicious air, and contended with the lamps, as if the spirits of wave and fire disputed which element could furnish forth the most delicious odours. And now, from behind the snowy draperies, trooped such forms as Adonis beheld when he lay on the lap of Venus. They came, some with garlands, others with lyres; they surrounded the youth, they led his steps to the banquet. They flung the chaplets round him in rosy chains. The earth—the thought of earth, vanished from his soul. He imagined himself in a dream, and suppressed his breath lest he should awake too soon: the senses, to which he had never yielded as yet, beat in his burning pulse, and confused his dizzy and reeling sight. And while thus amazed and lost, once again, but in brisk and Bacchic measures, rose the magic strains.

As the song ended, a group of three maidens, entwined with a chain of starred flowers, and who, while they imitated, might have shamed the Graces, advanced towards him in the gliding measures of the Ionian dance; such as the Nereids wreathed in moonlight on the yellow sands of the Ægean wave—such as Cytherea taught her handmaids in the marriage-feast of Psyche and her son.

Now approaching, they wreathed their chaplet round his head; now kneeling, the youngest of the three proffered him the bowl, from which the wine of Lesbos foamed and sparkled. The youth resisted no more, he grasped the intoxicating cup, the blood mantled fiercely through his veins. He sank upon the breast of the nymph who sat beside him, and turning with swimming eyes to seek for Arbaces, whom he had lost in the whirl of his emotions, he beheld him seated beneath a canopy at the upper end of the table, and gazing upon him with a smile that encouraged him to pleasure.

BOOK TWO

9. The Gladiators

In one of those parts of Pompeii which were tenanted not by the lords of pleasure, but by its minions and its victims; the haunt of gladiators and prize-fighters; of the vicious and the penniless; of the savage and the obscene; in the Alsatia of an ancient city, there was a shop which opened on to a crowded lane. Before the threshold was a group of men whose iron and well-strung muscles, whose short and Herculean necks, whose hardy and reckless countenances, indicated the champions of the arena. On a shelf, outside the shop, were ranged jars of wine and oil; and right over this was inserted in the wall a coarse painting, which exhibited gladiators drinking—so ancient and so venerable is the custom of signs! Within the room were placed several small tables, arranged somewhat in the modern fashion of boxes, and round these were seated several knots of men, some drinking, some dicing. The hour was the early forenoon, and nothing better, perhaps, that that unreasonable time itself denoted the habitual indolence of these tavern-loungers. Yet, despite the situation of the house and the character of its inmates, it indicated none of that sordid squalor which would have characterized a similar haunt in a modern city. The gay disposition of all the Pompeians, who sought, at least, to gratify the sense even where they neglected the mind, was typified by the gaudy colours which decorated the walls, and the shapes, fantastic but not inelegant, in which the lamps, the drinking-cups, the commonest household utensils, were wrought.

"By Pollux!" said one, as he leaned against the wall of the threshold, "the wine thou sellest us, old Silenus"—and as he spoke he slapped a portly personage on the back—"is enough to thin the best blood in one's veins."

The man thus caressingly saluted, and whose bared arms, white apron, and keys and napkin tucked carelessly within his girdle, indicated him to be the host of the tavern, had already passed into the autumn of his years; but his form was still so robust and athletic that he might have shamed even the sinewy shapes beside him, save that the cheeks were swelled and bloated, and the increasing stomach threw into shade the vast and massive chest which rose above it.

"None of thy scurrilous blusterings with me," growled the gigantic landlord, in the gentle semi-roar of an insulted tiger. "My wine is good enough for a carcase which shall so soon soak the dust of the spoliarium."

"Croakest thou thus, old raven!" returned the gladiator, laughing scornfully; "thou shalt live to hang thyself with despite when thou seest me win the palm crown; and when I get the purse at the amphitheatre, as I certainly shall, my first vow to Hercules shall be to forswear thee and thy vile potations evermore."

"Hear to him—hear to this modest Pyrgopolinices!" cried the host. "Sporus, Niger, Tetraides, he declares he shall win the purse from you. Why, by the gods! Each of your muscles is strong enough to stifle all his body, or I know nothing of the arena!"

"Ha!" said the gladiator, colouring with rising fury, "our lanista would tell a different story."

"What story could he tell against me, vain Lydon?" said Tetraides, frowning.

"Or me, who have conquered in fifteen fights?" said the gigantic Niger, stalking up to the gladiator.

"Or me?" grunted Sporus, with eyes of fire.

"Tush!" said Lydon, folding his arms, and regarding his rivals with a reckless air of defiance. "The time of trial will soon come; keep your valour till then."

"Ay, do," said the surly host; "and if I press down my thumb to save you, may the Fates cut my thread!"

"Your rope, you mean," said Lydon, sneeringly: "here is a sesterce to buy one."

The Titan wine-vendor seized the hand extended to him, and gripped it in so stern a vice that the blood spurted from the fingers' ends over the garments of the bystanders.

They set up a savage laugh.

"I will teach you, young braggart, to play the Macedonian with met I am no puny Persian, I warrant thee! What, man! Have I not fought twenty years in the ring, and never lowered my arms once? And have I not received the rod from the editor's own hand as a sign of victory, and as a grace to retirement on my laurels! And am I now to be lectured by a boy?" So saying, he flung the hand from him in scorn.

Without changing a muscle, but with the same smiling face with which he had previously taunted mine host, did the gladiator brave the painful grasp he had undergone. But no sooner was his hand released, than, crouching for one moment as a wild cat crouches, while the hair bristled on head and beard, with a fierce shrill yell he sprang at the throat of the giant, with an impetus that threw him, vast and sturdy as he was, from his balance—and down, with the crash of a falling rock, he fell—while over him fell also his ferocious foe.

He might have had no need of the rope so kindly recommended to him had he remained three minutes longer in that position. But, summoned to his assistance by the noise of his fall, a woman, who had hitherto kept in an inner apartment, rushed to the scene of the battle. This new ally was in herself a match for the gladiator; she was tall, lean, and with arms that could give other than soft embraces. In fact, the gentle helpmate of Burbo the wine-seller had, like himself, fought in the lists—even under the emperor's eye. And Burbo himself—Burbo, the unconquered in the field, according to report, now and then yielded the palm to his soft Stratonice. This sweet creature no sooner saw the imminent peril that awaited her worse half, than without other weapons than those which Nature had provided, she darted upon the incumbent gladiator, and, clasping him round the waist with her long and snake-like arms, lifted him by a sudden wrench from the body of her husband, leaving only his hands still clinging to the throat of his foe. So have we seen a dog snatched by the hind legs from the strife with a fallen rival in the arms of some envious groom; so have we seen one half of him high in air—passive and offenceless—while the other half, head, teeth, eyes, claws, seemed buried and engulfed in the mangled and prostrate enemy. Meanwhile the gladiators, lapped, and pampered, and glutted upon blood, crowded delightedly round the combatants—their nostrils distended—their lips grinning—their eyes gloatingly fixed on the bloody throat of the one, and the indented talons of the other.

"*Habet!*" cried they, with a sort of yell, rubbing their nervous hands.

"Non *habeo*, ye liars; I have not got it!" shouted the host, as with a mighty effort he wrenched himself from those deadly hands, and rose to his feet, breathless, panting, lacerated, bloody; and frothing, with reeling eyes, the glaring look and grinning teeth of his baffled foe, now struggling (but struggling with disdain) in the grip of the sturdy amazon.

"Fair play!" cried the gladiators: "one to one"—and, crowding round Lydon and the woman, they separated their pleasing host from his courteous guest.

But Lydon, feeling ashamed at his present position, and en-deavouring in vain to shake off the grasp of the virago, slipped his hand into his girdle, and drew forth a short knife. So menacing was his look, so brightly gleamed the blade, that Stratonice, who was used only to the pugilistic fashion of battle, started back in alarm.

"O gods!" cried she, "the ruffian—he has concealed weapons! Is that fair? Is that like a gentleman and a gladiator? No, indeed, I scorn such fellows!" With that she contemptuously turned her back on the gladiator, and hastened to examine the condition of her hus-band.

But he, as much inured to the constitutional exercise as an Eng-lish bulldog is to a contest with a more gentle antagonist, had al-ready recovered himself. He shook himself with a complacent grunt, satisfied that he was still alive, and then looked at his foe from head to foot with an air of more approbation than he had ever bestowed on him before: "By Castor!" said he, "thou art a stronger fellow than I took thee for! I see thou art a man of merit and virtue; give me thy hand, my hero!"

"Jolly old Burbo!" cried the gladiators, applauding; "staunch to the backbone. Give him thy hand, Lydon."

"Oh, to be sure," said the gladiator; "but now I have tasted his blood, I long to lap the whole."

"By Hercules!" returned the host, quite unmoved, "that is the true gladiator feeling. Pollux! To think how good training may make a man; why a beast could not be fiercer!"

"A beast! O dullard! We beat the beasts hollow," cried Tetraides.

"Well, well," said Stratonice, who was now employed in smoothing her hair and adjusting her dress, "if ye are all good friends again, I recommend you to be quiet and orderly; for some young noblemen, your patrons and backers, have sent to say they will come here to pay you a visit: they wish to see you more at their ease than at the schools, before they make up their bets on the great fight at the amphitheatre."

"Yes," continued Burbo, drinking off a bowl, or rather a pail of wine, "a man who has won my laurels can only encourage the brave. Lydon, drink, my boy! May you have an honourable old age like mine!"

"Come here," said Stratonice, drawing her husband to her affec-tionately by the ears, in that caress which Tibullus has so prettily described—"Come here!"

"Not so hard, she-wolf! Thou art worse than the gladiator," murmured the huge jaws of Burbo.

"Hist!" said she, whispering him; "Calenus has just stolen in disguised, by the back way. I hope he has brought the sesterces."

"Ho! Ho! I will join him," said Burbo; "meanwhile, I say, keep a sharp eye on the cups—attend to the score. Let them not cheat thee, wife; they are heroes, to be sure, but then they are arrant rogues; Cacus was nothing to them."

"Never fear me, fool!" was the conjugal reply; and Burbo, satisfied with the dear assurance, strode through the apartment, and sought the penetralia of his house.

"So those soft patrons are coming to look at our muscles," said Niger. "Who sent to previse thee of it, my mistress?"

"Lepidus. He brings with him Clodius, the surest better in Pompeii, and the young Greek, Glaucus."

"A wager on a wager," cried Tetraides; "Clodius bets on me, for twenty sesterces! What say you, Lydon?"

"He bets on me!" said Lydon.

"No, on me!" grunted Sporus.

"Dolts! Do you think he would prefer any of you to Niger?" said the athlete, thus modestly naming himself.

"Well, well," said Stratonice, as she pierced a huge amphora for her guests, who had now seated themselves before one of the tables, "great men and brave, as ye all think yourselves, which of you will fight the Numidian lion in case no malefactor should be found to deprive you of the opinion?"

"I who have escaped your arms, stout Stratonice," said Lydon, "might safely, I think, encounter the lion."

"But tell me," said Tetraides, "where is that pretty young slave of yours—the blind girl, with bright eyes? I have not seen her a long time."

"Oh! She is too delicate for you, my son of Neptune," said the hostess, "and too nice even for us, I think. We send her into the town to sell flowers and sing to the ladies; she makes us more money so than she would by waiting on you. Besides, she has often other employments which lie under the rose."

"Other employments!" said Niger; "why she is too young for them."

"Silence, beast!" said Stratonice; "you think there is no play but the Corinthian. If Nydia were twice the age she is at present, she would be equally fit for Vesta—poor girl!"

"But, hark ye, Stratonice," said Lydon: "how didst thou come by so gentle and delicate a slave? She were more meet for the handmaid of some rich matron of Rome than for thee."

"That is true," returned Stratonice; "and some day or other I shall make my fortune by selling her. How came I by Nydia, thou askest?"

"Ay!"

"Why, thou seest, my slave Staphyla—thou rememberest Staphyla, Niger?"

"Ay, a large-handed wench, with a face like a comic mask. How should I forget her, by Pluto, whose handmaid she doubtless is at this moment?"

"Tush, brute!—Well, Staphyla died one day, and a great loss she was to me, and I went into the market to buy me another slave. But, by the gods! They were all grown so dear, and money was so scarce, that I was about to leave the place in despair, when a merchant plucked me by the robe. 'Mistress,' said he, 'dost thou want a slave cheap? I have a child to sell—a bargain. She is but little, and almost an infant, it is true; but she is quick and quiet, docile and clever, sings well, and is of good blood, I assure you.' 'Of what country?' said I. 'Thessalian.' Now I knew the Thessalians were acute and gentle; so I said I would see the girl. I found her just as you see her now, scarcely smaller and scarcely younger in appearance. She looked patient and resigned enough, with her hands crossed on her bosom, and her eyes downcast. I asked the merchant his price: it was moderate, and I bought her at once. The merchant brought her to my house, and disappeared in an instant. Well, my friends, guess my astonishment when I found she was blind! Ha! Ha! A clever fellow that merchant! I ran at once to the magistrates, but the rogue was already gone from Pompeii. So I was forced to go home in a very ill humour, I assure you; and the poor girl felt the effects of it too. But, by degrees, we got reconciled to our purchase. True, she had not the strength of Staphyla, and was of very little use in the house, but she could soon find her way about the town, as well as if she had the eyes of Argus; and when one morning she brought us home a handful of sesterces, which she said she had got from selling some flowers she had gathered in our poor little garden, we thought the gods had sent her to us. So from that time we let her go out as she likes, filling her basket with flowers, which she wreathes into garlands after the Thessalian fashion, which pleases her gallants; and the great people seemed to take a fancy to her, for they always pay her more than they do any other flower girl, and she brings all of it home to us, which is more than any other slave would do. Besides her skill in the garlands, she sings and plays on the cithara, which also brings money; and lately—but that is a secret."

"*That* is a secret! What!" cried Lydon; "art thou turned sphinx?"

"Sphinx, no—why sphinx?"

"Cease thy gabble, good mistress, and bring us our meat—I am hungry," said Sporus, impatiently.

"And I too," echoed the grim Niger, whetting his knife on the palm of his hand.

The amazon stalked away to the kitchen, and soon returned with a tray laden with large pieces of meat half-raw; for so, as now, did the heroes of the prize-fight imagine they best sustained their hardihood and ferocity; they drew round the table with the eyes of famished wolves—the meat vanished, the wine flowed.

10. A Slave Rebels

In the earlier times of Rome the priesthood was a profession, not of lucre but of honour. It was embraced by the noblest citizens— it was forbidden to the plebeians. Afterwards it was equally open to all ranks; at least, that part of the profession which embraced the flamens, or priests—not of religion generally, but of peculiar gods. Even the priest of Jupiter, preceded by a lictor, and entitled by his office to the entrance of the senate, at first the especial dignitary of the patricians, was subsequently the choice of the people. Thus Calenus, the priest of Isis, was of the lower origin. His relations, though not his parents, were freedmen. He had received from them a liberal education, and from his father a small patrimony, which he had soon exhausted. He embraced the priesthood as a last resource from distress.

Calenus had but one surviving relative at Pompeii, and that was Burbo. Various dark and disreputable ties, stronger than those of blood, united their hearts and interests; and often the minister of Isis stole disguised and furtively from the supposed austerity of his devotions, and glided through the back door of the retired gladiator, a man infamous alike by vices and profession, rejoicing to throw off the last rag of a hypocrisy which, but for the dictates of avarice, his ruling passion, would at all times have sat clumsily upon a nature too brutal for even the mimicry of virtue.

Wrapped in one of those large mantles which came in use among the Romans in proportion as they dismissed the toga, whose ample folds well concealed the form, and in which a sort of hood (attached to it) afforded no less a security to the features, Calenus now sat in the small and private chamber of the wine-cellar, whence a small passage ran to that back entrance with which nearly all the houses of Pompeii were furnished.

Opposite to him sat the sturdy Burbo, carefully counting on a table between them a little pile of coins which the priest had just poured from his purse.

"You see," said Calenus, "that we pay you handsomely, and you ought to thank me for recommending you to so advantageous a market."

"I do, my cousin, I do," replied Burbo, affectionately, as he swept the coins into a leathern receptacle, which he then deposited in his girdle, drawing the buckle round his capacious waist. "And, by Isis, Pisis, and Nisis, or whatever other gods there may be in Egypt, my little Nydia is a very Hesperides—a garden of gold to me."

"She sings well, and plays like a muse," returned Calenus; "those are virtues that he who employs me always pays liberally."

"He is a god," cried Burbo, enthusiastically; "every rich man who is generous deserves to be worshipped. But come, a cup of wine, old friend: tell me more about it. What does she do? She is frightened, talks of her oath, and reveals nothing."

"Nor will I, by my right hand! I, too, have taken that terrible oath of secrecy."

"Oath! What are oaths to men like we are?"

"True, oaths of a common fashion; but this!"—and the stalwart priest shuddered as he spoke. "Yet," he continued, emptying a huge cup of unmixed wine, "I will own to thee, that it is not so much the oath that I dread as the vengeance of him who proposed it. By the gods! He is a mighty sorcerer, and could draw my confession from the moon, did I dare to make it to her. Talk no more of this. By Pollux! Wild as his banquets are, I am never quite at ease there. I love one jolly hour with thee, and one of the laughing girls that I meet in this chamber, all smoke-dried though it be, better than whole nights of those magnificent debauches."

"Ho! Sayest thou so? Then tomorrow night, please the gods, we will have a snug carousal."

"With all my heart," said the priest, rubbing his hands, and drawing himself nearer the table.

At this moment they heard a slight noise at the door, as of one feeling the handle. The priest lowered the hood over his head.

"Tush!" whispered the host, "it is but the blind girl," as Nydia opened the door, and entered the apartment.

"Ho! Girl, and how dost thou? Thou lookest pale—thou hast kept late revels? No matter, the young must be always the young," said Burbo, encouragingly.

The girl made no answer, but she dropped on one of the seats with an air of lassitude. Her colour went and came rapidly; she beat the floor impatiently with her small feet, then she suddenly raised her face, and said, with a determined voice: "Master, you may starve me if you will—you may beat—you may threaten death—but I will not go there again."

"How, fool!" said Burbo, in a savage voice, and his heavy brows met darkly over fierce and bloodshot eyes; "how, rebellious! Take care."

"I have said it," said the poor girl, crossing her hands on her breast.

"What! My modest one, sweet vestal, thou wilt go no more! Very well, thou shalt be carried."

"I will raise the city with my cries," said she, passionately; and the colour mounted to her brow.

"We will take care of that too; thou shalt go gagged."

"Then may the gods help me!" said Nydia, rising; "I will appeal to the magistrates."

"Thine oath remember!" said a hollow voice, as for the first time Calenus joined in the dialogue.

At these words a trembling shook the frame of the unfortunate girl; she clasped her hands imploringly. "Wretch that I am!" she cried, and burst violently into sobs.

Whether or not it were the sound of that vehement sorrow which brought the gentle Stratonice to the spot, her grisly form at this moment appeared in the chamber.

"How now? What hast thou been doing with my slave, brute?" said she, angrily, to Burbo.

"Be quiet, wife," said he, in a tone half-sullen, half-timid; "you want new girdles and fine clothes, do you? Well then, take care of your slave, or you may want them long; *Væ capiti tuo*—vengeance on thy head, wretched one!"

"What is this?" said the hag, looking from one to the other.

Nydia started as by a sudden impulse from the wall against which she had leaned; she threw herself at the feet of Stratonice; she embraced her knees, and looking up at her with those sightless but touching eyes:

"O my mistress!" she sobbed, "you are a woman—you have had sisters—you have been young like I am—feel for me—save me! I will go to those horrible feasts no more!"

"Stuff!" said the hag, dragging her up rudely by one of those delicate hands, fit for no harsher labour than that of weaving the flowers which made her pleasure of her trade—"stuff! Such scruples are not for slaves."

"Hark ye," said Burbo, drawing forth his purse, and chinking its contents: "you hear this music, wife; by Pollux if you do not break in yon colt with a tight rein, you will hear it no more."

"The girl is tired," said Stratonice, nodding to Calenus; "she will be more docile when you next want her."

"*You*? *You*? Who is here?" cried Nydia, casting her eyes round the apartment with so fearful and straining a survey, that Calenus rose in alarm from his seat.

"She *must* see with those eyes!" he muttered.

"Who is here? Speak in heaven's name! Ah, if you were blind like I am you would be less cruel," she said; and again burst into tears.

"Take her away," said Burbo impatiently; "I hate these whimperings."

"Come!" said Stratonice, pushing the poor child by the shoulders.

Nydia drew herself aside, with an air to which resolution gave dignity.

"Hear me," she said; "I have served you faithfully—I, who was brought up—Ah! My mother, my poor mother! Didst thou dream I should come to this?" She dashed the tears from her eyes and proceeded: "Command me in aught else, and I will obey: but I tell you now, hard as you are—I tell you that I will go there no more; or, if I am forced there, that I will implore the mercy of the praetor himself."

The hag's eyes glowed with fire; she seized the child by the hair with one hand, and raised on high the other—that formidable right hand, the least blow of which seemed capable of crushing the frail and delicate form that trembled in her grasp. That thought itself appeared to strike her, for she suspended the blow, changed her purpose, and, dragging Nydia to the wall, seized a rope from a hook, and the next moment the agonized shrieks of the blind girl rang piercingly through the house.

11. A Purchase Which Will Be Dear

"Holla, my brave fellows!" said Lepidus, stooping his head, as he entered the low doorway of the house of Burbo. "We have come to see which of you most honours your lanista." The gladiators rose from the table in respect to three gallants known to be amongst the gayest and richest youths of Pompeii, and whose voices were therefore the dispensers of amphitheatrical reputation.

"What fine animals!" said Clodius to Glaucus, "worthy to be gladiators!"

"It is a pity they are not warriors," returned Glaucus.

A singular thing it was to see the dainty and fastidious Lepidus, whom in a banquet a ray of daylight seemed to blind, whom in the bath a breeze of air seemed to blast—in whom Nature seemed twisted and perverted from every natural impulse, and curdled into one dubious thing of effeminacy and art—a singular thing was it to see this Lepidus, now all eagerness, energy, and life, patting the vast shoulders of the gladiators with blanched and girlish hand, feeling with a mincing grip their great brawn and iron muscles, all lost in calculating admiration at that manhood which he had spent his life in carefully banishing from himself.

"Ha! Niger!" he said, "how will you fight, and with whom?"

"Sporus challenges me," said the grim giant; "and we shall fight to the death."

"Ah! To be sure," grunted Sporus, with a twinkle of his small eye.

"He takes the sword, I the net and the trident; it will be rare sport. I hope the survivor will have enough to keep up the dignity of the crown."

"Never fear, we'll fill the purse, my Hector," said Clodius, "let me see—you fight against Niger? Glaucus, a bet—I back Niger."

"I told you so," cried Niger exultingly. "The noble Clodius knows me; count yourself dead already, my Sporus."

Clodius took out his tablet. "A bet—ten sestertia. What say you?"

"So be it," said Glaucus. "But whom have we here? I never saw this hero before;" and he glanced at Lydon, whose limbs were slighter than those of his companions, and who had something of grace, and something even of nobleness, in his face, which his profession had not yet wholly destroyed.

"It is Lydon, a youngster, practised only with the wooden sword as yet," answered Niger, condescendingly. "But he has the true blood in him, and has challenged Tetraides."

"*He* challenged *me*," said Lydon: "I accept the offer."

"And how do you fight?" asked Lepidus. "Chut, my boy, wait a while before you contend with Tetraides."

Lydon smiled disdainfully.

"Is he a citizen or a slave?" Clodius asked.

"A citizen—we are all citizens here."

"Stretch out your arm, my Lydon," said Lepidus, with the air of a connoisseur.

The gladiator, with a significant glance at his companions, extended an arm, which, if not so huge in its girth as those of his comrades, was so firm in its muscles, so beautifully symmetrical in its proportions, that the three visitors uttered simultaneously an admiring exclamation.

"Well, man, what is your weapon?" said Clodius, tablet in hand.

"We are to fight first with the cestus; afterwards, if both survive, with swords," returned Tetraides, sharply, and with an envious scowl.

"With the cestus?" cried Glaucus. "There you are wrong, Lydon; the cestus is the Greek fashion; I know it well. You should have encouraged flesh for that contest; you are far too thin for it—avoid the cestus."

"I cannot," said Lydon. "And why?"

"I have said—because he has challenged me."

"But he will not hold you to the precise weapon."

"My honour holds me!" returned Lydon, proudly.

"I bet on Tetraides, two to one, at the cestus," said Clodius. "Shall it be, Lepidus?—even betting, with swords."

"If you give me three to one, I will not take the odds," said Lepidus: "Lydon will never come to the swords. You are mighty courteous."

"What say you, Glaucus?"

"I will like the odds three to one."

"Ten sestertia to thirty."

"Yes."

Clodius wrote that bet in his book.

"Pardon me, noble sponsor mine," said Lydon, in a low voice to Glaucus: "but how much think you the victor will gain?"

"How much? Why, perhaps seven sestertia."

"You are sure it will be as much?"

"At least. But out on you!—a Greek would have thought of the honour, and not the money. O Italians! Everywhere ye are Italians!"

A blush mantled over the bronzed cheek of the gladiator.

"Do not wrong me, noble Glaucus; I think of both, but I should never have been a gladiator but for the money."

"Base! Mayst thou fall! A miser never was a hero."

"I am not a miser," said Lydon, haughtily, and he withdrew to the other end of the room.

"But I don't see Burbo; where is Burbo? I must talk with Burbo," cried Clodius.

"He is within," said Niger, pointing to the door at the extremity of the room.

"And Stratonice, the brave old lass, where is she?" Lepidus asked.

"Why, she was here just before you entered; but she heard something that displeased her yonder, and vanished. Pollux! Old Burbo had perhaps caught hold of some girl in the back room. I heard a wench's voice crying out; the old dame is as jealous as Juno."

"Ho! Excellent!" cried Lepidus, laughing "Come, Clodius, let us go shares with Jupiter; perhaps he has caught a Leda."

At this moment a loud cry of pain and terror startled the group.

"Oh, spare me! Spare me! I am so young. I am blind—is not *that* punishment enough?"

"O Pallus! I know that voice, it is my poor flower-girl!" exclaimed Glaucus, and he burst open the door; he beheld Nydia writhing in the grasp of the infuriated hag; the cord, already dabbled with blood, was raised in the air.

"Fury!" said Glaucus, and with his left hand he caught Nydia from her grasp. "How dare you use thus a girl—one of your own sex, a child!"

"Oh! Is that you—is that Glaucus?" exclaimed the flower girl, in a tone almost of transport. The tears stood arrested on her cheek.

"And how dare you interfere between a free woman and her slave? By the gods! Despite your fine tunic and your filthy perfumes, I doubt whether you are even a Roman at all."

"Fair words, mistress—fair words!" said Clodius, now entering with Lepidus. "This is my friend. He must be put under shelter from your tongue, sweet one; it rains stones!"

"Give me my slave!" shrieked the virago, placing her mighty grasp on the breast of the Greek, who now stood between her and the shrinking girl.

"Not if all your sister Furies could help you," answered Glaucus. "Fear not, Nydia; an Athenian never forsakes distress!"

"Holla!" said Burbo, rising reluctantly, "what turmoil is all this about a slave? Let go the young gentleman, wife—let him go: for his sake the pert thing shall be spared this once." So saying, he drew, or rather dragged off, his ferocious helpmate.

"Methought when we entered," said Clodius, "there was another man present?"

"He is gone."

For the priest of Isis had indeed thought it high time to vanish.

"Oh, a friend of mine! A brother cup man, a quiet dog, who does not love these snarlings," said Burbo, carelessly. "But go, child, you will tear the gentlemen's tunic if you cling to him so tightly; go, you are pardoned."

"Oh, do not—do not forsake me!" cried Nydia, clinging yet closer to the Athenian. Moved by her forlorn situation, her appeal to him, her own innumerable and touching graces, the Greek seated himself on one of the rude chairs. He held her on his knees—he wiped the blood from her shoulders with his long hair—he whispered to her a thousand of those soothing words with which we calm the grief of a child—and so beautiful did he seem in his gentle and consoling task, that even the fierce heart of Stratonice was touched.

"Well, who could have thought our blind Nydia had been so honoured?" said the virago, wiping her heated brow.

Glaucus looked up at Burbo.

"My good man," said he, "this is your slave; she sings well, she is accustomed to the care of flowers—I wish to make a present of such a slave to a lady. Will you sell her to me?" As he spoke, he felt the whole frame of the poor girl tremble with delight; she started up, she put her dishevelled hair from her eyes, she looked around, as if, alas! She had the power to see.

"Sell Nydia! No, indeed," said Stratonice, gruffly.

Nydia sank back with a long sigh, and again clasped the robe of her protector.

"Nonsense!" said Clodius, imperiously, "you must oblige me. What, man! What, old dame! Offend me, and your trade is ruined. Is not Burbo my kinsman Pansa's client? Am I not the oracle of the amphitheatre and its heroes? If I say the word, break up your wine-jars—you sell no more. Glaucus, the slave is yours."

Burbo scratched his head in evident embarrassment.

"The girl is worth her weight in gold to me."

"Name your price, I am rich," said Glaucus.

"I paid six sestertia for her, she is worth twelve now," muttered Stratonice.

"You shall have twenty; come to the magistrates at once, and then to my house for your money."

"I would not have sold the dear girl for a hundred but to oblige noble Clodius," said Burbo whiningly. "And you will speak to Pansa about the place of designator at the amphitheatre, noble Clodius? It would just suit me."

"Thou shalt have it," said Clodius; adding in a whisper to Burbo; "Yon Greek can make your fortune; money runs through him like a sieve: mark today with white chalk, my Priam."

"*An dabis*?" said Glaucus, in the formal question of sale and barter.

"*Dabitur*," answered Burbo

"Then, then, I am to go with you? O happiness!" murmured Nydia.

"Pretty one, yes; and thy hardest task henceforth shall be to sing thy Grecian hymns to the loveliest lady in Pompeii."

The girl withdrew from his clasp; a change came over her face, so bright the instant before; she sighed heavily, and then once more taking his hand, she said: "I thought I was to go to your house?"

"And so thou shalt for the present; come, we lose time."

12. The Rival Goes Ahead

Ione was one of those exceptional women who unite the rarest of earthly gifts—beauty and brains. No one ever possessed superior intellectual qualities without knowing them—the alliteration of modesty and merit is pretty enough, but where merit is great, the veil of modesty never disguises its contents from its possessor.

Ione knew her genius; but, with that charming versatility that belongs of right to women, she had the faculty so few of a kindred genius in the less malleable sex can claim—the faculty to bend and model her graceful intellect to all whom it encountered. The sparkling fountain threw its waters alike upon the strand, the cavern, and the flowers; it refreshed, it smiled, it dazzled everywhere. That pride, which is the necessary result of superiority, she wore easily—it concentred itself in independence. She pursued her own bright and solitary path. She asked no aged matron to direct and guide her—she walked alone by the torch of her own unflickering purity. She obeyed no tyrannical and absolute custom. She moulded custom to her own will, but this so delicately and with so feminine a grace, so perfect an exemption from error, that she could not be said to outrage custom, but rather to command it.

It was no wonder that she had completely chained and subdued the mysterious but burning soul of the Egyptian, a man in whom dwelt the fiercest passions. Her beauty and her soul alike enthralled him.

Set apart himself from the common world, he loved that daringness of character which also made itself, among common things, aloof and alone. He did not, or he would not see, that that very isolation put her yet more from him than from the vulgar. Far as the poles—far as night from day, his solitude was divided from hers.

If it were not strange that Ione thus enthralled the Egyptian, far less strange was it that she had captured, suddenly and irrevocably, the brighter heart of the Athenian. The gladness of a temperament which seemed woven from the beams of light had led Glaucus into pleasure. He obeyed no more vicious dictates when he wandered into the dissipations of his time, than the exhilarating voices of youth and health. He threw the brightness of his nature over every abyss and cavern through which he strayed. Of far more penetration than his companions deemed, he saw that they sought to prey upon his riches and his youth: but he despised wealth, save as the means of enjoyment, and youth was the great sympathy that united him to them. He felt, it is true, the impulse of nobler thoughts and higher aims, but the world was one vast prison, to which the Sovereign of Rome was the Imperial jailer; and the very virtues, which in the free days of Athens would have made him ambitious, made him inactive and supine. For in that unnatural and bloated civilisation, all that was noble in emulation was forbidden. Ambition in the regions of a despotic and luxurious court was but the contest of flattery and craft. Avarice had become the sole incentive of men who desired offices only as the license to pillage, and government was but the excuse of rapine.

But as Ione was independent in her choice of life, so was her modest pride proportionately vigilant and easily alarmed. The falsehood of the Egyptian was prompted by a deep knowledge of her nature. The story of coarseness, of indelicacy, in Glaucus, stung her to the quick. She felt it a reproach upon her character and her career, a punishment above all to her love; she felt, for the first time, how suddenly she had yielded to that love; she imagined it was that weakness which had incurred the contempt of Glaucus. Yet her love, perhaps, was no less alarmed than her pride. If one moment she murmured reproaches upon Glaucus—if one moment she renounced, she almost hated him—at the next she burst into passionate tears, her heart yielded to its softness, and she said in the bitterness of anguish: "He despises—he does not love me."

From the hour the Egyptian had left her, she had retired to her most secluded chamber, she had denied herself to the crowds that besieged her door. Glaucus was excluded with the rest; he wondered, but he guessed not why. He never attributed to her that woman-like caprice of which the love-poets of Italy so unceasingly complain. He was troubled, but his hopes were not dimmed, for he knew already that he loved and was beloved; what more could he desire as an amulet against fear?

At deepest night, then, when the streets were hushed, and the high moon only beheld his devotions, he stole to that temple of his heart—her home; and wooed her after the beautiful fashion of his country. He covered her threshold with the richest garlands, in which every flower was a volume of sweet passion; and he charmed the long summer night with the sound of the Lydian lute.

But the window above did not open; all was still and dark.

Yet Ione slept not, nor disdained to hear. Those soft strains ascended to her chamber; they soothed, they subdued her. While she listened, she believed nothing against her lover, but when they were stilled at last, and his step departed, the spell ceased; and, in the bitterness of her soul, she almost conceived in that delicate flattery a new affront.

I said she was denied to all, but there was one exception, there was one person who would not be denied, assuming over her actions and her house something like the authority of a parent; Arbaces, for himself, claimed an exemption from all the ceremonies observed by others. He entered the threshold with the license of one who feels that he is privileged and at home.

He was cheered and elated by his conquest over her brother. From the hour in which Apæcides fell beneath the voluptuous sorcery of that fete which we have described, he felt his empire over the young priest triumphant and assured. He knew that there is no victim so thoroughly subdued as a young and fervent man for the first time delivered to the thraldom of the senses.

When Apæcides recovered, with the morning light, from the profound sleep which succeeded to the delirium of wonder and of pleasure, he was, it is true, ashamed—terrified—appalled. His vows of austerity and celibacy echoed in his ear; his thirst after holiness— had it been quenched at so unhallowed a stream? But Arbaces knew well the means by which to confirm his conquest. From the arts of pleasure he led the young priest at once to those of his mysterious wisdom. He bared to his amazed eyes the initiatory secrets of the sombre philosophy of the Nile—those secrets plucked from the stars, and the wild chemistry, which, in those days, might well pass for the lore of a diviner magic. He seemed to the young eyes of the priest as a being above mortality, and endowed with supernatural gifts. The pure and stern lessons of that creed to which Olinthus had sought to make him convert, were swept away from his memory by the deluge of new passions. And the Egyptian, who was versed in the articles of that true faith, and who soon learned from his pupil the effect which had been produced upon him by its believers, sought, not unskilfully, to undo that effect by a tone of reasoning, half-sarcastic and half-earnest.

"This faith," said he, "is but a borrowed plagiarism from one of the many allegories invented by our priests of old. Observe," he added, pointing to a hieroglyphical scroll, "observe in these ancient figures the origin of the Christian's Trinity. Here are also three gods—the Deity, the Spirit, and the Son. Observe that the epithet of the Son is 'Saviour'—observe that the sign by which his human qualities are denoted is the cross. Note here, too, the mystic history of Osiris, how he put on death; how he lay in the grave; and how, thus fulfilling a solemn atonement, he rose again from the dead! In these stories we but design to paint an allegory from the operations of nature and the evolutions of the eternal heavens. But, the allegory unknown, the types themselves have furnished to credulous nations the materials of many creeds."

This was the last argument which completely subdued the priest. It was necessary to him, as to all, to believe in something; and undivided and, at last, unreluctant, he surrendered himself to that belief which Arbaces inculcated, and which all that was human in passion—all that was flattering in vanity—all that was alluring in pleasure, served to invite to, and contributed to confirm.

This conquest thus easily made, the Egyptian could now give himself wholly up to the pursuit of a far dearer and mightier object; and he hailed, in his success with the brother, an omen of his triumph over the sister.

He had seen Ione on the day following the revel we have witnessed; and which was also the day after he had poisoned her mind against his rival. The next day, and the next, he saw her also; and each time he laid himself out with consummate art, partly to confirm her impression against Glaucus, and principally to prepare her for the impressions he desired her to receive. The proud Ione took care to conceal the anguish she endured; and the pride of woman has an hypocrisy which can deceive the most penetrating, and the most astute. But Arbaces was no less cautious not to recur to a subject which he felt it was most politic to treat as of the lightest importance.

He recurred no more to the presumption of Glaucus; he mentioned his name, but not more often that that of Clodius or of Lepidus. He affected to class them together, as things of a low and ephemeral species; as things wanting nothing of the butterfly, save its innocence and its grace. Sometimes he slightly alluded to some invented debauch, in which he declared them companions; sometimes he adverted to them as the antipodes of those lofty and spiritual natures, to whose order that of Ione belonged. Blinded alike by her pride and his own, he dreamed not that she already loved; but he dreaded lest she might have formed for Glaucus the first fluttering prepossessions. And, secretly, he ground his teeth in rage and jealousy, when he reflected on the youth, the fascinations, and the brilliancy of that formidable rival whom he pretended to undervalue.

It was on the fourth day from that on which he had first sort to poison her mind against his younger rival that Arbaces and Ione sat together.

"You wear your veil at home." he said. "That is not fair to those whom you honour with your friendship."

"But to Arbaces," answered Ione, who, indeed, had cast the veil over her features to conceal eyes red with weeping, "to Arbaces, who looks only to the mind, what matters it that the face is concealed?"

"I do look only to the mind," replied the Egyptian: "show me then your face—for there I shall see it!"

"You grow gallant in the air of Pompeii," she said, with a forced tone of gaiety.

"Do you think, fair Ione, that it is only at Pompeii that I have learned to value you?" The Egyptian's voice trembled—he paused for a moment, and then resumed.

"There is a love, beautiful Greek, which is not the love only of the thoughtless and the young—there is a love which sees not with the eyes, which hears not with the ears; but in which soul is enamoured of soul. The countryman of thy ancestors, the cave-nursed Plato, dreamed of such a love—his followers have sought to imitate it; but it is a love that is not for the head to echo—it is a love that only high and noble natures can conceive—it hath nothing in common with the sympathies and ties of coarse affection—wrinkles do not revolt it—homeliness of feature does not deter; it asks youth, it is true, but it asks it only in the freshness of the emotions; it asks beauty, it is true, but it is the beauty of the thought and of the spirit. Such is the love, O Ione, which is a worthy offering to thee from the cold and the austere. Austere and cold thou deemest me—such is the love that I venture to lay upon thy shrine—thou canst receive it without a blush."

"And its name is Friendship!" replied Ione: her answer was innocent, yet it sounded like the reproof of one conscious of the design of the speaker.

"Friendship!" said Arbaces, vehemently. "No; that is a word too often profaned to apply to a sentiment so sacred. Friendship! It is a tie that binds fools and profligates! Friendship! It is the bond that unites the frivolous hearts of a Glaucus and a Clodius! Friendship! no, that is an affection of earth, of vulgar habits and sordid sympathies; the feeling of which I speak is borrowed from the stars—it partakes of that mystic and ineffable yearning, which we feel when we gaze upon them—it burns, yet it purifies—it is the lamp of naphtha in the alabaster vase, glowing with fragrant odours, but shining only through the purest vessels. No; it is not love, and it is not friendship, that Arbaces feels for Ione. Give it no name—earth hath no name for it—it is not of earth—why debase it with earthly epithets and earthly associations?"

Never before had Arbaces ventured so far, yet he felt his ground step by step; he knew he uttered a language which was at that time strange and unfamiliar, to which no precise idea could be attached, from which he could imperceptibly advance or recede, as occasion suited, as hope encouraged or fear deterred. Ione trembled, though she knew not why; her veil hid her features, and masked an expression, which, if seen by the Egyptian, would have at once damped and enraged him; in fact he was never more displeasing to her—the harmonious modulation of the most suasive voice that ever distinguished unhallowed thought fell discordantly on her ear.

Anxious to change the conversation, she replied, therefore, with a cold and indifferent voice. "Whomsoever Arbaces honours with the sentiment of esteem, it is natural that his elevated wisdom should colour that sentiment with its own hues; it is natural that his friendship should be purer than that of others, whose pursuits and errors he does not deign to share. But tell me, Arbaces, hast thou seen my brother of late? He has not visited me for several days; and when I last saw him, his manner disturbed and alarmed me much."

"Be cheered, Ione," replied the Egyptian. "It is true, that some little time since he was troubled and sad of spirit; those doubts beset him which were likely to haunt one of that fervent temperament, which ever ebbs and flows, and vibrates between anxieties and distress; he sought one who pitied and loved him; I have calmed his mind—I have removed his doubts—I have taken him from the threshold of Wisdom into its temple; and before the majesty of the goddess his soul is hushed and soothed."

"You rejoice me," answered Ione. "My dear brother, in his contentment I am happy."

The conversation then turned upon lighter subjects; the Egyptian exerted himself to please, he condescended even to entertain; the vast variety of his knowledge enabled him to adorn and light up every subject on which he touched; and Ione, forgetting the displeasing effect of his former words, was carried away, despite her sadness, by the magic of his intellect. Her manner became unrestrained and her language fluent; and Arbaces, who had waited his opportunity, now hastened to seize it.

"You have never seen," said he, "the interior of my home; it may amuse you to do so; it contains some rooms that may explain to you what you have often asked me to describe—the fashion of an Egyptian house; not, indeed, that you will perceive in the poor and minute proportions of Roman architecture the massive strength, the vast space, the gigantic magnificence, or even the domestic construction of the palaces of Thebes and Memphis; but something there is, here and there, that may serve to express to you some notion of that antique civilization which has humanized the world. Devote, then, to the austere friend of your youth, one of these bright summer evenings, and let me boast that my gloomy mansion has been honoured with the presence of the admired Ione."

Unconscious of the pollutions of the mansion, Ione readily assented to the proposal. The next evening was fixed for the visit; and the Egyptian, with a serene countenance, and a heart beating with fierce and unholy joy, departed. Scarce had he gone, when another visitor claimed admission.

13. Glaucus and Nydia

Nydia came, with light though cautious step, along the marble tablinum. She passed the portico, and paused at the flowers which bordered the garden. She had her water-vase in her hand, and she sprinkled the thirsting plants, which seemed to brighten at her approach. She bent to inhale their odour. She touched them timidly and caressingly. She felt along their stems, lest any withered leaf or creeping insect marred their beauty. And as she hovered from flower to flower, with her earnest and youthful countenance and graceful motions, you could not have imagined a fitter handmaid for the goddess of the garden.

"Nydia, my child!" said Glaucus.

At the sound of his voice she paused at once—listening, blushing, breathless; with her lips parted, her face upturned to catch the direction of the sound, she laid down the vase—she hastened to him; and it was wonderful to see how she threaded her dark way unerringly through the flowers, and came by the shortest route to the side of her new lord.

"Nydia," he said, tenderly stroking back her long and beautiful hair, "it is now three days since thou hast been under the protection of my household gods. Have they smiled on thee? Art thou happy?"

"Ah! So happy!" sighed the slave.

"And now that thou hast recovered somewhat from the hateful recollections of thy former state—and they have fitted thee with garments more meet for thy delicate shape—now, sweet child, that you hast accustomed thyself to a happiness, which may the gods grant thee ever! I am about to pray at thy hands a boon."

"Oh, what can I do for thee?" she answered, clasping her hands.

"Listen," he said, "and young as thou art, thou shalt be my confidant. Hast thou heard the name of Ione?"

"Yes! I have heard that she is of Neapolis, and beautiful."

"Beautiful! Her beauty is a thing to dazzle the day! Neapolis! Nay, she is Greek by origin; Greece only could furnish forth such shapes. Nydia, I love her!"

"I thought so," replied Nydia, calmly.

"I love, and thou shalt tell her so. I am about to send thee to her. Happy Nydia, thou wilt be in her chamber—thou wilt drink the music of her voice—thou wilt bask in the sunny air of her presence!"

"What! Wilt thou send me from thee?"

"Thou wilt go to Ione," answered Glaucus, in a tone that said, "What more canst thou desire?"

Nydia burst into tears.

Glaucus, raising himself, drew her towards him with the soothing caresses of a brother.

"My child, thou weepest in ignorance of the happiness I bestow upon thee. She is gentle and kind, and soft as the breeze of spring. She will be a sister to thy youth—she will appreciate thy winning talents—she will love thy simple graces as none other could, for they are like her own. Weepest thou still, fond fool? I will not force thee. Wilt thou not do for me this kindness?"

"If I can serve thee, command. See, I weep no longer—I am calm."

"That is my own Nydia," he continued. "Go, then, to her; if thou art disappointed in her kindness—if I have deceived thee, return when thou wilt. I do not *give* thee to another; I but lend. My home shall ever be thy refuge. Ah! Would it could shelter all the friendless and distressed! But if my heart whisper truly, I shall soon claim thee again. My home and Ione's will become the same, and thou shalt dwell with both."

A shiver passed through the slight frame of the blind girl, but she wept no more; she was resigned.

"Go, then, my Nydia, to Ione's house—they shall show thee the way. Take her the fairest flowers thou canst pluck; the vase which contains them I will give thee; thou must excuse its unworthiness. Thou shalt take, too, the lute that I gave thee yesterday, and from which thou knowest so well to awaken the charming spirit. Thou shalt give her also this letter, in which, after a hundred efforts, I have embodied something of my thoughts. Let thine ear catch every accent—every modulation of her voice, and tell me, when we meet again, if its music could flatter me or discourage. It is now, Nydia, some days since I have been admitted to Ione; there is something mysterious in this exclusion. Be my friend, plead for me; and oh! How vastly wilt thou overpay the little I have done for thee! Thou comprehendest, Nydia; thou art yet a child—have I said more than thou canst understand?"

"No."

"And thou wilt serve me?"

"Yes."

"Come to me when thou hast gathered the flowers, and I will give thee the vase I speak of, seek me in the chamber of Leda. Pretty one, thou dost not grieve now?"

"Glaucus, I am a slave; what business have I with grief or joy?

"Sayest thou so? No, Nydia, be free. I give thee freedom; enjoy it as thou wilt, and pardon me that I reckoned on thy desire to serve me."

"You are offended. Oh! I would not, for that which no freedom can give offend you, Glaucus. My guardian, my saviour, my protector, forgive the poor blind girl! She does not grieve even in leaving thee, if she can contribute to thy happiness."

"May the gods bless this grateful heart!" said Glaucus, greatly moved; and, unconscious of the fires he excited, he kissed her forehead.

"Thou forgivest me," said she, "and thou wilt say no more of freedom; my happiness is to be thy slave: thou hast promised thou wilt not give me to another—"

"I have promised."

"And now I will gather the flowers."

14. Lady and Slave

A slave entered the chamber of Ione. A messenger from Glaucus desired to be admitted.

Ione hesitated an instant.

"She is blind," said the slave; "she will do her commission to none but thee."

Hearing that the messenger was blind, Ione felt the impossibility of returning a chilling reply. Glaucus had chosen a herald that was indeed sacred; one who could not be denied.

"What can he want of me?" she thought, and her heart beat quickly. The curtain across the door was withdrawn; a soft and echoless step fell upon the marble; and Nydia, led by one of the attendants, entered with her precious gift.

She stood still a moment, as if listening for some sound that might direct her.

"Will the noble Ione," said she, in a soft low voice, "deign to speak, that I may lay my offerings at her feet?"

"Fair child," said Ione, touched and soothingly, "give not thyself the pain to cross the slippery floor. My attendant will bring to me what thou hast to present," and she motioned to the handmaid to take the vase.

"I may give these flowers to none but thee," answered Nydia; and, guided by her ear, she walked slowly to the place where Ione sat; and, kneeling when she came before her, proffered the vase.

Ione took it from her hand, and placed it on the table at her side. She then raised her gently, and would have seated her on the couch, but the girl modestly resisted.

"I have not yet discharged my office," said she; and she drew the letter of Glaucus from her vest. "This will, perhaps, explain why he who sent me chose so unworthy a messenger."

The Neapolitan took the letter with a hand the trembling of which Nydia at once felt, and sighed to feel. With folded arms and downcast looks, she stood before the proud and stately form of Ione—no less proud, perhaps in her attitude of submission. Ione waved her hand, and the attendants withdrew; she gazed upon the form of the young slave in surprise and beautiful compassion; then, retiring a little from her, she opened and read the letter:

"Glaucus to Ione sends more than he dares to utter. Is Ione ill? Thy slaves tell me 'No' and that assurance comforts me. Has Glaucus offended Ione?—ah! That question I may not ask from *them*. For five days I have been banished from thy presence. Has the sun shone?—I know it not. Has the sky smiled? It has had no smile for me. My sun and my sky are Ione. Am I too bold? Do I say that on the tablet which my tongue has hesitated to breathe? Alas! It is in absence that I feel most the spells by which thou hast subdued me. And absence, that deprives me of joy, brings me courage. Thou wilt not see me; thou has banished also the common flatterers that flock around thee. Canst thou confound them with me? Thou knowest well that I am not of them—that their clay is not mine. Have they slandered me to thee? Thou wilt not believe them. Did the Delphic oracle itself tell me thou wert unworthy, I would not believe it; and am I less incredulous than thou? I think of the last time we met—of the song which I sang to thee—of the look that thou gavest me in return. Disguise it as thou wilt, Ione, there is something kindred between us, and our eyes acknowledged it, though our lips were silent. Deign to see me, to listen to me, and after that exclude me if thou wilt. I meant not so soon to say I loved. But those words rush to my heart—they will have way Accept, then, my homage and my vows. We met first at the shrine of Pallas; shall we not meet before a softer and more ancient altar?

"Accept the flowers which I send—their sweet breath has a language more eloquent than words. I send them by one whom thou wilt receive for her own sake, if not for mine. She, like us, is a stranger; her father's ashes lie under brighter skies; but, less happy than we, she is blind and a slave. Poor Nydia! I seek as much as possible to repair to her the cruelties of Nature and Fate, in asking permission to place her with thee. She is gentle, quick, and docile. She is skilled in music and the song; and she is a very Chloris to the flowers. She thinks, Ione, that thou wilt love her; if thou dost not, send her back to me.

"One word more—let me be bold, Ione. Why thinkest thou so highly of that dark Egyptian? He hath not about him the air of honest men. We Greeks learn mankind from our cradle; we are not the less profound, in that we affect no sombre mien; our lips smile, but our eyes are grave—they observe—they note—they study. Arbaces is not one to be credulously trusted: can it be that he hath wronged me to thee? I left him with thee; thou sawest how my presence stung him; since then thou hast not admitted me. Believe nothing that he can say to my disfavour; if thou dost, tell me so at once; for this you owe me."

It seemed to Ione, as she read this letter, as if a mist had fallen from her eyes. What had been the supposed offence of Glaucus—that he had not really loved! And now, plainly, and in no dubious terms, he confessed that love. From that moment, his power was fully restored. At every tender word full of romantic and trustful passion, her heart smote her. Had she doubted his faith, and had she believed another? And had she refused to him the culprit's right to know his crime, to plead in his defence? The tears rolled down her cheeks—she kissed the letter—she placed it in her bosom; and then, turning to Nydia, who stood in the same place and in the same posture:

"Wilt thou sit, my child," she said, "while I write an answer?"

"You will answer it, then!" said Nydia, coldly. "Well, the slave that accompanied me can take it back."

"For you," said Ione, "stay with me—trust me, your service shall be light." Nydia bowed her head. "What is your name, fair girl?"

"They call me Nydia."

"Your country?"

"The land of Olympus—Thessaly."

"Thou shalt be to me a friend," said Ione caressingly, "as thou art already a countrywoman. Meanwhile, I beseech thee, stand not on that cold and glassy marble—There! Now that thou art seated, I can leave thee for an instant."

"Ione to Glaucus, greeting—Come to me tomorrow. I may have been unjust; but I will tell thee, at least, the fault that has been imputed to thee. Fear not the Egyptian—fear none. Thou sayest thou hast expressed too much—alas! In these hasty words I have already done so. Farewell!"

"As Ione reappeared with the letter, which she did not dare to read after she had written, Nydia started from her seat.

"You have written to Glaucus?"

"I have."

"And will he thank the messenger who gives him thy letter?" Ione forgot that her companion was blind; she blushed from the brow to the neck, and remained silent.

"I mean this," added Nydia in a calmer tone; "the lightest word of coldness from thee will sadden him—the lightest kindness will rejoice. If it be the first, let the slave take back thine answer; if it be the last, let me—I will return this evening."

"And why, Nydia," asked Ione, evasively, "wouldst thou be the bearer of my letter?"

"It is so, then!" said Nydia. "Ah! How could it be otherwise; who could be unkind to Glaucus?"

"My child," said Ione, a little more reservedly than before, "thou speakest warmly—Glaucus, then, is amiable in thine eyes?"

"Noble Ione! Glaucus has been that to me which neither fortune nor the gods have been—*a friend*!"

The sadness mingled with dignity with which Nydia uttered these simple words, affected Ione so that she bent down and kissed her. "Thou art grateful, and deservedly so. Go, Nydia—take this letter—but return again. If I am from home—as this evening, perhaps I shall be—thy chamber shall be prepared next my own. Nydia, I have no sister—wilt thou be one to me?"

The Thessalian kissed Ione's hand, and then said with some embarrassment: "One favour—may I dare ask it?"

"Thou canst not ask what I will not grant."

"They tell me that thou art beautiful beyond the loveliness of earth. Alas! I cannot see that which gladdens the world! Wilt thou suffer me, then, to pass my hand over thy face?"

She did not wait for Ione's answer, but, as she spoke, gently and slowly passed her hand over the bending and half averted features of the Greek—features which but one image in the world can depict and recall—that image is the mutilated, but all-wondrous, statue in her native city—her own Neapolis—that Parian face, before which all the beauty of the Florentine Venus is poor and earthly—that aspect so full of harmony—of youth—of genius—of the soul—which modern critics have supposed the representation of Psyche.

Her touch lingered over the braided hair and polished brow—over the downy and damask cheek—over the dimpled lip—the swan-like neck. "I know now that thou art beautiful," she said, "and I can picture thee to my darkness, henceforth, and forever!"

When Nydia left her, Ione sank into a deep but delicious reverie. Glaucus loved her; he owned it—yes, he loved her. She drew forth again that dear confession; she paused over every word, she kissed every line; she did not ask why he had been maligned, she only felt assured that it was so. She wondered how she had ever believed a syllable against him; she wondered how the Egyptian had been enabled to exercise a power against him; she felt a chill creep over her as she again turned to his warning against Arbaces, and her secret fear of that gloomy being, darkened into awe. She was awakened from these thoughts by her maidens, who came to announce to her that the hour appointed to visit Arbaces was arrived; she started, she had forgotten the promise. Her first impulse was to renounce it; her second was to laugh at her own fears of her eldest surviving friend. She hastened to add the usual ornaments to her dress, and, doubtful whether she should vet question the Egyptian more closely with respect to his accusation of Glaucus, or whether she should wait till, without citing the authority, she should insinuate to Glaucus the accusation itself, she took her way to the gloomy mansion of Arbaces.

15. Ione Within the Net

"O dearest Nydia!" exclaimed Glaucus, as he read her letter, "whitest-robed messenger that ever passed between heaven and earth—how, how shall I thank thee?"

"I am rewarded," said the poor Thessalian.

"Tomorrow—tomorrow! How shall I pass the hours till then?"

The enamoured Greek would not let Nydia escape him, though she sought several times to leave the chamber; he made her recite to him over and over again every syllable of the brief conversation that had taken place between her and Ione; a dozen times, forgetting her misfortune, he questioned her of the looks, of the countenance of his beloved; and then quickly again, excusing his fault, he bade her recommence the whole recital which he had thus interrupted. The moments painful to Nydia passed rapidly and delightfully to him, and the twilight had already darkened when he sent her again to Ione with a fresh letter and further flowers. Scarcely had she gone, when Clodius and several of his gay companions broke in upon him; they rallied him on his seclusion, and his absence from his customary haunts; they invited him to accompany them to various resorts in that lively city, where night and day proffered diversity of pleasures. He was too happy to be unsocial; he longed to cast off the exuberance of joy that oppressed him. He willingly accepted the proposal of his comrades, and laughingly they sallied out together down the populous and glittering streets.

In the meantime Nydia once more gained the house of Ione, who had long left it; she inquired indifferently whither Ione had gone.

The answer arrested and appalled her.

"To the house of Arbaces—of the Egyptian? Impossible!"

"It is true, my little one," said the slave, who had replied to her question. "She has known the Egyptian long."

"And has she visited him before?"

"Never till now," answered the slave. "If rumours be true, it might be better, perhaps, if she had not ventured now. But our mistress hears nothing of that which reaches us; the talk of the vestibulum reaches not to the peristyle."

"Never till now!" repeated Nydia. "Art thou sure?"

"Sure, pretty one; but what is that to thee or to us?"

Nydia hesitated a moment, and then, putting down the flowers with which she had been charged, she called to the slave who had accompanied her, and left the house without saying another word.

"She does not dream," she thought, "she cannot—of the dangers into which she has plunged. Fool that I am—shall I save her?—yes, for I love Glaucus better than myself."

When she arrived at the house of the Athenian, she learnt that he had gone out with a party of his friends, and none knew whither. He probably would not be home before midnight.

The Thessalian groaned; she sank upon a seat in the hall. "There is no time to be lost," she thought. Starting up, she turned to the slave who had accompanied her.

"Knowest thou," said she, "if Ione has any relative, any intimate friend at Pompeii?"

"Why, by Jupiter!" answered the slave, "art thou silly enough to ask the question? Every one in Pompeii knows that Ione has a brother, who, young and rich, has been—under the rose I speak—so foolish as to become a priest of Isis."

"A priest of Isis! O Gods! His name?"

"Apæcides."

"I know it all," muttered Nydia: "brother and sister, then, are to be both victims! Apæcides! Yes, that was the name I heard in— He well, then, knows the peril that surrounds his sister; I will go to him."

She sprang up at that thought, and taking the staff which always guided her steps, she hastened to the neighbouring shrine of Isis. Till she had been under the guardianship of the kindly Greek, that staff has sufficed to conduct the poor blind girl from corner to corner of Pompeii. Every street, every turning in the more frequented parts, was familiar to her; and as the inhabitants entertained a tender and half-superstitious veneration of those subject to her infirmity, the passengers had always given way to her timid steps.

But since she had been under the roof of Glaucus, he had ordered a slave to accompany her always; and the poor devil thus appointed, who was somewhat of the fattest, and who, after having twice performed the journey to Ione's house, now saw himself condemned to a third excursion (whither the gods only knew), hastened after her, deploring his fate, and solemnly assuring Castor and Pollux that he believed the blind girl had the talaria of Mercury as well as the infirmity of Cupid.

Nydia, however, required but little of his assistance to find her way to the popular temple of Isis. The space before it was now deserted, and she went without obstacle to the sacred rails.

"There is no one here," said the fat slave. "What dost thou want, or whom? Knowest thou not that the priests do not live in the temple?"

"Call out!" said she, impatiently; "night and day there is always one flamen, at least, watching in the shrines."

The slave called—no one appeared.

"Seest thou no one?"

"No one."

"Thou mistakest; I hear a sigh: look again."

The slave, wondering and grumbling, cast round his heavy eyes, and before one of the altars he beheld a form bending in meditation.

"I see a figure," said he; "and, by the white garments, it is a priest.

"O flamen of Isis!" cried Nydia; "servant of the Most Ancient, hear me!"

"Who calls?" said a low and melancholy voice.

"One who has no common tidings to impart to a member of your body; I come to declare and not to ask oracles."

"With whom wouldst thou confer? This is no hour for thy conference; depart, disturb me not: the night is sacred to the gods: the day to men."

"Methinks I know thy voice! Thou art he whom I seek. Art thou not the priest Apæcides?"

"I am that," replied the priest, emerging from the altar and approaching the rail.

"Thou art! The gods be praised!" Waving her hand to the slave, she bade him withdraw to a distance. "Hush!" said she, speaking quick and low; "art thou indeed Apæcides?"

"If thou knowest me, canst thou not recall my features?"

"I am blind," answered Nydia; "my eyes are in my ear, and that recognises thee: yet swear that thou art he."

"By the gods I swear it, by my right hand, and by the moon!"

"Hush! Speak low—bend near—give me thy hand: knowest thou Arbaces? Hast thou laid flowers at the foot of the dead? Ah! Thy hand is cold—hark ye!—hast thou taken the awful vow?"

"Who art thou? I do not know thee."

"But thou hast heard my voice; no matter, those recollections it should shame us both to recall. Listen, thou hast a sister."

"What of her?"

"Thou knowest the banquets of the dead—it pleases thee, perhaps, to share them—would it please thee to have thy sister there? With Arbaces her host?"

"Gods! He dare not!"

"I speak the truth; Ione is in the halls of Arbaces—for the first time. Thou knowest the peril of that first time! Thou art warned. I can do no more."

"Stay! Stay! If this be true, what—what can be done to save her? They may not admit me. I know not all the mazes of that intricate mansion. O Nemesis! Justly am I punished!"

"I will dismiss yon slave; I will lead thee to the private door of the house; I will whisper to thee the word which admits. Take some weapon: it may be needful!"

"Wait an instant," said Apæcides, retiring into one of the cells that flank the temple, and reappearing in a few moments wrapped in a large cloak, which was then much worn by all classes, and which concealed his sacred dress. "Now," he said, grinding his teeth, "if Arbaces—but he dare not! He dare not! Why should I suspect him? Is he so base a villain? I will not think it—yet, sophist! Dark bewilderer that he is! O gods protect!—hush! Are there gods? Yes, there is one goddess, at least, whose voice I can command; and that is—vengeance!"

Muttering these disconnected thoughts, Apæcides, followed by his silent and sightless companion, hastened through the most solitary paths to the house of the Egyptian.

The slave, abruptly dismissed by Nydia, shrugged his shoulders, muttered an adjuration, and, nothing loath, rolled off to his cubiculum.

16. The Solitude of the Egyptian

We must go back a few hours. At the first grey dawn, the Egyptian was seated, sleepless and alone, on the summit of the lofty pyramidal tower which flanked his house. A tall parapet around it served as a well, and conspired, with the height of the edifice and the gloomy trees that girded the mansion, to defy the prying eyes of curiosity or observation. A table, on which lay a scroll filled with mystic figures, was before him. On high, the stars were faint, and the shades of night melted from the sterile mountain-tops; only above Vesuvius there rested a deep and massy cloud, which for several days past had gathered darker and more solid over its summit. The struggle of night and day was more visible over the broad ocean, which stretched calm, like a gigantic lake, bounded by the circling shores that, covered with vines and foliage, and gleaming here and there with the white walls of sleeping cities, sloped to the scarce-rippling waves.

It was the hour above all others most sacred to the daring science of the Egyptian—the science which could read our changeful destinies in the stars.

He had filled his scroll, he had noted the moment and the sign; and, leaning upon his hand, he had surrendered himself to the thoughts which his calculation excited.

"Again do the stars forewarn me! Some danger assuredly awaits me!" said he, slowly; "some danger, violent and sudden. The stars wear for me the same mocking menace which, if our chronicles do not err, they once wore for Pyrrhus—for him doomed to strive for all things, to enjoy none—all attacking, nothing gaining—battles without fruit, laurels without triumph, fame without success; at last made craven by his own superstitions, and slain like a dog by a tile from the hand of an old woman! Verily, the stars flatter when they give me a type in this fool of war—when they promise to the ardour of my wisdom the same results as to the madness of his ambition— perpetual exercise—no certain goal—the Sisyphus task, the mountain and the stone!—the stone, a gloomy image!—it reminds me that I am threatened with somewhat of the same death as the Epirote. Let me look again. 'Beware,' say the shining prophets, 'how thou passest under ancient roofs, or besieged walls, or overhanging cliffs—a stone, hurled from above, is charged by the curses of destiny against thee!' And, at no distant date from this, comes the peril: but I cannot, of a certainty, read the day and hour. Well! If my glass run low, the sands shall sparkle to the last. Yet, if I escape this peril—ay, if I escape—bright and clear as the moon-light track along the waters glows the rest of my existence. I see honours, happiness, success, shining upon every billow of the dark gulf beneath which I must sink at last. How then, with such destinies beyond the peril, shall I succumb to it? My soul whispers hope, it sweeps exultingly beyond the boding hour, it revels in the future—its own courage is the fittest omen."

As he thus concluded his soliloquy, the Egyptian involuntarily rose. He paced rapidly the narrow space of that star-roofed floor, and, pausing at the parapet, looked again upon the grey and melancholy heavens. The chills of the faint dawn came refreshingly upon his brow, and gradually his mind resumed its natural and collected calm. He withdrew his gaze from the stars, as, one after one, they receded into the depths of heaven; and his eyes fell over the broad expanse below. Dim in the silenced port of the city rose the masts of the galleys: along that mart of luxury and of labour was stilled the mighty hum. No lights, save here and there from before the columns of a temple, or in the porticos of the voiceless forum, broke the wan and fluctuating light of the struggling morn. From the huge space of the amphitheatre, with its stony seats rising one above the other—coiled and round as some slumbering monster—rose a thin and ghastly mist, which gathered darker, and more dark, over the scattered foliage that gloomed in its vicinity. The city seemed as, after the awful change of seventeen ages, it seems now to the traveller—a City of the Dead.

From the serene and tideless sea, there came, softened by distance, a faint and regular murmur, like the breathing of sleep; and curving far, as with outstretched arms, into the green and beautiful land, it seemed unconsciously to clasp to its breast the cities sloping to its margin—Stabiæ, and Herculaneum, and Pompeii—those darlings of the deep. "Ye slumber," said the Egyptian, as he scowled over the cities, the boast and flower of Campania; "ye slumber!—would it were the eternal repose of death! As ye are now—jewels in the crown of empire—so once were the cities of the Nile! Their greatness hath perished from them, they sleep amidst ruins, their palaces and their shrines are tombs, the serpent coils in the grass of their streets, the lizard basks in the solitary halls. By that mysterious law of Nature, which humbles one to exalt the other, ye have thriven upon their ruins; thou, haughty Rome, hast usurped the glories of Sesostris and Semiramis—thou art a robber, clothing thyself with their spoils! And these—slaves in thy triumph—that I (the last son of forgotten monarchs) survey below, reservoirs of thine all-pervading power and luxury, I curse as I behold! The time shall come when Egypt shall be avenged! When the barbarian's steed shall make his manger in the Golden House of Nero! And thou that hast sown the wind with conquest shall reap the harvest in the whirlwind of desolation!"

As the Egyptian uttered a prediction which fate so fearfully fulfilled, a more solemn and boding image of ill omen never occurred to the dreams of painter or poet. The morning light, which can pale so wanly even the young cheek of beauty, gave his majestic and stately features almost the colours of the grave, with the dark hair falling massively around them, the dark robes flowing long and loose, the arms outstretched from the lofty eminence, and the glittering eyes, fierce with a savage gladness—half prophet and half-fiend!

He turned his gaze from the city and the ocean; before him lay the vineyards and meadows of the rich Campania. The gate and walls—ancient, half Pelasgic—of the city, seemed not to bound its extent. Villas and villages stretched on every side up the ascent of Vesuvius, not nearly then so steep or so lofty as at present. For as Rome itself is built on an exhausted volcano, so in similar security the inhabitants of the South, tenanted the green and vine-clad places around a volcano whose fires they believed at rest forever. From the gate stretched the long street of tombs, various in size and architecture, by which, on that side, the city is yet approached. Above all, rose the cloud-capped summit of the Dread Mountain, with the shadows, now dark, now light, betraying the mossy caverns and ashy rocks, which testified the past conflagrations, and might have prophesied—but man is blind—that which was to come.

But it was neither the rugged height of the still volcano, nor the fertility of the sloping fields, nor the melancholy avenue of tombs, nor the glittering villas of a polished and luxurious people, that now arrested the eyes of the Egyptian. On one part of the landscape, the mountain of Vesuvius descended to the plain in a narrow and uncultivated ridge, broken here and there by jagged crags and copses of wild foliage. At the base of this lay a marshy and unwholesome pool; and the intent gaze of Arbaces caught the outline of some living form moving by the marshes, and stooping as if to pluck its rank produce.

"So" he said aloud, "I have another companion in these unworldly night-watches. The witch of Vesuvius is abroad. What! Doth she, too, as the credulous image—doth she too, learn the lore of the great stars? Hath she been uttering foul magic to the moon, or culling (as her pauses betoken) foul herbs from the venomous marsh? Well, I must see this fellow-labourer. Whoever strives to know learns that no human lore is despicable. Despicable only you—slaves of luxury—sluggards in thought—who, cultivating nothing but the barren sense, dream that its poor can produce alike the myrtle and the laurel. No, the wise only can enjoy—when mind, brain, invention, experience, thought, learning, imagination, all contribute like rivers to swell the sea…Ione."

As Arbaces uttered that last and charmed word, his thoughts sunk at once into a deeper channel. His steps paused; once or twice he smiled joyously, and then, as he turned from his place of vigil, and sought his couch, he muttered: "If death frown so near, I will say at least that I have lived—Ione shall be mine!"

The character of Arbaces was one of those intricate and varied webs, in which even the mind that sat within it was sometimes confused and perplexed. In him, the son of a fallen dynasty, the outcast of a sunken people, was that spirit of discontented, pride, which ever rankles in one of a sterner mould, who feels himself inexorably shut from the sphere in which his father shone, and to which Nature as well as birth no less entitle himself. This sentiment has no benevolence; it wars with society, it sees enemies in mankind. But with this sentiment did not go its common companion, poverty. Arbaces possessed wealth which equalled that of most of the Roman nobles; and this enabled him to gratify to the utmost the passions which had no outlet in business or ambition. Travelling from clime to clime, and beholding Rome everywhere, he increased both his hatred of society, and his passion for pleasure. He was in a vast prison, which, however, he could fill with the ministers of luxury. He could not escape from the prison, and his only object, therefore, was to give it the character of a palace. The Egyptians, from the earliest time, were devoted to the joys of sense; Arbaces inherited both their appetite for sensuality and the glow of imagination which struck light from its rottenness. But still, unsocial in his pleasures as in his graver pursuits, and brooking neither superior nor equal, he admitted few to his companionship, save the willing slaves of his profligacy. He was the solitary lord of a crowded harem; but, with all, he felt condemned to that satiety which is the curse of men whose intellect is above their pursuits, and that which once had been the impulse of passion froze down to the ordinance of custom. From the disappointments of sense he sought to raise himself by the cultivation of knowledge; and as it was not his object to serve mankind, so he despised that knowledge which is practical and useful. His dark imagination loved to exercise itself in those visionary and obscure researches which are ever delightful to a wayward and solitary mind, and to which he himself was invited by the daring pride of his disposition and the mysterious traditions of his clime. Thus he pursued Science across her appointed boundaries, into the land of perplexity and shadow. From the truths of astronomy he wandered into astrological fallacy; from the secrets of chemistry he passed into the spectral labyrinth of magic; and he who could be sceptical as to the power of the gods, was credulously superstitious as to the power of man.

His conscience was solely of the intellect—it was awed by no moral laws. If man imposed these checks upon the herd, so he believed that man, by superior wisdom, could raise himself above them. "If" he reasoned, "I have the genius to impose laws, have I not the right to command my own creations? Still more, have I not the right to control—to evade—to scorn—the fabrications of meaner intellects than my own?" Thus, he justified his villainy by what ought to have made him virtuous—the elevation of his capacities.

Most men have more or less the passion for power; in Arbaces that passion corresponded exactly to his character. It was not the passion for an external and brute authority. He desired not the purple and the fasces, the insignia of vulgar command. His youthful ambition once foiled and defeated, scorn had supplied its place—his pride, his contempt for Rome, which had become the synonym of the world, did not permit him to aspire to sway over others, for that would render him at once the tool or creature of the emperor. He, the Son of the Great Race of Rameses—*he* execute the orders of, and receive his power from, another!—the mere notion filled him with rage. But in rejecting an ambition that coveted nominal distinctions, he indulged the more in the ambition to rule the heart. Honouring mental power as the greatest of earthly gifts, he loved to feel that power palpably in himself, by extending it over all whom he encountered. Thus had he ever sought the young—thus had he ever fascinated and controlled them.

He had seldom lived long in one place; but as he grew older, he grew more wearied of the excitement of new scenes, and he had sojourned among the delightful cities of Campania for a period which surprised even himself. In fact, his pride somewhat crippled his choice of residence. Rome herself was hateful to his indignant soul; nor did he love to find his riches rivalled by the minions of the court, and cast into comparative poverty by the mighty magnificence of the court itself. The Campanian cities proffered to him all that his nature craved—the luxuries of an unequalled climate—the imaginative refinements of a voluptuous civilization.

It is the curse of sensualists never to love till the pleasures of sense begin to pall; their hearts are exhausted. So, ever chasing love, the Egyptian had spent all the glory of his years without attaining the object of his desires. The beauty of tomorrow succeeded the beauty of today, and the shadows bewildered him in pursuit of the substance. When, two years before, he beheld Ione, he saw, for the first time, one whom he imagined he could love. He stood, then, upon that bridge of life, from which man sees before him distinctly a wasted youth on the one side, and the darkness of approaching age upon the other: a time in which we are more than ever anxious, perhaps, to secure to ourselves, ere it be too late, whatever we have been taught to consider necessary to the enjoyment of life of which the brighter half is gone.

With an earnestness and a patience which he had never before commanded for his pleasures, Arbaces had devoted himself to win the heart of Ione. It did not content him to love; he desired to be loved. In this hope he had watched the expanding youth of the beautiful Neapolitan; and, knowing the influence that the mind possesses over those who are taught to cultivate it, he had contributed willingly to form her genius and enlighten her intellect, in the hope that she would thus be able to appreciate what he felt would be his best claim to her affection; a character which, however criminal and perverted, was rich in its original elements of strength and grandeur. When he felt that character to be acknowledged, he willingly allowed, nay, encouraged her, to mix among the idle votaries of pleasure, in the belief that her soul, fitted for higher commune, would miss the companionship of his own, and that, in comparison with others, she would learn to love him. He had forgotten that, as the sunflower to the sun, so youth turns to youth, until his jealousy of Glaucus suddenly apprised him of his error. From that moment, though, as we have seen, he knew not the extent of his danger, a fiercer and more tumultuous direction was given to a passion long controlled.

He resolved to lose no further time upon cautious and perilous preparations; he resolved to place an irrevocable barrier between himself and his rivals; he resolved to possess himself of the person of Ione: not that, in his present love, so long nursed and fed by hopes purer than those of passion alone, he would have been contented with that mere possession. He desired the heart, the soul, no less than the beauty, of Ione; but he imagined that once separated by a daring crime from the rest of mankind—once bound to Ione by a tie that memory could not break, she would be driven to concentrate her thoughts in him—that his arts would complete his conquest, and that, according to the true moral of the Roman and the Sabine, the empire obtained by force would be cemented by gentler means. This resolution was yet more confirmed in him by his belief in the prophecies of the stars; they had long foretold to him this year, and even the present month, as the epoch of some dread disaster, menacing life itself. He was driven to a certain and limited date. He resolved to crowd, monarch-like, on his funeral pyre, all that his soul held most dear. In his own words, if he were to die, he resolved to feel that he had lived, and that Ione should be his own.

17. Ione in the House of Arbaces

When Ione entered the spacious hall of the Egyptian, the awe which had crept over her brother impressed itself also upon her: there seemed something ominous and warning in the still and mournful faces of those dread Theban monsters, whose majestic and passionless features the marble so well portrayed.

The tall Æthiopian slave grinned as he admitted her, and motioned to her to proceed. Halfway up the hall she was met by Arbaces himself, in festive robes, which glittered with jewels. Although it was broad day without, the mansion, according to the practice of the luxurious, was artificially darkened, and the lamps cast their still and odour-giving light over the rich floors, and ivory roofs.

"Beautiful Ione," said Arbaces, as he bent to touch her hand, "it is you who have eclipsed the day—it is your eyes that light up the halls."

"You must not talk to me thus," said Ione, smiling: "you forget that your lore has sufficiently instructed my mind to render these graceful flatteries unwelcome. It was you who taught me to disdain adulation: will you unteach your pupil?"

There was something so frank and charming in the manner of Ione as she thus spoke that the Egyptian was more than ever enamoured, and more than ever disposed to renew the offence he had committed; he however, answered quickly and gaily, and hastened to turn the conversation.

He led her through the various chambers of the house, which seemed to certain to her eyes, inexperienced to other splendour than the minute elegance of Campanian cities, the treasures of the world.

In the walls were set pictures of inestimable art; the lights shone over statues of the noblest age of Greece. Cabinets of gems, each cabinet itself a gem, filled up the interstices of the columns: the most precious woods lined the thresholds and composed the doors; gold and jewels seemed lavished all around. Sometimes they were alone in these rooms—sometimes they passed through silent rows of slaves, who, kneeling as she passed, proffered to her offerings of bracelets, of chains, of gems, which the Egyptian vainly entreated her to receive.

"I have often heard," said she, wonderingly, "that you were rich, but I never dreamed of the amount of your wealth."

"Would I could coin it all," replied the Egyptian, "into one crown, which I might place upon that snowy brow!"

"Alas! The weight would crush me; I should be a second Tarpeia," she answered, laughingly.

"But do not disdain riches. They know not what life is capable of who are not wealthy. Gold is the great magician of earth—it realizes our dreams—it gives them the power of a god—there is a grandeur, a sublimity, in its possession; it is the mightiest, yet the most obedient of slaves."

The artful Arbaces sought to dazzle the young Neapolitan by his treasures and his eloquence; he sought to awaken in her the desire to be mistress of what she surveyed; he hoped that she would confound the owner with the possessions, and that the charms of his wealth would reflect on himself. Meanwhile, Ione was secretly somewhat uneasy at the gallantries which escaped from those lips, which, till lately, had seemed to disdain the common homage which is paid to beauty: and, with that delicate subtlety which women alone possess, she sought to ward off shafts deliberately aimed, and to laugh or to talk away the meaning from his warming language.

Suddenly, as they stood in a hall which was surrounded by draperies of silver and white, the Egyptian clapped his hands, and, as if by enchantment, a banquet rose from the floor—a couch, or throne, with a crimson canopy, ascended simultaneously at the feet of Ione—and at the same instant, from behind the curtains, swelled invisible and softest music.

Arbaces placed himself at her feet, and children, young and beautiful as Loves, ministered to the feast.

The feast was over, the music sank to a low and subdued strain, and Arbaces thus addressed his beautiful guest:

"Hast thou never in this dark and uncertain world—hast thou never aspired, my pupil, to look beyond—hast thou never wished to put aside the veil of futurity, and to behold on the shores of Fate the shadowy images of things to be? For it is not the past alone that has its ghosts: each event to come has also its spectrum—its shade; when the hour arrives, life enters it, the shadow becomes corporeal, and walks the world. Thus, in the land beyond the grave, are ever two impalpable and spiritual hosts—the things that have been and the things that are! If by our wisdom we can penetrate that land, we see the one as the other, and learn, as I have learned, not alone the mysteries of the dead, but also the destiny of the living."

"As thou hast learned! Can wisdom attain so far?"

"Wilt thou prove my knowledge, Ione, and behold the representation of thine own fate? It is a drama more striking than those of Æschylus: it is one I have prepared for thee, if thou wilt see the shadows perform their part."

The Neapolitan trembled; she thought of Glaucus, and sighed as well as trembled; were their destinies to be united? Half incredulous, half believing, half awed, half alarmed by the words of her strange host, she remained some moments silent, and then answered:

"It may revolt—it may terrify; the knowledge of the future will perhaps only embitter the present!"

"Not so, Ione. I have myself looked upon thy future lot, and the ghosts of thy Future bask in the gardens of Elysium; amidst the asphodel and the rose they prepare garlands of thy sweet destiny, and the Fates, so harsh to others, weave only for thee the web of happiness and love. Wilt thou then come and behold thy fate, so that thou mayst enjoy it beforehand?"

She uttered a half audible assent; the Egyptian arose, and, taking her by the hand, he led her across the banquet-room, the curtains withdrew as by magic hands, and the music broke forth in a louder and gladder strain; they passed a row of columns, on either side of which the fountains cast aloft their fragrant waters; they descended by broad and easy steps into a garden. Eve had commenced; the moon was already high in heaven, and those sweet flowers that sleep by day, and fill, with ineffable odours, the air of night, were thickly scattered amidst alleys cut through the star-lit foliage—or, gathered in baskets, lay like offerings at the feet of the frequent statues that gleamed along their path.

"Whither wouldst thou lead me, Arbaces?" said Ione, wonderingly.

"Only yonder," said he, pointing to a small building which stood at the end of the vista. "It is a temple consecrated to the Fates—our rites require holy ground."

They passed into a narrow hall, at the end of which hung a sable curtain. As he lifted it, she entered, and found herself in total darkness.

"Be not alarmed," said the Egyptian, "the light will rise instantly." While he spoke, a soft, warm, gradual light diffused itself around; as it spread over each object, she perceived that she was in an apartment of moderate size, hung everywhere with black; a couch of draperies of the same hue was beside her. In the centre of the room was a small altar, on which stood a tripod of bronze. At one side, upon a lofty column of granite, was a colossal head of the blackest marble, which she perceived, by the crown of wheat-ears that encircled the brow, represented the great Egyptian goddess. Arbaces stood before the altar: he had laid his garland on the shrine, and seemed occupied with pouring into the tripod the contents of a brazen vase; suddenly from that tripod leaped into life a blue, quick, darting, irregular flame; he drew back to her side, and muttered some words in an unfamiliar language; the curtain at the back of the altar waved tremulously—it parted slowly, and, in the aperture which was thus made, Ione beheld an indistinct and pale landscape, which gradually grew brighter and clearer, till, as she gazed at it, she saw trees, and rivers, and meadows, and all the beautiful diversity of the richest earth. At length, before the landscape, a dim shadow glided; it rested opposite to her; slowly the same charm seemed to operate upon it as over the rest of the scene; it took form and shape, and lo!—in its feature and in its form Ione beheld herself!

Then the scene behind the spectre faded away, and was succeeded by the representation of a gorgeous palace; a throne was raised in the centre of its hall—the dim forms of slaves and guards were ranged round it, and a pale hand held over the throne the likeness of a diadem.

A new actor now appeared; he was clothed from head to foot in a dark robe—his face was concealed—he knelt at the feet of the shadowy Ione—he clasped her hand—he pointed to the throne, as if to invite her to ascend it.

The Neapolitan's heart beat violently. "Shall the shadow disclose itself?" Arbaces whispered beside her.

"Ah, yes!" answered Ione, softly, for Glaucus was in her thoughts.

Arbaces raised his hand—the spectre seemed to drop the mantle that concealed its form—and Ione shrank back, for it was Arbaces who thus knelt before her.

"This is indeed thy fate!" whispered the Egyptian's voice in her ear. "And thou art destined to be the bride of Arbaces."

Then the black curtain closed over the phantasmagoria; and Arbaces himself—the real, the living Arbaces—was at her feet.

"Oh, Ione!" said he, passionately gazing upon her.

"Listen to one who has long struggled vainly with his love. I adore thee! The fates do not lie—thou art destined to be mine—I have sought the world around, and found none like thee. From my youth upward, I have sighed for such as thou art. I have dreamed till I saw thee—I wake, and behold thee. Turn not away from me, Ione; think not of me as thou hast thought; I am not that being, cold, insensate, and morose which I have seemed to thee. Never woman had lover so devoted—so passionate as I will be to Ione. Do not struggle in my clasp; see—I release thy hand. Take it from me if thou wilt—well, be it so! But do not reject me, Ione—do not rashly reject—judge of thy power over him whom thou canst thus transform. I who never knelt to mortal being, kneel to thee. I who have commanded fate, receive from thee my own. Ione, tremble not, thou art my queen—my goddess—be my bride. All the wishes thou canst form shall be fulfilled. The ends of the earth shall minister to thee—pomp, power, luxury, shall be thy slaves. Arbaces shall have no ambition, save the pride of obeying thee. Ione, turn upon me those eyes—shed upon me thy smile. Dark is my soul when thy face is hidden from it—shine over me, my sun—my heaven—my delight!—Ione, Ione—do not reject my love!"

Alone, and in the power of this singular and fearful man, Ione was not yet terrified. The respect of his language, the softness of his voice, reassured her; and, in her own purity, she felt protection. But she was confused, astonished: it was some moments before she could recover the power to reply.

"Rise, Arbaces!" said she at length; and she resigned to him once more her hand, which she as quickly withdrew again, when she felt upon it the burning pressure of his lips. "Rise! And if thou art serious, if thy language be in earnest—"

"*If!*" said he, tenderly.

"Well, then, listen to me: you have been my guardian, my friend, my monitor; for this new character I was not prepared; think not," she added quickly, as she saw his dark eyes glitter with the fierceness of his passion—"think not, that I scorn—that I am untouched—that I am not honoured by this homage; but, say—canst hear me calmly?"

"Ay, though thy words were lightning, and could blast me!"

"*I love another!*" said Ione, blushingly, but in a firm voice.

"By the gods—by hell!" shouted Arbaces, rising to his fullest height, "dare not tell me that—dare not mock me—it is impossible! Whom hast thou seen—whom known? Oh, Ione, it is thy woman's art that speaks—thou wouldst gain time: I have surprised—I have terrified thee. Do with me as thou wilt—say that thou lovest not me; but say not that thou lovest another."

"Alas!" began Ione; and then, appalled before his sudden and unlooked-for violence, she burst into tears.

Arbaces came nearer to her—his breath glowed fiercely on her cheek; he wound his arms around her—she sprang from his embrace. In the struggle a tablet fell from her bosom on the ground: Arbaces perceived, and seized it—it was the letter that morning received from Glaucus. Ione sank upon the couch, half dead with terror.

Rapidly the eyes of Arbaces ran over the writing; the Neapolitan did not dare to gaze upon him: she did not see the deadly paleness that came over his countenance—she marked not his withering frown, nor the quivering of his lip. He read it to the end, and then, as the letter fell from his hand, he said, in a voice of deceitful calmness:

"Is the writer of this the man thou lovest?"

Ione sobbed, but answered not. "Speak!"

"It is—it is!"

"And—it is written here—his name is Glaucus!"

Ione, clasping her hands, looked round as for succour or escape.

"Then hear me," said Arbaces, sinking his voice into a whisper, "thou shalt go to thy tomb rather than to his arms! What! Thinkest thou Arbaces will brook such a rival as this puny Greek? What! Thinkest thou that he has watched the fruit ripen, to yield it to another! Pretty fool—no! Thou art mine—all—only mine: and thus—thus I seize and claim thee!" As he spoke, he caught Ione in his arms; and, in that ferocious grasp, was all the energy—less of love than of revenge. But to Ione despair gave supernormal strength; she again tore herself from him, and fell exhausted, with a loud cry, at the base of the column which supported the head of the Egyptian goddess, Arbaces paused for a moment, as if to regain his breath; and then once more moved to seize her.

At that instant the curtain was rudely torn aside, and the Egyptian felt a fierce grasp on his shoulder. He turned—he beheld before him the angry eyes of Glaucus, and the pale, worn, but menacing, countenance of Apæcides. "Ah!" he muttered, as he glared from one to the other, "what Fury hath sent ye here?"

"Até," answered Glaucus; and he closed at once with the Egyptian. Meanwhile, Apæcides raised his sister, now lifeless, from the ground; his strength, exhausted by mind long overwrought, did not suffice to bear her away; he placed her, therefore, on the couch, and stood over her with a knife, watching the contest between Glaucus and the Egyptian, and ready to use his weapon should Arbaces be victorious in the struggle.

There is, perhaps, nothing on earth so terrible as the naked and unarmed contest of animal strength, with no weapon but those which Nature supplies to rage. The antagonists were now locked in each other's grasp—the hand of each seeking the throat of the other—the face drawn back—the fierce eyes flashing—the muscles strained—the veins swelled—the lips apart—the teeth set—both were strong beyond the ordinary power of men, both animated by relentless wrath; they coiled, they wound around each other; they swayed from end to end of their confined arena—they uttered cries of ire and revenge—they were now before the altar—now at the base of the column where the struggle had commenced: they drew back for breath—Arbaces leaning against the column—Glaucus a few paces apart.

"O ancient goddess!" exclaimed Arbaces, clasping the column, and raising his eyes towards the sacred image it supported, "protect thy chosen—proclaim thy vengeance against this thing of an upstart creed, who with sacrilegious violence profanes thy resting-place and assails thy servant."

As he spoke, the still and vast features of the goddess seemed to glow with life; through the black marble, as through a transparent veil, flashed luminously a crimson and burning hue; around the head played and darted coruscations of livid lightning; the eyes became like balls of lurid fire, and seemed fixed in withering and intolerable wrath upon the countenance of the Greek. Awed and appalled by this sudden and mystic answer to the prayer of his foe, and not free from the hereditary superstition of his race, the cheeks of Glaucus paled before that strange and ghastly animation of the marble. He stood, seized with a divine panic, dismayed, aghast, half unmanned before his foe. Arbaces gave him not breathing time to recover. "*Die, wretch!*" he shouted, in a voice of thunder, as he sprang upon the Greek; "the Mighty Mother claims thee as a living sacrifice!"

Taken thus by surprise in the first consternation of his superstitious fears, the Greek lost his footing—the marble floor was as smooth as glass—he slid—he fell. Arbaces planted his foot on his fallen foe.

Apæcides, taught by his sacred profession, as well as by his knowledge of Arbaces, to distrust all miraculous interpositions, had not shared the dismay of his companion; he rushed forward, his knife gleamed in the air—the watchful Egyptian caught his arm as it descended—one wrench of his powerful hand tore the weapon from the weak grasp of the priest—one sweeping blow stretched him to the earth—with a loud and exulting cry Arbaces brandished the knife. Glaucus gazed upon his impending fate with unwinking eyes, and in the stern and scornful resignation of a fallen gladiator, when, at that awful instant, the floor shook under them with a rapid and convulsive throe—a mightier spirit than that of the Egyptian was abroad!—a great and crushing power, before which sank into sudden impotence his passion and his arts.

Far and wide beneath the soil went a hoarse and rumbling sound, the curtains of the chamber shook as at the blast of a storm—the altar rocked—and, high. over the place of contest, the column trembled—the sable head of the goddess tottered and fell from its pedestal—and as the Egyptian stooped above his intended victim, upon his bended form, between, the shoulder and the neck, struck the marble mass.

The shock stretched him like the blow of death, at once, suddenly, without sound or motion, or semblance of life, upon the floor, apparently crushed by the very divinity he had impiously animated and invoked.

"The Earth has preserved her children," said Glaucus, staggering to his feet. "Blessed be the dread convulsion! Let us worship the providence of the gods!" He assisted

Apæcides began to rise, raised Ione lightly in his arms, and they fled from the unhallowed spot. But scarce had they entered the garden when they were met on all sides by flying and disordered groups of women and slaves, whose festive and glittering garments contrasted in mockery the solemn terror of the hour; they did not appear to heed the strangers—they were occupied only with their own fears. After the tranquillity of sixteen years, that burning and treacherous soil again menaced destruction; they uttered but one cry, "THE EARTHQUAKE! THE EARTHQUAKE!" and passing unmolested from the midst of them, Apæcides and is companions, without entering the house, hastened down one of the alleys, and fled through an open gate.

BOOK THREE

18. The Forum of the Pompeians

It was early noon, and the forum was crowded alike with the busy and the idle. As in Paris at this day, so at that time in the cities of Italy, men lived almost wholly out of their own doors: the public buildings, the forum, the porticoes, the baths, the temples themselves, might be considered their real homes; it was no wonder that they decorated so gorgeously these favourite places of resort—they felt for them a sort of domestic affection as well as a public pride. And animated was, indeed, the aspect of the forum of Pompeii at that time. Along its broad pavement, composed of large flags of marble, were assembled various groups, conversing in that energetic fashion which appropriates a gesture to every word, and which is still the characteristic of the people of Southern Europe. Here, in seven stalls on one side of the colonnade, sat the money-changers, with their glittering heaps before them, and merchants and seamen in various costumes crowding round their stalls. On one side, several in long togas were seen bustling rapidly up to a stately edifice, where the magistrates administered justice. In this centre, pedestals supported various statues, of which the most remarkable was the stately form of Cicero. Around the court ran a regular and symmetrical colonnade of Doric architecture; and there several, whose business drew them early to the place, were taking the slight morning repast which made an Italian breakfast, talking vehemently on the earthquake of the preceding night, as they dipped pieces of bread in their cups of diluted wine. In the open space, too, were various petty traders exercising the art of their calling. Here one man was holding out ribbons to a fair dame from the country; another was vaunting to a stout farmer the excellence of his shoes; a third, a kind of stall-restaurateur, still common in the Italian cities, was supplying hungry mouths with hot messes from his small and itinerant stove, while—contrast strongly typical of the mingled bustle and intellect of the time—close by, a schoolmaster was expounding to his puzzled pupils the elements of the Latin grammar. A gallery above the portico, which was ascended by small wooden staircases, had also its throng; though, as here the immediate business of the place was mainly carried on, its groups wore a more quiet and serious air.

Every now and then the crowd below respectfully gave way as some senator swept along to the Temple of Jupiter (which filled up one side of the forum, and was the senators' hall of meeting), nodding with ostentatious condescension to such of his friends or clients as he distinguished amongst the throng. Mingling amidst the gay dresses of the better orders, hardy farmers made their way to the public granaries. Beyond the temple could be seen the triumphal arch, and the long street swarming with inhabitants. In one of the niches of the arch a fountain played, cheerily sparkling in the sunbeams; and above its cornice rose the bronzed equestrian statue of Caligula, strongly contrasting the gay summer skies. Behind the stalls of the money-changers was that building now called the Pantheon, and a crowd of the poorer Pompeians passed through the small vestibule which admitted to the interior, with panniers under their arms, pressing on towards a platform, placed between two columns, where such provisions as the priests had rescued from the sacrifices were exposed for sale.

At one of the public edifices appropriated to the business of the city, workmen were employed upon the columns, the noise of their labour rising above the hum of the multitude. Work which would never be finished, though the columns would endure for millenniums.

Facing the steps of the Temple of Jupiter, with folded arms, and a knit contemptuous brow, stood a man of about fifty years. His dress was remarkably plain—not so much from its material, as from the absence of all those ornaments which were worn by the Pompeians of every rank—partly from the love of show, partly, because they were chiefly wrought into those shapes deemed most efficacious in resisting the assaults of magic and the influence of the evil eye. His forehead was high and bald; the few locks that remained at the back of the head were concealed by a sort of cowl, which made a part of his cloak, to be raised or lowered at pleasure, and now drawn halfway over the head, as a protection from the rays of the sun. The colour of his garments was brown, no popular hue with the Pompeians. His girdle contained a small receptacle for ink, which hooked on, and tablets of no ordinary size. It was remarkable that the cincture held no purse, which was the almost indispensable appurtenance of the girdle, even when that purse had the misfortune to be empty.

It was not often that the gay and egotistical Pompeians busied themselves with observing the countenances and actions of their neighbours; but there was that in the lip and eye of this bystander so remarkably bitter and disdainful, as he surveyed the religious procession sweeping up the stairs of the temple, that it could not fail to arrest the notice of many.

"Who is yon cynic?" asked a merchant of his companion, a jeweller.

"It is Olinthus," replied the jeweller; "a reputed Nazarene."

The merchant shuddered. "A dread sect!" said he, in a fearful whisper. "It is said, that when they meet at nights they commence their ceremonies by the murder of a newborn babe: they profess a community of goods, too—the wretches! A community of goods! What would become of merchants, or jewellers either, if such notions were in fashion?"

"That is true," said the jeweller; "besides, they wear no jewels—they mutter imprecations when they see a serpent; and all our ornaments are serpentine here."

"Do but observe," said a third, who was a fabricant of bronze, "how yon Nazarene scowls at the piety of the sacrificial procession. He is murmuring curses on the temple, be sure. Do you know, Celcinus, that this fellow, passing by my shop the other day, and seeing me employed on a statue of Minerva, told me with a frown that, had it been marble, he would have broken it; but the bronze was too strong for him. 'Break a goddess!' said I. 'A goddess!' answered the atheist; 'it is a demon—an evil spirit!' Then he passed on his way cursing. Are such things to be borne? What marvel that the earth heaved so fearfully last night, anxious to reject the atheist from her bosom—an atheist, do I say? Worse still—a scorner of the Fine Arts! Woe to us fabricants of bronze, if such fellows as this give the law to society!"

"These are the incendiaries who started the fire of Rome," groaned the jeweller.

While such were the remarks provoked by the air and faith of the Nazarene, Olinthus himself became sensible of the effect he was producing; he looked round, and observed the intent faces of the accumulating throng, whispering as they gazed; and surveying them for a moment with an expression, first of defiance, and afterwards of compassion, he gathered his cloak round him and passed on, muttering audibly: "Deluded idolaters!—did not last night's convulsion warn ye? Alas! How will ye meet the last day?"

The crowd that heard these boding words gave them different interpretations, according to their different shades of ignorance and of fear; all, however, concurred in imagining them to convey some awful imprecation.

As he stalked through the crowd, and gained one of the more private places of egress from the forum, he perceived gazing upon him a pale and earnest countenance, which he was not slow to recognise.

Wrapped in a pallium that partially concealed his sacred robes, the young Apæcides surveyed the disciple of that new and mysterious creed, to which at one time he had been half a convert.

"Is *he*, too, an impostor? Does this man, so plain and simple in life, in garb, in mien—does he too, like Arbaces, make austerity the robe of the sensualist? Does the veil of Vesta hide the vices of the prostitute?"

Olinthus, accustomed to men of all classes, and combining with the enthusiasm of his faith a profound experience of his kind, guessed, perhaps by the index of the countenance, something of what passed within the mind of the priest. He met the survey of Apæcides with a steady eye, and a brow of serene and open candour.

"Peace be with thee!" said he, saluting him as he spoke.

"Peace!" echoed the priest, in so hollow a tone that it went at once to the heart of the Nazarene.

"In that wish," continued Olinthus, "all good things are combined—without virtue thou canst not have peace. Like the rainbow, Peace rests upon the earth, but its arch is raised to in heaven!"

"Alas!" began Apæcides, when he caught the gaze of the curious loiterers, inquisitive to know what could possibly be the theme of conversation between a Nazarene and a priest of Isis. He stopped short, and then added in a low tone: "We cannot converse here. I will follow thee to the banks of the river; there is a walk which at this time is usually deserted and solitary."

Olinthus bowed assent. He passed through the streets with a hasty step, but a quick and observant eye. Every now and then he exchanged a significant glance, a slight sign, with some passenger, whose garb usually betokened the wearer to belong to the humbler classes; for Christianity was in this the type of all other and less mighty revolutions—the grain of mustard seed was in the hearts of the lowly. Amidst the huts of poverty and labour the vast stream which afterwards poured its broad waters beside the cities and palaces of earth took its neglected source.

19. On the Campanian Seas

"But tell me, Glaucus," said Ione, as they glided down the rippling Sarnus in their boat of pleasure, "how camest thou with Apæcides to my rescue from that bad man?"

"Ask Nydia yonder," answered the Athenian, pointing to the blind girl, who sat a little distance from them, leaning pensively over her lyre, "she must have thy thanks, not we. It seems that she came to my house, and finding me from home, sought thy brother in his temple; he accompanied her to Arbaces; on their way they encountered me, with a company of friends, whom thy kind letter had given me a spirit cheerful enough to join. Nydia's quick ear detected my voice—a few words sufficed to make me the companion of Apæcides; I told not my associates why I left them—could I trust thy name to their light tongues and gossiping opinion? Nydia led us to the garden-gate, and we were about to plunge into the mysteries of that evil house, when we heard thy cry in another direction. Thou knowest the rest."

Ione raised her eyes to those of Glaucus, and he felt all the thanks she could not utter. "Come hither, my Nydia," said she, tenderly to the Thessalian.

"Did I not tell thee that thou shouldst be my sister and friend? Hast thou not already been more?—my guardian, my preserver!"

"It is nothing," answered Nydia coldly, and without stirring.

"Ah! I forgot," continued Ione, "I should come to thee;" and she moved along the benches till she reached the place where Nydia sat, and flinging her arms caressingly around her, covered her cheeks with kisses.

Nydia was that morning paler than her wont, and her countenance grew even more wan and colourless as she submitted to the embrace of the beautiful Neapolitan. "But how camest thou, Nydia," whispered Ione, "to surmise so faithfully the danger to which I was exposed? Didst thou know aught of the Egyptian?"

"Yes, I knew of his vices."

"And how?"

"Noble Ione, I have been a slave to the vicious—those whom I served were his minions."

"And thou hast entered his house, since thou knewest so well that private entrance?"

"I have played on my lyre to Arbaces," answered the Thessalian, with embarrassment.

"And thou hast escaped the contagion from which thou hast saved Ione!" returned the Neapolitan, in a voice too low for the ear of Glaucus.

"Noble Ione, I have neither beauty nor station; I am a child, and a slave, and blind. The despicable are ever safe."

It was with a pained, proud, indignant tone that Nydia made this humble reply; and Ione felt that she only wounded her by pursuing the subject. She remained silent, and the bark floated on to the sea.

"Confess that I was right, Ione," said Glaucus, "in prevailing on thee not to waste this beautiful noon in thy chamber—confess that I was right."

"Thou wert right, Glaucus," said Nydia, abruptly.

"The dear child speaks for thee," returned the Athænian.

"But permit me to move opposite to thee, or our light boat will be overbalanced."

"Thou wert to tell me why for so many days thy door was closed to me?"

"Oh, think of it no more! I gave my ear to what I know now was the malice of slander."

"And my slanderer was the Egyptian?"

Ione's silence assented.

"His motives are sufficiently obvious."

"Talk not of him," said Ione, covering her face with her hands, as if to shut out the very thought.

"Perhaps he may be already by the banks of the slow Styx," resumed Glaucus. "Yet in that case we should probably have heard of his death. Thy brother hath felt the dark influence of his gloomy soul. When we arrived last night at thy house, he left me abruptly. Will he ever vouchsafe to be my friend?"

"He is consumed with some secret care," answered Ione, fearfully. "Would that we could lure him from himself! Let us join in that effort."

"He shall be my brother."

"How calmly," said Ione, rousing herself from the gloom into which her thoughts of Apæcides had plunged her, "How calmly the clouds seem to repose in heaven; and yet you tell me, for I knew it not myself, that the earth shook beneath us last night."

"It did, and more violently, they say, than it has done since the great convulsion sixteen years ago; the land we live in yet nurses mysterious terror; and the reign of Pluto, which spreads beneath our burning fields, seems rent with unseen commotion. Didst thou not feel the earthquake, Nydia, where thou wert seated last night? And was it not the fear that it occasioned thee that made thee weep?"

"I felt the soil creep and heave beneath me, like some monstrous serpent," answered Nydia. "But, as I saw nothing, I did not fear; I imagined the convulsion to be a spell of the Egyptian's. They say he has power over the elements."

"Thou art a Thessalian, my Nydia," replied Glaucus, "and hast a national right to believe in magic."

"Magic—who doubts it?" answered Nydia simply; "dost thou?"

"Until last night (when a necromantic prodigy did indeed appal me), methinks I was not credulous in any other magic save that of love!" said Glaucus, in a tremulous voice, and fixing his eyes on Ione.

"Ah!" said Nydia, with a sort of shiver, and she awoke a few pleasing notes from her lyre. The sound suited well the tranquillity of the waters, and the sunny stillness of the noon.

"Play to us, dear Nydia," said Glaucus, "play, and give us one of thine old Thessalian songs; whether it be of magic or not, as thou wilt—let it, at least, be of love!"

"Of love!" repeated Nydia, raising her large, wandering eyes, that ever thrilled those who saw them with a mingled fear and pity; for they could never familiarize themselves to their aspect. So strange did it seem that those dark wild orbs were ignorant of the day, and either so fixed was their deep, mysterious gaze or so restless and perturbed their glance, that those who encountered them had that same vague and chilling, and half-prenatural impression, which comes with the presence of the insane—of those who having a life outwardly like our own, have a life within life—dissimilar—unsearchable—unguessed.

"Wilt thou that I sing of love?' said she, fixing those eyes upon Glaucus.

"Yes," replied he, looking down.

She moved a little way from the arm of Ione, still cast round her, as if that soft embrace embarrassed: and placing her light and graceful instrument on her knee, after a short prelude she sang the following strain:

"The wind and the Sun loved the Rose,
And the Rose loved one;
For who recks the wind where it blows?
Or loves not the sun?

Her petals she moved apart
As the light drew nigh;
It entered the rose's heart

As the wind went by.

Light came to the waiting flower,
And it worked its will.
It ruled in the noontide hour,
And the wind was still.

The wind with its least caress
Blows the rose awry.
Its love must be guerdonless,
And its proof to die."

"Thou singest but sadly, sweet girl," said Glaucus; "thy youth only feels as yet the dark shadow of Love; far other inspiration doth he wake, when he himself bursts and brightens upon us."

"I sing as I was taught," replied Nydia, sighing.

"Thy master was love-crossed then—try thy hand at a gayer air. Nay, girl, give the instrument to me." As Nydia obeyed, her hand touched his, and with that slight touch her hand trembled—her cheek flushed. Ione and Glaucus, occupied with each other, perceived not those signs of emotion, which preyed upon a heart that, nourished by imagination, dispensed with hope.

Still vainly seeking the eyes of Ione, as half downcast, half averted, they shunned his own, the Athenian, in a low and soft voice, thus expressed the feeling inspired by happier thoughts than those which had coloured the song of Nydia:

"As a barque on the sea of its passion for thee,
My heart setteth forth on its quest,
For its course it relies on the stars of thine eyes,
And thy smile is its haven of rest.

Than should clouds be above, or the light of thy love
Should beacon no longer ahead,
It would sink, if it might, while the stars are in sight,
And it knew not its trust were misled."

As the last words of the song trembled over the sea, Ione raised her eyes—they met those of her lover. Happy Nydia!—happy in the affliction, that could not see the gaze that said so much.

But, though the Thessalian could not see, she divined the meaning of their silence. She pressed her hands tightly across her breast, as if to keep down its bitter and jealous thoughts; and then she hastened to speak—for that silence was intolerable to her.

"After all, O Glaucus!" said she, "there is nothing very mirthful in your strain!"

"Yet I meant it to be so, when I took up the lyre, pretty one. Perhaps happiness will not permit us to be mirthful."

"How strange it is," said Ione, changing the conservation to a lighter tone, "that for the last several days yonder cloud has hung motionless over Vesuvius! Yet not motionless, for sometimes it changes form, and now it looks like some vast giant, with an arm outstretched over the city. Dost thou see the likeness—or is it only my fancy?"

"I see it also. It is astonishingly distinct. The giant seems seated on the brow of the mountain, the different shades of the cloud appear to form a white robe that sweeps over its vast breast and limbs; it seems to gaze with a steady face upon the city below, to point with one hand over its glittering streets, and to raise the other towards the higher heaven."

"Could that mountain have any connection with last night's earthquake? They say that, ages ago, it gave forth such fires as Etna still does."

"It is possible," said Glaucus doubtfully.

"Thou sayest thou art slow to believe in magic?" said Nydia suddenly. "I have heard that a potent witch dwells amongst the scorched caverns of the mountain, and the cloud may be the dim shadow of the demon she confers with."

"Thou art full of the romance of thy native Thessaly," said Glaucus, "and a strange mixture of sense and all conflicting superstitions."

"We are ever superstitious in the dark," replied Nydia. "Tell me," she added after a slight pause, "tell me, O Glaucus! Do all that are beautiful resemble each other? They say you are beautiful, and Ione also. Are your faces then the same? I fancy not, yet it ought to be so!"

"Fancy no such grievous wrong to Ione," answered Glaucus, laughing. "But we do not, alas, resemble each other, as the homely and the beautiful sometimes do. Ione's hair is dark, mine light; Ione's eyes are—what colour, Ione? I cannot see, turn them to me. Oh, are they black? No, they are too soft. Are they blue? No, they are too deep: they change with every ray of the sun—I know not their colour: but mine, sweet Nydia, are grey, and bright only when Ione shines on them! Ione's cheek is—"

"I do not understand one word of thy description," interrupted Nydia, peevishly. "I comprehend only that you do not resemble each other, and I am glad of it."

"Why, Nydia?" said Ione.

Nydia coloured slightly. "Because," she replied coldly. "I have always imagined you under different forms, and one likes to know one is right."

"And what hast thou imagined Glaucus to resemble?" asked Ione softly.

"Music!" replied Nydia, looking down.

"Thou art right," thought Ione.

"And what likeness hast thou ascribed to Ione?"

"I cannot tell yet," answered the blind girl. "I have not yet known her long enough to find a shape and sign for my guesses."

"I will tell thee, then," said Glaucus, passionately. "She is like the sun that warms—like the wave that refreshes."

"The sun sometimes scorches, and the wave sometimes drowns," answered Nydia.

"Take then these roses," said Glaucus, "let their fragrance suggest to thee Ione."

"Alas, the roses will fade!" said the Neapolitan archly.

Thus conversing, they wore away the hours; the lovers conscious only of the brightness and smiles of love; the blind girl feeling only its darkness—its tortures—the fierceness of jealousy and its woe!

And now, as they drifted on, Glaucus once more resumed the lyre, and woke its strings with a careless hand to a strain so wildly and gladly beautiful, that even Nydia was aroused from her reverie, and uttered a cry of admiration.

"Thou seest, my child," cried Glaucus, "that I can yet redeem the character of love's music, and that I was wrong in saying that happiness could not be gay. Listen, Nydia! Listen, dear Ione!"

THE COMING OF LOVE

Like a star in the skies above,
Like a dream from the waves of sleep,
She rose, the incarnate Love,
She rose from the charmed deep;
And over the Cyprian isle
The skies were a cloudless smile,
And the wood's green depths were stirred
By the One Immortal Word:

The Word that had leapt to birth
From the womb of the pregnant earth.

From the deepest vale below,
To the sky's high dome above,
There was nothing that did not know,
And leap to the call of Love.
No leaf of the laughing land
No cloud of the heights of sky,
From the hills where the temples stand
To the caves where the sea-winds lie,
But the call they heard of the deathless Word,
And thrilled to the same reply.

And now, as a birth anew,
The Visible Word I see
In the eyes and the lips of you
That smile as the dawn on me.
No pearl from the ocean floor
That rose on the sunlit sea,
Shell-borne to the waiting shore,
The Life of the Earth to be,
Wast more than art thou to my longing now
If thou be kind to me.

20. The Congregation

Followed by Apæcides, the Nazarene gained the side of the Sarnus—that river soon to be shrunk to a pretty stream, which then
rushed gaily to the sea, covered with countless vessels, and reflect-
ing on its waves the gardens, the vines, the palaces, and the temples
of Pompeii. From its noisy frequented banks, Olinthus directed his
steps to a path which ran amidst a shady vista of trees, at the distance of a few paces from the river. This walk was in the evening a
favourite resort of the Pompeians, but during the heat and business
of the day was seldom visited, save by groups of playful children,
some meditative poet, or some disputative philosophers. At the side
farthest from the river, frequent copses of box interspersed the more
delicate and evanescent foliage, and these were cut into a thousand
quaint shapes, sometimes into the forms of fauns and satyrs, sometimes into the mimicry of Egyptian pyramids, sometimes into the
letters that composed the name of a popular and eminent citizen.

This walk now, as the noonday sun shone perpendicularly through the checkered leaves, was entirely deserted; at least no other forms than those of Olinthus and the priest infringed upon the solitude. They sat themselves on one of the benches placed at intervals between the trees, and facing the faint breeze that came languidly from the river, whose waves danced and sparkled before them—a singular and contrasted pair; the believer in the latest—the priest of the most ancient—worship in the world.

"Since thou leftst me so abruptly," said Olinthus, "hast thou been happy? Has thy heart found contentment under these priestly robes? Hast thou, still yearning for the voice of God, heard it whisper comfort to thee from the oracles of Isis? That sigh, that averted countenance, give me the answer my soul predicted."

"Alas!" answered Apæcides, sadly, "thou seest before thee a wretched and distracted man! From my childhood upward I have idolized the dreams of virtue! I have envied the holiness of men who, in caves and lonely temples, have been admitted to the companionship of beings above the world; my days have been consumed with feverish and vague desires; my nights with mocking but solemn visions. Seduced by the mystic prophecies of an impostor, I have indued these robes—my nature (I confess it to thee frankly)—my nature has revolted at what I have seen and been doomed to share! Searching after truth, I have become the minister of falsehoods. On the evening in which we last met, I was buoyed by hopes created by that same impostor, whom I ought already to have better known. I have—no matter—no matter! Suffice it, I have added perjury and sin to rashness and sorrow. The veil is now rent forever from my eyes; I behold a villain where I obeyed a demigod; the earth darkens in my sight; I am in the deepest abyss of gloom. I know not if there be gods above; if we are the things of chance; if beyond the bounded and melancholy present there is annihilation or hereafter—tell me, then, thy faith; solve me these doubts, if thou has indeed the power."

"I do not marvel," answered the Nazarene, "that thou hast thus erred, or that thou art thus sceptic. Eighty years ago there was no assurance to man of God, or of a certain and definite future beyond the grave. New laws are declared to him who has ears—a heaven, a true Olympus, is revealed to him who has eyes—heed then, and listen."

And with all the earnestness of a man believing ardently himself, and zealous to convert, the Nazarene poured forth to Apæcides the assurance of scriptural promise. He spoke first of the sufferings and miracles of Christ—he wept as he spoke: he turned next to the glories of the Saviour's Ascension—to the clear predictions of revelation. He described a pure and unsensual heaven destined to the virtuous—fires and torments that were the doom of guilt.

The doubts which spring up to the mind of later reasoners were not such as would occur to an early heathen. He had been accustomed to believe that the gods had lived upon earth, and taken upon themselves the forms of men; had shared in human passions, in human labours, and in human misfortunes. What was the travail of his own Alcmæna's son, whose altars now smoked with the incense of countless cities, but a toil for the human race? Had not the great Dorian Apollo expiated a mystic sin by descending to the grave? Those who were the deities of heaven had been law-givers or benefactors on earth, and gratitude had led to worship. It seemed, therefore, a doctrine neither new nor strange, that Christ had been sent from heaven, that an immortal had indued mortality, and tasted the bitterness of death. And the end for which He thus toiled and suffered—how far more glorious did it seem to Apæcides than that for which the deities of old had visited the nether world, and passed through the gates of death! Was it not worthy of a God to descend to these dim valleys, in order to clear up the clouds gathered over the dark mount beyond—to satisfy the doubts of sages—to convert speculation into certainty—by example to point out the rules of life—by revelation to solve the enigma of the grave—and prove that the soul did not yearn in vain when it dreamed of immortality?

"Come," said the Nazarene, as he perceived the effect he had produced, "come to the humble hall in which we meet—a select and chosen few; listen there to our prayers; mingle in our simple sacrifice—not of victims, nor of garlands, but offered by white-robed thoughts upon the altar of the heart. The flowers that we lay there are imperishable—they bloom over us when we are no more; nay, they accompany us beyond the grave, they spring up beneath our feet in heaven, they delight us with an eternal odour, for they are of the soul, they partake of its nature; these offerings are temptations overcome, and sins repented. Come! Lose not another moment; prepare already for the great, the awful journey, from darkness to light, from sorrow to bliss, from corruption to immortality!"

There seemed to Apæcides, naturally pure of heart, something ineffably generous and benign in that spirit of conversion which animated Olinthus—a spirit that found its own bliss in the happiness of others—that sought in its wide sociality to make companions for eternity. He was touched, softened, and subdued. He was not in a mood that could bear to be left alone; curiosity, too, mingled with his purer stimulants—he was anxious to see those rites of which so many dark and contradictory rumours were afloat. He paused a moment, looked over his garb, thought of Arbaces, shuddered with horror; lifted his eyes to the broad brow of the Nazarene, intent, anxious, watchful—but for his benefit, for his salvation! He drew his cloak round him, so wholly to conceal his robes, and said: "Lead on, I follow thee."

Olinthus pressed his hand joyfully, and then, descending to the river-side, hailed one of the boats that plied there constantly; they entered it; an awning overhead, while it sheltered them from the sun, screened also their persons from observation. From one of the boats that passed them floated a soft music, and its prow was decorated with flowers—it was gliding towards the sea.

"So," said Olinthus sadly, "unconscious and mirthful in their delusions, sail the votaries of luxury into the great ocean of storm and shipwreck; we pass them, silent and unnoticed, to gain the land."

Apæcides, lifting his eyes, caught through the aperture in the awning a glimpse of the face of one of the inmates of that gay barque—it was the face of Ione. The priest sighed, and once more sank back upon his seat. They reached the shore where, in the suburbs, an alley of small mean houses stretched towards the bank; they dismissed the boat, landed, and Olinthus, preceding the priest, threaded the labyrinth of lanes, and arrived at last at the closed door of a habitation somewhat larger than its neighbours. He knocked thrice—the door was opened and closed again, as Apæcides followed him across the threshold.

They passed a deserted atrium, and gained an inner chamber of moderate size, which, when the door was closed, received its only light from a small window cut over the door itself. But, halting at the threshold of this chamber, and knocking at the door, Olinthus said: "Peace be with you!"

A voice from within returned: "Peace with whom?"

"The Faithful!" answered Olinthus, and the door opened; twelve or fourteen persons were sitting in a semi-circle, silent, and seemingly absorbed in thought, and opposite to a crucifix rudely carved in wood.

They lifted up their eyes when Olinthus entered, without speaking; the Nazarene himself, before he accosted them, knelt down, and by his moving lips, and his eyes fixed steadfastly on the crucifix, Apæcides saw that he prayed. This rite performed, Olinthus turned to the congregation: "Men and brethren," said he, "start not to behold amongst you a priest of Isis; he hath sojourned with the blind, but the Spirit hath fallen on him—he desires to see, to hear, and to understand."

"Let him," said one of the assembly; and Apæcides beheld in the speaker a man still younger than himself, of a countenance equally worn and pallid, of an eye which equally spoke of the restless and fiery operations of a working mind.

"Let him," repeated a second voice, and he who thus spoke was in the prime of manhood; his bronzed skin and Asiatic features bespoke him a son of Syria—he had been a robber in his youth.

"Let him," said a third voice; and the priest, again turning to regard the speaker, saw an old man with a long gray beard, whom he recognized as a slave to the wealthy Diomed.

"Let him," repeated simultaneously the rest—men who, with two exceptions, were evidently of the inferior ranks. In these exceptions, Apæcides noted an officer of the guard, and an Alexandrian merchant.

"We do not," recommenced Olinthus, "we do not bind you to secrecy; we impose no oaths on you (as some of our weaker brethren would do) not to betray us. It is true, indeed, that there is no absolute law against us; but the multitude, more savage than their rulers, thirst for our lives. So my friends, when Pilate would have hesitated, it was the people who shouted: 'Christ to the cross!' But we bind you not to our safety. Betray us to the crowd—impeach, calumniate, malign us if you will—we are above death, we should walk cheerfully to the den of the lion, or the rack of the torturer—we can trample down the darkness of the grave, and what is death to a criminal is eternity to the Christian."

A low and applauding murmur ran through the assembly. "Thou comest amongst us as an examiner, mayest thou remain a convert! Our religion? You behold it! Yon cross our sole image, yon scroll the mysteries of our Cære and Eleusis! Our morality? It is in our lives!—sinners we all have been. Who can now accuse us of a crime? We have baptised ourselves from the past. Think not that this is of us, it is of God. Approach, Medon," beckoning to the old slave who had spoken third for the admission of Apæcides, "thou art the sole man amongst us who is not free. But in heaven, the last shall be first; so with us. Unfold your scroll, read and explain."

Useless would it be for us to accompany the lecture of Medon, or the comments of the congregation. Familiar now are those doctrines, then strange and new. To us there would seem little congenial in the doubts that occurred to a heathen priest, and little learned from the answers they received from men uneducated, rude, and simple, possessing only the knowledge that they were greater than they seemed.

There was one thing that greatly touched the Neapolitan; when the lecture was concluded, they heard a very gentle knock at the door; the password was given, the door opened, and two young children, the elder of whom might have told its seventh year, entered timidly; they were the children of the master of the house, that dark and hardy Syrian whose youth had been spent in pillage and bloodshed. The eldest of the congregation (it was the old slave) opened to them his arms; they fled to their shelter—they crept to his breast—and his hard features smiled as he caressed them. And then these bold and fervent men, nursed in vicissitude, beaten by the rough winds of life—men of mailed and impervious fortitude, ready to affront a world, prepared for torment and armed for death—men who presented all imaginable contrast to the weak nerves, the light hearts, the tender fragility of childhood, crowded round the infants, smoothing their rugged brows and composing their bearded lips to kindly and fostering smiles; and then the old man opened the scroll, and he taught the infants to repeat after him that beautiful prayer which we still dedicate to the Lord, and still teach to our children; and then he told them, in simple phrase, of God's love to the young. This lovely custom of their initiation was long cherished by the early Church, in memory of the words which said: "Suffer little children to come unto me, and forbid them not;" and was perhaps the origin of the superstitious calumny which ascribed to the Nazarenes the crime which the Nazarene, when victorious, attributed to the Jew: the decoying of children to hideous rites, at which they were secretly immolated.

And the stern paternal penitent seemed to feel in the innocence of his children a return to early life—life ere yet it sinned; he followed the motion of their young lips with an earnest gaze; he smiled as they repeated, with hushed and reverent looks, the holy words; and when the lesson was done, and they ran gladly to his knee, he clasped them to his breast, kissing them again and again.

It was at this time that an inner door opened gently, and a very old man entered the chamber, leaning on a staff. At his presence, the whole congregation rose; there was an expression of deep, affectionate respect upon every countenance. Apæcides felt attracted towards him by an irresistible sympathy. No man ever looked upon that face without love; for there had dwelt the smile of the deity, the incarnation of divinest hope—and the glory of the smile had never passed away.

"My children, God be with you!" said the old man, stretching his arms; and as he spoke, the infants ran to his knee.

"Father," said Olinthus, "thou on whose form the miracle of the Redeemer worked; thou who wert snatched from his grave to become the living witness of His mercy and His power; behold, a stranger in our meeting—a new lamb gathered to the fold!"

"Let me bless him," said the old man; the throng gave way. Apæcides approached him as by an instinct; he fell on his knees before him—the old man laid his hand on the priest's head, and blessed him, but not aloud.

The children were on either side of the convert; his heart was theirs—he had become one of them—to enter into the kingdom of Heaven.

21. The Stream of Love Runs On

Days are like years in the love of the young, when no bar, no obstacle, is between their hearts—when the sun shines, and the course runs smooth—when love is prosperous and confessed. Ione no longer concealed from Glaucus the attachment she felt for him, and their talk was only of their love. Over the rapture of the present, the hopes of the future glowed like the heaven above the gardens of spring. In the youth of their hearts it seemed as if care, and change, and death, were unknown. Perhaps they loved each other the more because the condition of the world left to Glaucus no aim and no wish but to love; because the distractions common in free states to men's affections did not exist for the Athenian; because his country wooed him not to the bustle of civil life; because ambition furnished no counterpoise to love; and, therefore, over their schemes and their projects, love only reigned.

They had now advanced far into August—the next month their marriage was fixed, and the threshold of Glaucus was already wreathed with garlands; and nightly, by the door of Ione, he poured forth the rich libations. He existed no longer for his gay companions; he was ever with her. In the mornings they beguiled the sun with music; in the evenings they forsook the crowded haunts of the gay for excursions on the water, or along the fertile vine clad plains that lay beneath the fatal mount of Vesuvius. The earth shook no more; the lively Pompeians forgot even that there had gone forth so terrible a warning of their approaching doom. Glaucus imagined that convulsion, in the vanity of his heathen religion, an especial interposition of the gods, less on behalf of his own safety than that of Ione. He offered up the sacrifices of gratitude at the temples of his faith; and even the altar of Isis was covered with his votive garlands.

Of Arbaces, they heard only that he still lived; stretched on the bed of suffering, he recovered slowly from the effect of the shock he had sustained—he left the lovers unmolested—but it was only to brood over the hour and the method of revenge.

Alike in their mornings at the house of Ione, and in their evening excursions, Nydia was their constant, and often their sole companion. They did not guess the secret fires which consumed her; the abrupt freedom with which she mingled in their conversation—her capricious and often peevish moods found indulgence in the recollection of the service they owed her, and their compassion for her affliction. They felt an interest in her, perhaps the greater and more affectionate from the very strangeness and waywardness of her nature, her singular alternations of passion and softness—the mixture of ignorance and genius—of delicacy and rudeness—of the quick humours of the child, and the proud calmness of the woman. Although she refused to accept freedom, she was constantly suffered to be free; she went where she would; they felt for one so darkly fated, and so susceptible of every wound, the same pitying and compliant indulgence the mother feels for a sickly child—dreading to impose authority, even where they imagined it for her benefit. She availed herself of this license by refusing the companionship of the slave whom they wished to attend her. With the slender staff by which she guided her steps, she went now, as in her former unprotected state, along the populous streets; it was almost miraculous to perceive how quickly and dexterously she threaded every crowd, avoiding every danger, and finding her benighted way through the most intricate windings of the city. But her chief delight was still in visiting the few feet of ground which made the garden of Glaucus—in tending the flowers that at least repaid her love. Sometimes she entered the chamber where he sat, and sought a conversation, which she nearly always broke off abruptly—for conversation with Glaucus only tended to one subject—Ione; and that name from his lips inflicted agony upon her.

As darkness favours the imagination, so, perhaps, her blindness contributed to fill with wild and delirious visions the love of the unfortunate girl. The voice of Glaucus had been the first that had sounded musically to her ear; his kindness had made a deep impression upon her mind; when he had left Pompeii in the former year, she had treasured up in her heart every word he had uttered; and when any one told her that this friend and patron was the most brilliant and the most graceful of the young revellers of Pompeii, she had felt a pleasing pride in nursing his recollection. Even the task of tending his flowers, which she imposed upon herself, served to keep him in her mind; she associated him with all that was most charming to her impressions; and when she had refused to express what image she fancied Ione to resemble, it was partly, perhaps, that whatever was bright and soft in nature she had already combined with the thought of Glaucus.

Doomed to be rescued by him—doomed to take shelter under his roof—doomed to breathe, but for so brief a time, the same air—and doomed, in the first rush of a thousand happy, grateful, delicious sentiments of an overflowing heart, to hear that he loved another; to be commissioned to that other, the messenger, the minister; to feel all at once the utter nothingness which she was—which she must ever be, but which, till then, her young mind had not taught her—that utter nothingness to him who was all to her; what wonder that, in her wild and passionate soul, all the elements jarred discordant? Sometimes she dreaded only lest Glaucus should discover her secret; sometimes she felt indignant that it was not suspected; it was a sign of contempt—could he imagine that she presumed so far? Her feelings to Ione ebbed and flowed with every hour; now she loved her because he did; now she hated her for the same cause. There were moments when she could have murdered her unconscious mistress; moments when she could have laid down life for her.

One morning, when she repaired to her usual task in the garden of the Athenian, she found Glaucus under the columns of the peristyle, with a merchant of the town; he was selecting jewels for his destined bride. He had already fitted up her apartment; the jewels he bought that day were placed also within it—they were never fated to grace the fair form of Ione; they may be seen still among the disinterred treasure of Pompeii, in the chambers of the studio at Naples.

"Come hither, Nydia; put down thy vase, and come hither. Thou musk take this chain from me—stay—there, I have put it on.—There, Servilius, doth it not become her?

"Wonderfully!" answered the jeweller; for jewellers are always well-bred and flattering men. "But when these earrings glitter in the ears of the noble Ione, then, by Bacchus, you will see whether my art adds anything to beauty.

"Ione?" repeated Nydia, who had hitherto acknowledged by smiles and blushes the gift of the Athenian.

"Yes," replied Glaucus, carelessly toying with the gems. "I am choosing a present for Ione, but there is none worthy of her."

He was startled as he spoke by an abrupt gesture of Nydia; she tore the chain violently from her neck, and dashed it on the ground.

"How is this? What, Nydia, dost thou not like the bauble? Art thou offended?"

"You treat me ever as a slave and as a child," replied the Thessalian, with a breast heaving with ill-suppressed sobs, and she turned hastily away to the opposite corner of the garden.

Glaucus did not attempt to follow, or to soothe; he was offended; he continued to examine the jewels, and to comment on their fashion—to object to this and to praise that, and finally to be talked by the merchant into buying all.

When he had completed his purchase and dismissed the jeweller, he retired to his chamber, dressed, mounted his chariot and went to Ione. He thought no more of the blind girl or her offence; he had forgotten both the one and the other.

He spent the forenoon with his beautiful Neapolitan, repaired thence to the baths, supped (if we can justly so translate the three o'clock cœna of the Romans) alone and abroad, and returning home to change his dress ere he again repaired to the house of Ione, he passed the peristyle with the absorbed reverie and absent eyes of a man in love, and did not note the form of the blind girl, in the same place where he had left her. But though he saw her not, her ear recognized the sound of his step. She had been counting the moments to his return. He had scarcely entered his favourite chamber, which opened on the peristyle, and seated himself musingly on his couch, when he felt his robe timorously touched, and, turning, he beheld Nydia kneeling before him, and holding up to him a handful of flowers—a gentle and appropriate peace-offering; her eyes, darkly upheld to his own, streaming with tears.

"I have offended thee," said she, sobbing, "and for the first time. I would die rather than cause thee a moment's pain—say that thou wilt forgive me. See! I have taken up the chain; I have put it on; I will never part from it—it is thy gift."

"My dear Nydia," returned Glaucus, and raising her, he kissed her forehead, "think no more of it! But why, my child, wert thou so suddenly angry? I could not divine the cause!"

"Do not ask!" said she, colouring violently. "I am a thing full of faults and humours; you know I am but a child—you say so often: is it from a child that you can expect a reason for every folly?"

"But, prettiest, you will soon be a child no more; and if you would have us treat you as a woman, you must learn to govern these singular impulses and gales of passion. Think not I chide; no, it is for your happiness only I speak."

"It is true," said Nydia, "I must learn to govern myself. I must hide, I must suppress, my heart. This is a woman's task and duty; methinks her virtue is hypocrisy."

"Self-control is not deceit, my Nydia," returned the Athenian, "and that is the virtue necessary alike to man and to woman; it is the true senatorial toga, the badge of the dignity it covers.

"Self-control! Well, what you say is right! When I listen to you, Glaucus, my wildest thoughts grow calm and sweet, and a delicious serenity falls over me. Advise, ah! Guide me, my preserver!"

"Thy affectionate heart will be thy best guide, Nydia, when thou hast learned to regulate its feelings."

"Ah! That will be never," sighed Nydia, wiping away her tears.

"Say not so; the first effort is the only difficult one."

"I have made many first efforts," answered Nydia, innocently. "But you, do you find it so easy to control yourself? Could you conceal your love for Ione?"

"Love! Dear Nydia; ah! That is quite another matter," answered the young preceptor.

"I thought so!" returned Nydia, with a melancholy smile. "Glaucus, wilt thou take my poor flowers? Do with them as thou wilt—thou canst give them to Ione," added she, with a little hesitation.

"Nay, Nydia," answered Glaucus kindly, divining something of jealousy in her language, though he imagined it only the jealousy of a vain and susceptible child; "I will not give thy pretty flowers to any one. Sit here and weave them into a garland; I will wear it this night; it is not the first those delicate fingers have woven for me."

The poor girl delightedly sat down beside Glaucus. She drew from her girdle a ball of the many-coloured threads, or rather slender ribbons, used in the weaving of garlands, and which (for it was her professional occupation) she carried constantly with her, and began quickly and gracefully to commence her task. Upon her cheeks the tears were already dried, a faint but happy smile played round her lips—child-like, indeed, she was sensible only of the joy of the present hour; she was reconciled to Glaucus; he had forgiven her—she was beside him—he played caressingly with her silken hair—Ione was not by—none other demanded, divided, his care. Yes, she was happy and forgetful; it was one of the few moments in her brief and troubled life that it was sweet to treasure, to recall.

"Thou hast beautiful locks," said Glaucus. "They were once, I guess well, a mother's delight."

Nydia sighed; she had not been a slave; but she shunned the mention of her parentage, and, whether obscure or noble, it was never known by her benefactors, nor by any one in those distant shores, even to the last. A child of sorrow and mystery, she came and went as some bird that enters our chamber for a moment; it flutters for a while before us, but we know not whence it came, nor to what region it goes.

Nydia sighed, and, after a short pause, without answering the remark, said:

"But do I weave too many roses in my wreath? They tell me it is thy favourite flower."

"And ever favoured, my Nydia, be it by those who have the soul of poetry; it is the flower of love, of festivals; it is also the flower we dedicate to silence and death; it blooms on our brows in life, while life be worth the having: it is scattered above our sepulchre when we are no more."

"Ah! Would," said Nydia, "instead of this perishable wreath, that I could take thy web from the hand of the Fates, and insert the roses there!"

"Pretty one! Thy wish is worthy of a voice so attuned to song; and whatever my doom, I thank thee."

"Whatever thy doom! Is it not already destined to all things bright and fair? My wish was vain. The Fates will be as tender to thee as I should."

"It might not be so, Nydia, were it not for love. While youth lasts, I may forget my country. But what Athenian, in his graver manhood, can think of Athens as she was, and be contented that he is happy while she is fallen?"

Nydia answered nothing to this, but stretched a hand to her lyre, and sang in a low tone a song which he had made, and taught her.

"Who shall assume the bays
The heroes wore?
Wreaths of the greater days
That dawn no more.
For slave and freeman grows
Naught but the fading rose,
Laurels are left to those
The famed of yore.

Hope lost and Freedom fled,
What yet remains?
Match we the mighty dead—
The heroes' gains?
Nay, but the rose is ours

Flowers for a life of flowers.
Long as the sunlit hours,
Pleasures for pains.

Wreathe then, the roses, wreathe!
For, wreathing, so
Sweet are the scents we breathe,
The joys we know.
All that is fair or bright
Caught in the arms of night
Yields us its soft delight,
Though glory go."

22. Julia

What happiness to Ione—what bliss to be ever by the side of Glaucus, to hear his voice! And she can see him!"

Such was the soliloquy of the blind girl, as she walked alone at twilight to the house of her mistress, whither Glaucus had already preceded her. Suddenly she was interrupted in her fond thoughts by a female voice.

"Blind flower-girl, whither goest thou? Where is thy pannier? Hast thou sold all thy flowers?"

The person thus accosting Nydia was a lady of a handsome, bold, and unmaidenly countenance; it was Julia, the daughter of Diomed. Her veil was half raised as she spoke; she was accompanied by Diomed himself, and by a slave carrying a lantern before them— the merchant and his daughter were returning home from a supper at one of their neighbour's houses.

"Dost thou not remember my voice? I am the daughter of Diomed."

"Forgive me, noble Julia, I have no flowers to sell."

"I heard that thou wert purchased by the beautiful Greek, Glaucus; is that true, pretty slave?"

"I serve the Neapolitan, Ione."

"Ah! It is true, then—"

"Come, come!" interrupted Diomed, with his cloak up to his mouth, "the night grows cold; I cannot stay here while you prate; let her follow you home, if you wish to speak to her."

"Do, child," said Julia, with the air of one not accustomed to be refused; "I have much to ask of thee; come."

"I cannot this night, it grows late," answered Nydia. "I must be at home. I am not free, noble Julia."

"What! The meek Ione will chide thee? Ay, I doubt not she is a second Tholestris. But come. Then, tomorrow; do—remember I have been thy friend of old."

"I will obey thy wishes," answered Nydia; and Diomed again impatiently summoned his daughter; she was obliged to proceed, with the main question she had desired to put to Nydia unasked.

Meanwhile Ione had received a visit from her brother. The first since he had assisted in saving her from the Egyptian.

Now he met her with a strange calmness on his features, a more quiet and self-possessed expression in his sunken eyes, than she had seen for years.

"May the gods bless thee, my brother!"

"The gods! Speak not thus vaguely; perchance there is but one God!"

"Brother!"

"What if the sublime faith of the Nazarene be true? What if God be a monarch—One—Invisible—Alone? What if these numerous, countless deities, whose altars fill the earth, be but evil demons, seeking to wean us from the true creed? This may be the case. Ione!"

"Alas! Can we believe it? Or, if we believed, would it not be a melancholy faith?" answered the Neapolitan.

"What! All this beautiful world made only human! The mountain disenchanted of its Dread—the waters of their Nymph—that beautiful prodigality of faith, which makes everything divine, consecrating the meanest flowers, bearing celestial whispers in the faintest breeze—wouldst thou deny this, and make the earth mere dust and clay? No, Apæcides; all that is brightest in our hearts is that very credulity which peoples the universe with gods."

Ione answered as a believer in the poetry of the old mythology would answer. We may judge by that reply how obstinate and hard the contest which Christianity had to endure. The Graceful Superstition was never silent; the most household actions of their lives were entwined with it—it was a portion of life itself, as the flowers are a part of the thyrsus. At every incident they recurred to a god, every cup of wine was prefaced by a libation; the very garlands on their thresholds were dedicated to some divinity; their ancestors themselves, made holy, presided as Lares over their hearths and halls.

But these superstitions were not to the early Christians the object of contempt so much as of horror. They did not believe, with the quiet scepticism of the heathen philosopher, that the gods were inventions of the priests; nor even, with the vulgar, that, according to the dim light of history, they had been mortals like themselves. They imagined the heathen divinities to be evil spirits—they transplanted to Italy and to Greece the gloomy demons of India and the East; and in Jupiter or in Mars they shuddered at the representative of Moloch or of Satan.

Apæcides had not yet adopted formally the Christian faith, but he was already on the brink of it. He already participated in the doctrines of Olinthus—he already imagined that the lively inventions of the heathen were suggestions of the arch-enemy of mankind. He hastened to reply vehemently, and yet so confusedly, that Ione feared for his reason more than she dreaded his violence.

"Ah brother!" said she, "these hard duties of thine have shattered thy very sense. Come to me, Apæcides, my brother, my own brother; give me thy hand, chide me not now, I understand thee not; think only that Ione could not offend thee!"

"Ione," said Apæcides, drawing her towards him, and regarding her tenderly, "can I think that this beautiful form, this kind heart, may be destined to an eternity of torment?"

"Dii meliora! The gods forbid!" said Ione, in the customary form of words by which her contemporaries thought an omen might be averted.

The words, and still more the superstition they implied, wounded the ear of Apæcides. He rose, muttering to himself, turned from the chamber, then, stopping halfway, gazed wistfully on Ione, and extended his arms.

Ione flew to them in joy; he kissed her earnestly, and then said:

"Farewell, sister! When next we meet, thou mayst be to me as nothing; take this embrace—full yet of all the tender reminiscences of childhood, when faith and hope, creeds, customs, interests, objects, were the same to us. Now, the tie is to be broken!"

With these strange words he left he house. The great and severest trial of the primitive Christians was indeed this; their conversation separated them from their dearest bonds. They could not associate with those whose commonest actions, whose commonest forms of speech, were impregnated with idolatry. They shuddered at the blessing of love; to their ears it was uttered in a demon's name. This, their misfortune, was their strength; if it divided them from the rest of the world, it was to unite them proportionally to each other.

Glaucus found Ione in tears. He drew from her a recital of her interview with her brother; but in her confused account of language itself so confused to one not prepared for it, he was equally at a loss to conceive the intentions or the meaning of Apæcides.

"Hast thou heard much," asked she, "of this new sect of the Nazarenes?"

"I have heard enough of the votaries," returned Glaucus, "but of their exact tenets know I naught, save that in their doctrine there seemeth something preternaturally chilling and morose. They live apart from their kind; they affect to be shocked even at our simple uses of garlands; they have no sympathies with the cheerful amusements of life; they utter awful threats of the coming destruction of the world; they appear, in one word, to have brought their unsmiling and gloomy creed out of the cave of Trophonius.

"Yet," continued he, after a slight pause, "they have not wanted men of great power and genius, nor converts, even among the Areopagites of Athens. Well do I remember to have heard my father speak of one strange guest at Athens, many years ago; methinks his name was Paul. My father was amongst a mighty crowd that gathered on one of our immemorial hills to hear this sage of the East expound; through the wide throng there rang not a single murmur!—the jest and the roar with which our native orators are received, were hushed for him; and when he stood on the loftiest summit of that hill, raised above the breathless crowd below, his mien and countenance awed every heart, even before a sound left his lips. He was a man, I have heard my father say, of no tall stature, but of noble and impressive mien. His robes were dark and ample; the declining sun, for it was evening, shone aslant upon his form as it rose aloft, motionless and commanding; his countenance was much worn and marked, as of one who had braved alike misfortune and the sternest vicissitudes of many climes; but his eyes were bright with an almost unearthly fire; and when he raised his arm to speak, it was with the majesty of a man into whom the Spirit of God had rushed."

"'Men of Athens!' he said, 'I find amongst ye an altar with this inscription—TO THE UNKNOWN GOD. Ye worship in ignorance the same Deity I serve. Unknown till now, to you be it revealed.'"

"Then he declared how this great Maker of all things, who had appointed unto man his several tribes and his various homes—the Lord of earth and the universal heaven, dwelt not in temples made with hands; that His presence, His spirit, were in the air we breathed; our life and our being were with Him. 'Think you,' he cried, 'that the Invisible is like your statues of gold and marble? Think you that He needeth sacrifice from you; He who made heaven and earth?' Then he spoke of fearful and coming times, of the end of the world, of a second rising of the dead, whereof an assurance had been given to man in the resurrection of the mighty being whose religion he came to preach."

"When he thus spoke, the philosophers who were mingled with the people muttered their sage contempt; but the people were touched and thrilled; and they trembled, though they knew not why, for the stranger had the voice and majesty of a man to whom 'The Unknown God' had committed the preaching of His faith."

Ione listened with rapt attention, and the serious and earnest manner of the narrator betrayed the impression that he himself had received from one who had been amongst the audience that, on the hill of the heathen Mars, had heard the first tidings of the word of Christ!

23. Why Lydon Fought

The door of Diomed's house was open, and Medon, the old slave, stood at the bottom of the steps. The luxurious mansion of the rich merchant of Pompeii is still to be seen outside the gates of the city, at the commencement of the Street of Tombs; it was a gay neighbourhood, despite the dead. On the opposite side, but at some yards nearer the gate, was a spacious hostelry, at which those brought by business or pleasure to Pompeii often stopped to refresh themselves. In the space before the entrance of the inn now stood wagons, and carts, and chariots, some just arrived, some just quitting, in all the bustle of an animated and popular resort of public entertainment. Before the door, some farmers, seated on a bench by a small circular table, were talking over their morning cups, on the affairs of their calling. On the side of the door itself was painted gaily and freshly the eternal sign of the chequers. By the roof of the inn stretched a terrace, on which were the wives of the farmers, some seated, some leaning over the railing, and conversing with their friends below. In a deep recess, at a little distance, was a covered seat, on which two or three poorer travellers were resting themselves, and shaking the dust from their garments. On the others side stretched a wide space, originally the burial-ground of a more ancient race than the present denizens of Pompeii, and now converted into the Ustrinum, or place for the burning of the dead. Above this rose the terraces of a gay villa, half hidden by trees. The tombs themselves, with their graceful and varied shapes, and the flowers and the foliage that surrounded them, made no melancholy feature in this prospect. Hard by the gate of the city, in a small niche, stood the still form of the well-disciplined Roman sentry, the sun shining brightly on his polished crest, and the lance on which he leaned. The gate itself was divided into three arches, the centre one for vehicles, the others for foot-passengers; and on either side rose the massive walls which girt the city, composed, patched, repainted at a thousand different epochs, according as war, time, or earthquake, had shattered the vain protection. At frequent intervals rose square towers, whose summits broke in picturesque rudeness the regular line of the wall, and contrasted well with modern buildings gleaming whitely by.

The curving road, which in that direction leads from Pompeii to Herculaneum, wound out of sight amidst hanging vines, above which frowned the sullen majesty of Vesuvius.

"Hast thou heard the news, old Medon?" said a young woman, with a pitcher in her hand, as she paused by Diomed's door to gossip a moment with the slave, ere she repaired to the neighbouring inn to fill the vessel, and coquet with the travellers.

"What news?" asked the slave, raising his eyes moodily from the ground.

"Why, there passed through the gate this morning, no doubt ere thou wert well awake, such a visitor to Pompeii!"

"Ay," said the slave, indifferently. "Yes, a present from the noble Pomponianus."

"A present! I thought thou saidst a visitor!"

"It is both visitor and present. Know, O dull and stupid, that it is a most beautiful young tiger, for our approaching games in the amphitheatre. Hear you that, Medon? Oh, what pleasure! I declare I shall not sleep a wink till I see it; they say it has such a roar!"

"Poor fool!" said Medon, sadly and cynically.

"I am no fool, old churl! It is a pretty thing, a tiger, especially if we could but find somebody for him to eat. We have now a lion and a tiger; only consider that, Medon! For the want of two good criminals, perhaps we shall be forced to see them eat each other. Bye-the-bye, your son is a gladiator, a handsome man and a strong; could you not persuade him to fight the tiger? Do now, you would oblige me mightily; nay, you would be a benefactor to the whole town."

"Vah! Vah!" said the slave with great asperity. "Think of thine own danger ere thou pratest of my poor boy's death."

"My own danger!" said the girl, frightened and looking hastily round. "Avert the omen! Let thy words fall on thine own head!" And as she spoke she touched a talisman suspended round her neck. "'Thine own danger!' What danger threatens me?"

"Had the earthquake but a few nights since no warning?" said Medon. "Has it not a voice? Did it not say to us all, 'Prepare for death; the end of all things is at hand?'"

"Stuff," said the young woman, settling the folds of her tunic. "Now thou talkest as they say the Nazarenes talk—methinks thou art one of them. Well, I can prate with thee, gray croaker, no more; thou growest worse and worse—Vale! O Hercules, send us a man for the lion—and another for the tiger!"

Holding up her tunic from the dusty road, the young woman stepped lightly across to the crowded hostelry.

"My poor son!" said the slave, half aloud," is it for things like this thou art to be butchered? Oh, faith of Christ, I could worship thee in all sincerity, were it but for the horror which thou inspirest for these bloody lists."

The old man's head sank dejectedly. He remained silent and absorbed, but every now and then with the corner of his sleeve he wiped his eyes. His heart was with his son; he did not see the figure that approached from the gate with a quick step, and a somewhat fierce and reckless gait. He did not lift his eyes till it paused opposite the place where he sat, and with a soft voice addressed him by the name of Father.

"Lydon, is it indeed thou?" said the old man, joyfully. "Ah, thou wert present to my thoughts."

"I am glad to hear it," said my gladiator, respectfully touching the knees and beard of the slave; "and soon may I be always present with thee, not in thought only."

"Yes, my son—but not in this world," replied the slave, mournfully.

"Talk not thus, O my sire—look cheerfully, for I feel so—I am sure that I shall win the day; and then, the gold I gain buys thy freedom. Oh, father, it was but a few days since that I was taunted; by one, too, whom I would gladly have undeceived, for he is more generous than the rest of his equals. He is not Roman—he is of Athens—by him I was taunted with the lust of gain—when I demanded what sum was the prize of victory. Alas, he little knew the soul of Lydon!"

"My boy! My boy!" said the old slave, as slowly ascending the steps, he conducted his son to his own little chamber, communicating with the entrance hall (which in this villa was the peristyle, not the atrium. The first door conducted to the staircase; the second was but a false recess, in which there stood a statue of bronze.) "Generous, affectionate, pious as thy motives are," said Medon, when they were thus secured from observation, "thy deed itself is guilt; thou art to risk thy blood for thy father's freedom—that might be forgiven; but the prize of victory is the blood of another. That is a deadly sin;

no object can purify it. Rather would I be a slave forever than purchase liberty on such terms!"

"Hush, father!" replied Lydon, somewhat impatiently; "thou has picked up in this new creed of thine, of which I pray thee not to speak to me, for the gods who gave me strength denied me wisdom, and I understand not one word of what thou preachest—thou has picked up, I say, in this new creed, some singular fantasies of right and wrong. Pardon me, if I offend thee; but reflect! Against whom shall I contend? Oh! could'st thou know those wretches with whom, for thy sake, I assort, thou wouldst think I purified earth by removing one of them. Beasts, whose very lips drop blood; things, all savage, unprincipled in their courage; ferocious, heartless, senseless; they know not fear, it is true—but neither know they gratitude, nor charity, nor love; they are made but for their own career, to slaughter without pity, to die without dread! Can thy gods, whosoever they be, look with wrath on a conflict with such as these, and in such a cause?"

The poor old slave, himself deprived of the lights of knowledge, and only late a convert to the Christian faith, knew not with what arguments to enlighten an ignorance at once so dark, and yet so beautiful in its error. His first impulse was to throw himself on his son's breast—his next to start away—to wring his hands; and in the attempt to reprove, his broken voice lost itself in weeping.

"And if," resumed Lydon—"if thy Deity (methinks thou wilt own but one?) be indeed that benevolent and pitying Power which thou assertest Him to be, He will know also that thy very faith in Him first confirmed me in that determination thou blamest."

"How! What mean you?" said the slave.

"Why, thou knowest that I, sold in my childhood as a slave, was set free at Rome by the will of my master, whom I had been fortunate enough to please. When I hastened to Pompeii to see thee—I found thee already aged and infirm, under the yoke of a capricious and pampered lord—thou hadst lately adopted this new faith, and its adoption made thy slavery doubly painful to thee; it took away all the softening charm of custom, which reconciles us so often to the worst. Didst thou not complain to me that thou wert compelled to offices that were not merely odious to thee as a slave but guilty as a Nazarene? Didst thou not tell me that thy soul shook with remorse when thou wert compelled to place even a crumb of cake before the Lares that watch over yon impluvium? That thy soul was torn by a perpetual struggle? Didst thou not tell me that even by pouring wine before the threshold, and calling on the name of some Grecian deity, thou didst fear thou wert incurring penalties worse than those of

Tantalus, an eternity of tortures more terrible than those of the Tartarean fields? Didst thou not tell me this? I wondered, I could not comprehend; nor, by Hercules, can I now; but I was thy son, and my sole task to be compassionate and relieve."

"Oh, that thou couldst hear Olinthus!" sighed the old man, more and more affected by the virtue of his son, but not less strongly convinced of the criminality of his purpose.

"I will hear the whole world talk, if thou wilt," answered the gladiator, gaily; "but not till thou art a slave no more. Ah, we shall be so happy—the prize can purchase all. Cheer thee, my sire! And now I must away—day wears—the lanista awaits me. Come! Thy blessing!"

As Lydon thus spoke, he had already quitted the dark chamber of his father; and speaking eagerly, though in a whispered tone, they now stood again at the porter's post.

"O bless thee! My brave boy!" said Medon, fervently; "and may the great Power that reads all hearts see the nobleness of thine, and forgive its error!"

The tall shape of the gladiator passed swiftly down the path; the eyes of the slave followed till the last glimpse was gone: and then sinking on his seat, his eyes again fastened themselves on the ground, his form mute and unmoving as a thing of stone.

"May I enter?" said a sweet voice. "Is thy mistress within?"

The slave mechanically motioned to the visitor to enter, but she who addressed him could not see the gesture—she repeated her question timidly, but in a louder voice.

"Have I not told thee?" said the slave, peevishly; "enter."

"Thanks," said the speaker, plaintively; and the slave, roused by the tone, looked up, and recognised the blind flower girl. Sorrow can sympathise with affliction—he raised himself, and guided her steps to the head of the adjacent staircase, where, summoning a female slave, he consigned to her the charge of the blind girl.

24. The Dressing-Room of Julia

The elegant Julia sat in her chamber, with her slaves around her. Like the cubiculum which adjoined it, the room was small, but much larger than the usual apartments appropriated to sleep, which were so diminutive that few who have not seen the bedchambers, even in the gayest mansions, can form any notion of the petty pigeon-holes in which the citizens of Pompeii thought it desirable to pass the night. But, in fact, "bed" with the ancients was not that grave, serious, and important part of domestic mysteries which it is with us. The couch itself was more like a very narrow and small sofa, light enough to be transported easily, and by the occupant himself, from place to place; and it was, no doubt, constantly shifted from chamber to chamber, according to the caprices of the inmate, or the changes of the season; for that side of the house which was crowded in one month, might, perhaps, be avoided in the next. There was also among the Italians of that period a singular and fastidious apprehension of too much daylight; their darkened chambers, which first appear to us the result of a negligent architecture, were the effect of elaborate study. In their porticoes and gardens, they courted the sun when it pleased their luxurious tastes. In the interior of their houses they sought rather for coolness and shade.

Julia's apartment at that season was in the lower part of the house, immediately beneath the state-rooms, and looking upon the garden, with which it was on a level. The wide glazed door alone admitted the morning rays: yet her eyes, accustomed to a certain darkness, were sufficiently acute to perceive what colours were the most becoming—what shade of the delicate rouge suited her dark glance, and the youthful freshness of her cheeks.

On the table before which she sat was a small circular mirror of polished steel round which, in precise order, were ranged the cosmetics and unguents—the perfumes and paints—the jewels and combs—the ribbons and gold pins, which were destined to add to the natural attractions of beauty the assistance of art and the capricious dictates of fashion. Through the dimness of the room, glowed brightly the vivid and various colourings of the wall in dazzling frescoes. Before the dressing-table, and under the feet of Julia, was spread a carpet woven from the looms of the East. Near at hand, on another table, was a silver basin and ewer; an extinguished lamp, of exquisite workmanship, in which the artist had represented a Cupid reposing under the spreading branches of a myrtle-tree; and a small roll of papyrus, containing the softest elegies of Tibullus. Before the door, which communicated with the cubiculum. hung a curtain richly broidered with gold flowers.

Julia leaned indolently back on her seat, while the hairdresser slowly piled, one above the other, a mass of small curls, dexterously weaving the false with the true, and carrying the whole fabric to a height that seemed to place the head rather at the centre than the summit of the human form.

Her tunic, of a deep amber, which set off her dark hair and somewhat embrowned complexion, swept in ample folds to her feet, which were encased in slippers, fastened round the slender ankles by white thongs; while a profusion of pearls were embroidered in the slippers, which were of purple, and turned slightly upward, as do the Turkish slippers of later days. An old slave, skilled by long experience in all the arcana of the toilet, stood beside the hairdresser, with the broad and studded girdle of her mistress over her arm, and giving, from to time, instructions to the mason of the ascending pile.

"Put that pin rather more to the right—lower—stupid one! Do you not observe how even those beautiful eye-brows are? One would think you were dressing Corinna, whose face is all of one side. Now put in the flowers—what, fool!—not that dull pink—you are not suiting colours to that dim cheek of Chloris."

"Gently!" said the lady, stamping her small foot violently: "you pull my hair as if you were plucking up a weed!"

"Dull thing!" continued the directress of the ceremony. "Do you not know how delicate is your mistress?—you are not dressing the coarse horsehair of the widow Fulvia. Now, then, the ribbon—that's right. Fair Julia, look in the mirror; saw you ever anything so lovely as yourself?"

When, after innumerable comments, difficulties and delays, the intricate tower was at length completed, the next preparation was that of giving to the eyes the soft languish produced by a dark powder applied to the lids and brows; a small patch, cut in the form of a crescent, skilfully placed by the rosy lips, attracted attention to their dimples, and to the teeth, to which already every art had been applied in order to heighten the dazzle of their natural whiteness.

To another slave, hitherto idle, was now consigned the charge of arranging the jewels—the ear-rings of pearl (two to each ear)—the massive bracelet of gold—the chain formed of rings of the same metal, to which a talisman cut in crystals was attached—the graceful buckle on the left shoulder, in which was set an exquisite cameo of Psyche—the girdle of purple ribbon, richly wrought with threads of gold, and clasped by interlacing serpents—and last, the various rings fitted to every joint of the white and slender fingers. The toilet was now arranged, according to the latest mode of Rome. The fair Julia regarded herself with a last gaze of complacent vanity, and, reclining again upon her seat, bade the youngest of her slaves, in a listless tone, read to her the enamoured couplets of Tibullus. This was still proceeding, when a female slave admitted Nydia into the presence of the lady of the place.

"*Salve*, Julia!" said the flower-girl, arresting her steps within a few paces from the spot were Julia sat, and crossing her arms upon her breast. "I have obeyed your commands."

"You have done well, flower-girl," answered the lady. "Approach—you may take a seat."

One of the slaves placed a stool by Julia, and Nydia seated herself.

Julia looked hard at the Thessalian for some moments in rather an embarrassed silence. She then motioned her attendants to withdraw, and to close the door. When they were alone, she said, looking mechanically from Nydia, and forgetful that she was with one who could not observe her countenance: "You serve the Neapolitan, Ione."

"I am with her at present."

"Is she as handsome as they say?"

"I know not. How can *I* judge?"

"Ah! I should have remembered. But thou hast ears, if not eyes. Do thy fellow-slaves tell thee she is handsome? Slaves talking with one another forget to flatter even their mistress."

"They tell me she is beautiful."

"Hem!—they say that she is tall?"

"Yes."

"Why, so am I—Dark-haired?"

"I have heard so."

"So am I. And doth Glaucus visit her much?"

"Daily," returned Nydia, with a half-suppressed sigh.

"Daily, indeed! Does he find her handsome?"

"I should think so, since they are so soon to be wedded."

"Wedded!" cried Julia, turning pale even through the false rose on her cheek, and starting from her couch. Nydia did not perceive the emotion she had caused. Julia remained a long time silent; but her heaving breast and angry eyes would have betrayed, to one who could have seen, the wound her vanity sustained.

"They tell me thou art a Thessalian," said she, at last breaking silence.

"Yes."

"Thessaly is the land of magic and witches, of talismans and love-philtres," said Julia.

"It has ever been celebrated for its sorcerers," returned Nydia, timidly.

"Knowest thou, then, of any love-charms?"

"I!" said the flower-girl, colouring; "*I!* How should I? No, assuredly not!"

"The worse for thee; I could have given thee gold enough to have purchased thy freedom hadst thou been wiser."

"But what," asked Nydia, "can induce the beautiful and wealthy Julia to ask that question of her servant? Has she not money, and youth, and loveliness? Are they not love-charms enough to dispense with magic?"

"To all but one person in the world," answered Julia haughtily: "but methinks thy blindness is infectious; and—but no matter."

"And that one person?"

"Is *not* Glaucus," replied Julia, with the customary deceit of her sex. "Glaucus—no!"

Nydia drew her breath more freely, and after a short pause Julia recommenced.

"But talking of Glaucus, and his attachment to this Neapolitan reminded me of the influence of love-spells, which, for aught I know or care, she may have exercised upon him. Blind girl, I love, and—shall Julia live to say it?—am loved not in return! I would see this ingrate at my feet—not in order that I might raise, but that I might spurn him. When they told me thou wert Thessalian, I imagined thy young mind might have learned the dark secrets of thy clime."

"Alas! No," murmured Nydia; "would it had!"

"Thanks, at least, for that kindly wish," said Julia, unconscious of what was passing in the breast of the flower-girl.

"But tell me—thou hearest the gossip of slaves, always prone to these dim beliefs; always ready to apply to sorcery for their own low loves—hast thou ever heard of an Eastern magician in this city, who possesses the art of which thou art ignorant? No vain chiromancer, no juggler of the market-place, but some more potent and mighty magician of India or of Egypt?"

"Of Egypt?—yes!" said Nydia, shuddering. "What Pompeian has not heard of Arbaces?"

"Arbaces! True," replied Julia, grasping at the recollection. "They say he is a man above all the petty and false impostures of dull pretenders—that he is versed in the learning of the stars, and the secrets of the ancient Nox; why not in the mysteries of love?"

"If there be one magician living whose art is above that of others, it is that dread man," answered Nydia; and she felt her talisman while she spoke.

"He is too wealthy to divine for money?" continued Julia, sneeringly. "Can I not visit him?"

"It is an evil mansion for the young and beautiful," replied Nydia. "I have heard, too, that he—"

"An evil mansion!" said Julia, catching only the first sentence. "Why so?"

"The orgies of his midnight leisure are impure and polluted—at least, so says rumour."

"By Ceres, by Pan, and by Cybele! Thou dost but provoke my curiosity, instead of exciting my fears," returned the wayward and pampered Pompeian. "I will seek and question him of his lore. If to these orgies love be admitted—why then more likely that he knows its secrets!"

Nydia did not answer.

"I will seek him this very day," resumed Julia; "nay, why not this very hour?"

"At daylight, and in his present state, thou hast assuredly the less to fear," answered Nydia, yielding to her own sudden and secret wish to learn if the dark Egyptian were indeed possessed of those spells to rivet and attract love, of which the Thessalian had so often heard.

"And who dare insult the daughter of Diomed?" said Julia, haughtily, "I will go."

"May I visit thee afterwards to learn the result?" asked Nydia, anxiously.

"Kiss me for thy interest in Julia's honour," answered the lady. "Yes, assuredly. This eve we sup abroad—come hither at the same hour tomorrow, and thou shalt know all: I may have to employ thee too; but enough for the present. Stay, take this bracelet for the new thought thou hast inspired me with; remember, if thou servest Julia, she is grateful and she is generous."

"I cannot take thy present," said Nydia, putting aside the bracelet; "but young as I am, I can sympathise unbought with those who love—and love in vain."

"Sayest thou so!" returned Julia. "Thou speakest like a free woman—and thou shalt yet be free—farewell!"

25. Julia Seeks Arbaces

Arbaces was seated in a chamber which opened on a kind of balcony or portico that fronted his garden. His cheek was pale and worn with the suffering he had endured, but his iron frame had already recovered from the severest effects of that accident which had frustrated him in the moment of victory. The air that came fragrantly to his brow revived his languid senses, and the blood circulated more freely than it had done for days through his shrunken veins.

"So, then," thought he, "the storm of fate has broken and blown over—the evil which my lore predicted, threatening life itself, has chanced—and yet I live! It came as the stars foretold; and now the long, bright, prosperous career which was to succeed that evil, if I survive it, smiles beyond: I have passed—I have subdued the latest danger of my destiny. I have but to lay out the gardens of my future fate—unterrified and secure. First, then, of all my pleasures, even before that of love, shall come revenge! This boy Greek—who has crossed my passions—thwarted my designs—baffled me even when the blade was about to drink his accursed blood—shall not a second time escape me! But for the method of my vengeance? Of that let me ponder well! Oh! Até, if thou art indeed a goddess, fill me with thy direst inspiration!" The Egyptian sank into an intent reverie, which did not seem to present to him any clear or satisfactory suggestions. He changed his position restlessly, as he revolved scheme after scheme, which no sooner occurred than it was dismissed. While thus absorbed, a boy slave timidly entered the chamber.

A female, evidently of rank, from her dress and that of the single slave who attended her, waited below and sought an audience with Arbaces.

"A female!" His heart beat quickly. "Is she young?"

"Her face is concealed by her veil; but her form is slight, yet round as that of youth."

"Admit her," said the Egyptian; for a moment his vain heart dreamed the stranger might be Ione.

But the first glance, as she entered, undeceived him.

"Pardon me that I rise with pain," said Arbaces, gazing on the stranger: "I am still suffering from recent illness."

"Do not disturb thyself, O great Egyptian!" returned Julia, seeking to disguise the fear she had already experienced, beneath the ready resort of flattery; "and forgive an unfortunate one who seeks consolation from thy wisdom"

"Draw near, fair stranger, and speak without apprehension or reserve." Julia placed herself on a seat beside the Egyptian, and wonderingly gazed around an apartment whose elaborate and costly luxuries shamed even the ornate enrichment of her father's mansion; fearfully, too, she regarded the hieroglyphical inscriptions on the walls—the faces of the mysterious images, which at every corner gazed upon her—the tripod at a little distance—and, above all, the grave and remarkable countenance of Arbaces himself.

"And what," said his low, deep voice, "brings thee to the house of the Eastern stranger?"

"His fame," replied Julia.

"In what?" said he, with a strange, slight smile.

"Canst thou ask, O wise Arbaces? Is not thy knowledge the gossip theme of Pompeii?"

"Some little lore have I, indeed, treasured up; but in what can such serious and sterile secrets benefit the ear of beauty?"

"Alas!" said Julia, a little cheered by the accustomed accents of adulation; "does not sorrow fly to wisdom for relief, and they who love unrequitedly, are not they the chosen victims of grief?"

"Ha!" said Arbaces, "can unrequited love be the lot of so fair a form, whose modelled proportions are visible even beneath the folds of thy graceful robe? Deign to lift thy veil, that I may see at least if the face correspond in loveliness with the form."

Not unwilling, perhaps, to exhibit her charms, and thinking they were likely to interest the magician in her fate, Julia, after some slight hesitation, raised her veil, and revealed a beauty which, but for art, had been indeed attractive to the fixed gaze of the Egyptian.

"Thou comest to me for advice in unhappy love," said he. "Well turn that face on the ungrateful one: what other love-charm can I give thee?"

"Oh, cease these courtesies!" said Julia; "it is a love-charm indeed that I would ask from thy skill."

"Fair stranger!" replied Arbaces, somewhat scornfully. "Love spells are not among the secrets I have wasted the midnight oil to attain."

"Is it indeed so? Then pardon me, great Arbaces, and farewell."

"Stay," said Arbaces, who was not unmoved by the beauty of his visitor; and, had he been in the flush of a more assured health, might have attempted to console the fair Julia by other means than those of supernatural wisdom. "Stay; although I confess that I have left the witchery of philtres and potions to those whose trade is in such knowledge, yet am I myself not so dull to beauty but that in earlier youth I may have employed them in my own behalf. I may give thee advice, at least, if thou wilt be candid with me. Tell me then first, art thou unmarried, as thy dress betokens?"

"Yes," said Julia. "And, being unblest with fortune, wouldst thou allure some wealthy suitor?"

"I am richer than he who disdains me."

"Strange and more strange! And thou lovest him who lovest not thee?"

"I know not if I love him," answered Julia, haughtily; "but I know that I would see myself triumph over a rival—I would see him who rejected me my suitor—I would see her whom he has preferred, in her turn despised."

"A natural ambition and a womanly," said the Egyptian, in a tone too grave for irony. "Yet more, fair maiden; wilt thou confide to me the name of thy lover? Can he be Pompeian, and despise wealth, even if blind to beauty?"

"He is of Athens."

"Ha!" cried the Egyptian, impetuously, as the blood rushed to his cheek; "there is but one Athenian, young and noble, in Pompeii. Can it be Glaucus of whom thou speakest!"

"Ah! Betray me not—so indeed they call him."

The Egyptian sank back, gazing vacantly on the averted face of the merchant's daughter, and muttering to himself—this conference, with which he had hitherto only trifled, amusing himself with the credulity and vanity of his visitor—might it not minister to his revenge?

"I see thou canst not assist me", said Julia, offended by his continued silence. "Guard at least my secret. Once more farewell."

"Maiden," said the Egyptian, in an earnest and serious tone, "thy suit hath touched me—I will minister to thy will. Listen to me: I have not myself dabbled in these lesser mysteries, but I know one who hath. At the base of Vesuvius, less than a league from the city, there dwells a powerful witch; beneath the rank dews of the moon, she has gathered the herbs which possess the virtue to chain Love in eternal fetters. Her art can bring thy lover to thy feet. Seek her, and mention to her the name of Arbaces; she fears that name, and will give thee her most potent philtres."

"Alas!" answered Julia. "I know not the road to the home of her of whom thou speakest: the way, short though it be, is long to traverse for a girl who leaves, unknown, the house of her father. The country is entangled with wild vines, and dangerous with precipitous caverns. I dare not trust to mere strangers to guide me; the reputation of women of my rank is easily tarnished—and though I care not who knows that I love Glaucus, I would not have it imagined that I obtained his love by a spell."

"Were I but three days advanced in health," said the Egyptian, rising and walking (as if to try his strength) across the chamber, but with irregular and feeble steps, "I myself would accompany thee. Well, thou must wait."

"But Glaucus is soon to wed that hated Neapolitan."

"Wed!"

"Yes, in the early part of next month."

"So soon! Art thou well advised to this?"

"From the lips of her own slave."

"It shall not be!" said the Egyptian, impetuously. "Fear nothing, Glaucus shall be thine. Yet how, when thou hast obtained it, canst thou administer to him this potion?"

"My father has invited him, and, I believe, the Neapolitan also, to a banquet, on the day following tomorrow: I shall then have the opportunity."

"So be it!" said the Egyptian, with eyes flashing such fierce joy, that Julia's gaze sank trembling beneath them. "Tomorrow eve, then, order thy litter—thou hast one at thy command?"

"Surely—yes," returned the purse-proud Julia.

"Order thy litter—at two miles' distant from the city is a house of entertainment, frequented by the wealthier Pompeians, for the excellence of its baths, and the beauty of its gardens. There thou canst pretend to shape thy course—there, ill or dying, I will meet thee by the statue of Silenus, in the copse that skirts the garden. Let us wait till, with the evening star, the goats of the herdsmen are gone to rest; when the dark twilight conceals us, and none shall cross our steps. Go home, and fear not. By Hades, swears Arbaces the sorcerer of Egypt, that Ione shall never wed with Glaucus!"

"And that Glaucus shall be mine?" added Julia, filling up the incomplete sentence.

"Thou hast said it!" replied Arbaces; and Julia, half frightened at this unhallowed appointment, but urged on by jealousy and the pique of rivalry even more than love, resolved to fulfil it.

Left alone, Arbaces burst forth: "Bright stars that never lie, ye already begin the execution of your promises—success in love, and victory over foes, for the rest of my smooth existence. In the very hour when my mind could devise no clue to the goal of vengeance, have ye sent this fair fool for my guide!" He paused in deep thought. "Yes" said he again, but in a calmer voice, "I could not myself have given to her the poison that shall be indeed a philtre!—his death might be tracked to my door. But the witch—aye, there is the fit, the natural agent of my designs!"

He summoned one of his slaves, and made him hasten to track the steps of Julia, and acquaint himself with her name and condition. This done, he stepped forth into the portico. The skies were serene and clear; but he, deeply read in the signs of their various changes, beheld in one mass of cloud, far on the horizon, which the wind began slowly to agitate, that a storm was brooding above.

"It is like my vengeance," said he, as he gazed; "the sky is clear, but the clouds move on."

26. The Witch's Cavern

It was when the meats of noon died gradually from the earth that Glaucus and Ione went forth to enjoy the cooled and grateful air, in a style of carriage which was then used both for travelling and for excursions into the country. It was commodious, containing three or four persons with ease, having a covering which could be raised at pleasure; and, in short, answering very much the purpose of (though very different in shape from) the modern britska. About ten miles from the city, there was at that day an old ruin, the remains of a temple, evidently Grecian; and as, for Glaucus and Ione, everything Grecian possessed interest, they had agreed to visit these ruins.

Their road lay among vines and olive-groves, till, winding more and more towards the higher ground of Vesuvius, the path grew rugged; the mules moved slowly, and with labour; and at every opening in the wood they beheld those gray and horrent caverns indenting the parched rock, which Strabo described, but which the revolutions of time and the volcano have removed from the present aspect of the mountain. The sun, sloping towards his descent, cast long shadows over the mountain: here and there they still heard the rustic reed of the shepherd amongst copses of beech wood and wild-oak. Sometimes they saw the silk-haired and graceful capella, with wreathing horn and bright gray eye, which still, beneath Ausonian skies, recalls the eclogues of Maro, browsing on the hills; and the grapes, already purple with the deepening summer, glowed out from the arched festoons which hung pendent from tree to tree. Above them, light clouds floated in the serene heavens, sweeping so slowly athwart the firmament that they scarcely seemed to stir; while, on their right, they caught glimpses of waveless sea, with some light barque skimming its surface; and the sunlight breaking over the deep in countless and softest hues peculiar to that delicious sea.

"How beautiful," said Glaucus, in a half-whispered tone, "is that expression by which we call Earth our Mother! With what a kindly equal love she pours her blessings upon her children! And even to those sterile spots to which Nature has denied beauty, she yet contrives to dispense her smiles; witness the arbutus and the vine, which she wreathes over the arid and burning soil of the extinct volcano. Ah! In such an hour and scene as this, well might we imagine that the laughing face of the faun should peep forth from those green festoons; or that we might trace the steps of the mountain nymph through the thick mazes of the glade. But the nymph ceased, beautiful Ione, when *thou* wast created!"

They arrived at the ruins: they examined them with that fondness with which we trace the hallowed vestiges of our own ancestry—they lingered there till Hesperus appeared in the rosy heavens; and then, returning homeward in the twilight, they were more silent than they had been; for, in the shadow and beneath the stars, they felt more oppressively their mutual love.

It was at this time that the storm which the Egyptian had predicted began to creep visibly over them. At first, a low and distant thunder gave warning of the approaching conflict of the elements; and then rapidly rushed above the dark ranks of the serried clouds. The suddenness of storms in that climate is something almost preternatural, and might well suggest to early superstition the notion of a divine agency—a few large drops broke heavily among the boughs that overhung their path, and then, swift and intolerably bright, the forked lightning darted across their very eyes, and was swallowed up by the increasing darkness.

"Swifter, good carrucarius!" cried Glaucus to the driver, "the tempest comes on apace."

The slave urged on the mules—they went swiftly over the uneven and stony road—the clouds thickened, near and more near broke the thunder, and fast came the dashing rain.

"Dost thou fear?" whispered Glaucus, as he sought excuse in the storm to come nearer.

"Not with thee," answered she softly.

At that instant, the carriage, fragile and ill-contrived (as for practical uses, despite their graceful shapes, most of such inventions were at that time), struck violently into a deep rut, over which lay a log of fallen wood; the driver, with a curse, stimulated his mules yet faster for the obstacle, the wheel was torn from the socket, and the carriage suddenly overset.

Glaucus, quickly extricating himself from the vehicle, hastened to assist Ione, who was fortunately unhurt; with some difficulty they raised the carruca and found that it ceased any longer even to afford them shelter; the springs that fastened the covering were snapped asunder, and the rain poured fast and fiercely into the interior.

In this dilemma, what was to be done? They were yet some distance from the city—no house, no aid, seemed near.

"There is," said the slave, "a smith about a mile off; I could seek him, and he might fasten the wheel—but, Jupiter! How the rain beats! My mistress will be soaked before I come back."

"Run thither at least," said Glaucus; "we must find the best shelter we can till you return."

The lane was overshadowed with trees, beneath the amplest of which Glaucus drew Ione. He endeavoured, by stripping his own cloak, to shield her from the rapid rain; but it descended with a fury that broke through all puny obstacles: and then the lightning struck one of the trees immediately before them, and split with a mighty crash its huge trunk in twain. This awful incident apprised them of the danger they braved in their present shelter, and Glaucus looked anxiously round for some less perilous place of refuge. "We are now," said he, "halfway up the ascent of Vesuvius; there ought to be some cavern, or hollow in the rocks, could we but find it."

While saying this, he moved from the trees, and looking wistfully towards the mountain, discovered through the gloom a red and tremulous light at no considerable distance. "That must come," said he, "from the hearth of some shepherd or vine-dresser—it will guide us to some hospitable retreat. Wilt thou stay here, while I—yet no—that would be to leave thee to danger."

"I will go with you cheerfully. Open as the space seems, it is better than the treacherous shelter of these boughs."

Half leading, half carrying her, and accompanied by their trembling female slave, he advanced towards the light, which now burnt red and steadfastly. At length, the space was no longer open; wild vines entangled their steps, and hid from them, save by imperfect intervals, the guiding gleam. But faster and fiercer came the rain, and the lightning assumed its most deadly and blasting form; they were still, therefore, impelled onward, hoping at last, if the light eluded them, to arrive at some cottage, or friendly cavern. The vines grew more and more intricate—the light was entirely snatched from them; but a narrow path continued to lead them towards its direction. The rain ceased suddenly; precipitous and rough crags of scorched lava frowned before them, rendered more fearful by the lightning that illumined the dark and dangerous soil. Sometimes the blaze lingered over the iron-gray heaps of scoria, covered in part with ancient mosses or stunted trees, as if seeking in vain for some gentler product of earth, more worthy of its ire; and sometimes, leaving the whole of that part of the scene in darkness, the lightning, broad and sheeted, hung redly over the ocean, tossing far below until its waves seemed glowing into fire; and so intense was the blaze that it brought vividly into view even the sharp outline of the more distant windings of the bay, from the eternal Misenum, with its lofty brow, to the beautiful Sorrentum and the giant hills beyond.

They had stopped in perplexity and doubt, when suddenly, as the darkness that gloomed between the fierce flashes of lightning once more wrapped them round, they saw near, but high, before them the mysterious light. Another blaze, in which heaven and earth were reddened, made visible to them the whole expanse; no house was near, but, just where they had beheld the light, they thought they saw in the recess of a cavern the outline of a human form. The darkness once more returned; the light, no longer paled beneath the fires of heaven, shone forth again: they resolved to ascend towards it; they wound their way among vast fragments of stone, overhung with wild bushes; but they gained nearer and nearer to the light, and at length stood opposite the mouth of a cavern, apparently formed by huge splinters of rock that had fallen transversely athwart each other: and, looking into the gloom, each drew back with a superstitious chill.

A fire burned in the far recess of the cave; and over it was a small cauldron; on a tall thin column of iron stood a rude lamp; over that part of the wall, at the base of which burned the fire, hung, in many rows, as if to dry, a profusion of herbs and weeds. A fox, couched before the fire, gazed upon the strangers with its bright red eyes—its hair bristling—and a low growl sounding from between its teeth; in the centre of the cave was an earthen statue, which had three heads of a singular and fantastic cast: they were formed by the real skulls of a dog, a horse, and a boar; a low tripod stood before this wild representation of the popular Hecate.

But it was not these appendages and appliances of the cave that thrilled the blood of those who gazed fearfully therein—it was the face of its inmate. Before the fire, with the light shining full upon her features, sat a woman of considerable age. Her countenance betrayed the remains of a regular but high and aquiline order of feature: with stony eyes turned upon them—with a look that met and fascinated theirs—they beheld in that fearful countenance the very image of a corpse—the glazed and lustreless regard, the blue and shrunken lips, the drawn and hollow jaw—the dead, lank hair, of a pale gray—the livid green, ghastly skin, which seemed surely tinged and tainted by the grave!

"It is a dead thing!" said Glaucus.

"Nay—it stirs—it is a ghost or larva," faltered Ione, as she clung to the Athenian's breast.

"Oh, away—away!" groaned the slave, "it is the witch of Vesuvius!"

"Who are ye?" said a hollow and ghostly voice. "And what do ye here?"

The sound, terrible and death-like as it was—suiting well the countenance of the speaker, and seeming rather the voice of some bodiless wanderer of the Styx than living mortal, would have made

Ione shrink back into the pitiless fury of the storm, but Glaucus, though not without some misgiving, drew her into the cavern.

"We are storm-beaten wanderers," he said, "drawn here by the light; we crave shelter and the comfort of your hearth."

As he spoke, the fox rose and advanced towards them, showing its white teeth and deepening its menacing growl.

"Down, slave!" said the witch; and at the sound of her voice the beast dropped at once, covering its face with its brush, and keeping only its quick, vigilant eye fixed upon the invaders of its repose. "Come to the fire if ye will!" said she, turning to Glaucus and his companions. "I never welcome living thing—save the owl, the fox, the toad and the viper—so I cannot welcome ye; but come to the fire without welcome—why stand upon form?"

The language in which the hag addressed them was strange and barbarous Latin, interspersed with many words of some more ancient dialect. She did not stir from her seat, but gazed stonily upon them as Glaucus released Ione from her outer garments, and after placing her on a log of wood, which was the only other seat he perceived at hand—fanned with his breath the embers into a more glowing flame. The slave, encouraged by the boldness of her superiors, divested herself also of her long palla, and crept timorously to the opposite corner of the hearth.

"We disturb you, I fear," said the silver voice of Ione, in conciliation.

The witch did not reply—she seemed like one who had awakened for a moment from the dead, and then relapsed into eternal slumber.

"Tell me," said she, and after a long pause, "are ye brother and sister?"

"No," said Ione.

"Are ye married?"

"Not so," replied Glaucus.

"Ho, lovers!—ha!-ha!-ha!" and the witch laughed so loud and so long that the caverns rang again.

Ione's heart stood still at that strange mirth. Glaucus muttered a rapid counter-spell to the omen—and the slave turned as pale as the cheek of the witch herself.

"Why dost thou laugh, old crone?" said Glaucus, somewhat sternly, as he concluded his invocation.

"Did I laugh?" said the hag absently.

"She is in her dotage," whispered Glaucus: but as he said this he caught the eye of the hag fixed upon him with a malignant and vivid glare.

"Thou liest!" she said abruptly.

"Thou art an uncourteous welcomer," returned Glaucus.

"Hush! Provoke her not," Ione whispered.

"I will tell thee why I laughed when I discovered ye were lovers," said the old woman. "It was because it is a pleasure to the old and withered to look upon young hearts like yours—and to know the time will come when you will loathe each other—loathe—ha!-ha!-ha!"

It was now Ione's turn to pray against the unpleasing prophecy.

"The gods forbid!" said she. "Yet, poor woman, thou knowest little of love, or thou wouldst know that it never changes."

"Was I young once, think ye?" returned the hag, quickly. "And I am old, and hideous, and deathly now? Such as is the form, so is the heart." With these words she sank again into a stillness profound and fearful, as if the cessation of life itself.

"Hast thou dwelt here long?" said Glaucus, after a pause, feeling uncomfortably oppressed beneath a silence so appalling.

"Ah, long!—yes."

"It is a dread abode."

"Ha! Thou mayst well say that—Hell is beneath us!" replied the hag, pointing her bony fingers to the earth. "And I will tell thee a secret—the dim things below are preparing wrath for thee above—you, the young, and the thoughtless, and the beautiful."

"Thou utterest but evil words, ill-becoming the hospitable," said Glaucus; "and in future I will brave the tempest rather than thy welcome."

"Thou wilt do well. None should seek me—save the wretched!"

"And why the wretched?" asked the Athenian.

"I am the witch of the mountain," replied the sorceress, with a ghastly grin. "My trade is to give hope to the hopeless: for the crossed in love I have philtres; for the avaricious, promises of treasure; for the malicious, potions of revenge; for the happy and the good, I have only what life has—curses! Trouble me no more."

With this the grim tenant of the cave relapsed into a silence so obstinate and sullen, that Glaucus in vain endeavoured to draw her into farther conversation. She did not evince, by any alteration of her locked and rigid features, that she even heard him. Fortunately, however, the storm began now to relax; the rain grew less; and at last, as the clouds parted, the moon burst forth in the purple opening of heaven, and streamed full and clear into that desolate abode. Never had she shone, perhaps, on a group more worthy of the painter's art. The young, the all-beautiful Ione, seated by that rude fire—her lover, already forgetful of the presence of the hag, at her feet, gazing upward to her face—the pale and affrighted slave at a little distance—and the ghastly hag resting her deadly eyes upon them; yet seemingly serene and fearless (for the companionship of love hath such a power) were these beautiful beings, things of another sphere, in that dark unholy cavern, with its gloomy quaintness of appurtenance. The fox regarded them from its corner with a keen and fiery eye; and as Glaucus now turned towards the witch, he perceived for the first time, just under her seat, the bright gaze and crested head of a large snake: whether it were that the vivid colouring of the Athenian's cloak, thrown over the shoulders of Ione, attracted the reptile's anger—its crest began to glow and rise, as if menacing and preparing itself to spring upon the Neapolitan—Glaucus caught quickly at one of the half-burned logs upon the hearth—and, as if enraged at the action, the snake came forth from its shelter, and with a loud hiss raised itself on end until its height nearly approached that of the Greek.

"Witch!" cried Glaucus, "command thy creature, or thou wilt see it dead."

"It has been despoiled of its venom!" said the witch, aroused at his threat; but ere the words had left her lip, the snake had sprung upon Glaucus; quick and watchful, the agile Greek leaped lightly aside, and struck so fell and dexterous a blow on the head of the snake, that it fell prostrate and writhing among the embers of the fire.

The hag sprang up, and stood confronting Glaucus with a face which would have befitted the fiercest of the Furies, so utterly dire and wrathful was its expression—yet even in horror and ghastliness preserving the outline and trace of beauty—and utterly free from that coarse grotesque at which the imaginations of the North have sought the source of terror.

"Thou hast," said she, in a slow and steady voice—which belied the expression of her face, so much was it passionless and calm—"thou hast had shelter under my roof, and warmth at my hearth: thou hast returned evil for good; thou hast smitten and haply slain the thing that loved me and was mine: nay, more, the creature, above all others, consecrated to gods and deemed venerable by man.—Now hear thy punishment. By the moon, who is the guardian of the sorceress—by Orcus, who is the treasurer of wrath—I curse thee! And thou art cursed! May thy love be blasted—may thy name be blackened—may the infernals mark thee—may thy heart wither and scorch—may thy last hour recall to thee the prophet voice of the Sage of Vesuvius! And thou"—she added, turning sharply towards

Ione, and raising her right arm, when Glaucus burst impetuously on her speech:

"Hag!" cried he, "forbear! Me thou hast cursed, and I commit myself to the gods—I defy and scorn thee! But breathe but one word against this maiden, and I will convert the oath on thy foul lips to thy dying groan. Beware!"

"I have done," replied the hag, laughing wildly; "for in thy doom is she who loves thee accursed. And not the less, that I heard her lips breathe thy name, and know by what word to commend thee to the demons. Glaucus—thou art doomed!" So saying, the witch turned from the Athenian, and kneeling down beside her wounded favourite she turned to them her face no more.

"O Glaucus!" said Ione, greatly terrified, "what have we done? Let us hasten from this place; the storm has ceased. Good mistress, forgive him—recall thy words—he meant but to defend himself—accept this peace-offering to unsay the curse:" and Ione, stooping, placed her purse on the hag's lap.

"Away!" said she, bitterly—"away! The oath once woven, the Fates only can untie. Away!"

"Come, dearest!" said Glaucus, impatiently. "Thinkest thou that the gods above us or below hear the impotent ravings of dotage? Come!"

Long and loud rang the echoes of the cavern with the dread laugh of the witch, who deigned no further reply.

They breathed more freely when they gained the open air: yet the scene they had witnessed, the words and the laughter, still fearfully dwelt with Ione; and even Glaucus could not thoroughly shake off the impression they bequeathed. The storm had subsided—save, now and then, a low thunder muttered in the distance amidst the darker clouds, or a momentary flash of lightning affronted the sovereignty of the moon. With some difficulty they regained the road, where they found the vehicle already sufficiently repaired for their departure, and the carrucarius calling loudly upon Hercules to tell him where his charges had vanished.

Glaucus vainly endeavoured to cheer the exhausted spirits of Ione; and scarce less vainly to recover the elastic tone of his own natural gaiety. They soon arrived before the gate of the city: as it opened to them, a litter borne by slaves impeded the way.

"It is too late for egress," cried the sentinel to the inmate of the litter.

"Not so," said a voice, which the lovers started to hear: it was a voice they well recognized. "I am bound to the villa of Marcus Polybius. I shall return shortly. I am Arbaces, the Egyptian."

The scruples of him of the gate were removed, and the litter passed close beside the carriage that bore the lovers.

"Arbaces, at this hour!—scarce recovered too, methinks!—whither and for what can he leave the city?" said Glaucus.

"Alas!" replied Ione, bursting into tears, "my soul feels still more and more the omen of evil. Preserve us, O ye Gods! Or at least," she murmured, "preserve my Glaucus!"

27. The Lord of the Burning Belt

Arbaces had tarried only till the cessation of the tempest to seek the saga of Vesuvius. Borne by those of his trustier slaves in whom in all more secret expeditions he was accustomed to confide, he lay extended along his litter, resigning his sanguine heart to the contemplation of vengeance gratified and love possessed. The slaves in so short a journey moved at little less than the ordinary pace of mules; and Arbaces soon arrived at the commencement of a narrow path which, skirting the thick vines, led at once to the habitation of the witch. Here he rested the litter; and bidding the slaves conceal themselves and the vehicle among the vines from the observation of any chance passenger, he mounted alone, with steps still feeble but supported by a long staff, the drear and sharp ascent.

Not a drop of rain fell from the tranquil heaven; but the moisture dripped mournfully from the laden boughs of the vines, and collected in pools in the hollows of the rocky way.

"Strange passions these for a philosopher," thought Arbaces, "that lead one like I just new from the bed of death, and lapped even in health amidst the roses of luxury, across such nocturnal paths as this; but Passion and Vengeance treading to their goal can make an Elysium of a Tartarus." High, clear, and melancholy shone the moon above the road of that dark wayfarer, glassing herself in every pool that lay before him, and sleeping in shadow along the sloping mount. He saw before him the same light that had guided the steps of his intended victims, but, no longer contrasted by the blackened clouds, it shone less redly clear.

He paused, as he approached the mouth of the cavern, to recover breath; and then, with wonted collected and stately mien, he crossed the unhallowed threshold.

The fox sprang up at the ingress of this newcomer, and by a long howl announced another visitor to his mistress.

The witch had resumed her seat, and her aspect of grave-like and grim repose. By her feet, upon a bed of dry weeds which half covered it, lay the wounded snake; but the quick eye of the Egyptian caught its scales glittering in the reflected light of the opposite fire, as it writhed—now contracting, now lengthening its folds, in pain and unsated anger.

"Down, slave!" said the witch, as before, to the fox, and, as before, the animal dropped to the ground—mute, but vigilant.

"Rise, servant of Nox and Erebus!" said Arbaces, commandingly. "A superior in thine art salutes thee! Rise, and welcome him."

At these words the hag turned her gaze upon the Egyptian's towering form and dark features. She looked long and fixedly upon him, as he stood before her in his Oriental robe, with folded arms, and steadfast and haughty brow. "Who art thou," she said at last, "that callest thyself greater in art than the Saga of the Burning Fields, and the daughter of the perished Etrurian race?"

"I am he," answered Arbaces, "from whom all cultivators of magic, from north to south, from east to west, from the Ganges and the Nile to the vales of Thessaly and the shores of the yellow Tiber, have stooped to learn."

"There is but one such man in these places," answered the witch, "one whom the men of the outer world, unknowing his loftier attributes and more secret fame, call Arbaces the Egyptian: to us of a higher nature and deeper knowledge, his rightful appellation is Hermes of the Burning Girdle."

"Look again," returned Arbaces, "I am he."

As he spoke he drew aside his robe, and revealed a cincture seemingly of fire, that burned around his waist, clasped in the centre by a plate whereon was engraven some sign apparently vague and unintelligible, but which was evidently not unknown to the saga. She rose hastily, and threw herself at the feet of Arbaces. "I have seen then," said she, in a voice of deep humility, "the Lord of the Mighty Girdle—accept my homage."

"Rise," said the Egyptian; "I have need of thee."

So saying, he placed himself on the same log of wood on which Ione had rested, and motioned to the witch to resume her seat.

"Thou sayest," said he, as she obeyed, "that thou art a daughter of the ancient Etrurians; the mighty walls of whose rock-built cities yet frown above the robber race that hath seized upon their ancient reign. Partly came that ancient people from Greece, partly were they exiles from a more burning and primeval soil. In either case art thou of Egyptian lineage, for the Grecian masters of the aboriginal helot were among the restless sons whom the Nile banished from her bosom. Equally, then, O Saga! Thy descent is from ancestors that swore allegiance to mine own. By birth, as by knowledge, art thou the subject of Arbaces. Hear me, then, and obey!"

The witch bowed her head.

"Whatever art we possess in sorcery," he continued, "we are sometimes driven to natural means to attain our object. The ring, the crystal, the ashes and the herbs do not give unerring divinations; neither do the higher mysteries of the moon yield even the possessor of the girdle a dispensation from the necessity of employing human measures for a human object. Mark me, then; thou art deeply skilled in the secrets of the more deadly herbs; thou knowest those which arrest life, which burn and scorch the soul from out her citadel, or freeze the channels of young blood into that ice which no sun can melt. Do I overrate thy skill? Speak, and truly!"

"Mighty Hermes, such lore is, indeed, mine own. Deign to look at these ghostly and corpse-like features; they have waned from the hues of life merely by watching over the rank herbs which simmer night and day in yon cauldron."

The Egyptian moved his seat from so unblessed or so unhealthful a vicinity, as the witch spoke.

"It is well," said he; "thou hast learned that maxim of all the deeper knowledge which saith: 'Despise the body to make wise the mind.' But to my task. There cometh to thee by tomorrow's starlight a vain maiden, seeking of thine art a love-charm to fascinate from another the eyes that should utter but soft tales to her own; instead of thy philtres, give the maiden one of thy most powerful poisons. Let the lover breathe his vows to the Shades."

The witch trembled from head to foot.

"Oh, pardon! Pardon! Dread master," said she falteringly; "but this I dare not. The law in these cities is sharp and vigilant; they will seize, they will slay me."

"For what purpose, then, thy herbs and thy potions, vain Saga?" said Arbaces sneeringly.

The witch hid her loathsome face with her hands.

"Oh! Years ago," said she, in a voice unlike her usual tones, so plaintive was it, and so soft, "I was not the thing that I am now—I loved. I fancied myself beloved."

"And what connection hath thy love with my commands?"

"Patience, I implore. I loved another, and less fair than I—yes, by Nemesis! Less fair—allured from me my chosen. I was of the Etrurian tribe to whom most of all were known the secrets off the gloomier magic. My mother was herself a saga: she shared my resentment; from her hands I received the potion that was to restore me his love; and from her, also, the poison that was to destroy my rival. Oh, crush me, dread walls! My trembling hands mistook the phials, my lover fell indeed at my feet; but dead! Dead! Since then, what has been life to me? I became suddenly old, I devoted myself to the sorceries of my race; still by an irresistible impulse I curse myself with an awful penance; still I seek the most noxious herbs; still I concoct the poisons; still I imagine that I am to give them to my hated rival: still I pour them into the phial; still I fancy that they shall blast her beauty to the dust; still I wake and see the quivering body, the foaming lips, the glazing eyes of my Aulus—murdered, and by me!"

The skeleton frame of the witch shook beneath strong convulsions.

Arbaces gazed upon her with a curious though contemptuous eye.

"And this foul thing has yet human emotions!" thought he. "She still cowers over the ashes of the same fire that consumes Arbaces! Such are we all! Mystic is the tie of those mortal passions that unite the greatest and the least."

He did not reply till she had somewhat recovered, and now sat rocking herself in her seat, with glassy eyes fixed on the opposite frame, and large tears rolling down her livid cheeks.

"A grievous tale is thine," said Arbaces. "But these emotions are fit only for our youth—age should harden our hearts to all things but ourselves; as every year adds a scale to the shellfish, so should each year wall and incrust the heart. Think of those frenzies no more. And now, listen to me again! By the revenge that was dear to thee, I command thee to obey me! It is for vengeance that I seek thee! This youth whom I would sweep from my path has crossed me, despite my spells: this thing of purple and broidery, of smiles and glances, soulless and mindless, with no charm but that of beauty—accursed be it—this insect—this Glaucus—I tell thee, by Orcus and by Nemesis, he must die."

And working himself up at every word, the Egyptian, forgetful of his debility—of his strange companion—of everything but his own vindictive rage, strode, with rapid though halting steps, the gloomy cavern.

"Glaucus! Saidst thou, mighty master?" said the witch, abruptly; and her dim eyes glared at the name with all that fierce resentment at the memory of small affronts common amongst the solitary and shunned.

"Ay, so he is called; but what matters the name? Let it not be heard as that of a living man three days from this date!"

"Hear me!" said the witch, breaking from a short reverie into which she was plunged after this last sentence of the Egyptian. "Hear me! I am thy thing and thy slave: spare me! If I give, to the maiden thou speakest of, that which would destroy the life of Glaucus, I shall be surely detected—the dead ever find avengers. Nay, dread man! If thy visit to me be tracked, if thy hatred to Glaucus be known, thou mayst have need of thy archest magic to protect thyself!"

"Ha!" said Arbaces, stopping suddenly short; and as a proof of that blindness with which passion darkens the eyes even of the most acute, this was the first time that the risk that he himself ran by this method of vengeance had occurred to a mind ordinarily wary and circumspect.

"But," continued the witch, "if instead of that which shall arrest the heart, I give that which shall sear and blast the brain—which shall make him who quaffs it unfit for the uses and career of life—an abject, raving, benighted thing—smiting sense to drivelling, youth to dotage—will not thy vengeance be equally sated—thy object equally attained?"

"Oh, witch! No longer the servant, but the sister—the equal of Arbaces—how much brighter is woman's wit, even in vengeance, than ours! How much more exquisite than death is such a doom!"

"And," continued the hag, gloating over her fell scheme, "in this is but little danger: for by ten thousand methods, which men forbear to seek, can our victim become mad. He may have been among the vines and seen a nymph—or the vine itself may have had the same effect—ha, ha! They never inquire too scrupulously into these matters in which the gods may be agents. And let the worst arrive—let it be known it is a love-charm—why, madness is a common effect of philtres; and even the fair she who gave it finds indulgence in the excuse. Mighty Hermes, have I ministered to thee cunningly?"

"Thou shalt have twenty years' longer date for this," returned Arbaces. "I will write anew the epoch of thy fate on the face of the pale stars. Thou shalt not serve in vain the Master of the Flaming Belt. And here, Saga, carve thee out, by these golden tools, a warmer cell in that cavern—one service to me shall countervail a thousand divinations by sieve and shears to the gaping rustics." So saying, he cast upon the floor a heavy purse, which clinked not unmusically to the ear of the hag, who loved the consciousness of possessing the means to purchase comforts she disdained. "Farewell," said Arbaces, "fail not—outwatch the stars in concocting thy beverage—thou shalt lord it over thy sisters at the Walnut-tree, when thou tellest them that thy patron and thy friend is Hermes the Egyptian. Tomorrow night we meet again."

He stayed not to hear the valediction or the thanks of the witch; but passed into the moonlit air, and hastened down the mountain.

The witch, who followed his steps to the threshold, stood long at the entrance of the cavern, gazing fixedly on his receding form; and as the sad moonlight streamed upon her shadowy form and deathlike face, emerging from the dismal rocks, it seemed as if one gifted, indeed, by supernatural magic had escaped from the dreary Orcus; and, the foremost of its ghostly throng, stood at its black portals—vainly summoning his return, or vainly sighing to rejoin him. The hag then, slowly re-entering the cave, groaningly picked up the heavy purse, took the lamp from its stand, and, passing to the remotest depths of her cell, a black and abrupt passage, which was not visible save at a near approach, being closed round with jutting crags, yawned before her; she went several yards along this gloomy path, which sloped gradually downwards, as if towards the bowels of the earth, and, lifting a stone, deposited her treasure in a hole beneath, which as the lamp pierced its secrets, showed other coins of various value, wrung from the credulity or gratitude of her visitors.

"I love to look at you," said she, apostrophizing the moneys; "for when I see you, I feel that I am indeed of power. And I am to have twenty years' longer life to increase your store! O thou great Hermes!"

She replaced the stone, and continued her path onward for some paces, until she reached a deep irregular fissure in the earth. Here, as she bent—strange, rumbling, hoarse, and distant sounds might be heard, while, ever and anon, with a loud and grating noise which, to use a homely but faithful simile, seemed to resemble the grinding of steel upon wheels, volumes of dark smoke issued forth, and moved spirally along the cavern.

"The Shades are noisier than their wont," said the hag, shaking her gray locks; and, looking into the cavity, she beheld, far down, glimpses of a long streak of light, intensely but darkly red. "Strange!" she said, shrinking back; "it is only within the last two days that dull deep light hath been visible—what can it portend?"

The fox, who attended the steps of his fell mistress, uttered a dismal howl, and ran cowering back to the inner cave; a cold shuddering seized the hag herself at the cry of the animal, which, causeless as it seemed, the superstitions of the time considered deeply ominous. She muttered her placatory charm, and tottered back into her cavern, where, amidst herbs and incantations, she prepared to execute the order of the Egyptian.

"He called me dotard," said she, as the smoke curled from the hissing cauldron; "when the jaws drop, and the grinders fall, and the heart scarce beats, it is a pitiable thing to dote; but when," she added, with a savage and exulting grin, "the young, the beautiful, and the strong are suddenly smitten into idiocy—ah, that is terrible! Burn flame, simmer herb—swelter toad—I cursed him, and he shall be cursed!"

On that night, and at the same hour which witnessed the unholy interview between Arbaces and the saga, Apæcides was baptized.

28. The Love Draught

"And you have the courage then, Julia, to seek the Witch of Vesuvius this evening; in company, too, with that fearful man?"

"Why, Nydia," replied Julia timidly; "dost thou really think there is anything to dread? These old hags, with their enchanted mirrors, their trembling sieves, and their moon-gathered herbs, are, I imagine, but crafty impostors, who have learned, perhaps, nothing but the very charm for which I apply to their skill, and which is drawn from the knowledge of the field's herbs. Wherefore should I dread?"

"Dost thou not fear thy companion?"

"What, Arbaces? By Dian, I never saw lover more courteous than that same magician! And were he not so dark, he would be even handsome."

Blind as she was, Nydia had the penetration to perceive that Julia's mind was not one that the gallantries of Arbaces were likely to terrify. She therefore dissuaded her no more; but nursed in her excited heart the wild and increasing desire to know if sorcery had indeed a spell to fascinate love to love.

"Let me go with thee, noble, Julia," said she at length. "My presence is no protection, but I should like to be beside thee."

"Thine offers pleases me much," replied the daughter of Diomed. "Yet how canst thou contrive it? We may not return until late—they will miss thee."

"Ione is indulgent," replied Nydia. "If thou wilt permit me to sleep beneath thy roof, I will say that thou, an early patroness and friend, hast invited me to pass the day with thee, and sing thee my Thessalian songs; her courtesy will readily grant to thee so light a boon."

"Nay, ask for thyself!" said the haughty Julia. "I stoop to request no favour from the Neapolitan!"

"Well, be it so. I will take my leave now; make my request, which I know will be readily granted; and return shortly."

"Do so, and thy bed shall be prepared in my own chamber."

With that, Nydia left the fair Pompeian.

On her way back to Ione, she was met by the chariot of Glaucus, on whose fiery and curveting steed was riveted the gaze of the crowded street.

He kindly stopped for a moment.

"Blooming as thine own roses, my gentle Nydia! and how is thy fair mistress?—recovered, I trust, from the effects of the storm?"

"I have not seen her this morning," answered Nydia, "but—"

"But what? Draw back—the horses are too near thee."

"But, think you Ione will permit me to pass the day with Julia, the daughter of Diomed? She wishes it, and was kind to me when I had few friends."

"The god bless thy grateful heart! I will answer for Ione's permission."

"Then I may stay over the night, and return tomorrow?" said Nydia, shrinking from the praise she so little merited.

"As thou and Julia please. Commend me to her; and, hark ye, Nydia, when thou hearest her speak, note the contrast of her voice with that of the silver-toned Ione. *Vale!*"

His spirits entirely recovered from the effects of the past night, his locks waving in the wind, his joyous and elastic heart bounding with every spring of his Parthian steed, a very prototype of his country's god, full of truth and of love—Glaucus was borne rapidly to his mistress.

Enjoy while ye may the present—who can read the future?

As the evening darkened, Julia, reclined within her litter, which was capacious enough also to admit her blind companion, took her way to the rural baths indicated by Arbaces. To her natural levity of disposition, her enterprise brought less of terror than of pleasurable excitement; above all, she glowed at the thought of her coming triumph over the hated Neapolitan.

A small but gay group was collected round the door of the villa, as her litter passed by it to the private entrance of the baths appropriated to the women.

"Methinks, by this dim light," said one of the bystanders, "I recognise the slaves of Diomed."

"True, Clodius," said Sallust: "it is probably the litter of his daughter Julia. She is rich, my friend; why dost thou not proffer thy suit to her?"

"Why, I had once hoped that Glaucus would have married her. She does not disguise her attachment; and then, as he gambles freely and with ill success—"

"The sesterces would have passed to thee, wise Clodius. A wife is a good thing—when she belongs to another man!"

"But," continued Clodius, "as Glaucus is to wed the Neapolitan, I think I must try my chance with the dejected maid. After all, the lamp of Hymen will be gilt, and the vessel will reconcile one to the odour of the flame. I shall only protest, my Sallust, against Diomed making thee trustee to his daughter's fortune."

"Ha! Ha! Let us within, my *comissator*; the wine and the garlands wait us."

Dismissing her slaves to that part of the house set apart for their entertainment, Julia entered the baths with Nydia and, declining the offers of the attendants, passed by a private door into the garden behind.

"She comes by appointment, be sure," said one of the slaves.

"What is that to thee?" said a superintendent sourly; "she pays for the baths, and does not waste the saffron. Such appointments are the best part of the trade. Hark! Do you not hear the widow Fulvia clapping her hands? Run, fool—run!"

Julia and Nydia, avoiding the more public part of the garden, arrived at the place specified by the Egyptian. In a small circular plot of grass the star gleamed upon the statue of Silenus—the merry god reclined upon a fragment of rock—the lynx of Bacchus at his feet—and over his mouth he held, with extended arm, a bunch of grapes, which he seemingly laughed to welcome ere he devoured.

"I see not the magician," said Julia, looking round. But, as she spoke, the Egyptian slowly emerged from the neighbouring foliage, and the light fell palely over his sweeping robes.

"*Salve*, sweet maiden!—But, ha! Whom hast thou here? We must have no companions!"

"It is but the blind flower-girl, wise magician," replied Julia: "herself a Thessalian."

"Oh! Nydia!" said the Egyptian; "I know her well."

Nydia drew back and shuddered.

"Thou hast been at my house," said he, approaching his voice to Nydia's ear: "thou knowest the oath!—Silence and secrecy, now as then, or beware!"

"Yet," he added, musingly to himself, "why confide more than is necessary, even in the blind—Julia, canst thou not trust thyself alone with me? Believe me, the magician is less formidable than he seems."

As he spoke, he gently drew Julia aside.

"The witch loves not many visitors at once," said he; "leave Nydia here till your return; she can be of no assistance to us: and, for protection—your own beauty suffices—your own beauty and your own rank; yes, Julia, I know thy name and birth. Come, trust thyself to me, fair rival of the youngest of the Naiads!"

The vain Julia was not, as we have seen, easily affrighted; she was moved by the flattery of Arbaces, and she readily consented to Nydia awaiting her return; nor did Nydia press her presence. At the sound of the Egyptian's voice all her terror of him returned; she felt a sentiment of pleasure at learning she was not to travel in his companionship.

She returned to the Bath-house, and in one of the private chambers waited their return. Many and bitter were the thoughts of this wild girl as she sat there in her eternal darkness. She thought of her own desolate fate, far from her native land, far from the bland cares that once assuaged the April sorrows of childhood—deprived of the light of day, with none but strangers to guide her steps, accursed by the one soft feeling of her heart, loving and without hope, save the dim and unholy ray which shot across her mind, as her Thessalian fancies questioned the force of spells and the gifts of magic!

Time passed: a light step entered the chamber where Nydia indulged her gloomy meditations.

"Oh, thanked be the immortal gods!" said Julia, "I have returned, I have left that terrible cavern! Come, Nydia! Let us away!"

It was not till they were seated in the litter that she again spoke.

"Oh!" said she, tremblingly, "such a scene! Such fearful incantations! And the dead face of the hag!—But, let us talk not of it. I have obtained the potion—she pledges its effect. My rival shall be suddenly indifferent to his eye, and I, I alone, the idol of Glaucus!"

"Glaucus!" exclaimed Nydia.

"Ay! I told thee, girl, at first, that it was not the Athenian whom I loved: but I see now that I may trust thee wholly—it is the beautiful Greek!"

What then were Nydia's emotions! She had connived, she had assisted, in tearing Glaucus from Ione; but only to transfer, by all the power of magic, his affections yet more hopelessly to another. Her heart swelled almost to suffocation—she gasped for breath. In the darkness of the vehicle, Julia did not perceive the agitation of her companion; she went on rapidly dilating on the promised effect of her acquisition, and on her approaching triumph over Ione, every now and then abruptly digressing to the horror of the scene she had quitted—the unmoved mien of Arbaces, and his authority over the dreadful saga.

Meanwhile, Nydia recovered her self-possession: a thought came: she slept in the chamber of Julia—she might possess herself of the potion.

They arrived at the house of Diomed, and descended to Julia's apartment, where the night's repast awaited them.

"Drink, Nydia, thou must be cold; the air was chill tonight; as for me, my veins are yet ice."

And Julia unhesitatingly quaffed deep draughts of the spiced wine.

"Thou hast the potion," said Nydia. "Let me hold it in my hands. How small the phial is! Of what colour is the draught?"

"Clear as crystal," replied Julia, as she retook the philtre; "thou couldst not tell it from this water. The witch assures me it is tasteless. Small though the phial, it suffices for a life's fidelity: it is to be poured into any liquid; and Glaucus will only know what he has quaffed by the effect."

"Exactly like this water in appearance?"

"Yes, sparkling and colourless as this. How bright it seems! It is as the very essence of moonlit dews. Bright thing! How thou shinest on my hopes through thy crystal vase!"

"And how is it sealed?"

"But by one little stopper—I withdraw it now—the draught gives no odour. Strange, that that which speaks to neither sense should thus command all!"

"Is the effect instantaneous?"

"Usually—but sometimes it remains dormant for a few hours."

"Oh, how sweet is this perfume!" said Nydia, suddenly, as she took up a small bottle on the table, and bent over its fragrant contents.

"Thinkest thou so? The bottle is set with gems of some value. Thou wouldst not have the bracelet yestermorn; wilt thou take the bottle?"

"It ought to be such perfumes as these that should remind one who cannot see of the generous Julia. If the bottle be not too costly—"

"Oh! I have a score of costlier ones: take it, child!"

Nydia bowed her gratitude, and placed the bottle in her vest.

"And the draught would be equally efficacious, whoever administers it?"

"If the most hideous hag beneath the sun bestowed it, such is its asserted virtue that Glaucus would deem her beautiful, and none but she!"

Julia, warmed by wine, and the reaction of her spirits, was now all animation and delight; she laughed loud, and talked on a hundred matters—nor was it till the night had advanced far towards morning that she summoned her slaves and undressed.

When they were dismissed, she said to Nydia:

"I will not suffer this holy draught to quit my presence until the hour comes for its uses. Lie under my pillow, bright spirit, and give me happy dreams!"

So saying, she placed the potion under her pillow. Nydia's heart beat violently.

"Why dost thou drink that unmixed water, Nydia? Take the wine by its side."

"I am fevered," replied the blind girl, "and the water cools me. I will place this bottle by my bedside: it refreshes in these summer nights, when the dews of sleep fall not on our lips. Fair Julia, I must leave thee early—so Ione bids—perhaps before thou art awake; accept, therefore, now by congratulations."

"Thanks: when next we meet, you may find Glaucus at my feet."

They had retired to their couches, and Julia, worn out by the excitement of the day, soon slept. But anxious and burning thoughts rolled over the mind of the wakeful Thessalian. She listened to the calm breathing of Julia; and her ear, accustomed to the finest distinctions of sound, speedily assured her of the deep slumber of her companion.

"Now befriend me, Venus!" said she softly.

She rose gently, and poured the perfume from the gift of Julia upon the marble floor—she rinsed it several times carefully with the water that was beside her, and then easily finding the bed of Julia (for night to her was as day) she pressed her trembling hand under the pillow and seized the potion. Julia stirred not, her breath regularly fanned the burning cheek of the blind girl. Nydia, then, opening the phial, poured its contents into the bottle, which easily contained them; and then refilling the former reservoir of the potion with that limpid water which Julia had assured her it so resembled, she once more placed the phial in its former place. She then stole again to her couch, and waited—with what thoughts!—the dawning of the day.

The sun had risen—Julia slept still—Nydia noiselessly dressed herself, placed her treasure carefully in her vest, took up her staff, and hastened to quit the house.

BOOK FOUR

29. Sacred Walls Have Ears

Whoever regards the early history of Christianity will perceive how necessary to its triumph was that fierce spirit of zeal, which, fearing no danger, accepting no compromise, inspired its champions and sustained its martyrs. The sectarian sternness which confined virtue and heaven to a chosen few, which saw demons in other gods, and the penalties of hell in another religion, made the believer naturally anxious to convert all to whom he felt the ties of human affection; and the circle thus traced by benevolence to man was yet more widened by a desire for the glory of God. The same fervour which made the Churchman of the Middle Ages a bigot without mercy, made the Christian of the early days a hero without fear.

Of these more fiery, daring, and earnest natures, not the least ardent was Olinthus. No sooner had Apæcides been received by the rites of baptism into the bosom of the Church, than the Nazarene hastened to make him conscious of the impossibility of the office and robes of priesthood. He could not profess to worship God, and continue even outwardly to honour the idolatrous altars of the Fiend.

Nor was this all: the sanguine and impetuous mind of Olinthus beheld in the power of Apæcides the means of divulging to the deluded people the juggling mysteries of the oracular Isis. He thought heaven had sent this instrument in order to disabuse the eyes of the crowd, and prepare the way, perchance, for the conversion of a whole city. He did not hesitate to appeal to all the new-kindled enthusiasm of Apæcides, to arouse his courage, and to stimulate his zeal. They met, according to previous agreement, the evening after the baptism of Apæcides, in the grove of Cybele.

"At the next solemn consultation of the oracle," said Olinthus, "advance thyself to the railing, proclaim aloud to the people the deception they endure, invite them to enter, themselves to witness of the gross but artful mechanism of imposture thou has described to me. Fear not—the Lord, who protected Daniel, shall protect thee; the community of Christians will be amongst the crowd, and urge on

164 * *THE LAST DAYS OF POMPEII*

the shrinking; and in the first flush of the popular indignation and shame, I myself, upon those very altars, will plant the palm-branch typical of the Gospel—and to my tongue shall descend the rushing Spirit of the living God."

Heated and excited as he was, this suggestion was not unpleasing to Apæcides. He was rejoiced at so early an opportunity of distinguishing his faith in his new sect, and to his holier feelings were added those of a vindictive loathing at the imposition he had himself suffered, and a desire to avenge it. Neither Olinthus nor the proselyte perceived the impediments to the success of their scheme which might be found in the reverent superstition of the people themselves, who would probably be loth, before the sacred altars of the great Egyptian goddess, to believe even the testimony of her priest against her power...

Apæcides assented to this proposal with a readiness which delighted Olinthus. They parted with the understanding that Olinthus should confer with the more important of his Christian brethren on his great enterprise, to obtain assurances of their support. It chanced that one of the festivals of Isis was to be held on the second day after this conference, and offered a ready occasion for the design. They appointed to meet once more on the next evening at the same spot; and at that meeting were finally to be settled the order and details of the event.

It happened that the latter part of this conference had been held near the *sacellum*, or small chapel, described previously; and so soon as the forms of the Christian and the priest had disappeared from the grove, a dark and ungainly figure emerged from behind the building.

"I have tracked you with some effect, my brother flamen," soliloquised the eavesdropper; "you, the priest of Isis, have not for mere idle discussion conferred with this gloomy Christian. Alas! That I could not hear all. I find, at least, that you meditate revealing the sacred mysteries, and that tomorrow you meet again at this place to plan it. May Osiris sharpen my ears to detect the whole of your audacity! When I have learned more, I must confer at once with Arbaces."

Thus muttering, Calenus wrapped his cloak round him, and strode thoughtfully homeward.

30. Apæcides Sees Ione

It was the day for Diomed's banquet to the most select of his friends. The graceful Glaucus, the beautiful Ione, the official Pansa, the high-born Clodius, the immortal Fulvius, the exquisite Lepidus, the epicurean Sallust, were not the only honourers of his festival. He expected an invalid senator from Rome, and a great warrior from Herculaneum, who had fought with Titus against the Jews, and having enriched himself prodigiously in the wars, was always told by his friends that his country was eternally indebted to his disinterested exertions. The party extended to a yet greater number: for although it was thought in-elegant among the Romans to entertain less than three or more than nine at their banquets, this rule was disregarded by the ostentatious; and it is recorded that one of the most splendid of these entertainers usually feasted a select party of three hundred. Diomed, however, more modest, contented himself with doubling the number of the Muses. His party consisted of eighteen.

It was the morning of the banquet; and Diomed himself, though he greatly affected the gentleman and the scholar, retained enough of his mercantile experience to know that a master's eye makes a ready servant. Accordingly, with his tunic ungirdled on his portly stomach, his slippers on his feet, a small wand in his hand, wherewith he now directed the gaze, and now corrected the back, of some duller menial, he went from chamber to chamber of his costly villa.

He did not disdain even a visit to that sacred apartment in which the priests of the festival prepare their offerings. On entering the kitchen, his ears were agreeably stunned by the noise of dishes and pans, of oaths and commands. Small as was this indispensable chamber in all the houses of Pompeii, it was, nevertheless, usually fitted with all that amazing variety of stoves and shapes, stew pans and saucepans, cutters and moulds, without which a cook of spirit, no matter whether he be ancient or modern, declares it impossible that he can give you anything to eat. And as fuel was then, as now, dear and scarce in those regions. great seems to have been the dexterity exercised in preparing as many things as possible with a little fire. An admirable contrivance of this nature may be still seen in the Neapolitan Museum: a portable kitchen, about the size of a folio volume, containing stoves for four dishes, and an apparatus for heating water or other beverages.

Across the small kitchen flitted many forms which the quick eye of the master did not recognize.

"Oh! Oh!" grumbled he to himself, "that accursed Congrio hath invited a whole legion of cooks to assist him. They won't serve for nothing, and this is another item in the total of my day's expenses. By Bacchus! Thrice lucky shall I be if the slaves do not help themselves to some of the drinking vessels: ready, alas, are their hands, capacious are their tunics. *Me miserum!*"

The cooks, however, worked on, seemingly heedless of the apparition of Diomed.

"Ho, Euclio, your egg-pan! What, is this the largest? It only holds thirty-three eggs: in the houses *I* usually serve, the smallest egg-pan holds fifty, if need be!"

"Thee unconscionable rogue!" thought Diomed. "He talks of eggs as if they were a sesterce a hundred!"

"By Mercury!" cried a pert little culinary disciple, scarce in his novitiate; "who ever saw such antique sweetmeat shapes as these?—it is impossible to do credit to one's art with such rude materials. Why, Sallust's commonest sweet-meat shape represents the whole siege of Troy; Hector and Paris, and Helen—with little Astyanax and the Wooden Horse into the bargain!"

"Silence, fool!" said Congrio, the cook of the house, who seemed to leave the chief part of the battle to his allies. "My master, Diomed, is not one of those expensive good-for-naughts who must have the last fashion, cost what it will!"

"Thou liest, base slave!" cried Diomed, in a great passion—"and thou costest me already enough to have ruined Lucullus himself! Come out of thy den, I want to talk to thee."

The slave, with a sly wink at his confederates, obeyed the command.

"How," Diomed asked, with a face of solemn anger, "didst thou dare to invite all those rascals into my house?—I see thief written in every line of their faces."

"Yet I assure you, master, that they are men of most respectable character—the best cooks of the place; it is a great favour to get them. But for my sake—"

"Thy sake, unhappy Congrio!" interrupted his master, "and by what purloined moneys of mine, by what reserved filchings from marketings, by what goodly meats converted into grease, and sold in the suburbs, by what false charges for bronzes marred, and earthenware broken—has thou been enabled to make them serve thee for thy sake?"

"Nay, master, do not impeach my honesty! May the gods desert me if—"

"Swear not!" again interrupted the choleric Diomed, "for then the gods will smite thee for a perjurer, and I shall lose my cook on the eve of dinner. But enough of this at present. Keep a sharp eye on thy ill-favoured assistants, and tell me no tales tomorrow of vases broken, and cups miraculously vanished, or thy whole back shall be one pain. And, hark thee! Thou knowest thou hast made me pay for those Phrygian partridges enough, by Hercules, to have feasted a sober man for a year together—see that they be not one iota over-roasted. The last time, O Congrio, that I gave a banquet to my friends, when thy vanity did so boldly undertake the becoming appearance of a Melian crane—thou knowest it came up like a stone from Ætna—as if all the fires of Phlegethon had been scorching out its juices. Be modest this time, Congrio—wary and modest. Modesty is the nurse of great actions; and in all other things, as in this, if thou wilt not spare thy master's purse, at least consult thy master's glory."

"There shall not be such a one seen at Pompeii since the days of Hercules."

"Softly, softly—thy cursed boasting again! But I say. Congrio, yon *homunculus*—yon pigmy assailant of my cranes—yon pert-tongued neophyte of the kitchen, was there aught but insolence on his tongue when he maligned the comeliness of my sweetmeat shapes? I would not be out of the fashion, Congrio."

"It is but the custom of us cooks," replied Congrio, gravely, "to undervalue our tools, in order to increase the effect of our art. The sweetmeat shape is a fair shape, and a lovely; but I would recommend my master, at the first occasion, to purchase some new ones of a—"

"That will suffice," exclaimed Diomed, who seemed resolved never to allow his slave to finish his sentences. "Now, resume thy charge—shine—eclipse thyself. Let men envy Diomed his cook—let the slaves of Pompeii style thee Congrio the great! Go! Yet stay—thou hast not spent all the moneys I gave thee for the marketing?"

"'All?'—alas! The nightingales' tongues and the Roman sausages and the oysters from Britain, and other things, too numerous to recite, are yet left unpaid for. But what matter? Everyone trusts the Head Cook of Diomed the wealthy!"

"Oh, unconscionable prodigal!—what waste!—what profusion!—I am ruined! But go, hasten—inspect!—taste!—perform!—surpass thyself! Let the Roman senator not despise the poor Pompeian. Away, slave—and remember, the Phrygian partridges."

The chef disappeared within his natural domain, and Diomed rolled back his portly presence to the more courtly chambers. All was to his liking—the flowers were fresh, the fountains played briskly, the mosaic pavements were as smooth as mirrors.

"Where is my daughter Julia?" he asked.

"At the bath."

"Ah! That reminds me!—time wanes!—and I must bathe also."

* * * * * * *

Meanwhile Apæcides, in the exhaustion of his emotions, had slept far into the morning, and the vertical sun already poured its fervid beams over the sacred place when he rose to perform his duties before the altars.

"*Salve*, Apæcides!" said a voice, whose natural asperity was smoothed by long artifice into an almost displeasing softness of tone. "Thou art late; has the goddess revealed herself to thee in visions?"

"Could she reveal her true self to the people, Calenus, how incenseless would these altars be!"

"That," replied Calenus, "may be true, but the deity is wise enough to hold commune with none but priests."

"A time may come when she will be unveiled without her own acquiescence."

"It is not likely: she has triumphed for countless ages. And that which has so long stood the test of time rarely succumbs to the lust of novelty. But hark ye, young brother! These sayings are indiscreet."

"It is not for thee to silence them," replied Apæcides, haughtily.

"So hot!—yet I will not quarrel with thee. Why, my Apæcides, has not the Egyptian convinced thee of the necessity of dwelling together in unity? Has he not convinced thee of the wisdom of deluding the people and enjoying ourselves? If not, oh brother, he is not that great magician he is esteemed."

"Thou, then, has shared his lessons?" said Apæcides, with a hollow smile.

"Ay! But I stood less in need of them than thou. Nature had already gifted me with the love of pleasure, and the desire of gain and power. Long is the way that leads the voluptuary to the severities of life; but it is only one step from pleasant sin to the sheltering hypocrisy. Beware the vengeance of the goddess, if the shortness of that step be disclosed!"

"Beware, thou, the hour when the tomb shall be rent, and the rottenness exposed," returned Apæcides, solemnly.

"*Vale!*"

With these words he left the flamen to his meditations. When he got a few paces from the temple, he turned to look back. Calenus had already disappeared in the entry room of the priests, for it now approached the hour of that repast which, called *prandium* by the ancients, answers in point of date to the breakfast of the moderns. The white and graceful fane gleamed brightly in the sun. Upon the altars before it rose the incense and bloomed the garlands. The priest gazed long and wistfully upon the scene—it was the last time that it was ever beheld by him!

He then turned and pursued his way slowly towards the house of Ione; for before, possibly, the last tie that united them was cut in twain—before the uncertain peril of the next day was incurred, he was anxious to see his last surviving relative, his fondest, as his earliest friend.

He arrived at her house, and found her in the garden with Nydia.

"This is kind, Apæcides," said Ione, joyfully; "and how eagerly I have wished to see thee!—what thanks do I not owe thee? How churlish hast thou been to answer none of my letters—to abstain from coming to receive the expressions of my gratitude!"

"My sweet Ione, thou owest me none, for thy cause was mine. Let us avoid that subject, let us recur not to that impious man—how hateful to both of us! I may have a speedy opportunity to teach the world the nature of his pretended wisdom and hypocritical severity. But let us sit down; I am wearied with the heat of the sun; let us sit in yonder shade, and, for a little while longer, be to each other what we have been."

Beneath a wide plane-tree, with cistus and arbutus clustering round them, the living fountain before, the green-sward beneath their feet; the gay cicada, once so dear to Athens, rising merrily amidst the grass; the butterfly, beautiful emblem of the soul, dedicated to Psyche, and which has continued to furnish illustrations to the Christian bard, rich in the glowing colours caught from Sicilian skies, hovering about the sunny flowers, itself like a winged flower—in this spot, and this scene, brother and sister sat together for the last time on earth. You may tread now on the same place; but the garden is no more, the columns are shattered, the fountain has ceased to play. Let the traveller search amongst the ruins of Pompeii for the house of Ione. Its remains are yet visible.

They sat down, and Nydia, glad to be alone, retired to the farther end of the garden.

"Ione," said the young convert, "place your hand on my brow; let me feel your cool touch. Speak to me, too; for your gentle voice is like a breeze that hath freshness as well as music. Speak to me, but *forbear* to *bless me!* Utter not one word of those forms of speech which our childhood was taught to consider sacred!"

"Alas! and what then shall I say? Our language of affection is so woven with that of worship, that the words grow chilled and trite if I banish from them allusion to our gods."

"*Our gods!*" murmured Apæcides, with a shudder: "thou slightest my request already."

"Shall I speak then to thee only of Isis?"

"The Evil Spirit! No, rather be dumb forever, unless at least thou canst—but away, away this talk! In thy sweet presence a calm falls over my spirit. For a little while I forget. For oh! if hereafter I escape, no matter what peril; and it be permitted me to address thee on one sacred and awful subject; should I find thine ear closed and thy heart hardened, what hope for myself could countervail the despair for thee? Ah, no—no—thou wilt listen to me yet! Dost thou remember how we went into the fields by Baiæ hand in hand together, to pluck the flowers of spring? Even so, hand in hand, shall we enter the Eternal Garden, and crown ourselves with imperishable asphodel!"

Wondering and bewildered by words she could not comprehend, but excited even to tears by the plaintiveness of their tone, Ione listened to the outpourings of a full and oppressed heart. In truth, Apæcides himself was softened much beyond his ordinary mood, which to outward seeming was usually either sullen or impetuous. For the noblest desires are of a jealous nature, they engross, they absorb the soul.

"I will talk to thee then of our early years," said Ione. "Shall yon blind girl sing to thee of the days of childhood? Her voice is sweet and musical, and she hath a song on that theme which contains none of those allusions it pains thee to hear."

"Dost thou remember the words?" asked Apæcides.

"Methinks yes; for the tune, which is simple, fixed them on my memory."

"Sing to me then thyself." Ione beckoned to a slave, who stood in the portico, and, sending for her lute, sang, when it arrived, to a tender and simple air:

"It is not that our childhood's days

Escaped their April showers,
Nor that we found in childhood's ways
No snake amidst the flowers.
Young though we were, the grief was there;
And keen to feel, though brief to bear,
And lost in happier hours.

It is not that our later years
The better joys forget,
Nor that we have no choice from tears,
From memories and regret.
But now more slow is grief to go,
And never shines the Iris bow
Our hearts remember yet."

Wisely and delicately had Ione chosen that song, sad though its burthen seemed; for when we are deeply mournful, discordant above all other is the voice of mirth: the fittest spell is that borrowed from melancholy itself, for dark thoughts can be softened when they cannot be brightened. Apæcides, yielding to the influence of the silver voice that reminded him of the past, and told but of half the sorrow born to the present, forgot his more immediate and fiery sources of anxious thought. He spent hours in making Ione alternately sing to, and converse with him; and when he rose to leave her, it was with a calmed and lulled mind.

"Ione," said he, as he pressed her hand, "should you hear my name blackened and maligned, will you credit the aspersion?"

"Never, my brother, never!"

"Dost thou not imagine, according to thy belief, that the evil-doer is punished hereafter, and the good rewarded?"

"Can you doubt it?"

"Dost thou think, then, that he who is truly good should sacrifice every selfish interest in his zeal for virtue?"

"He who doth so is the equal of the gods."

"And thou believest that, according to the purity and courage with which he thus acts, shall be his portion of bliss beyond the grave?"

"So we are taught to hope "

"Kiss me, my sister. One question more. Thou art to be wedded to Glaucus: perchance that marriage may separate us more hopelessly—but not of this speak I. Thou art to be married to Glaucus—dost thou love him? Nay, my sister, answer me by words."

"Yes!"

"Dost thou feel that, for his sake thou couldst renounce pride, brave dishonour, and incur death? I have heard that when women really love, it is to that excess."

"Brother, all this could I do for Glaucus, and feel that it were not a sacrifice. There is no sacrifice to those who love, in what is borne for the one we love."

"Enough! Shall woman feel thus for man, and man feel less devotion to his God?"

He spoke no more. His countenance seemed instinct and inspired with a divine life. He turned to meet the eyes of Ione—earnest, wistful, fearful—he kissed her fondly, strained her warmly to his breast, and in a moment more he had left the house.

Long did Ione remain in the same place, mute and thoughtful. The maidens again and again came to warn her of the deepening noon, and her engagement to Diomed's banquet. At length she woke from her reverie, and prepared, not with the pride of beauty, but listless and melancholy, for the festival: one thought alone reconciled her to the promised visit—she would meet Glaucus—she could confide to him her alarm and uneasiness for her brother.

31. A Classic Banquet

Meanwhile Sallust and Glaucus were slowly strolling towards the house of Diomed. Despite the habits of his life, Sallust was not devoid of many estimable qualities. He would have been an active friend, a useful citizen—in short an excellent man, if he had not taken it into his head to be a philosopher. Brought up in the schools in which Roman plagiarism echoed Grecian wisdom, he had imbued himself with those doctrines by which the later Epicureans corrupted the simple maxims of the great master. He gave himself altogether to pleasure, and imagined there was no sage like a boon companion. Still he had a considerable degree of learning, wit, and good-nature; and the hearty frankness of his vices seemed like virtue itself beside the corruption of Clodius and the effeminacy of Lepidus. Glaucus liked him the best of his companions; and he, in turn, appreciating the nobler qualities of the Athenian, loved him almost as much as a cold muræna, or a bowl of the best Falernian.

"This is a vulgar old fellow, this Diomed," said Sallust; "but he has some good qualities—in his cellar!"

"And some charming ones—in his daughter."

"True, Glaucus: but you are not much moved by them. I fancy Clodius is desirous to be your successor."

"He is welcome. At the banquet of Julia's beauty, no guest, be sure, is unwelcome."

"You are severe: but she has, indeed, something of the Corinthian about her—they will be well-matched, after all! What good-natured fellows we are, to associate with that gambling good-for-naught!"

"Pleasure unites strange varieties," answered Glaucus. "He amuses me—"

"And flatters—but then he pays himself well! He powders his praise with gold-dust."

"You often hint that he plays unfairly—think you so really?"

"My dear Glaucus, a Roman noble has his dignity to keep up—dignity is very expensive—Clodius must cheat like a scoundrel, in order to live like a gentleman."

"Ha, ha!—well, of late I have renounced the dice. Ah! Sallust, when I am wedded to Ione, I trust I may yet redeem a youth of follies. We are both born for better things than those in which we sympathize now—born to render our worship in nobler temples than the sty of Epicurus."

"Alas!" returned Sallust in a rather melancholy tone, "what do we know more than this—life is short—beyond the grave all is dark? There is no wisdom like that which says 'enjoy'."

"By Bacchus! I doubt sometimes if we do enjoy the utmost of which life is capable."

"I am a moderate man," returned Sallust, "and do not ask 'the utmost'. We are like malefactors, and intoxicate ourselves with wine and myrrh, as we stand on the brink of death; but, if we did not do so the abyss would look very disagreeable. I own that I was inclined to be gloomy until I took so heartily to drinking—that is a new life, my Glaucus."

"Yes! But it brings us next morning to a new death."

"Why, the next morning is unpleasant, I own; but then, if it were not so, one would never be inclined to read. I study betimes—because, by the gods! I am generally unfit for anything else till noon."

"Fie, Scythian!"

"Pshaw! The fate of Pentheus to him who denies Bacchus."

"Well, Sallust, with all your faults, you are the best profligate I ever met; and verily, if I were in danger of life, you are the only man in all Italy who would stretch out a finger to save me."

"Perhaps *I* should not, if it were in the middle of supper. But, in truth, we Italians are fearfully selfish."

"So are all men who are not free," said Glaucus, with a sigh.

"Freedom, then, must be a very fatiguing thing," answered Sallust. "But here we are at our host's."

As Diomed's villa was one of the most considerable in Pompeii, and built much according to the specific instructions for a suburban villa laid down by the Roman architect, it may not be uninteresting briefly to describe the plan of the apartments through which the visitors passed.

They entered by the small vestibule at which Medon was stationed, and passed at once into a colonnade, technically termed the peristyle; for the main difference between the suburban villa and the town mansion consisted in placing the colonnade in exactly the same place as that which, in the town mansion, was occupied by the atrium. In the centre of the peristyle was an open court, which contained the impluvium.

From this peristyle descended a staircase to the offices; another narrow passage on the opposite side communicated with a garden; various small apartments surrounded the colonnade, appropriated to country visitors. Another door to the left on entering communicated with a small triangular portico, which belonged to the baths; and behind was the wardrobe, in which were kept the holiday suits of the slaves, and, perhaps, of the master. Seventeen centuries afterwards were found those relics of ancient finery calcined and crumbling; kept longer, alas! than their thrifty lord foresaw.

Return we to the peristyle, and endeavour now to present to the reader a *coup-d'œil* of the whole suite of apartments, which immediately stretched before the steps of the visitors.

But now imagine the columns of the portico hung with festoons of flowers; the columns themselves in the lower part painted red, and the walls around glowing with various frescoes; then, beyond a curtain, three parts drawn aside, the eye catches tablinum or saloon, closed at will by glazed doors, now slid back into the walls. On either side of this tablinum, were small rooms, one of which was a kind of cabinet of gems; and these apartments, as well as the tablinum, communicated with a long gallery, which opened at either end upon terraces; and between the terraces, and communicating with the central part of the gallery, was a hall, in which the banquet was that day prepared.

All these apartments, though almost on a level with the street, were one story above the garden; and the terraces communicating with the gallery were continued into corridors, raised above the pillars, which, to the right and left, skirted the garden below.

Beneath, and on a level with the garden, ran the apartments already described as chiefly appropriated to Julia.

In the gallery, Diomed received his guests.

The merchant affected greatly the man of letters, and, therefore, he also affected a passion for everything Greek; he paid particular attention to Glaucus.

"You will see, my friend," said he, with a wave of his hand, "that I am a little classical here—a little Cecropian—eh? The hall in which we shall sup is borrowed from the Greeks. It is an Œcus Cyzicene. Noble Sallust, they have not, I am told, this sort of apartment in Rome."

"Oh!" replied Sallust, with a half-smile; "you Pompeians combine all that is most eligible in Greece and Rome: may you combine the viands as well as the architecture!"

"You shall see—you shall see, my Sallust," replied the merchant. "We have a taste at Pompeii, and we have also money."

"They are two excellent things," replied Sallust. "But, behold, the lady Julia!"

The main difference in the manner of life observed among the Athenians and Romans, was that, with the first, the modest women rarely or never took part in entertainments; with the latter, they were the common ornaments of the banquet; but when they were present at the feast it usually terminated at an early hour.

Magnificently robed in white, interwoven with pearls and threads of gold, Julia entered the apartment.

Scarcely had she received the salutation of the two guests, ere Pansa and his wife, Lepidus, Clodius, and the Roman senator entered almost simultaneously; then came the widow Fulvia; then the poet Fulvius, like to the widow in name if in nothing else; the warrior from Herculaneum, accompanied by his umbra, next stalked in; afterwards, the less eminent of the guests, Ione, yet tarried.

It was the mode among the courteous ancients to flatter whenever it was in their power: accordingly it was a sign of ill breeding to seat themselves immediately on entering the house of their host. After performing the salutation, which was usually accomplished by a cordial shake of the right hand, and sometimes an embrace, they spent several minutes in surveying the apartment, and admiring the bronzes, the pictures, or the furniture, with which it was adorned.

"A beautiful statue this of Bacchus!" said the Roman senator.

"A mere trifle!" replied Diomed

"What charming paintings!" said Fulvia.

"Mere trifles!" answered the owner.

"Exquisite candelabra!" cried the warrior.

"Exquisite!" echoed the umbra.

"Trifles, trifles!" reiterated the merchant.

Meanwhile, Glaucus found himself by one of the windows of the gallery, which communicated with the terraces, and Julia by his side.

"Is it an Athenian virtue, Glaucus," said the merchant's daughter, "to shun those whom we once sought?"

"Fair Julia—no!"

"Yet, methinks, it is one of the qualities of Glaucus."

"Glaucus never shuns a *friend*!" replied the Greek, with some emphasis on the last word.

"May Julia rank among the number of his friends?"

"It would be an honour to the emperor to find a friend in one so lovely."

"You evade my question," returned the enamoured Julia. "But tell me, is it true that you admire the Neapolitan Ione?"

"Does not beauty constrain our admiration?"

"Ah! Subtle Greek, still do you fly the meaning of my words. But say, shall Julia be indeed your friend?"

"If she will favour me, blessed by the gods!"

"Yet, even while you speak, your eye is restless—you move away involuntarily—you are impatient to join Ione!"

For at that moment Ione had entered, and Glaucus had indeed betrayed the emotion noticed by the jealous beauty.

"Can admiration to one woman make me unworthy the friendship of another? Sanction not so, O Julia, the libels of the poets on your sex!"

"Well, you are right—or I will learn to think so. Glaucus, yet one moment! You are to wed Ione; is it not so?"

"If the Fates permit, such is my blessed hope."

"Accept, then, from me, in token of our new friendship, a present for your bride. Nay, it is the custom of friends, you know, always to present to bride and bridegroom some such little marks of their esteem and favouring wishes."

"Julia! I cannot refuse any token of friendship from one like you. I will accept the gift as an omen from Fortune herself."

"Then, after the feast, when the guests retire, you will descend with me to my apartment, and receive it from my hands. Remember!" said Julia, as she joined the wife of Pansa, and left Glaucus to seek Ione.

The window Fulvia and the spouse of the ædile were engaged in high and grave discussion.

"O Fulvia! I assure you that the last account from Rome declares that the frizzling mode of dressing the hair is growing antiquated; they only now wear it built up in a tower, like Julia's, or arranged as a helmet—the *Galerian* fashion, like mine, you see: it has a fine effect, I think. I assure you, Vespius" (this was the name of the Herculaneum hero) "admires it greatly."

"And nobody wears the hair like yon Neapolitan, in the Greek way?"

"What, parted in front, with the knot behind? Oh, no; how ridiculous it is; it reminds one of the statue of Diana! Yet this Ione is handsome, eh?"

"So the men say; but then she is rich; she is to marry the Athenian—I wish her joy. He will not be long faithful, I suspect; those foreigners are very inconstant."

"Oh, Julia!" said Fulvia, as the merchant's daughter joined them; "have you seen the tiger yet?"

"No!"

"Why all the ladies have been to see him. He is so handsome!"

"I hope we shall find some criminal or other for him and the lion," replied Julia. "Your husband" (turning to Pansa's wife) "is not so active as he should be in this matter."

"Why, really the laws are too mild," replied the dame of the helmet. "There are so few offences to which the punishment of the arena can be awarded; and then, too, the gladiators are growing effeminate! The stoutest bestiarii declare they are willing enough to fight a boar or a bull; but as for a lion or a tiger, they think the game too much in earnest."

"Oh! Have you seen the new house of Fulvius, the dear poet?" asked Pansa's wife.

"No; is it handsome?"

"Very!—such good taste. But they say, my dear, that he has such improper pictures! He won't show them to the women: how ill-bred!"

"Those poets are always odd," said the widow. "But he is an interesting man; what pretty verses he writes! We improve very much in poetry; it is impossible to read the old stuff now."

"I declare I am of your opinion," returned the lady of the helmet. "There is so much more force and energy in the modern school."

The warrior sauntered up to the ladies.

"It reconciles me to peace," said he, "when I see such faces."

"Oh! You heroes are ever flatterers," returned Fulvia, hastening to appropriate the compliment specially to herself.

"By this chain, which I received from the emperor's own hand," replied the warrior, playing with a short chain which hung round the neck like a collar, instead of descending to the breast, according to the fashion of the peaceful—"By this chain, you wrong me! I am a blunt man—a soldier should be so."

"How do you find the ladies of Pompeii generally?" asked Julia.

"By Venus, most beautiful! They favour me a little, it is true, and that inclines my eyes to double their charms."

"We love a warrior," said the wife of Pansa.

"I see it, by Hercules! It is even disagreeable to be too celebrated in these cities. At Herculaneum they climb the roof of my atrium to catch a glimpse of me through the compluvium; the admiration of one's citizens is pleasant at first, but burthensome afterwards."

"True, true, O Vespius!" cried the poet, joining the group: "I find it so myself!"

"You!" said the stately warrior, scanning the small form of the poet with ineffable disdain. "In what legion have you served?"

"You may see my spoils, my exuviæ, in the forum itself," returned the poet, with a significant glance at the women. "I have been among the tent-companions, the *contuburnales*, of the great Mantuan himself."

"I know no general from Mantua," said the warrior, gravely. "What campaign have you served?"

"That of Helicon."

"I never heard of it."

"Nay, Vespius, he does but joke," said Julia laughing.

"Joke! By Mars, am I a man to be joked?"

"Yes, Mars himself was in love with the mother of jokes," said the poet, a little alarmed. "Know, then, O Vespius, that I am the poet Fulvius. It is I who make warriors immortal!"

"The gods forbid!" whispered Sallust to Julia. "If Vespius were made immortal, what a specimen of tiresome braggadocio would be transmitted to posterity!"

The soldier looked puzzled; when, to the relief of himself and his companions, the signal for the feast was given.

Diomed, who was rather ceremonious, had appointed a *nomenclator*, or appointer of places, to each guest.

The festive board was composed of three tables; one at the centre, and one at each wine. It was only at the outer sides of these tables that the guest reclined; the inner space was left untenanted, for the greater convenience of the waiters. The extreme corner of one of the wings was appropriated to Julia as the lady of the feast; that next her, to Diomed. At one corner of the centre table was placed the ædile; at the opposite one the Roman senator—these were the posts of honour. The other guests were arranged so that the young should sit next each other, and the more advanced in years be similarly matched. An agreeable provision enough, but one which must often have offended those who wished to be thought still young.

The chair of Ione was next to the couch of Glaucus. The seats were veneered with tortoise-shell, and covered with quilts stuffed with feathers, and ornamented with costly embroideries. The modern ornaments of epergne or plateau were supplied by images of the gods, wrought in bronze, ivory and silver. The sacred salt-cellar and the familiar Lares were not forgotten. Over the table and the seats, a rich canopy was suspended from the ceiling. At each corner of the table were lofty candelabra—for though it was early noon, the room was darkened—while from tripods, placed in different parts of the room, distilled the odours of myrrh and frankincense; and upon the abacus, or sideboard, large vases and various ornaments of silver were ranged, much with the same ostentation (but with more than the same taste) that might be seen at a modern feast.

The custom of grace was invariably supplied by that of libation to the gods; and Vesta, as queen of the household, usually received first that graceful homage.

This ceremony being performed, the slaves showered flowers upon the couches and floor, and crowned each guest with garlands, intricately woven with ribbons, tied by the rind of the linden-tree, and each intermingled with ivy and amethyst—supposed preventives against the effects of wine; the wreaths of the women only were exempted from these leaves, for it was not the fashion for them to drink wine in public.

It was then that Diomed thought it advisable to institute a basileus, or director of the feast—an important office sometimes chosen by lot; sometimes by the master of the entertainment.

Diomed was a little puzzled as to his election. The invalid senator was too grave and too infirm for the proper fulfilment of his duty; the ædile Pansa was adequate enough to the task; but then, to choose the next in official rank to the senator, was an affront to the senator himself. While deliberating between the merits of the others, he caught the mirthful glance of Sallust, and by a sudden inspiration named the jovial epicure to the rank of director, or *arbiter bibendi*.

Sallust received the appointment with becoming humility.

"I shall be a merciful king," said he, "to those who drink deep; to a recusant, Minos himself shall be less inexorable. Beware!"

The slaves handed round basins of perfumed water, by which lavation the feast commenced: and now the table groaned under the initiatory course.

The conversation, at first desultory and scattered, allowed Ione and Glaucus to carry on those sweet whispers which are worth all the eloquence in the world. Julia watched them with frowning eyes.

"How soon shall her place be mine!" thought she.

But Clodius, who sat in the centre table, so that he could well observe the countenance of Julia, guessed her pique, and resolved to profit by it. He addressed her across the table in set phrases of gallantry; and as he was of high birth and of a showy person, the vain Julia was not so much in love as to be insensible to his attentions.

The slaves, in the interim, were constantly kept upon the alert by the vigilant Sallust, who chased one cup by another with a celerity which seemed as if he were resolved upon exhausting the capacious cellars. The worthy merchant began to repent his choice, as amphora after amphora was pierced and emptied. The slaves were all under the age of manhood (the youngest being about ten years old—it was they who filled the wine; the eldest, some five years older, mingled it with water). They seemed to share in the zeal of Sallust; and the face of Diomed began to glow as he watched the provoking complacency with which they seconded the exertions of the king of the feast.

"Pardon me, O senator!" said Sallust; "I see you flinch; your purple hem cannot save you—drink!"

"By the gods!" said the senator, coughing, "my lungs are already on fire; you proceed with so miraculous a swiftness, that Phæton himself were nothing to you I am infirm, O pleasant Sallust: you must exonerate me "

"Not I, by Vesta! I am an impartial monarch—drink!"

The poor senator, compelled by the laws of the table, was forced to comply. Alas! Every cup was bringing him nearer and nearer to the Stygian pool.

"Gently! Gently! My king," groaned Diomed; "we already begin to—"

"Treason!" interrupted Sallust; "no stern Brutus here!—no interference with royalty!"

"But our female guests—"

"Love a toper! Did not Ariadne dote upon Bacchus?"

The feast proceeded; the guests grew more talkative and noisy; the dessert was already on the table; and the slaves bore round water with myrrh and hyssop for the finishing lavation. At the same time, a small circular table that had been placed in the space opposite the guests, suddenly, and as by magic, opened in the centre, and cast up a fragrant shower, sprinkling the table and the guests; while as it ceased the awning above them was drawn aside, and the guests perceived that a rope had been stretched across the ceiling, and that one of those nimble dancers for which Pompeii was celebrated was now treading his airy measures right over their heads.

This apparition, removed but by a cord from one's pericranium, and indulging the most vehement leaps, apparently with the intention of alighting upon that cerebral region, was accepted by the Pompeian revellers with delighted curiosity, and applauded, in proportion as the dancer appeared with the most difficulty to miss falling upon the head of whatever guest he particularly selected to dance above. He paid the senator, indeed, the peculiar compliment of literally falling from the rope, and catching it again with his hand, just as the whole party imagined the skull of the Roman was as much fractured as that of the poet whom the eagle took for a tortoise. At length, to the great relief of at least Ione, who had not accustomed herself to this entertainment, the dancer suddenly paused as a strain of music was heard from without. He danced again still more wildly; the air changed, the dancer paused again; no, it could not dissolve the charm which was supposed to possess him! He represented one who by a strange disorder is compelled to dance, and whom only a certain air of music can cure. At length the musician seemed to hit on the right tune; the dancer gave one leap, swung himself down from the rope, alighted on the floor, and vanished.

One art now yielded to another; and the musicians stationed on the terrace struck up a soft and mellow air, to which were sung the following words, made almost indistinct by the barrier between, and the exceeding lowness of the minstrelsy:

FESTIVE MUSIC SHOULD BE LOW

"Hark! Through these flowers our music sends its greeting
To your loved halls, where Psilas shuns the day;
When the young god his Cretan nymph was meeting
He taught Pan's rustic pipe this gliding lay.
Soft as the dews of wine
Shed in this banquet hour,
The rich libation of Sound's stream divine,
O reverent harp, to Aphrodite pour!

Wild rings the trump o'er ranks to glory marching;
Music's sublimer bursts for wars are meet.
But sweet lips murmuring under wreaths o'er-arching,
Find the low whispers like their own most sweet.
Steal, my lull'd music, steal,

Like woman's half-heard tone,
So that whoe'er shall hear shall think to feel
In thee the voice of lips that seek his own."

At the end of the song, Ione's cheek blushed more deeply than
before, for Glaucus had contrived, under cover of the table, to steal
her hand.

"It is a pretty song," said Fulvius, patronizingly.

"Ah, if you would oblige us!" murmured the wife of Pansa.

"Do you wish Fulvius to sing?" asked the kind of the feast, who
had just called on the assembly to drink the health of the Roman
senator, a cup to each letter of his name.

"Can you ask?" said the matron, with a complimentary glance
at the poet.

Sallust snapped his fingers, and whispered to the slave who
came to learn his orders. The latter disappeared, and returned in a
few moments with a small harp in one hand, and a branch of myrtle
in the other.

The slave approached the poet, and with a low reverence presented to him the harp.

"Alas! I cannot play," said the poet.

"Then you must sing to the myrtle. It is a Greek fashion: Diomed loves the Greeks—I love the Greeks—you love the Greeks—
we all love the Greeks—and between you and me this is not the only
thing we have stolen from them. However, I introduce this custom—
I, the king: sing, subject, sing!"

The poet, with a bashful smile, took the myrtle in his hands, and
after a short prelude sang in a pleasant and well-tuned voice:

THE CORONATION OF LOVES

"The merry Loves one holiday
Were all at gambols madly;
But loves too long can seldom play
Without behaving sadly.
They laughed, they toyed, they romped about,
And then for change they all fell out.
Fie, fie! How can they quarrel so?
My Lesbia—ah, for shame, love!
Methinks 'tis scarce an hour ago
When we did just the same, love.

The loves, 'tis thought, were free till then,

They had no king or laws, dear;
But gods, like men, should subject be
Say all the ancient saws, dear.
And so our crew resolved for quiet,
To choose a king to curb their riot.
A kiss: ah! What a grievous thing
For both, methinks, 'twould be, child,
If I should take some prudish king,
And cease to be so free, child!

Among their toys a Casque they found,
It was the helm of Ares;
With horrent plumes the crest was crown'd,
It frightened all the Lares.
So fine a king was never known—
They placed the helmet on the throne.
My girl, since Valour wins the world,
They chose a mighty master;
But thy sweet flag of smiles unfurl'd
Would win the world much faster!

The Casque soon found the Loves too wild
A troop for him to school them;
For warriors know how one such child
Has aye contrived to fool them.
They plagued him so, that in despair
He took a wife the plague to share.
If kings themselves thus find the strife
Of earth, unshared, severe, girl;
Why just to halve the ills of life,
Come, take your partner here, girl."

This song, which suited the gay and lively fancy of the Pompeians, was received with considerable applause, and the widow insisted on crowning her namesake with the branch of myrtle to which he had sung. It was easily twisted into a garland, and the immortal Fulvius was crowned amidst the clapping of hands and shouts of *Io triumphe!* The song and the harp now circulated round the party, a new myrtle branch being handed about, stopping as each person who could be prevailed upon to sing.

The sun began now to decline, though the revellers, who had worn away several hours, perceived it not in their darkened chamber; and the senator, who was tired, and the warrior, who had to return to Herculaneum, rising to depart, gave the signal for the general dispersion. "Tarry yet a moment, my friends," said Diomed; "if you will go so soon, you must at least take a share in our concluding game."

So saying, he motioned to one of the ministri, and as he whispered him, the slave went out, and presently returned with a small bowl containing various tablets carefully sealed, and, apparently at the nominal price of the lowest piece of silver; and the sport of this lottery (which was the favourite diversion of Augustus, who introduced it) consisted in the inequality, and sometimes the incongruity, of the prizes, the nature and amount of which were specified within the tablets. For instance, the poet, with a wry face, drew one of his own poems (what physician ever less willingly swallowed his own draught?), the warrior drew a case of bodkins, which gave rise to certain novel witticisms relative to Hercules and the distaff; the widow Fulvia obtained a large drinking-cup; Julia, a gentleman's buckle; and Lepidus, a lady's patch-box. The most appropriate lot was drawn by the gambler Clodius, who reddened with anger on being presented with a set of cogged dice. A certain damp was thrown upon the gaiety which these various lots created by an accident that was considered ominous; Glaucus drew the most valuable of all the prizes, a small marble statue of Fortune, of Grecian workmanship: but, on handing it to him, the slave suffered it to drop, and it broke in pieces.

A shiver went round the assembly, and each voice cried spontaneously on the gods to avert the omen.

Glaucus alone, though perhaps as superstitious as the rest, affected to be unmoved.

"Sweet Neapolitan," whispered he tenderly to Ione, who had turned pale as the broken marble itself, "I accept the omen. It signifies, that in obtaining thee, Fortune can give no more—she breaks *her* image when she blesses me with *thine*."

In order to divert the impression which this incident had occasioned, Sallust, now crowning his cup with flowers, gave the health of their host. This was followed by a similar compliment to the emperor; and then, with a parting cup to Mercury to send them pleasant slumbers, they concluded the entertainment by a last libation, and broke up the party.

Carriages and litters were little used in Pompeii, partly owing to the extreme narrowness of the streets, partly to the convenient smallness of the city. Most of the guests, replacing their sandals, which they had put off in the banquet-room, and putting on their cloaks, left the house on foot attended by their slaves.

Meanwhile, having seen Ione depart, Glaucus, turning to the staircase which led down to the rooms of Julia, was conducted by a slave to an apartment in which he found the merchant's daughter already seated.

"Glaucus!" said she, looking down "I see that you really love Ione—she is indeed beautiful."

"Julia is charming enough to be generous," replied the Greek. "Yes, I love Ione; amidst all the youth who court you, may you have one worshipper as sincere."

"I pray the gods to grant it. See, Glaucus, these pearls are the present I destine for your bride: may Juno give her health to wear them!"

So saying, she placed a case in his hand, containing a row of pearls of some size and price. It was so much the custom for persons about to be married to receive these gifts, that Glaucus could have little scruple in accepting the necklace, though the gallant and proud Athenian had resolved to requite the gift by one of thrice its value. Julia then, stopping short his thanks, poured forth some wine into a small bowl.

"You have drunk many toasts with my father," said she, smiling—"one now with me. Health and fortune to your bride!"

She touched the cup with her lips and then presented it to him. The customary etiquette required that he should drain the whole contents; he accordingly did so. Julia, unknowing the deceit which Nydia had practised upon her, watched him with sparkling eyes; although the witch had told her that the effect *might* not be immediate, yet she sanguinely trusted to an expeditious operation in favour of her charms. She was disappointed when she found him coldly replace the cup, and converse with her in the same unmoved but gentle tone as before. And though she detained him as long as she decorously could, no change took place in his manner.

"But tomorrow," thought she, exultingly recovering her disappointment—"tomorrow, alas for Glaucus!"

Alas for him, indeed!

32. The Man Who Had Known Death

Restless and anxious, Apæcides consumed the day in wandering through the most sequestered walks in the vicinity of the city. The sun was slowly setting as he paused beside a lonely part of the Sarnus, ere yet it wound amidst the evidences of luxury and power. Only through openings in the woods and vines were caught glimpses of the white gleaming city, in which was heard in the distance no din, no sound, no "busiest hum of men." Amidst the green banks crept the lizard and the grasshopper, and here and there in the brake some solitary bird burst into sudden song, as suddenly stilled. There was deep calm around, but not the calm of night; the air still breathed of the freshness and life of day; the grass still moved to the stir of the insect horde; and on the opposite bank the graceful and white capella passed browsing through the herbage, and paused at the wave to drink.

As Apæcides stood gazing upon the waters, he heard beside him the low bark of a dog.

"Be still, poor friend," said a voice at hand, "the stranger's step harms not thy master." The convert recognized the voice, and, turning, he beheld the old man whom he had seen in the congregation of the Nazarenes.

The old man was sitting upon a fragment of stone covered with ancient mosses; beside him were his staff and scrip; at his feet lay a small shaggy dog, the companion in many pilgrimages.

The face of the old man was as balm to the excited spirit of the neophyte: he approached and, craving his blessing, sat down beside him.

"Thou art provided as for a journey, father, said he, "wilt thou leave us yet?"

"My son," replied the old man, "the days in store for me on earth are few and scanty; I employ them as becomes me, travelling from place to place, comforting those whom God has gathered together in His name, and proclaiming the glory of His Son, as testified to His servant."

"Thou hast looked, they tell me, on the face of Christ?"

"And the face received me from the dead. Know, young proselyte to the true faith, that I am he of whom thou readest in the scroll of the Apostle. In far Judea, in the city of Nain, there dwelt a widow, humble of spirit and said of heart; for of all the ties of life one son alone was spared to her. And she loved him with a melancholy love, for he was the likeness of the lost. And the son died. The reed on which she leaned was broken, the oil was dried up in the widow's cruse. They bore the dead upon his bier; and near the gate of the city, where the crowd were gathered, there came a silence over the sounds of woe, for the Son of God was passing by. The mother, who followed the bier, wept—all who looked upon her saw that her heart was crushed. And the Lord pitied her, and He touched the bier and said: 'I SAY UNTO THEE, ARISE.' And the dead man woke and looked upon the face of the Lord. I rose, I spoke, I was living, and in my mother's arms—yes, I am the dead revived! The people shouted, the funeral horns rang forth merrily; there was a cry: 'God has visited His people!' I heeded them not—I felt—I saw—nothing—but the face of my Redeemer!"

The old man paused, deeply moved; and the youth felt his blood creep, and his hair stir. He was in the presence of one who had known the Mystery of Death!

"Till that time," renewed the widow's son, "I had been as other men: taking no heed, but of the things of love and life; nay, I had inclined to the gloomy faith of the earthly Sadducee. But, raised from the dead, from awful and desert dreams that these lips never dare reveal—re-called upon earth, to testify the powers of Heaven—once more mortal, the witness of immortality; I drew a new being from the grave. O faded—O lost Jerusalem! Him from whom came my life, I beheld adjudged to agonized and parching death! Far in the mighty crowd, I saw the light rest and glimmer over the cross; I heard the hooting mob, I cried aloud, I raved, I threatened—none heeded me—I was lost in the whirl and the roar of thousands! But even then, in my agony and His own, methought the glazing eye of the Son of man sought me out. His lip smiled, as when it conquered death—it hushed me, and I became calm. He who had defied the grave for another—what was the grave to Him?"

The old man paused, and, when he resumed, it was in a calmer tone.

"From that night I resigned all earthly thought but that of serving HIM. A preacher and a pilgrim, I have traversed the earth, proclaiming His Divinity, and bringing converts to His fold. I come as the wind, and as the wind depart; sowing, as the wind sows, the seeds that enrich the world.

"Son, on earth we shall meet no more. Forget not this hour—what are the pleasures and pomps of life? As the lamp shines, so life glitters for an hour; but the soul's light is the star that burns forever, in the heart of illimitable space."

33. The Poisoned Cup

When Glaucus arrived home, he found Nydia seated under the portico of his garden. She had sought his house in the hope that he might return at an early hour: anxious, fearful, anticipative, she resolved upon seizing the earliest opportunity of availing herself of the love-charm, while at the same time she half hoped the opportunity might be deferred.

He crossed the portico just as the first stars became visible, and heaven assumed its most purple robe.

"Ho, my child, wait you for me?"

"Nay, I have been tending the flowers, and did but linger a little while to rest myself."

"It has been warm," said Glaucus, placing himself also on one of the seats beneath the colonnade.

"Very."

"Wilt thou summon Davus? The wine I have drunk heats me, and I long for some cooling drink."

Here at once, suddenly and unexpectedly, the very opportunity that Nydia awaited presented itself; of himself, at his own free choice, he afforded to her that occasion. She breathed quickly. "I will prepare for you myself," said she, "the summer draught that Ione loves—of honey and weak wine cooled in snow."

"Thanks. If Ione loves it, enough; I would be grateful were it poison."

Nydia frowned, and then smiled; she withdrew for a few moments, and returned with the cup containing the beverage. Glaucus took it from her hand. What would not Nydia have given then for one hour's prerogative of sight, to have watched her hopes ripening to effect—to have seen the first dawn of imagined love—to have worshipped, with more than Persian adoration, the rising of that sun which her credulous soul believed was to break on her dreary night! Far different, as she stood then and there, were the thoughts. the emotions of the blind girl, from those of the vain Pompeian under a similar suspense. In the last, what poor and frivolous passion had made up the daring whole! What petty pique, what small revenge, what expectation of a paltry triumph, had swelled the attributes of that sentiment she dignified with the name of love! But in the wild heart of the Thessalian all was pure, uncontrolled, unmodified passion, debased by no elements of a more sordid feeling. Filled with love as with life itself, how could she resist the occasion of winning love in return!

She leaned for support against the wall, and her face, before so flushed, was now white; and with her delicate hands clasped convulsively together, her lips apart, her eyes on the ground, she waited the next words Glaucus should utter.

Glaucus had raised the cup to his lips, he had drained about a fourth of its contents, when his eye suddenly glancing upon the face of Nydia, he was so forcibly struck by its alteration, by its intense, and painful, and strange expression, that he paused abruptly, and still holding the cup near his lips, exclaimed:

"Why, Nydia! Nydia! I say, art thou ill or in pain? Nay, thy face speaks for thee. What ails my poor child?" As he spoke, he put down the cup and rose from his seat to approach her, when a sudden pang shot coldly of his heart, and was followed by a chill, confused, dizzy sensation at the brain. The floor seemed to glide from under him—his feet seemed to move on air—a mighty and unearthly gladness rushed upon his spirit—but he felt too buoyant for the earth—he longed for wings, nay, it seemed in the buoyancy of his new existence as if he possessed them. He burst involuntarily into a loud and thrilling laugh. He clapped his hands—he bounded aloft—he was as a Pythoness inspired; suddenly as it came this preternatural transport passed, though only partially, away. He now felt his blood rushing loudly and rapidly through his veins; it seemed to swell, to exult, to leap along, as a stream that has burst its bounds, and hurried to the ocean. It throbbed in his ear with a mighty sound, he felt it mount to his brow, he felt the veins in the temples stretch and swell as if they could no longer contain the violent and increasing tide—then darkness fell over his eyes—darkness, but not entire; for through the dim shade he saw the opposite walls glow out, and the figures painted thereon seemed, ghost-like, to creep and glide. What was most strange, he did not feel himself *ill*—he did not sink or quail beneath the frenzy that was gathering within him. The novel feelings seemed bright and vivid—he felt as if a younger health had been infused into his frame. He was gliding on to madness—and he knew it not!

Nydia had not answered his first question—she had not been able to reply—his wild and fearful laugh had roused her from her passionate suspense: she could not see his fierce gesture—she could not mark his reeling and unsteady step as he paced unconsciously to and fro; but she heard the words, broken, incoherent, insane, that gushed from his lips. She became terrified and appalled—she hastened to him, feeling with her arms until she touched his knees, and then falling on the ground she embraced them, weeping with terror and excitement.

"O, speak to me! Speak! You do not hate me?—speak, speak!"

"By the bright goddess, a beautiful land this Cyprus! Ho! How they fill us with wine instead of blood! Now they open the veins of the Faun yonder, to show how the tide within bubbles and sparkles. Come hither, jolly old god! Thou ridest on a goat, eh?—what long silky hair he has! He is worth all the coursers of Parthia. But a word with thee—this wine of thine is too strong for us mortals. Oh! Beautiful! The boughs are at rest! The green waves of the forest have caught the Zephyr and drowned him! Not a breath stirs the leaves—and I view the Dreams sleeping with folded wings upon the motionless elm; and I look beyond, and I see a blue stream sparkle in the silent noon; a fountain—a fountain springing aloft! Ah! My fount, thou wilt not put out the rays of my Grecian sun, though thou tryest ever so hard with thy nimble and silver arms. And now, what form steals yonder through the boughs? She glides like a moon-beam—she has a garland of oak-leaves on her head. In her hand is a vase upturned, from which she pours pink and tiny shells, and spar-kling water. Oh! look on yon face! Man never before saw its like. See! we are alone; only I and she in the wide forest. There is no smile upon her lips—she moves, grave and sweetly sad. Ha! Fly, it is a nymph!—it is one of the wild Napæae! Whoever sees her be-comes mad—fly, see, she discovers me!"

"Oh! Glaucus! Glaucus! Do you not know me? Rave not so wildly, or thou wilt kill me with a word!"

A new change seemed now to operate upon the jarring and dis-ordered mind of the unfortunate Athenian. He put his hands upon Nydia's silken hair; he smoothed the locks—he looked wistfully upon her face, and then, as in the broken chain of thought one or two links were yet unsevered, it seemed that her countenance brought its associations of Ione; and with that remembrance his madness be-came yet more powerful, and it was swayed and tinged by passion, as he burst forth: "I swear by Venus, by Diana, and by Juno, that though I have now the world on my shoulders, as my countryman Hercules (ah! Dull Rome! Whoever was truly great was of Greece; why, you would be godless if it were not for us!)—I say, as my countryman Hercules said before me, I would let it fall into chaos for one smile from Ione. Ah, beautiful—Adored," he added, in a voice inexpressibly fond and plaintive, "thou lovest me not. Thou art unkind to me. The Egyptian hath belied me to thee—thou knowest not what hours I have spent beneath thy casement—thou knowest not how I have outwatched the stars, thinking thou, my Sun, wouldst rise at last—and thou lovest me not, thou forsakest me! Oh! Do not leave me now! I feel that my life will not be long; let me gaze on thee unto the last. I am of the bright land of thy fathers—I have trod the heights of Phyle—I have gathered the hyacinth and rose amidst the olive-groves of Ilyssus. Thou shouldst not desert me, for thy fa-thers were brothers to my own. And they say this land is lovely, and these climes serene, but I will bear thee with me—Ho! Dark form, why risest thou like a cloud between me and mine? Death sits calmly dread upon thy brow—on thy lip is the smile that slays: thy name is Orcus, but on earth men call thee Arbaces. See, I know thee; fly, dim shadow, thy spells avail not!"

"Glaucus! Glaucus!" murmured Nydia, releasing her hold and falling, beneath the excitement of her dismay, remorse and anguish, insensible on the floor.

"Who calls? said he, in a loud voice. "Ione, it is she! They have borne her off—we will save her—where is my stylus? Ha, I have it! I come, Ione, to the rescue! I come! I come!"

So saying, the Athenian with one bound passed the portico, he traversed the house, and rushed with swift but vacillating steps, muttering audibly to himself, down the star-lit streets. The direful potion burnt like fire in his veins, for its effect was made still more sudden from the wine he had drunk previously. Used to the excesses of nocturnal revellers, the citizens, with smiles and winks, gave way to his reeling steps; they naturally imagined him under the influence of the Bromian god, not vainly worshipped at Pompeii; but they who looked twice upon his face started in a nameless fear, and the smile withered from their lips. He passed the more populous streets; and, pursuing mechanically the way to Ione's house, he traversed a more deserted quarter, and entered now the lonely grove of Cybele, in which Apæcides had held his interview with Olinthus.

34. Murder

Impatient to learn whether the fell drug had yet been administered by Julia to his hated rival, and with what effect, Arbaces resolved, as the evening came on, to seek her house, and satisfy his suspense. It was customary for men at that time to carry abroad with them tablets and stylus attached to their girdles, and with the girdle they were put off when at home. In fact, under the appearance of a literary instrument, the Romans carried about with them in that same stylus a very sharp and formidable weapon. It was with his stylus that Cassius stabbed Cæsar in the senate house. Taking his girdle and cloak, Arbaces left his house, supporting his steps, which were still somewhat feeble (though hope and vengeance had conspired greatly with his own medical science, which was profound, to restore his natural strength) by his long staff: Arbaces took his way to the villa of Diomed.

Softly bright the moonbeams fell over the antique grove consecrated to Cybele—the stately trees, whose date went beyond tradition, cast their long shadows over the soil, while through the openings in their boughs shone the frequent stars. The whiteness of the small sacellum in the centre of the grove, amidst the dark foliage, had in it something abrupt and startling; it recalled the purpose to which the wood was consecrated—its holiness and solemnity.

With a swift, stealthy pace, Calenus, gliding under the shade of the trees, reached the chapel, and, gently putting back the boughs that closed round its rear, settled himself in his concealment; a concealment so complete, with the fane in front and the trees behind, that no unsuspicious passenger could possibly have detected him. All was solitary in the grove.

From the height on which it was placed, shone through the intervals of the trees the broad purple sea, rippling in the distance, the white villas of Stabiæ in the curving shore, and the dim Lectiarian hills mingling with the delicious sky. Presently the tall figure of Arbaces, on his way to the house of Diomed, entered the extreme end of the grove; and at the same instant Apæcides, bound to his appointment with Olinthus, crossed the Egyptian's path.

"Hem! Apæcides," said Arbaces, recognising the priest at a glance; "when last we met, you were my foe. I have wished since then to see you, for I would have you still my pupil and my friend."

Apæcides started at the voice of the Egyptian; and, halting abruptly, gazed upon him with a countenance full of contending, bitter, and scornful emotions.

"Villain and impostor!" said he at length; "thou hast recovered then from the jaws of the grave! But think not again to weave around me thy guilty meshes. *Retiarius*, I am armed against thee!"

"Hush!" said Arbaces, in a very low voice—but his pride, which in that descendant of kings was great, betrayed the wound it received from the insulting epithets of the priest in the quiver of his lip and the flush of his tawny brow. "Hush! More low! Thou mayest be overheard, and if other ears than mine had drunk those sounds—why—"

"Dost thou threaten—what if the whole city had heard me?"

"The manes of my ancestors would not have suffered me to forgive thee. But, hold, and hear me. Thou art enraged that I would have offered violence to thy sister. Nay, peace, peace, but one instant, I pray thee. Thou art right; it was the frenzy of passion and of jealousy—I have repented bitterly of my madness. Forgive me; I, who never implored pardon of living man, beseech thee now to forgive me. Nay, I will atone the insult—I ask thy sister in marriage;— start not, consider—what is the alliance of yon holiday Greek compared to mine? Wealth unbounded—birth that in its far antiquity leaves your Greek and Roman names the things of yesterday— science—but that thou knowest! Give me thy sister, and my whole life shall atone a moment's error."

"Egyptian, were even I to consent, my sister loathes the very air thou breathest: but I have my own wrongs to forgive—I may pardon thee that thou hast made me a tool to thy deceits, but never that thou hast seduced me to become the abettor of thy vices—a polluted and perjured man. Tremble!—even now I prepare the hour in which thou and thy false gods shall be unveiled. Thy lewd and Circean life shall be dragged to day—thy mumming oracles disclosed—the fane of the idol Isis shall be a byword and a scorn—the name of Arbaces a mark for the hisses of execration! Tremble!"

The flush on the Egyptian's brow was succeeded by a livid paleness. He looked behind, before, around, to feel assured that none were by; and then he fixed his dark dilating eyes on the priest, with such a gaze of wrath and menace, that one, perhaps, less supported than Apæcides by the fervent daring of a divine zeal, could not have faced with unflinching look that lowering aspect. But the young convert met it unmoved, and returned it with one of proud defiance.

"Apæcides," said the Egyptian, in a tremulous and inward tone, "beware! What is it thou wouldst meditate? Speakest thou—reflect, pause before thou repliest—from the hasty influences of wrath, as yet divining no settled purpose, or from some fixed design?"

"I speak from the inspiration of the True God, whose servant I now am," answered the Christian, boldly; "and in the knowledge that by His grace human courage has already fixed the date of thy hypocrisy and thy demon's worship, ere thrice the sun has dawned, thou wilt know all! Dark sorcerer, tremble, and farewell!"

All the fierce and lurid passions which he inherited from his nation and his clime, at all times but ill concealed beneath the blandness of craft and the coldness of philosophy, were released in the breast of the Egyptian. Rapidly one thought chased another; he saw before him an obstinate barrier to even a lawful alliance with Ione—the fellow-champion of Glaucus in the struggle which had baffled his designs—the reviler of his name—the threatened desecrator of the goddess he served while he disbelieved—the avowed and approaching revealer of his own impostures and vices. His love, his repute, nay, his very life, might be in danger—the day and hour seemed even to have been fixed for some design against him. He knew by the words of the convert that Apæcides had adopted the Christian faith; he knew the indomitable zeal which led on the proselytes of that creed. Such was his enemy; he grasped his stylus—that enemy was in his power! They were now before the chapel; one hasty glance once more he cast around; he saw none near—silence and solitude alike tempted him.

"Die, then, in thy rashness!" he muttered. "Away, obstacle to my rushing fates!"

And just as the young Christian had turned to depart, Arbaces raised his hand high over the left shoulder of Apæcides, and plunged his sharp weapon twice into his breast.

Apæcides fell to the ground pierced to the heart—he fell mute, without even a groan, at the very base of the sacred chapel.

Arbaces gazed upon him for a moment with the fierce animal joy of conquest over a foe. But presently the full sense of the danger to which he was exposed flashed upon him; he wiped his weapon carefully in the long grass with the garments of his victim, drew his cloak round him, and was about to depart, when he saw, coming up the path, right before him, the figure of a young man, whose steps reeled and vacillated strangely as he advanced: the quiet moonlight streamed full upon his face, which seemed, by the whitening ray, colourless as marble. The Egyptian recognised the face and form of Glaucus. The unfortunate and benighted Greek was chanting a mad, disconnected song, composed from snatches of hymns and sacred odes, all jarringly woven together.

"Ha!" thought the Egyptian, instantaneously divining his state, and its terrible cause; "so, then, the hell-draught works, and destiny hath sent thee hither to crush two of my foes at once!"

Quickly, even ere this thought occurred to him, he had withdrawn on one side of the chapel, and concealed himself among the boughs; from that lurking-place he watched, as a tiger in his lair, the advance of his second victim. He noted the wandering restless fire in the bright and beautiful eyes of the Athenian; the convulsions that distorted his features and writhed his lip. He saw that the Greek was utterly deprived of reason. Nevertheless, as Glaucus came up to the dead body of Apæcides, from which the dark red stream flowed slowly over the grass, so strange and ghastly a spectacle could not fail to arrest him, be nighted and erring as was his glimmering sense. He paused, placed his hand to his brow, as if to collect himself, and then saying:

"What, ho! Endymion, sleepest thou so soundly? What has the moon said to thee? Thou makest me jealous; it is time to wake," he stooped down with the intention of lifting up the body.

Forgetting—feeling not—his own debility, the Egyptian sprang from his hiding-place, and as the Greek bent, struck him forcibly to the ground, over the very body of the Christian; then, raising his powerful voice to its loudest pitch, he shouted:

"Ho, citizens—oh! Help me!—hither—hither! A murder—a murder before your very fane! Help, or the murderer escapes!" As he spoke, he placed his foot on the breast of Glaucus: an idle and superfluous precaution; for the potion operating with the fall, the Greek lay there motionless and insensible, save that now and then his lips gave vent to some vague and raving sounds.

And now, fast and breathless, several citizens came thronging to the place, some with torches, which the moon rendered unnecessary, but which flared red and tremulously against the darkness of the trees as they surrounded the spot.

"Lift up the corpse," said the Egyptian, "and guard well the murderer."

They raised the body, and great was their horror and sacred indignation to discover a priest of the adored and venerable Isis; but still greater, perhaps, was their surprise when they found the accused in the brilliant and admired Athenian.

"Glaucus!" cried the bystanders with one accord; "is it credible?"

"I would sooner," whispered one man to his neighbour, "believe it to be the Egyptian himself."

Here a centurion thrust himself into the gathering crowd with an air of authority.

"How! Blood spilt! Who is the murderer?"

The bystanders pointed to Glaucus.

"He!—by Mars, he has rather the air of being the victim. Who accuses him?"

"I," said Arbaces, drawing himself up haughtily; and the jewels which adorned his dress flashing in the eyes of the soldier, instantly convinced that worthy warrior of the witness's respectability.

"Pardon me—your name?" said he.

"Arbaces; it is well known, methinks, in Pompeii. Passing through the grove, I beheld before me the Greek and the priest in earnest conversation. I was struck by the reeling motions of the first, his violent gestures, and the loudness of his voice; he seemed to me either drunk or mad. Suddenly I saw him raise his stylus—I darted forward—too late to arrest the blow. He had twice stabbed his victim, and was bending over him, when in my horror and indignation, I struck him to the ground. He fell without a struggle, which makes me yet more suspect that he was not altogether in his senses when the crime was perpetrated; for, recently recovered from a severe illness, my blow was comparatively feeble, and the frame of Glaucus, as you see, is strong and youthful."

"His eyes are open now—his lips move," said the soldier. "Speak, prisoner, what sayest thou to the charge?"

"The charge—ha—ha! Why, it was merrily done; when the old hag set her serpent at me, and Hecate stood by laughing from ear to ear—what could I do? But I am ill—I faint—the serpent's fiery tongue hath bitten me. Bear me to bed, and send for your physician; old Æsculapius himself will attend me, if you let him know that I am Greek. Oh, mercy—mercy—I burn!—marrow and brain, I burn!"

And, with a thrilling and fierce groan, the Athenian fell back in the arms of the bystanders.

"He raves," said the officer, compassionately; "and in his delirium he has struck the priest. Hath any one present seen him today?"

"I," said one of the spectators, "beheld him in the morning. He passed my shop and accosted me. He seemed well and sane as the stoutest of us."

"And I saw him half an hour ago," said another, "passing up the streets, muttering to himself with strange gestures, and just as the Egyptian has described."

"Corroboration of the witness! It must be too true. He must at all events to the prætor; a pity, so young and so rich! But the crime is dreadful: a priest of Isis, in his very robes, too, and at the base of our most ancient chapel!"

At these words the crowd were reminded more forcibly than in their excitement and curiosity they had yet been, of the heinousness of the sacrilege. They shuddered in pious horror.

"No wonder the earth has quaked," said one, "when it held such a monster!"

And one voice was heard shrilly and joyously above the rest:

"The beasts will not want a gladiator now,
'Ho, ho! For the merry, merry show!' "

It was the voice of the young woman whose conversation with Medon has been recorded.

"True—true—it chances in season for the games!" cried several; and at that thought all pity for the accused seemed vanished. His youth—his beauty, but fitted him better for the purpose of the arena.

"Bring hither some planks—or if at hand, a litter—to bear the dead," said Arbaces; "a priest of Isis ought scarcely to be carried to his temple by vulgar hands, like a butchered gladiator."

At this the bystanders reverently laid the corpse of Apæcides on the ground, with the face upwards; and some of them sent in search of some contrivance to bear the body, untouched by the profane.

It was just at that time that the crowd gave way to right and left as a sturdy form forced itself through, and Olinthus the Christian stood immediately confronting the Egyptian. But his eyes, at first, only rested with in-expressible grief and horror on that gory side and up-turned face, on which the agony of violent death yet lingered.

"Murdered!" he said. "It is thy zeal that has brought thee to this? Have they detected thy noble purpose, and by death prevented their own shame?"

He turned his head abruptly, and his eyes fell full on the solemn features of the Egyptian.

As he looked, you might see in his face, and even the slight shiver of his frame, the repugnance and aversion which the Christian felt for one whom he knew to be so dangerous and so criminal. It was indeed the gaze of the bird upon the basilisk—so silent was it and so prolonged. But shaking off the sudden chill that had crept over him, Olinthus extended his right arm towards Arbaces, and said, in a deep and loud voice: "Murder hath been done upon this corpse! Where is the murderer? Stand forth, Egyptian! For, as the Lord liveth, I believe *thou* art the man!"

An anxious and perturbed change might for one moment be detected on the dusky features of Arbaces; but it gave way to the frowning expression of indignation and scorn, as, awed and arrested by the suddenness and vehemence of the charge, the spectators pressed nearer and nearer upon the two more prominent actors.

"I know," said Arbaces, proudly, "who is my accuser, and I guess wherefore he thus arraigns me. Men and citizens, know this man for the most bitter of the Nazarenes. What marvel that in his malignity he dares accuse even an Egyptian of the murder of a priest of Egypt!"

"I know him! I know the dog!" shouted several voices. "It is Olinthus the Atheist—he denies the gods!"

"Peace, brethren," said Olinthus, with dignity, "and hear me! This murdered priest of Isis before his death embraced the Christian faith—he revealed to me the dark sins, the sorceries of yon Egyptian—the mummeries and delusions of the fane of Isis. He was about to declare them publicly. *He*, a stranger, unoffending, without enemies! Who should shed his blood but one of those who feared his witness? Who might fear that testimony the most?—Arbaces, the Egyptian!"

"You hear him!" said Arbaces; "you hear him! he blasphemes! Ask him if he believes in Isis?"

"Do I believe in an evil demon?" returned Olinthus, boldly.

A groan passed through the assembly. Nothing daunted, prepared at every time for peril, and in the present excitement losing all prudence, the Christian continued:

"Back, idolaters! This clay is not for your vain and polluting rites—it is to us—to the followers of Christ, that the last offices due to a Christian belong. I claim this dust in the name of the great Creator who has recalled the spirit!"

With so solemn and commanding a voice and aspect the Christian spoke these words, that even the crowd for-bore to utter aloud the execration of fear and hatred which in their hearts they conceived. And never, perhaps, since Lucifer and the Archangel contended for the body of the mighty Lawgiver, was there a more striking subject for the painter's genius than that scene exhibited. The dark trees—the stately fane—the moon full on the corpse of the deceased—the torches tossing wildly in the rear—the various faces of the motley audience—the insensible form of the Athenian, supported, in the distance; and, in the foreground, and above all, the forms of Arbaces and the Christian; the first drawn to its full height, far taller than the herd around; his arms folded, his brows knit, his eyes fixed, his lip slightly curled in defiance and disdain. The last bearing, on a brow worn and furrowed, the majesty of an equal command—the features stern, yet frank—the aspect bold, yet open—the quiet dignity of the whole form impressed with an ineffable earnestness, hushed, as it were, in a solemn sympathy with the awe he himself had created. His left hand pointing to the corpse—his right hand raised to heaven.

The centurion pressed forward again.

"Hast thou, Olinthus, any proof of the charge thou hast made against Arbaces?"

Olinthus remained silent—the Egyptian laughed contemptuously.

"Dost thou claim the body of a priest of Isis as one of the Nazarene sect?"

"I do."

"Swear then by yon fane, yon statue of Cybele, by yon most ancient sacellum in Pompeii, that the dead man embraced your faith!"

"Vain man! I disown your idols! I abhor your temples! How can I swear by Cybele?"

"Away, away with the atheist! away!—away with him to death!"

"*To the beasts*!" added a female voice in the centre of the crowd: "*we shall have one apiece now for the lion and tiger!*"

"If, O Nazarene, thou disbelievest in Cybele, which of our gods dost thou own?" resumed the soldier, unmoved by the cries around.

"None!"

"Hark to him! Hark!" cried the crowd.

"O vain and blind!" continued the Christian, raising his voice; "Can you believe in images of wood and stone? Do you imagine that they have eyes to see, or ears to hear, or hands to help ye? Is yon mute thing carved in man's art a goddess?—hath it made mankind?—alas! By mankind it was made. Lo! Convince yourselves of its nothingness—of your folly."

And as he spoke, he strode across to the fane, and ere any of the bystanders were aware of his purpose, he, in his compassion or zeal, struck the statue of wood from its pedestal.

"See!" cried he, "your goddess cannot avenge herself. Is this a thing to worship?"

Further words were denied to him; so gross and daring a sacrilege—of one, too, of the most sacred of their places of worship—filled even the most lukewarm with rage and horror. With one accord the crowd rushed upon him, seized, and but for the interference of the centurion, would have torn him to pieces.

"Peace!" said the soldier, authoritatively "refer we this insolent blasphemer to the proper tribunal!—time has already been wasted. Bear both the culprits to the magistrates; place the body of the priest on the litter—carry it to his own home."

At this moment a priest of Isis stepped forward. "I claim these remains, according to the custom of the priesthood."

"The flamen be obeyed," said the centurion. "How is the murderer?"

"Were his crimes less, I could pity him. On!"

Arbaces, as he turned, met the eye of that priest of Isis—it was Calenus; and something there was in that glance, so significant and sinister, that the Egyptian muttered to himself:

"Could he have witnessed the deed?"

A girl darted from the crowd, and gazed hard on the face of Olinthus. "*By Jupiter, a stout knave! I say, we shall have a man for the tiger now; one for each beast!*"

"Ho!" shouted the mob; "a man for the lion, and another for the tiger! What luck! Io, Pæan!"

35. Arbaces Offers Terms

The night was somewhat advanced, but the gay lounging-places of the Pompeians were still crowded. The various idlers talked in large knots and groups, as if they sought by numbers to divide the half-painful, half-pleasurable anxiety which belonged to the subject on which they conversed: it was a subject of life and death.

A young man passed briskly by the graceful portico of the Temple of Fortune—so briskly, indeed, that he came with no slight force full against the rotund and comely form of that respectable citizen Diomed, who was retiring homeward to his suburban villa.

"Holloa!" groaned the merchant, recovering with some difficulty his equilibrium; "have you no eyes? Or do you think I have no feeling? By Jupiter! You have well-nigh driven out the divine particle; such another shock, and my soul will be in Hades!"

"Ah, Diomed! Is it you? Forgive my inadvertence. I was absorbed in thinking of the reverses of life. Our poor friend, Glaucus, eh! Who would have guessed it?"

"Well, but tell me, Clodius, is he really to be tried by the senate?"

"Yes: they say the crime is of so extraordinary a nature, that the senate itself must adjudge it; and so the lictors are to induct him formally."

"He has been accused publicly?"

"To be sure; where have you been, not to hear that?"

"Why, I have only just returned from Neapolis, whither I went on business the very morning after his crime—so shocking, and at my house the same night that it happened!"

"There is no doubt of his guilt," said Clodius, shrugging his shoulders; "and as these crimes take precedence of all little undignified peccadilloes, they will hasten to finish the sentence previous to the games."

"The games! Good gods!" replied Diomed, with a slight shudder; "can they adjudge him to the beasts?—so young, so rich!"

"True; but, then, he is a Greek. Had he been a Roman, it would have been a thousand pities. These foreigners can be borne with in their prosperity; but in adversity we must not forget that they are in reality slaves. However, we of the upper classes are always tender-hearted; and he would certainly get off tolerably well, if he were left to us: for, between ourselves, what is a paltry priest of Isis!—what is Isis herself? But the common people are superstitious; they clamour for the blood of the sacrilegious one. It is dangerous not to give way to pubic opinion."

"And the blasphemer—the Nazarene, or whatever else he be called?"

"Oh, poor dog! if he will sacrifice to Cybele, or Isis, he will be pardoned—if not, the tiger has him. At least, I suppose so; but the trial will decide. We talk while the urn's still empty. And the Greek may yet escape. But enough of this gloomy subject. How is the fair Julia?"

"Well, I fancy."

"Commend me to her. But hark! The door yonder creaks on its hinges; it is the house of the prætor. Who comes forth? By Pollux! It is the Egyptian! What can he want with our official friend?"

"Some conference touching the murder, doubtless," replied Diomed; "but what was supposed to be the inducement to the crime? Glaucus was to have married the priest's sister."

"Yes; some say Apæcides refused the alliance. It might have been a sudden quarrel. Glaucus was evidently drunk—so much as to have been quite insensible when taken up, and I hear is still delirious—whether with wine, terror, remorse, the Furies, or the Bacchanals, I cannot say."

"Poor fellow!—he has good counsel?"

"The best—Caius Pollio, an eloquent fellow enough. Pollio has been hiring all the poor gentlemen and well-born spendthrifts of Pompeii to dress shabbily and sneak about, swearing their friendship to Glaucus (who would not have spoken to them to be made emperor!—I will do him justice, he was a gentleman in his choice of acquaintance) and trying to melt the stony citizens into pity. But it will not do; Isis is mightily popular just at this moment."

"And I have some merchandise at Alexandria. Yes, Isis ought to be protected."

"True; so farewell: we shall meet soon; if not, we must have a friendly bet at the Amphitheatre. All my calculations are confounded by this cursed misfortune of Glaucus! He had bet on Lydon, the gladiator; I must make up my tablets elsewhere. Vale!"

Leaving the less active Diomed to regain his villa, Clodius strode on, humming a Greek air, and perfuming the night with the odours that steamed from his snowy garments and flowing locks.

"If," thought he, "Glaucus feed the lion, Julia will no longer have a person to love better than me; she will certainly dote on me—and so, I suppose, I must marry. By the gods! The twelve lines begin to fail—men look suspiciously at my hand when it rattles the dice. That infernal Sallust insinuates cheating; and if it be discovered that the ivory is cogged, why farewell to the merry supper and the perfumed billet—Clodius is undone! Better marry, then, while I may, renounce gaming, and push my fortune (or rather the gentle Julia's) at the imperial court."

Thus muttering the schemes of his ambition, if by that high name the projects of Clodius may be called, the gamester found himself suddenly accosted; he turned and beheld the dark brow of Arbaces.

"Hail, noble Clodius! Pardon my interruption; and inform me, I pray you, which is the house of Sallust?"

"It is but a few yards hence, wise Arbaces. But does Sallust entertain tonight?"

"I know not," answered the Egyptian; "nor am I one of those whom he would seek as a boon companion. But thou knowest that this house holds the person of Glaucus, the murderer."

"Ay! He, good-hearted epicure, believes in the Greek's innocence! You remind me that he has become his surety. Well, Sallust's house is better than a prison, especially that wretched hole in the forum. But for what can you seek Glaucus?"

"Why, noble Clodius, if we could save him from execution, it would be well. The condemnation of the rich is a blow upon society itself. I should like to confer with him—for I hear he has recovered his senses—and ascertain the motives of his crime; they may be so extenuating as to plead in his defence."

"You are benevolent, Arbaces."

"Benevolence is the duty of one who aspires to wisdom," replied the Egyptian, modestly. "Which way lies Sallust's mansion?"

"I will show you," said Clodius, "if you will suffer me to accompany you a few steps. But, pray what has become of the poor girl who was to have wed the Athenian—the sister of the murdered priest?"

"Alas! Well-nigh insane. Sometimes she utters imprecations on the murderer—then suddenly stops short—then cries: 'But why curse? Oh, my brother! Glaucus was not thy murderer—never will I believe it!' Then she begins again, and again stops short, and mutters awfully to herself: 'Yet if it were indeed he?'"

"Unfortunate Ione!"

"But it is well for her that those solemn cares to the dead which religion enjoins have hitherto greatly absorbed her attention from Glaucus and herself: and, in the dimness of her senses, she scarcely seems aware that Glaucus is apprehended and on the eve of trial. When the funeral rites due to Apæcides are performed, her apprehension will return; and then I fear me much that her friends will be revolted by seeing her run to succour and aid the murderer of her brother!"

"Such scandal should be prevented."

"I trust I have taken precautions to that effect. I am her lawful guardian, and have just succeeded in obtaining permission to escort her, after the funeral of Apæcides, to my own house; there, please the gods! She will be secure."

"You have done well, sage Arbaces. And now, yonder is the house of Sallust. The gods keep you! Yet, hark you, Arbaces—why so gloomy and unsocial? Men say you *can* be gay—why not let me initiate you into the pleasures of Pompeii? I flatter myself no one knows them better."

"I thank you, noble Clodius: under your auspices I might venture, I think, to wear the philyra: but, at my age, I should be an awkward pupil."

"Oh, never fear; I have made converts of fellows of seventy. The rich, too, are never old."

"You flatter me. At some future time, I will remind you of your promise."

"You may command Marcus Clodius at all times—and so, *vale!*"

"Now," said the Egyptian, soliloquizing, "I am not wantonly a man of blood, I would willingly save this Greek, if, by confessing the crime, he will lose himself forever to Ione, and forever free me from the chance of discovery; and I can save him by persuading Julia to own the philtre, which will be held his excuse. But if he do not confess the crime, why Julia must be shamed from the confession, and he must die!—die, lest he prove my rival with the living— die, that he may be proxy with the dead! Will he confess?—can he not be persuaded that in his delirium he struck the blow? To me it would give far greater safety than even his death. Hem! We must hazard the experiment."

Sweeping along the narrow street, Arbaces now approached the house of Sallust, where he beheld a dark form wrapped in a cloak, and stretched at length across the threshold of the door.

So still lay the figure, and so dim was its outline, that any other than Arbaces might have felt a superstitious fear, lest he beheld one of those grim *lemures*, who, above all other spots, haunted the threshold of the homes they formerly possessed. But not for Arbaces were such dreams.

"Rise!" said he, touching the figure with his foot, "thou obstructest the way!"

"Ha! who art thou?" cried the form, in a sharp tone; and as she raised herself from the ground, the star-light fell full on the pale face and fixed but sightless eyes of Nydia the Thessalian. "Who art thou? I know the burden of thy voice."

"Blind girl! What dost thou here at this late hour? Fie!—is this seeming thy sex or years? Home, girl."

"I know thee," said Nydia, in a low voice, "thou art Arbaces the Egyptian." Then, as if inspired by some sudden impulse, she flung herself at his feet, and clasping his knees, exclaimed, in a wild passionate tone: "Oh, dread and potent man! Save him!—save him! He is not guilty—it is I! He lies within, ill, dying, and I—I am the hateful cause. And they will not admit me to him—they spurn the blind girl from the hall. Oh, heal him! Thou knowest some herb—some spell—some counter-harm, for it is a potion that hath wrought this frenzy!"

"Hush, child! I know all!—thou forgettest that I accompanied Julia to the saga's home. Doubtless her hand administered the draught; but her reputation demands thy silence. Reproach not thyself—what must be, must: meanwhile, I seek the criminal—he may yet be saved. Away!"

Thus saying, Arbaces extricated himself from the clasp of the despairing Thessalian, and knocked loudly at the door.

In a few moments the heavy bars were heard to yield, and the porter, half opening the door, demanded who was there.

"Arbaces—important business to Sallust, relative to Glaucus. I come from the prætor."

The porter, half yawning, half groaning, admitted the tall form of the Egyptian. Nydia sprang forward. "How is he?" she cried; "tell me—tell me!"

"Ho, mad girl! Is it thou still?—for shame! Why, they say he is sensible."

"The gods be praised!—and you will not admit me? Ah! I beseech thee—"

"Admit thee!—no. A pretty salute I should prepare for these shoulders. Go home."

The door closed. Nydia, with a deep sigh, laid herself down once more on the cold stones; and, wrapping her cloak round her face, resumed her weary vigil.

Meanwhile Arbaces had already gained the triclinium, where Sallust, with his favourite freedman, sat late at supper.

"What! Arbaces! And at this hour!—Accept this cup."

"Nay, gentle Sallust; it is on business, not pleasure, that I venture to disturb thee. How doth thy charge?—they say in the town that he has recovered sense."

"Alas! And truly," replied the good-natured but thoughtless Sallust, "but so shattered are his nerves and frame that I scarcely recognize the gay carouser I was wont to know. Yet, strange to say, he cannot account for the cause of the sudden frenzy that seized him—he retains but a dim consciousness of what hath passed, and, despite thy witness, wise Egyptian, solemnly upholds his innocence of the death of Apæcides."

"Sallust," said Arbaces gravely, "there is much in thy friend's case that merits a peculiar indulgence; and could we learn from his lips the confession and the cause of his crime, much might yet be hoped from the mercy of the senate; for the senate, thou knowest, hath the power either to mitigate or to sharpen the law. Therefore it is that I have conferred with the highest authority of the city, and obtained his permission to hold a private conference this night with the Athenian, before the trial comes on."

"Well, said Sallust, "thou wilt be worthy of thy Eastern name and fame if thou canst learn aught from him; but thou mayst try. Poor Glaucus!—and he had such an excellent appetite! He eats nothing now!"

The benevolent epicure was moved sensibly at this thought. He sighed, and ordered his slaves to refill his cup.

"Night wanes," said the Egyptian; "suffer me to see thy ward now."

Sallust nodded assent, and led the way to a small chamber, guarded without by two dozing slaves. The door opened; at the request of Arbaces, Sallust withdrew—the Egyptian was alone with Glaucus.

One of those tall and graceful candelabra common to that day, supporting a single lamp, burned beside the narrow bed. Its rays fell palely over the face of the Athenian, and Arbaces was moved to see how sensibly that countenance had changed. The rich colour was gone, the cheek was sunk, the lips were pallid; fierce had been the struggle between reason and madness, life and death. The youth, the strength of Glaucus had conquered; but the freshness of blood and soul—the life of life, its glory and its zest, were gone forever.

The Egyptian seated himself quietly beside the bed; Glaucus still lay mute and unconscious of his presence. At length, after a considerable pause, Arbaces thus spoke: "Glaucus we have been enemies. I come to thee alone, and in the dead of night—thy friend, perhaps thy saviour."

As the steed starts from the path of the tiger, Glaucus sprang up breathless—alarmed panting at the abrupt voice, the sudden apparition of his foe. Their eyes met, and neither, for some moments, had power to withdraw his gaze. The flush went and came over the face of the Athenian, and the bronzed cheek of the Egyptian grew a shade more pale. At length with an inward groan, Glaucus turned away, drew his hand across his brow, sank back, and muttered:

"Am I still dreaming?"

"No, thou art awake. By this right hand and my father's head, thou seest one who may save thy life. Hark! I know what thou hast done, but I know also its excuse, of which thou thyself art ignorant. Thou hast committed murder, it is true—a sacrilegious murder: frown not—start not—these eyes saw it. But I can save thee—I can prove how thou wert bereaved of sense, and made not a free-thinking and free-acting man. But in order to save thee, thou must confess thy crime. Sign but this paper, acknowledging thy hand in the death of Apæcides, and thou shalt avoid the fatal urn."

"What words are these?—Murder and Apæcides! Did I not see him stretched on the ground bleeding and a corpse? And wouldst thou persuade me that I did the deed? Man, thou liest! Away!"

"Be not rash—Glaucus, be not hasty; the deed is proved. Come, come, thou mayst well be excused for not recalling the act of thy delirium, and which thy sober senses would have shunned even to contemplate. But let me try to refresh thy exhausted and weary memory. Thou knowest thou wert walking with the priest, disputing about his sister; thou knowest he was intolerant, and half a Nazarene, and he sought to convert thee, and there were hot words. He calumniated thy mode of life, and swore he would not marry Ione to thee—and then, in thy wrath and frenzy, thou didst strike the sudden blow. Come, come; you can recollect this!—read this papyrus, it runs to that effect—sign it, and thou art saved."

"Barbarian, give me the written lie, that I may tear it! I the murderer of Ione's brother! I confess to have injured one hair of the head of him she loved! Let me rather perish a thousand times!"

"Beware!" said Arbaces, in a low and hissing tone; "there is but one choice—thy confession and thy signature, or the ampitheatre and the lion's maw!"

As the Egyptian fixed his eyes upon the sufferer, he hailed with joy the signs of evident emotion that seized the latter at these words. A slight shudder over the Athenian's frame—his lip fell—an expression of sudden fear and wonder betrayed itself in his brow and eye.

"Great gods," he said, in a low voice, "what reverse is this? It seems but a little day since life laughed out from amidst roses—Ione mine—youth, health, love, lavishing on me their treasures; and now—pain, madness, shame, death! And for what? What have I done? Oh, am I mad still?"

"Sign, and be saved!" said the soft, sweet voice of the Egyptian.

"Tempter, never!" cried Glaucus, in the reaction of rage. "Thou knowest me not: thou knowest not the soul of an Athenian! The sudden face of death might appal me for a moment, but the fear is over. Dishonour appals forever! Who will debase his name to save his life? Who exchange clear thoughts for sullen days? Who will belie himself to shame, and stand blackened in the eyes of glory and love?

If to earn a few years of polluted life there be so base a coward, dream not, dull barbarian of Egypt! To find him in one who has trod the same sod as Harmodius, and breathed the same air as Socrates. Go! Leave me to live without self-reproach—or to perish without fear!"

"Bethink thee well! The lion's fangs: the hoots of the brutal mob; the vulgar gaze on thy dying agony and mutilated limbs; thy name degraded; thy corpse unburied; the shame thou wouldst avoid clinging to thee forever!"

"Thou ravest! *Thou* art the madman! Shame is not in the loss of other men's esteem—it is in the loss of our own. Wilt thou go? My eyes loathe the sight of thee! Hating ever, I despise thee now!"

"I go," said Arbaces, stung and exasperated, but not without some pitying admiration of his victim. "I go; we meet twice again— once at the trial, once at the death! Farewell!"

The Egyptian rose slowly, gathered his robes about him, and left the chamber. He sought Sallust for a moment, whose eyes began to reel with the vigils of the cup: "He is still unconscious, or still obstinate; there is no hope for him."

"Say not so," replied Sallust, who felt but little resentment against the Athenian's accuser, for he possessed no great austerity of virtue, and was rather moved by his friend's reverses than persuaded of his innocence—"say not so, my Egyptian! So good a drinker shall be saved if possible. Bacchus against Isis!"

"We shall see," said the Egyptian.

Suddenly the bolts were again withdrawn—the door unclosed; Arbaces was in the open street; and poor Nydia once more started from her long watch.

"Wilt thou save him?" she cried, clasping her hands.

"Child, follow me home; I would speak to thee—it is for his sake I ask it."

"And thou wilt save him?"

No answer came to the thirsting ear of the blind girl; Arbaces had already proceeded far up the street; she hesitated a moment, and then followed his steps in silence.

"I must secure this girl," said he, musingly, "lest she give evidence of the philtre; as to the vain Julia, she will not betray herself."

36. Arbaces Seizes Ione

When the last duties of her brother were performed, Ione's mind awoke to thought of her affianced, and the dread charge against him.

Not attaching even a momentary belief to the unnatural accusation, but nursing the darkest suspicion against Arbaces, she felt that justice to her lover and to her murdered relative demanded her to seek the prætor, and communicate her impression, unsupported as it might be. Questioning her maidens, who had hitherto—kindly anxious to save her the additional agony—refrained from informing her of the state of Glaucus, she learned that he had been dangerously ill; that he was in custody, under the roof of Sallust; that the day of his trial was appointed.

"Averting gods!" she exclaimed; "and have I been so long forgetful? Have I seemed to shun him? O! Let me hasten to do him justice—to show that I, the nearest relative of the dead, believe him innocent of the charge. Let me soothe—tend—cheer him! and if they will not believe me; if they will not yield to my conviction; if they sentence him to exile or to death, let me share the sentence!"

Instinctively she hastened her pace, confused and bewildered, scarce knowing whither she went; now designing first to seek the prætor, and now to rush to the chamber of Glaucus. She hurried on—she passed the gate of the city—she was in the long street leading up the town. The houses were opened, but no one was yet astir in the streets; the life of the city was scarce awake—when lo! She came suddenly upon a small knot of men standing beside a covered litter. A tall figure stepped from the midst of them, and Ione beheld Arbaces.

"Fair Ione!" said he, gently, not appearing to heed her alarm; "my ward, my pupil! forgive me if I disturb thy pious sorrows; but the prætor, solicitous of thy honour, and anxious that thou mayst not rashly be implicated in the coming trial; knowing the strange embarrassment of thy state (seeking justice for thy brother, but dreading punishment to thy betrothed)—sympathizing, too, with thy unprotected and friendless condition, and deeming it harsh that thou shouldst be suffered to act unguided and mourn alone—hath wisely and paternally confided thee to the care of thy lawful guardian. Behold the writing which intrusts thee to my charge!"

"Dark Egyptian!" cried Ione, drawing herself proudly aside; "begone! It is thou that hast slain my brother! Is it to thy care, thy hands yet reeking with his blood, that they will give the sister? Ha! thou turnest pale! Thy conscience smites thee! Pass on, and leave me to my woe!"

"Thy sorrows unstring thy reason, Ione," said Arbaces, attempting in vain his usual calmness of tone. "I forgive thee. Thou wilt find me now, as ever, thy surest friend. But the public streets are not the fitting place for us to confer—for me to console thee. Approach, slaves! Come, my sweet charge, the litter awaits thee."

Her amazed and terrified attendants gathered round her, and clung to her knees.

"Arbaces," said the eldest of the maidens, "this is surely not the law! For nine days after the funeral, is it not written that the relatives of the deceased shall not be molested in their homes, or interrupted in their solitary grief?"

"Woman!" returned Arbaces, imperiously waving his hand, "to place a ward under the roof of her guardian is not against the funeral laws. I tell thee I have the fiat of the prætor. This delay is indecorous. Place her in the litter."

So saying, he threw his arm firmly round the shrinking form of Ione. She drew back, gazed earnestly in his face, and then burst into hysterical laughter:

"Ha, ha! This is well—well! Excellent guardian—paternal law! Ha, ha!" And, startled herself at the dread echo of that shrill and maddened laughter, she sank, as it died away, lifeless upon the ground. A minute more, and Arbaces had lifted her into the litter. The bearers moved swiftly on, and the unfortunate Ione was soon borne from the sight of her weeping handmaids.

37. An Adventure Happens to Ione

It will be remembered that, at the command of Arbaces, Nydia followed the Egyptian to his home, and conversing there with her, he learned from the confession of her despair and remorse, that her hand and not Julia's, had administered to Glaucus the fatal potion. At another time the Egyptian might have conceived a philosophical interest in sounding the depths and origin of the strange passion which, in blindness and slavery, this singular girl had dared to cherish; but at present he spared no thought from himself. As, after her confession, the poor Nydia threw herself on her knees before him, and be-sought him to restore the health and save the life of Glaucus—for in her youth and ignorance she imagined the dark magician all-powerful to effect both—Arbaces, with unheeding ears, was noting only the new expediency of detaining Nydia a prisoner until the trial and fate of Glaucus were decided. For if, when he judged her merely the accomplice of Julia in obtaining the philtre, he had felt it was dangerous to the full success of his vengeance to allow her to be at large—to appear, perhaps, as a witness—to avow the manner in which the sense of Glaucus had been darkened, and thus win indulgence to the crime of which he was accused—how much more was she likely to volunteer her testimony when she herself had administered the draught, and, inspired by love, would be only anxious, at any expense of shame, to retrieve her error and preserve her beloved! Besides, how unworthy of the rank and repute of Arbaces to be implicated in the disgrace of pandering to the passion of Julia, and assisting in the unholy rites of the Saga of Vesuvius! Nothing less, indeed, than his desire to induce Glaucus to own the murder of Apæcides, as a policy evidently the best both for his own permanent safety and his successful suit with Ione, could have led him to contemplate the confession of Julia.

As for Nydia, necessarily cut off by her blindness from much of the knowledge of active life, and who, a slave and stranger, was naturally ignorant of the perils of the Roman law, she thought rather of the illness and delirium of her Athenian, than of the crime of which she had vaguely heard him accused, or the chances of the impending trial. Poor wretch that she was, whom none addressed, none cared for, what did she know of the senate and the sentence—the hazard of the law—the ferocity of the people—the arena and the lion's den? She was accustomed only to associate with the thought of Glaucus everything that was prosperous and lofty—she could not imagine that any peril, save from the madness of her love, could menace that sacred head. He seemed to her set apart for the blessings of life. She only had disturbed the current of his felicity; she knew not, she dreamed not, that the stream, once so bright, was dashing on to darkness and death. It was therefore to restore the brain that she had marred, to save the life that she had endangered, that she implored the assistance of the great Egyptian.

"Daughter," said Arbaces, waking from his reverie, "thou must rest here; it is not meet for thee to wander along the streets, and be spurned from the threshold by the rude feet of slaves. I have compassion on thy soft crime—I will do all to remedy it. Wait here patiently for some days, and Glaucus shall be restored." So saying, and without waiting for her reply, he hastened from the room, drew the bolt across the door, and consigned the care and wants of his prisoner to the slave who had the charge of that part of the mansion.

Alone, then, and musingly, he waited the morning light, and with it repaired, as we have seen, to possess himself of the person of Ione.

His primary object with respect to the unfortunate Neapolitan was really that which he had stated to Clodius, to prevent her interesting herself actively in the trial of Glaucus, and also to guard against her accusing him, (which she would, doubtless, have done) of his former act of perfidy and violence towards her, his ward—denouncing his causes for vengeance against Glaucus—unveiling the hypocrisy of his character—and casting doubt upon his veracity in the charge which he had made against the Athenian. Not till he had encountered her that morning—not till he had heard her loud denunciations—was he aware that he had also another danger to apprehend in her suspicion of his crime. He hugged himself now in the thought that these ends were effected; that one, at once the object of his passion and his fear, was in his power. He believed more than ever the flattering promises of the stars; and when he sought Ione in that chamber in the inmost recesses of his mysterious mansion to which he had consigned her, he thought more of the loveliness which no frenzy could distort, than of the woe which he had brought upon her. In that sanguine vanity common to men who through life have been invariably successful, whether in fortune or love, he flattered himself that when Glaucus had perished—when his name was solemnly blackened by the award of a legal judgment, his title to her love forever forfeited by condemnation to death for the murder of her own brother—her affection would be changed to horror; and that his tenderness and passion, assisted by all the arts with which he well knew how to dazzle women's imaginations, might elect him to that throne in her heart from which his rival would be so awfully expelled. This was his hope: but, should it fail, his unholy and fervid passion whispered: "At the worst, now she is in my power."

"Yes," said he, striding to and fro his solitary chamber—"yes, the law that gave me the person of my ward gives me the possession of my bride. Far across the broad main will we sweep on our search after novel luxuries and unexperienced pleasures. Cheered by my stars, supported by the omens of my soul, we will penetrate to those vast and glorious worlds which my wisdom tells me lie yet untracked in the recesses of the circling sea. There may this heart, possessed of love, grow once more alive to ambition—there, amongst nations uncrushed by the Roman yoke, and to whose ear the name of Rome has not yet been wafted, I may found an empire, and transplant my ancestral creed; renewing the ashes of the dead Theban rule: continuing on yet grander shores the dynasty of my crowned fathers, and waking in the noble heart of Ione the grateful consciousness that she shares the lot of one who, far from the aged rottenness of this slavish civilization, restores the primal elements of greatness, and unites in one mighty soul the attributes of the prophet and the king."

From this exultant soliloquy, Arbaces was aroused to attend the trial of the Athenian.

The worn and pallid cheek of his victim touched him less than the firmness of his nerves and the dauntlessness of his brow; for Arbaces was one who had little pity for what was unfortunate, but a strong sympathy for what was bold. The congenialities that bind us to others ever assimilate to the qualities of our own nature. The hero weeps less at the reverses of his enemy than at the fortitude with which he bears them. All of us are human, and Arbaces, criminal as he was, had his share of our common feelings. Had he but obtained from Glaucus the written confession of his crime, which would, better than even the judgment of others, have lost him with Ione, and removed from Arbaces the chance of future detection, the Egyptian would have been willing to save his rival. Even now, his hatred was over—his desire of revenge was slaked; he crushed his prey, not in enmity, but as an obstacle in his path. Yet was he not the less resolved, the less crafty and persevering, in the course he pursued, for the destruction of one whose doom was become necessary to the attainment of his objects; and while, with apparent reluctance and compassion, he gave against Glaucus the evidence which condemned him, he secretly, and through the medium of the priesthood, fomented the popular indignation which made an effectual obstacle to the pity of the senate. He had sought Julia; he had detailed to her the confession of Nydia; he had easily, therefore, lulled any scruple of conscience which might have led her to extenuate the offence of Glaucus by avowing her share in his frenzy: and the more readily, for her vain heart had loved the fame and the prosperity of Glaucus—not Glaucus himself; she felt no affection for a disgraced man—nay, she almost rejoiced in a disgrace that humbled the hated Ione. If Glaucus could not be her slave, neither could he be the adorer of her rival. This was sufficient consolation for any regret at his fate. Volatile and fickle, she began again to be moved by the earnest suit of Clodius, and was not willing to hazard the loss of an alliance with that base but highborn noble by any public exposure of her past weakness and immodest passion for another. All things then smiled upon Arbaces—all things frowned upon the Athenian.

38. Nydia Is a Sorceress

When the Thessalian found that Arbaces returned to her no more—when she was left, hour after hour, to all the torture of that miserable suspense which was rendered by blindness doubly intolerable, she began, with outstretched arms, to feel around her prison for some channel of escape; and finding the only entrance secure, she called aloud, with the vehemence of a temper naturally violent, and now sharpened by impatient agony.

"Ho, girl!" said the slave in attendance, opening the door; "art thou bit by a scorpion? Or thinkest thou that we are dying of silence here, and only to be preserved, like the infant Jupiter, by a hullaba-loo?"

"Where is thy master? And wherefore am I caged here? Let me go forth!"

"Alas! Little one, has thou not seen enough of Arbaces to know that his will is imperial? He hath ordered thee to be caged; and caged thou art, and I am thy keeper. Thou canst not have liberty; but thou mayst have what are much better things—food and wine."

"*Proh Jupiter!*" cried the girl, wringing her hands; "and why am I thus imprisoned? What can the great Arbaces want with so poor a thing as I am?"

"That I know not, unless it be to attend on thy new mistress, who has been brought hither this day."

"What! Ione here?"

"Yes, poor lady; she likes it little, I fear. Yet, by the Temple of Castor! Arbaces is a gallant man to the women. Thy lady is his ward, thou knowest."

"Wilt thou take me to her?"

"She is ill-frantic with rage and spite. Besides, I have no orders to do so; and I never think for myself. When Arbaces made me slave of these chambers, he said: 'I have but one lesson to give thee—while thou servest me, thou must have neither ears, eyes, nor thought; thou must be but one quality—obedience.'"

"But what harm is there in seeing Ione?"

"That I know not; but if thou wantest a companion, I am willing to talk to thee, little one, for I am solitary enough in my dull cubicu-lum. And, by the way, thou art Thessalian—knowest thou not some cunning amusement of knife and shears, some pretty trick of telling fortunes, as most of thy race do, in order to pass the time?"

"Nay, but if thou wilt speak, that hast thou heard of the state of Glaucus?"

"Why, my master has gone to the Athenian's trial. Glaucus will smart for it!"

"For what?"

"The murder of the priest Apæcides."

"Ha!" said Nydia, pressing her hands to her forehead; "some-thing of this I have indeed heard, but understand not. Yet who will dare to touch a hair of this head?"

"That will the lion, I fear."

"Averting gods! What wickedness dost thou utter?"

"Why, only that, if he be found guilty, the lion, or maybe the tiger, will be his executioner."

Nydia leaped up as if an arrow had entered her heart; she uttered a piercing scream; then, falling before the feet of the slave, she cried, in a tone that melted even his rude heart:

"Ah! Tell me thou jestest—thou utterest not the truth—speak, speak!"

"Why, by my faith, blind girl, I know nothing of the law; it may not be as bad as I say. But Arbaces is his accuser, and the people desire a victim for the arena. Cheer thee! But what hath the fate of the Athenian to do with thine?"

"No matter, no matter—he hath been kind to me: thou knowest not then what they will do? Arbaces his accuser! O fate! The people—the people! Ah! They can look upon his face—who will be cruel to the Athenian! Yet was not Love itself cruel to him?"

So saying, her head drooped; she sank into silence; scalding tears flowed down her cheeks; and all the kindly efforts of the slave were unable either to console or distract her.

When his household cares obliged the ministrant to leave her room, Nydia began to recollect her thoughts. Arbaces was the accuser of Glaucus; Arbaces had imprisoned her here; was not that a proof that her liberty might be serviceable to Glaucus? Yes, she was evidently inveigled into some snare; she was contributing to the destruction of her beloved! Oh, how she panted for release! Fortunately, for her sufferings, all sense of pain became merged in the desire of escape; and as she began to revolve the possibility of deliverance, she grew calm and thoughtful. She possessed much of the craft of her sex, and it had been increased by her early servitude. What slave was ever destitute of cunning? She resolved to practise upon her keeper; and, calling suddenly to mind his superstitious query as to the Thessalian art, she hoped by that handle to work out some method of release. These doubts occupied her mind during the rest of the day and the long hours of night; and, accordingly, when Sosia visited her the following morning, she hastened to divert his garrulity into that channel in which it had before evinced a natural disposition to flow.

She was aware, however, that her only chance of escape was at night; and accordingly she was obliged, with a bitter pang at the delay, to defer till then her purposed attempt.

"The night," said she, "is the sole time in which we can well decipher the decrees of Fate—then it is thou must seek me. But what desirest thou to learn?"

"By Pollux! I should like to know as much as my master: but that is not to be expected. Let me know, at least, whether I shall save enough to purchase my freedom, or whether this Egyptian will give it me for nothing. He does such generous things sometimes. Next, supposing that be true, shall I possess myself of that snug taberna among the Myropolia which I have long had in my eye? 'Tis a genteel trade that of a perfumer, and suits a retired slave who has something of a gentleman about him?"

"Ay! So you would have precise answers to those questions?—there are various ways of satisfying you. There is the Lithomanteia, or Speaking-stone, which answers your prayer with an infant's voice; but, then, we have not that precious stone with us—costly is it and rare. Then there is the Gastromanteia, whereby the demon casts pale and deadly images upon water, prophetic of the future. But this art requires also glasses of a peculiar fashion, to contain the consecrated liquid, which we have not. I think, therefore, that the simplest method of satisfying your desire would be by the Magic of Air."

"I trust," said Sosia, tremulously, "that there is nothing very frightful in the operation? I have no love for apparitions."

"Fear not; thou wilt see nothing; thou wilt only hear by the bubbling of water whether or not thy suit prospers. First, then, be sure, from the rise of the evening star, that thou leavest the garden-gate somewhat open, so that the demon may feel himself invited to enter therein; and place fruits and water near the gate as a sign of hospitality; then, three hours after twilight, come here with a bowl of the coldest and purest water, and thou shalt learn all, according to the Thessalian lore my mother taught me. But forget not the garden-gate—all rests upon that: it must be open when you come, and for three hours previously."

"Trust me," replied the unsuspecting Sosia. "I know what a gentleman s feelings are when a door is shut in his face, as the cookshop's hath been in mine many a day; and I know, also, that a person of respectablllty, as a demon of course is, cannot but be pleased, on the other hand, with any little mark of courteous hospitality. Meanwhile, pretty one, here is thy morning's meal."

"And what of the trial?"

"Oh, the lawyers are still at it—talk, talk—it will last over till tomorrow."

"Tomorrow?—you are sure of that?"

"So I hear."

"And Ione?"

"By Bacchus! she must be tolerably well, for she was strong enough to make my master stamp and bite his lip this morning. I saw him quit her apartment with a brow like a thunderstorm."

"Lodges she near this?"

"No—in the upper apartments. But I must not stay prating here longer. *Vale!*"

39. A Wasp in the Spider's Web

The second night of the trial had set in; and it was nearly the time at which Sosia was to brave the dread Unknown, when there entered, at that very garden-gate which the slave had left ajar not, indeed, one of those mysterious spirits of earth or air, but the heavy and most human form of Calenus, the priest of Isis. He scarcely noted the humble offerings of indifferent fruit, and still more indifferent wine, which the pious Sosia had deemed good enough for the invisible stranger they were intended to allure. "Some tribute," thought he, "to the garden god. By my father's head! If his deityship were never better served, he would do well to give up the godly profession. Ah! Were it not for us priests, the gods would have a sad time of it. And now for Arbaces—I am treading a quick-sand but it ought to cover a mine. I have the Egyptian's life in my power—what will he value it at?"

As he thus soliloquized, he crossed through the open court into the peristyle, where a few lamps here and there broke upon the empire of the starlit night; and, issuing from one of the chambers that bordered the colonnade, suddenly encountered Arbaces.

"Ho! Calenus, seekest thou me?" said the Egyptian; and there was a little embarrassment in his voice.

"Yes, wise Arbaces—I trust my visit is not unseasonable?"

"Nay—it was but this instant that my freedman Callias sneezed thrice at my right hand; I knew, therefore, some good fortune was in store for me—and, lo! The gods have sent me Calenus."

"Shall we within to your chamber, Arbaces?"

"As you will; but the night is clear and balmy—I have some remains of languor yet lingering on me from my recent illness—the air refreshes me—let us walk in the garden—we are equally alone there."

"With all my heart," answered the priest; and the two passed slowly to one of the many terraces which, bordered by marble vases and sleeping flowers, intersected the garden.

"It is a lovely night," said Arbaces, "blue and beautiful as that on which, twenty years ago, the shores of Italy first broke upon my view. My Calenus, age creeps upon us—let us, at least, feel that we have lived."

"Thou, at least, mayst arrogate that boast," said Calenus, beating about, as it were, for an opportunity to communicate the secret which weighed upon him, and feeling his usual awe of Arbaces still more impressively that night, from the quiet and friendly tone of dignified condescension which the Egyptian assumed. "Thou, at least, mayst arrogate that boast. Thou hast had countless wealth—a frame on whose close-woven fibres disease can find no space to enter—prosperous love—inexhaustible pleasure—and, even at this hour, triumphant revenge."

"Thou alludest to the Athenian. Ay, with tomorrow's sun the fiat of his death will go forth. The senate does not relent. But thou mistakest: his death gives me no other gratification than that it releases me from a rival in the affections of Ione. I entertain no other sentiment of animosity against that unfortunate homicide."

"Homicide!" repeated Calenus, slowly and meaningly; and, halting as he spoke, he fixed his eyes upon Arbaces. The stars shone pale and steadily on the proud face of their prophet, but they betrayed there no change; the eyes of Calenus fell disappointed and abashed. He continued rapidly: "Homicide! It is well to charge him with that crime; but thou, of all men, knowest that he is innocent."

"Explain thyself," said Arbaces coldly; for he had prepared himself for the hint secret fears had foretold.

"Arbaces," answered Calenus, sinking his voice into a whisper, "I was in the sacred grove, sheltered by the chapel and the surrounding foliage. I overheard—I marked the whole. I saw thy weapon pierce the heart of Apæcides. I blame not the deed—it destroyed a foe and an apostate."

"Thou sawest the whole!" said Arbaces dryly: "So I imagined—thou wert alone?"

"Alone!" returned Calenus, surprised at the Egyptian's calmness. "And wherefore wert thou hid behind the chapel at that hour?"

"Because I had learned the conversion of Apæcides to the Christian faith—because I knew that on that spot he was to meet the fierce Olinthus—because they were to meet there to discuss plans for unveiling the sacred mysteries of our goddess to the people—and I was there to detect, in order to defeat them."

"Hast thou told living ear what thou didst witness?"

"No, my master; the secret is locked in thy servant's breast."

"What! Even thy kinsman Burbo guesses it not? Come, the truth!"

"By the gods—"

"Hush! We know each other—what are the gods to us?"

"By the fear of thy vengeance, then—no!"

"And why hast thou hitherto concealed from me this secret? Why hast thou waited till the eve of the Athenian's condemnation before thou hast ventured to tell me that Arbaces is a murderer? And, having tarried so long, why revealest thou now that knowledge?"

"Because—because—" stammered Calenus, colouring and in confusion.

"Because," interrupted Arbaces, with a gentle smile, and tapping the priest on the shoulder with a kindly and familiar gesture, "because, my Calenus (see now, I will read thy heart, and explain its motives), because thou didst wish thoroughly to commit and entangle me in the trial, so that I might have no loophole of escape: that I might stand firmly pledged to perjury and to malice, as well as to homicide; that having myself whetted the appetite of the populace to blood, no wealth, no power, could prevent my becoming their victim; and thou tellest me thy secret now, ere the trial be over, and the innocent condemned, to show what a desperate web of villany thy word tomorrow could destroy; to enhance in this, the ninth hour, the price of thy forbearance; to show that my own arts, in arousing the popular wrath, would, at thy witness, recoil upon myself, and that, if not for Glaucus, for me would gape the jaws of the lion! Is it not so?"

"Arbaces," replied Calenus, losing all the vulgar audacity of his natural character, "verily thou *art* a Magian; thou readest the heart as it were a scroll."

"It is my vocation," answered the Egyptian, laughing gently. "Well, then, forbear; and when all is over, I will make thee rich."

"Pardon me," said the priest, as the quick suggestion of that avarice, which was his master-passion, bade him trust no future chance of generosity; "pardon me; thou saidst right—we know each other. If thou wouldst have me silent, thou must pay something in advance, as an offer to Harpocrates. If the rose, sweet emblem of discretion, is to take root firmly, water her this night with a stream of gold."

"Witty and poetical!" answered Arbaces, still in that bland voice which lulled and encouraged, when it ought to have alarmed and checked, his griping comrade. "Wilt thou not wait the morrow?"

"Why this delay? Perhaps when I can no longer give my testimony without shame for not having given it ere the innocent man suffered, thou wilt forget my claim; and, indeed, thy present hesitation is a bad omen of thy future gratitude."

"Well, then, Calenus, what wouldst thou have me pay thee?"

"Thy life is very precious, and thy wealth is very great," returned the priest, grinning.

"Wittier and more witty. But speak out—what shall be the sum?"

"Arbaces, I have heard that in thy secret treasure below, beneath those rude Oscan arches, which prop thy stately halls, thou hast piles of gold, of vases, and of jewels, which might rival the receptacles of the wealth of the deified Nero. Thou mayst easily spare out of those piles enough to make Calenus among the richest priests of Pompeii, and yet not miss the loss."

"Come, Calenus," said Arbaces, winningly, and with a frank and generous air, "thou art an old friend, and hast been a faithful servant. Thou canst have no wish to take away my life, nor I a desire to stint thy reward: thou shalt descend with me to that treasury thou referrest me to; thou shalt feast thine eyes with the blaze of uncounted gold and the sparkle of priceless gems; and thou shalt, for thine own reward, bear away with thee this night as much as thou canst conceal beneath thy robes. Nay, when thou hast once seen what thy friend possesses, thou wilt learn how foolish it would be to injure one who has so much to bestow. When Glaucus is no more, thou shalt pay the treasury another visit. Speak I frankly and as a friend?"

"Oh, greatest, best of men!" cried Calenus, almost weeping with joy, "canst thou thus forgive my injurious doubts of thy justice, thy generosity?"

"Hush! One other turn, and we will descend to the Oscan arches."

40. Nydia Escapes

Impatiently Nydia awaited the arrival of the no less anxious Sosia. Fortifying his courage by plentiful potations, of a better liquor than that provided for the demon, the credulous ministrant stole into the blind girl's chamber.

"Well, Sosia, and art thou prepared? Hast thou the bowl of pure water?"

"Verily, yes: but I tremble a little. You are sure I shall not see the demon? I have heard that those gentlemen are by no means of a handsome person or a civil demeanour."

"Be assured! And hast thou left the garden-gate gently open?"

"Yes; and placed some beautiful nuts and apples on a little table close by."

"That's well. And the gate is open now, so that the demon may pass through it?"

"Surely it is."

"Well, then, open this door; there—leave it just ajar. And now, Sosia, give me the lamp."

"What! You will not extinguish it?"

"No; but I must breathe my spell over its ray. There is a spirit in fire. Seat thyself."

The slave obeyed; and Nydia, after bending for some moments silently over the lamp, rose and in a low voice chanted this invocation:

"Viewless spectre of the air,
Hear the blind Thessalian's prayer!
By Erictho's art, that shed
Dews of life when life was fled,
By Ione Ithaca's wise king,
Who could wake the crystal spring
To the voice of prophecy,
By the lost Eurydice,
Summon'd from the shadowy throng,
At the sound of magic song—
By the Colchian's awful charms,
When fair-hair'd Jason left her arms,
Spectre of the airy halls,
Humbly one who owns thee calls!
Breathe along the brimming bowl,
And instruct the fearful soul
In the shadowy things that be
Hidden in futurity.
Come, wild demon of the air,
Answer thy disciple's prayer,
That no god of air or earth—
Not the Paphian Queen of Mirth,
Nor the vivid Lord of Light,
Nor the triple Maid of Night,
Nor the Thunderer's self be now

Blest and honour'd more than thou!"

"The spectre *is* certainly coming," said Sosia. "I feel him running along my hair!"

"Place thy bowl of water on the ground. Give me thy napkin, and let me fold up thy face and eyes."

"Ay! That's the custom with these charms. Not so tight though: gently—gently!"

"There—thou canst not see?"

"See, by Jupiter! No! Nothing but darkness."

"Address, then, to the spectre whatever question thou wouldst ask him, in a low-whispered voice three times. If thy question be answered in the affirmative, thou wilt hear the water ferment and bubble before the demon breathes upon it; if in the negative, the water will be quite silent."

"But you will not play any trick with the water, eh?"

"Let me place the bowl under thy feet—so. Now thou wilt perceive that I cannot touch it without thy knowledge."

"Very fair. Bacchus! Befriend me. Thou knowest that I have always loved thee better than all the other gods, that I will dedicate to thee that silver cup I stole last year from the butler, if thou wilt but befriend me with this water-loving demon. And thou, O Spirit! Listen and hear me. Shall I be enabled to purchase my freedom next year? Thou knowest: for, as thou livest in the air, the birds have doubtless acquainted thee with every secret of this house—thou knowest that I have filched and pilfered all that I honestly—that is, safely—could lay finger upon for the last three years, and I yet want two thousand sesterces of the full sum. Shall I be able, O good Spirit, to make up the deficiency in the course of this year? Speak! Ha! Does the water bubble? No; all is still as a tomb. Well, then, if not this year in two years?—Ah! I hear something; the demon is scratching at the door; he'll be here presently. In two years, my good fellow? Come now, two; that's a very reasonable time. What! Dumb still! Two years and a half—three—four? Ill fortune to you, friend demon! You are not a lady, that's clear, or you would not keep silence so long. Five—six—sixty years? And may Pluto seize you! I'll ask no more." And Sosia, in a rage, kicked down the water over his legs. He then, after much fumbling, and more cursing, managed to extricate his head from the napkin in which it was completely folded—stared round—and discovered that he was in the dark.

"What, ho! Nydia; the lamp is gone. Ah, traitress; and thou art gone too; but I'll catch thee—thou shalt smart for this!"

The slave groped his way to the door; it was bolted from without: he was a prisoner instead of Nydia. What could he do? He did not dare to knock loud—to call out—less Arbaces should overhear him, and discover how he had been duped; and Nydia, meanwhile, had probably already gained the garden-gate, and was fast on her escape.

"But, thought he, "she will go home, or at least, be somewhere in the city. Tomorrow, at dawn, when the slaves are at work in the peristyle, I can make myself heard; then I can go forth and seek her. I shall be sure to find and bring her back, before Arbaces knows a word of the matter. Ah! That's the best plan. Little traitress, my fingers itch at thee: and so to leave only a bowl of water, too! Had it been wine, it would have been some comfort."

Meanwhile Nydia, with that singular precision and dexterous rapidity of motion which was peculiar to her, had passed lightly along the peristyle, threaded the opposite passage that led into the garden, and, with a beating heart, was about to proceed towards the gate, when she heard the sound of approaching steps, and distinguished the dreaded voice of Arbaces. She paused for a moment in doubt and terror; then it flashed across her recollection that there was another passage little used except for the admission of the fair partakers of the Egyptian's secret revels, which wound along the basement of that massive fabric towards a door which also communicated with the garden. By good fortune it might be open. At that thought, she hastily retraced her steps, descending the narrow stairs at the right, and was soon at the entrance of the passage. Alas! the door at the entrance was closed and secured. While she was yet assuring herself that it was locked, she heard behind her the voice of Calenus, and, a moment after, that of Arbaces in low reply. She could not stay there; they were probably passing to that very door. She sprang onward, and felt herself on unknown ground. The air grew damp and chill; this reassured her. She thought she might be among the cellars of the luxurious mansion, or, at least, in some rude spot not likely to be visited by its haughty lord, when, again, her quick ear caught steps and the sound of voices. On, on, she hurried, extending her arms, which now frequently encountered pillars of thick and massive form. With a tact, doubled in acuteness by her fear, she escaped these perils, and continued her way, the air growing more and more damp as she proceeded; yet, still, as she paused for breath, she heard the advancing stept and the indistinct murmur of voices. At length she was abruptly stopped by a wall that seemed the limit of her path. Was there no spot in which she could hide? No aperture? No cavity? There was none! She stopped, and wrung her hands in despair, then again, nerved as the voices neared upon her, she hurried on by the side of the wall; and coming suddenly against one of the sharp buttresses that jutted boldly forth, she fell to the ground. Though bruised, her senses did not leave her; she uttered no cry; nay, she hailed the accident that had led her to something like a screen; and creeping close up to the angle formed by the buttress, so that on one side at least she was sheltered from view, she gathered her slight form into its smallest compass, and breathlessly awaited her fate.

Meanwhile Arbaces and the priest were taking their way to that secret chamber whose stores were so vaunted by the Egyptian. They were in a vast subterranean hall; the low roof was supported by short, thick pillars of an architecture far remote from the Grecian graces of that luxuriant period. The single and pale lamp, which Arbaces bore, shed but an imperfect ray over the bare and rugged wall, in which the rude stones, without cement, were fitted curiously and uncouthly into each other. The disturbed reptiles glared dully on the intruders, and then crept into the shadow of the walls.

Calenus shivered as he looked around and breathed the damp, unwholesome air.

"Yet," said Arbaces, with a smile, perceiving his shudder, "it is these rude abodes that furnish the luxuries of the halls above. They are like the labourers of the world—we despise their ruggedness, yet they feed the very pride that disdains them."

"And whither goes yon dim gallery to the left?" asked Calenus; "in this depth of gloom it seems without limit, as if winding into Hades."

"On the contrary, it does but conduct to the upper day," answered Arbaces carelessly: "it is to the right that we steer."

The hall, like many in the more habitable regions of Pompeii, branched off at the extremity into two wings or passages; the length of which, not really great, was to the eye exaggerated by the sullen gloom against which the lamp faintly struggled. To the right the two comrades now directed their steps.

"The gay Glaucus will be lodged tomorrow in apartments not much drier, and far less spacious than this," said Calenus, as they passed by the very spot where, completely wrapped in the shadow of the broad projecting buttress, cowered the Thessalian.

"Ay, but then he will have dry room, and ample enough, in the arena on the following day. And to think," continued Arbaces, slowly, and very deliberately, "to think that a word of thine could save him, and consign Arbaces to his doom!"

"That word shall never be spoken," said Calenus.

"Right, my Calenus! It never shall," returned Arbaces, familiarly leaning his arm on the priest's shoulder: "and now, halt—we are at the door."

The light trembled against a small door deep set in the wall, and guarded strongly by many plates and bindings of iron, that intersected the rough dark wood. From his girdle Arbaces drew a small ring, holding three or four keys. Oh, how beat the griping heart of Calenus, as he heard the rusty wards growl as if resenting the admission to the treasures they guarded!

"Enter, my friend" said Arbaces, "while I hold the lamp on high, that thou mayst glut thine eyes on the yellow heaps."

The impatient Calenus did not wait to be twice invited; he hastened towards the aperture.

Scarce had he crossed the threshold, when the strong hand of Arbaces plunged him forward.

"*The word shall never be spoken!*" said the Egyptian, with a loud, exultant laugh, and closed the door upon the priest.

Calenus had been precipitated down several steps, but not feeling at the moment the pain of his fall, he sprang up again to the door, and beating at it fiercely with his clenched fist, he cried aloud in what seemed more a beast's howl than a human voice, so keen was his agony and despair: "Oh, release me, release me, and I will ask no gold!"

The words but imperfectly penetrated the massive door, and Arbaces again laughed. Then, stamping his foot violently, replied, perhaps to give vent to his long-stifled passions:

"All the gold of Dalmatia," cried he, "will not buy thee a crust of bread. Starve, wretch! Thy dying groans will never wake even the echo of these vast halls: nor will the air ever reveal, as thou gnawest, in thy desperate famine, thy flesh from thy bones, that so perishes the man who threatened, and could have undone, Arbaces! Farewell!"

"Oh pity—mercy! Inhuman villain; was it for this—?"

The rest of the sentence was lost to the ear of Arbaces as he passed backward along the dim hall. A toad, plump and bloated, lay unmoving before his path; the rays of the lamp fell upon its unshaped hideousness and upward eye. Arbaces turned aside that he might not harm it.

"Thou art loathsome and obscene," he muttered, "but thou canst not injure me: therefore thou art safe in my path."

The cries of Calenus, dulled and choked by the barrier that confined him, yet faintly reached the ear of the Egyptian. He paused and listened intently.

"This is unfortunate," thought he; "for I cannot sail till that voice is dumb forever. My stores and treasures lie, not in yon dungeon, it is true, but in the opposite wing. My slaves, as they move them, must not hear his voice. But what fear of that? In three days, if he still survive, his accents, by my father's beard, must be weak enough! No, they could not pierce even through his tomb. By Isis, it is cold! I long for a deep draught of the spiced Falernian."

With that, the remorseless Egyptian drew his gown more closely round him, and resought the upper air.

41. Nydia and Calenus

What words of terror, yet of hope, had Nydia overheard! The next day Glaucus was to be condemned; yet there lived one who could save him, and adjudge Arbaces to his doom, and that one breathed within a few steps of her hiding-place! She caught his cries and shrieks—his imprecations—his prayers, though they fell choked and muffled on her ear. He was imprisoned, but she knew the secret of his cell: could she but escape—could she but seek the prætor, he might yet in time be given to light, and preserve the Athenian. Her emotions almost stifled her; her brain reeled—she felt her sense give way—but by a violent effort she mastered herself; and after listening intently for several minutes, till she was convinced that Arbaces had left the space to solitude and herself, she crept on as her ear guided her to the door that had closed upon Calenus. Here she more distinctly caught his accents of terror and despair. Thrice she attempted to speak, and thrice her voice failed to penetrate the folds of the heavy door. At length finding the lock, she applied her lips to its small aperture, and the prisoner distinctly heard a soft tone breathe his name.

His blood curled—his hair stood on end. That awful solitude, what mysterious and preternatural being could penetrate? "Who's there?" he cried, in new alarm; "what spectre—what dread larva, calls upon the lost Calenus?"

"Priest," replied the Thessalian, "unknown to Arbaces, I have been, by the permission of the gods, a witness to his perfidy. If I myself can escape from these walls, I may save thee. But let thy voice reach mine ear through this narrow passage, and answer what I ask."

"Ah, blessed spirit," said the priest, exultingly, and obeying the suggestion of Nydia, "save me, and I will sell the very cups on the altar to pay thy kindness."

"I want not thy gold—I want thy secret. Did I hear aright?—Canst thou save the Athenian Glaucus from the charge against his life?"

"I can—I can—therefore (may the Furies blast the foul Egyptian!) hath Arbaces snared me thus, and left me to starve and rot!

"They accuse the Athenian of murder; canst thou disprove the accusation?"

"Only free me, and the proudest head of Pompeii is not more safe than his. I saw the deed done—I saw Arbaces strike the blow; I can convict the true murderer and acquit the innocent man. But if I perish, he dies also. Dost thou interest thyself for him? Oh, blessed stranger, in my heart is the urn which condemns or frees him!

"And wilt thou give full evidence of what thou knowest?"

"Will!—Oh! Were hell at my feet—yes! Revenge on the false Egyptian! Revenge! Revenge! Revenge!"

As Calenus shrieked forth those last words, Nydia felt that in his worst passions was her certainty of his justice to the Athenian. Her hearth beat: was it—was it to be her proud destiny to preserve her idolized—her adored? "Enough," said she; "the powers that conducted me hither will carry me through all. Yes, I feel that I shall deliver thee. Wait in patience and hope."

"But be cautious, be prudent, sweet stranger. Attempt not to appeal to Arbaces—he is marble. Seek the prætor—say what thou knowest—obtain his writ of search, bring soldiers, and smiths of cunning—these locks are wondrous strong! Time flies—I may starve—starve! If you are not quick! Go—go! Yet stay—it is horrible to be alone—the air is like a charnel—and the scorpions—ha! and the pale larvæ! Oh! Stay!"

"Nay," said Nydia, terrified by the terror of the priest, and anxious to confer with herself—"nay, for thy sake, I must depart. Take Hope for thy companion—farewell!"

So saying, she glided away, and felt with extended arms along the pillared space until she had gained the farther end of the hall and the mouth of the passage that led to the upper air. But there she paused; she felt that it would be more safe to wait awhile, until the night was so far blended with the morning that the whole house would be buried in sleep, and so that she might quit it unobserved. She, therefore, once more laid herself down, and counted the weary moments. In her sanguine heart, joy was the predominant emotion. Glaucus was in deadly peril—but *she* should save him!

42. Arbaces and Ione

When Arbaces had warmed his veins by large draughts of spiced and perfumed wine, he felt more than usually elated and exultant of heart. There is a pride in triumphant ingenuity, even though its object be guilty, and afterwards may come the horrible reactions of remorse.

But remorse was not a feeling which Arbaces was likely to experience for the fate of the base Calenus. He swept from his remembrance the thought of the priest's agonies and lingering death: he felt only that a great danger was past, and a possible foe silenced, all left to him now would be to account to the priesthood for the disappearance of Calenus; and this he imagined it would not be difficult to do. Calenus had often been employed by him in various religious missions to the neighbouring cities. On some such errand he could now assert that he had been sent, with offerings to the shrines of Isis at Herculaneum and Neapolis, placatory of the goddess for the recent murder of her priest Apæcides. When Calenus had expired, his body might be thrown, previous to the Egyptian's departure from Pompeii, into the deep stream of the Sarnus; and, if discovered, suspicion would probably fall upon the Nazarene atheists, as an act of revenge for the death of Olinthus at the arena. After rapidly running over these plans for screening himself, Arbaces dismissed from his mind all recollection of the wretched priest; and, animated by the success which had lately crowned his schemes, he surrendered his thoughts to Ione. The last time he had seen her, she had driven him from her presence by a reproaching and bitter scorn, which his arrogant nature was unable to endure. He now felt emboldened to renew that interview; for his passion for her was like similar feelings in other men—it made him restless for her presence, even though in that presence he were exasperated and humbled. From delicacy to her grief he laid not aside his dark and unfestive robes, but, renewing the perfumes on his hair, and arranging his tunic in its most becoming folds, he sought the chamber of the Neapolitan. Accosting the slave in attendance without, he inquired if Ione had retired to rest; and learning that she was up, and unusually quiet and composed, he ventured into her presence. He found his beautiful ward sitting before a small table, and leaning her face upon her hands in an attitude of thought. Yet the expression of the face itself possessed not its wonted bright and Psyche-like expression of sweet intelligence; the lips were apart—the eye vacant and unheeding—and the long dark hair, falling neglected and dishevelled upon her neck, gave by the contrast additional paleness to a cheek which had already lost the roundness of its contour.

Arbaces gazed upon her a moment. She, too, lifted up her eyes; and when she saw who was the intruder, shut them with an expression of pain, but did not stir.

"Ah!" said he, in a low and earnest tone, as respectfully nay, humbly, he advanced and seated himself at a little distance from the table—"Ah! That my death could remove thy hatred, then would I gladly die! Thou wrongest me, Ione; but I will bear the wrong without a murmur, only let me see thee sometimes. Chide, reproach, scorn me, if thou wilt—I will teach myself to bear it. And is not even thy bitterest tone sweeter to me than the music of the most artful lute? In thy silence the world seems to stand still—there is no earth, no life, without the light of thy countenance and the melody of thy voice."

"Give me back my brother and my betrothed," said Ione, in a calm and imploring tone, and a few large tears rolled unheeded down her cheeks

"Would that I could restore the one and save the other!" returned Arbaces, with apparent emotion. "Yes; to make thee happy I would renounce my ill-fated love, and gladly join thy hand to the Athenian's. Perhaps he will yet come unscathed from his trial." (Arbaces had prevented her learning that the trial had already commenced.) "If so, thou art free to judge or condemn him thyself. And think not, O Ione, that I would follow thee longer with a prayer of love. I know that it would be vain. Suffer me only to weep—to mourn with thee. Forgive a violence deeply repented, and that shall offend no more. Let me be to thee only what I once was—a friend, a father, a protector. Ah, Ione! Spare me and forgive."

"I forgive thee. Save but Glaucus, and I will renounce him. O mighty Arbaces! Thou art powerful in evil or in good; save the Athenian, and the poor Ione will never see him more." As she spoke, she rose with weak and trembling limbs, and, falling at his feet, she clasped his knees: "Oh! If thou really lovest me—if thou art human—remember my father's ashes, remember my childhood, think of all the hours we passed happily together, and save my Glaucus!"

Strange convulsions shook the frame of the Egyptian; his features worked fearfully—he turned his face aside, and said, in a hollow voice: "If I could save him, even now, I would; but the Roman law is stern and sharp. Yet if I *could* succeed—if I *could* rescue and set him free—wouldst thou be mine—my bride?"

"Thine?" repeated Ione, rising, "thine!—thy bride? My brother's blood is unavenged: *who* slew him? O Nemesis, can I even sell, for the life of Glaucus, the solemn trust? Arbaces—*thine*? Never."

"Ione, Ione!" cried Arbaces, passionately, "why these mysterious words?—why dost thou couple my name with the thought of thy brother's death?"

"My dreams couple it—and dreams are from the gods."

"Vain fantasies! Is it for a dream that thou wouldst wrong the innocent, and hazard thy sole chance of saving thy lover's life?"

"Hear me!" said Ione, speaking firmly, and with a deliberate and solemn voice: "if Glaucus be saved by thee, I will never be borne to his home a bride. But I cannot master the horror of other rites: I cannot wed thee. Interrupt me not; but mark me, Arbaces!— if Glaucus die, on that same day I baffle thine arts, and leave to thy love only my dust! Yes—thou mayst put the knife and the poison from my reach—thou mayst imprison—thou mayst chain me, but the brave soul resolved to escape is never without means. These hands, naked and unarmed though they be, shall tear away the bonds of life. Fetter them, and these lips shall refuse the air. Thou art learned—thou hast read how women have died rather than meet dishonour. If Glaucus perish, I will not unworthily linger. By all the gods of the heaven, and earth, and seal!"

High, proud, dilating in her stature, like one inspired, her air and voice struck awe into the heart of her listener.

"Brave heart!" said he, after a short pause; "thou art indeed worthy to be mine. Oh! That I should have dreamed of such a partner in my lofty destinies, and never found it but in thee! Ione," he continued rapidly, "dost thou not see that we are born for each other? Canst thou not recognize something kindred to thine own energy—thine own courage—in this high and self-depended soul? We were formed to unite our sympathies—formed to breathe a new spirit into this gross world—formed for the mighty ends which my soul, sweeping dawn the gloom of time, foresees with a prophet's vision. With a resolution equal to thine own, I defy thy threats of an inglorious suicide. I hail thee as mine own! Queen of climes undarkened by the eagle's wing, unravished by his beak, I bow before thee in homage and in awe—but I claim thee in worship and in love! Together will we cross the ocean—together will we found our realm; and far-distant ages shall acknowledge the long race of kings born from the marriage-bed of Arbaces and Ione!"

"Thou ravest! These mystic declamations are suited rather to some palsied crone selling charms in the market-place than to the wise Arbaces. Oh, Arbaces! Hear me, and be swayed!"

"Enough, Ione. All that I can do for Glaucus shall be done; but blame me not if I fail. Inquire of my foes, even, if I have not sought, if I do not seek, to turn aside the sentence from his head; and judge me accordingly. Sleep, then, Ione. Night wanes. I leave thee to its rest—and mayst thou have kinder dreams of one who has no existence but in thine."

Without waiting a reply, Arbaces hastily withdrew; afraid, perhaps, to trust himself further to the passionate prayer which racked him with jealousy, even while it touched him to compassion. But compassion came too late. Had Ione even pledged him her hand as his reward, he could not now, his evidence given—the populace excited—have saved the Athenian. Still, made sanguine by his very energy of mind, he threw himself on the chances of the future, and believed he should yet triumph over the woman who had so entangled his passions.

As his attendants assisted to unrobe him for the night, he thought of Nydia. He felt it was necessary that Ione should never learn of her lover's frenzy, lest it might excuse his imputed crime; and it was possible that her attendants might inform her that Nydia was under his roof, and she might desire to see her. As this idea crossed him, he turned to one of his freedmen:

"Go, Callias," said he, "to Sosia, and tell him, that on no pretence is he to suffer Nydia out of her chamber. But stay—first seek those in attendance upon my ward, and caution them not to inform her that the blind girl is under my roof. Go—quick!"

The freedman hastened to obey. After having discharged his commission with respect to Ione's attendants, he sought the worthy Sosia. He found him not in the little cell which was apportioned for his cubiculum; he called his name aloud, and from Nydia's chamber, close at hand, he heard his voice reply: "Oh, Callias, is it you that I hear?—the gods be praised! Open the door, I pray you!"

Callias withdrew the bolt, and the rueful face of Sosia obtruded itself.

"What!—in the chamber with that young girl, Sosia! *Prob pudor*! Are there no fruits ripe enough on the wall, but that thou must tamper with such green—?"

"Name not the little witch!" interrupted Sosia, impatiently, "she will be my ruin!" And he forthwith imparted to Callias the history of the Air Demon, and the escape of the Thessalian.

"Hang thyself, then, unhappy Sosia! I am just charged from Arbaces with a message to thee—on no account art thou to suffer her, even for a moment, from that chamber!"

"*Me miserum!*" exclaimed the slave. "What can I do!—by this time she may have visited half Pompeii. But tomorrow I will undertake to catch her in her old haunts. Keep but my counsel, my dear Callias."

"I will do all that friendship can, consistent with my own safety. But are you sure she has left the house? She may be hiding here yet."

"How is that possible? She could easily have gained the garden; and the door, as I told thee, was open. "Nay, not so; for, at that very hour thou specifiest, Arbaces was in the garden with the priest Calenus. I went there in search of some herbs for my master's bath tomorrow. I saw the table set out; but the gate I am sure was shut: depend upon it, that Calenus entered by the garden, and naturally closed the door after him."

"But it was not locked."

"Yes; for I myself, angry at a negligence which might expose the bronzes in the peristyle to the mercy of any robber, turned the key, took it away, and—as I did not see the proper slave to whom to give it, or I should have rated him finely—here it actually is, still in my girdle."

"Oh, merciful Bacchus! I did not pray to thee in vain, after all. Let us not lose a moment! Let us to the garden instantly—she may yet be there!"

The good-natured Callias consented to assist the slave; and after vainly searching the chambers at hand, and the recesses of the peristyle, they entered the garden.

It was about this time that Nydia had resolved to quit her hiding-place, and venture forth. Lightly, tremulously, holding her breath—now gliding by the flower-wreathed columns that bordered the peristyle—now darkening the still moonshine that fell over its tesselated centre—now ascending the terrace of the garden—now gliding amidst the gloomy and breathless trees, she gained the fatal door—to find it locked! We have all seen that expression of pain, of uncertainty, of fear, which a sudden disappointment of touch casts over the face of the blind. But what words can paint the intolerable woe which was now visible on the features of the Thessalian? Again and again her small, quivering hands wandered over the inexorable door. Poor thing that thou wert! in vain had been all thy noble courage, thy innocent craft, thy doublings to escape the hound and huntsman! Within but a few yards from thee, laughing at thy endeavours—thy despair—knowing thou wert now their own, and watching with cruel patience their own moment to seize their prey—thou art saved from seeing thy pursuers!

"Hush, Callias!—let her go on. Let us see what she will do when she has convinced herself that the door is honest."

"Look! she raises her face to the heavens—she mutters—she sinks down despondent! No! By Pollux, she has some new scheme! She will not resign herself! By Jupiter, a tough spirit! See, she springs up—she thinks of some other chance! I advise thee, Sosia, to delay no longer: seize her ere she quit the garden,—now!"

"Ah! Runaway! I have thee—eh?" said Sosia, seizing upon the unhappy Nydia.

As a hare's last cry in the fangs of the dogs—as the sharp voice of terror uttered by a sleep-walker suddenly awakened—broke the shriek of the blind girl, when she felt the abrupt grip of her jailer. It was a shriek of such utter agony, such entire despair, that it might have rung hauntingly in their ears forever. She felt as if the last plank of the sinking Glaucus were torn from his grasp. It had been a suspense of life and death; and death had now won the game.

"Gods! That cry will alarm the house! Arbaces sleeps full lightly. Gag her!" cried Callias.

"Ah! Here is the very napkin with which the young witch conjured away my reason! Come! That's right; now thou art dumb as well as blind."

And, catching the light weight in his arms, Sosia soon gained the house, and reached the chamber from which Nydia had escaped. There, removing the gag, he left her to a solitude so racked and terrible, that, out of Hades, its anguish could scarcely be exceeded.

43. The Dungeon

It was now late on the third and last day of the trial of Glaucus and Olinthus. A few hours after the court had broken up and judgment been given, a small party of the fashionable youth at Pompeii were assembled round the fastidious board of Lepidus.

"So Glaucus denied his crime to the last?" said Clodius.

"Yes: but the testimony of Arbaces was convincing; he saw the blow given," answered Lepidus.

"What could have been the cause?"

"Why, the priest was a gloomy and sullen fellow. He probably rated Glaucus about his gay life and gaming habits, and swore he would not consent to his marriage with Ione. High words arose;

Glaucus seems to have been full of the passionate god, and struck in sudden exasperation. The excitement of wine, the desperation of abrupt remorse, brought on the delirium under which he suffered for some days; and I can readily imagine, poor fellow, that, yet confused by that delirium, he is even now unconscious of the crime he committed! Such, at least, is the shrewd conjecture of Arbaces, who seems to have been most kind and forbearing in his testimony."

"Yes; he has made himself generally popular by it. But, in consideration of these extenuating circumstances, the senate should have relaxed the sentence."

"And they would have done so, but for the people; but they were outrageous. The priests had spared no pains to excite them; and they imagined—ferocious brutes!—because Glaucus was rich and a gentleman, that he was likely to escape; and therefore they were inveterate against him. It seems that he was never formally enrolled as a Roman citizen; and thus the senate is deprived of the power to resist the people, though, after all, there was but a majority of three against him. Ho! The Chian!"

"He looked sadly altered; but how composed and fearless!"

"Ay, we shall see if his firmness will last over tomorrow. But what merit is there in courage, when that atheistical hound, Olinthus, manifested the same?"

"The blasphemer! Yes," said Lepidus, with pious wrath, "no wonder that one of the decurions was, but two days ago, struck dead by lightning in a serene sky. The gods feel vengeful against Pompeii while the vile desecrator is alive within its walls."

"Yet so lenient was the senate, that had he but expressed penitence, and scattered a few grains of incense on the altar of Cybele, he would have been let off. I doubt whether these Nazarenes, had they the state religion, would be as tolerant to us, supposing we had kicked down the image of their Deity, blasphemed their rites, and denied their faith."

"They give Glaucus one chance, in consideration of the circumstances; they allow him, against the lion, the use of the same stylus wherewith he smote the priest."

"Hast thou seen the lion? Hast thou looked at his teeth and fangs, and wilt thou call *that* a chance? Why, sword and buckler would be mere reed and papyrus against the rush of the mighty beast! No, I think the true mercy has been not to leave him long in suspense; and it is fortunate for him that our benign laws are slow to pronounce, but swift to execute; and that the games of the amphitheatre had been, by a sort of providence, so long since fixed for tomorrow. He who awaits death dies twice."

"As for the atheist," said Clodius, "he is to face the grim tiger naked-handed. Well, these combats are past betting on! Who will take the odds?"

A peal of laughter announced the ridicule of the question.

"Poor Clodius!" said the host; "to lose a friend is something; but to find no one to bet on the chance of his escape is a worse misfortune to thee."

"Why, it is provoking; it would have been some consolation to him and to me to think he was useful to the last."

"The people," said the grave Pansa, "are delighted with the result. They were so much afraid the sports at the ampitheatre would go off without a criminal for the beasts; but now, to get two criminals is indeed a joy for the poor fellows! They work hard; they ought to have some amusement."

"There speaks the popular Pansa, who never moves without a string of clients as long as an Indian triumph. He is always prating about the people. Gods! He will end by being a Gracchus!"

"Certainly I am no insolent patrician," said Pansa, with a generous air.

"Well," observed Lepidus, "it would have been dangerous to have been merciful at the eve of a beast-fight. If ever *I*, though a Roman bred and born, come to be tried, pray Jupiter there may be either no beasts in the *vivaria*, or plenty of criminals in the jail."

"And pray," said one of the party, "what has become of the poor girl whom Glaucus was to have married? A widow without being a bride—that is hard!"

"Oh," returned Clodius, "she is safe under the protection of her guardian, Arbaces. It was natural she should go to him when she had lost both lover and brother."

"By sweet Venus, Glaucus was fortunate among the women! They say the rich Julia was in love with him."

"A mere fable, my friend," said Clodius, coxcombically. "I was with her today. If she ever conceived any feeling of the sort I flatter myself that I have consoled her."

"Hush, gentlemen!" said Pansa; "do you not know that Clodius is employed at the house of Diomed in blowing hard at the torch? It begins to burn, and will soon shine on the bright shrine of Hymen."

"Is it so?" said Lepidus. "What! Clodius become a married man?—Fie!"

"Never fear," answered Clodius; "old Diomed is delighted at the notion of marrying his daughter to a nobleman, and will come down largely with the sesterces. You will see that I shall not lock them up in the atrium. It will be a white day for his jolly friends, when Clodius marries an heiress."

"Say you so?" cried Lepidus; "come then, a full cup to the health of the fair Julia!"

While such was the conversation in the gaudy triclinium of Lepidus, far different the scene which scowled before the young Athenian.

After his condemnation, Glaucus was admitted no more to the gentle guardianship of Sallust, the only friend of his distress. He was led along the forum till the guards stopped at a small door by the side of the temple of Jupiter. The door opened in the centre in a somewhat singular fashion, revolving round on its hinges, like a modern turnstile, so as only to leave half the threshold open at once. Through this narrow aperture they thrust the prisoner, placed before him a loaf and pitcher of water, and left him in darkness, and, as he thought, in solitude. So sudden had been the revolution of fortune which had prostrated him from the height of youthful pleasure and successful love to the lowest abyss of ignominy, and the horror of a most bloody death, that he could scarcely convince himself that he was not held in the meshes of some fearful dream. His elastic and glorious frame had triumphed over a potion, the greater part of which he had fortunately not drained. He had recovered sense and consciousness, but still a dim and mistry depression clung to his nerves and darkened his mind. His natural courage and Greek nobility, enabled him to vanquish all unbecoming apprehension, and, in the judgment-court to face his awful lot with a steady mien. But the consciousness of innocence scarcely sufficed to support him when the gaze of men no longer excited his haughty valour, and he was left to loneliness and silence. He felt the damps of the dungeon sink chillingly into his enfeebled frame. *He*—the fastidious, the luxurious, the refined—he who had hitherto braved no hardship and known no sorrow. Beautiful bird that he was! why had he left his far and sunny clime—the olive-groves of his native hills—the music of immemorial streams? Why had he wantoned on his glittering plumage amidst these harsh and ungenial strangers, dazzling the eyes with his gorgeous hues, charming the ear with his blithesome song—thus suddenly to be arrested—caged in darkness—a victim and a prey—his gay flights forever over—his hymns of gladness forever stilled! The hoot of the mob, amidst whose plaudits he had so often guided his graceful car and bounding steeds, still rang gratingly in his ear. The cold and stony faces of his former friends still rose before his eyes. None now were by to soothe, to sustain, the admired, the adulated stranger. These walls opened but on the dread arena of a violent and shameful death. And Ione! Of her, too, he had heard naught; no encouraging word, no pitying message; she, too, had forsaken him; she believed him guilty—and of what crime?— the murder of a brother! He ground his teeth—he groaned aloud— and ever and anon a sharp fear shot across him. In that fell and fierce delirium which had so unaccountably seized his soul, which had so ravaged the disordered brain, *might he not*, indeed, unknowing to himself, have committed the crime of which he was accused? Yet, as the thought flashed upon him, it was as suddenly checked; for, amidst all the darkness of the past, he could distinctly recall the dim grove of Cybele, the upward face of the pale dead, the pause that he had made beside the corpse, and the sudden shock that felled him to the earth. He felt convinced of his innocence; and yet who, to the latest time, long after his mangled remains were mingled with the elements, would believe him guiltless, or uphold his fame? As he recalled his interview with Arbaces, and the causes of revenge which had been excited in the heart of that dark and fearful man, he could not but believe that he was the victim of some deep-laid and mysterious snare—the clue and train of which he was lost in attempting to discover: and Ione—Arbaces loved her—might his rival's success be founded upon his ruin? That thought cut him more deeply than all; and his noble heart was more stung by jealousy than appalled by fear. Again he groaned aloud.

A voice from the recess of the darkness answered that burst of anguish. "Who is my companion in this awful hour? Athenian Glaucus, is it thou?"

"So, indeed, they called me in mine hour of fortune: they may have other names for me now. And thy name, stranger?"

"Is Olinthus, thy co-mate in the prison as the trial."

"What, he whom they call the Atheist? Is it the injustice of men that hath taught thee to deny the providence of the gods?"

"Alas!" answered Olinthus: "thou, not I, art the true Atheist, for thou deniest the sole true God—the Unknown One—to whom thy Athenian fathers erected an altar. It is in this hour that I know my God. He is with me in the dungeon; His smile penetrates the darkness; on the eve of death my heart whispers immortality, and earth recedes from me but to bring the weary soul nearer unto heaven."

"Tell me," said Glaucus, abruptly, "did I not hear thy name coupled with that of Apæcides in my trial? Dost thou believe me guilty?"

"God alone reads the heart! But my suspicion rested not upon thee."

"On whom, then?"

"Thy accuser, Arbaces."

"Ha! Thou cheerest me; and wherefore?"

"Because I know the man's evil breast, and he had cause to fear him who is now dead."

With that Olinthus proceeded to inform Glaucus of the conversion of Apæcides, the plan they had proposed for the detection of the impostures of the Egyptian priest-craft, and of the seductions practised by Arbaces upon the youthful weakness of the proselyte. "Therefore," continued Olinthus, "had the deceased encountered Arbaces, reviled his treasons, and threatened detection, the place, the hour, might have favoured the wrath of the Egyptian, and passion and craft alike dictated the fatal blow."

"It must have been so!" cried Glaucus, joyfully. "I am happy."

"Yet what, o unfortunate, avails to thee now the discovery? Thou art condemned and fated; and in thine innocence thou wilt perish."

"But I shall *know myself* guiltless; and in my mysterious madness I had fearful, though momentary, doubts. Yet tell me, man of a strange creed, thinkest thou that, for small errors, or for ancestral faults, we are forever abandoned and cursed by the powers above, whatever name thou allotest to them?"

"God is just, and abandons not His creatures for their mere human frailty. God is merciful, and curses none but the wicked who repent not."

"Yet it seemeth to me as if, in the divine anger, I had been smitten by a sudden madness, a supernatural and solemn frenzy, wrought not by human means."

"There are demons on earth," answered the Nazarene, fearfully, "as well as there are God and His Son in heaven; and since thou acknowledgest not the last, the first may have had power over thee."

Glaucus did not reply, and there was a silence for some minutes. At length the Athenian said, in a changed, and soft, and half-hesitating voice: "Christian, believest thou, among the doctrines of thy creed, that the dead live again—that they who have loved here are united hereafter—that beyond the grave our good name shines pure from the mortal mists that unjustly dim it in the gross-eyed world—and that the streams which are divided by the desert and the rock meet in the solemn Hades, and flow once more into one?"

"Believe I that, O Athenian? No, I do not believe—I *know!* And it is that beautiful and blessed assurance which supports me now. O Cyllene!" continued Olinthus, passionately, "bride of my heart! Torn from me in the first month of our nuptials, shall I not see thee yet, and ere many days be past? Welcome, welcome, death, that will bring me to heaven and thee!"

There was something in this sudden burst of human affection which struck a kindred chord in the soul of the Greek. He felt, for the first time, a sympathy greater than that of mere affliction between him and his companion. He crept nearer towards Olinthus; for the Italians, fierce in some points, were not unnecessarily cruel in others: they spared the separate cell and the superfluous chain, and allowed the victims of the arena the sad comfort of such freedom and such companionship as the prison would afford.

"Yes," continued the Christian with holy fervour, "the immortality of the soul—the resurrection—the reunion of the dead—is the great principle of our creed—the great truth a God suffered death itself to attest and proclaim. No fabled Elysium—no poetic Orcus—but a pure and radiant heritage of heaven itself, is the portion of the good."

"Tell me, then, thy doctrines, and expound to me thy hopes," said Glaucus, earnestly.

Olinthus was not slow to obey that prayer; and there—as oftentimes in the early ages of the Christian creed—it was in the darkness of the dungeon, and over the approach of death, that the dawning Gospel shed its soft and consecrating rays.

44. A Chance for Glaucus

The hours passed in lingering torture over the head of Nydia.

Sosia, as if afraid he should be again outwitted, had refrained from visiting her until late in the morning of the following day, and then he but thrust in the periodical basket of food and wine, and hastily reclosed the door. That day rolled on, and Nydia felt herself pent—barred—inexorably confined, when that day was the judgement day of Glaucus, and when her release would have saved him! Yet knowing, almost impossible as seemed her escape, that the sole chance for the life of Glaucus rested on her, this young girl, frail, passionate, and acutely susceptible as she was—resolved not to give way to a despair that would disable her from seizing whatever opportunity might occur. She kept her senses; she took food and wine that she might sustain her strength—that she might be prepared.

She revolved scheme after scheme of escape, and was forced to dismiss all. Yet Sosia was her only hope, the only instrument with which she could tamper. He had been superstitious in the desire of ascertaining whether he would eventually purchase his freedom.

Blessed gods! Might he not be won by the bribe of freedom itself? Was she not nearly rich enough to purchase it? Her slender arms were covered with bracelets, the presents of Ione, and on her neck she yet wore that very chain which had occasioned her jealous quarrel with Glaucus, and which she had afterwards promised vainly to wear forever. She waited burningly till Sosia should again appear; but as hour after hour passed, and he came not, she grew impatient. Every nerve beat with fever; she could endure the solitude no longer—she shrieked aloud—she beat herself against the door. Her cries echoed along the hall, and Sosia, in peevish anger, hastened to see what was the matter.

"Ho! Ho! What is this?" said he, surlily. "Young slave, if thou screamest out thus, we must gag thee again. My shoulders will smart for it, if thou art heard by my master."

"Kind Sosia, chide me not—I cannot endure to be so long alone," answered Nydia; "the solitude appals me. Sit with me, I pray, a little while. Nay, fear not that I should attempt to escape; place thy seat before the door. Keep thine eye on me—I will not stir from this spot."

Sosia, who was a considerable gossip himself, was moved by this address. He pitied one who had nobody to talk with—it was his case too. He took the hint of Nydia, placed a stool before the door, leaned his back against it, and replied: "I do not wish to be churlish; and so far as a little innocent chat goes, I have no objection to indulge you. But mind, no tricks—no more conjuring!"

"No, no; tell me, dear Sosia, what is the hour?"

"It is already evening—the goats are going home."

"O gods! How went the trial?"

"Both condemned!"

Nydia repressed a shriek. "Well—well, I thought it would be so. When do they suffer?"

"Tomorrow, in the ampitheatre. If it were not for thee, little wretch! I should be allowed to go with the rest and see it."

Nydia leant back for some moments. Nature could endure no more—she had fainted. But Sosia did not perceive it, for it was the dusk of eve, and he was full of his own privations. He went on lamenting the loss of so delightful a show, and accusing the injustice of Arbaces for singling him out from all his fellows to be converted into a jailer; and ere he had half finished, Nydia, with a deep sigh, recovered the sense of life.

"Thou sighest, blind one, at my loss! Well, that is some comfort. As long as you acknowledge how much you cost me, I will endeavour not to grumble. It is hard to be ill-treated, and yet not pitied."

"Sosia, how much dost thou require to make up the purchase of thy freedom?"

"How much? Why, about two thousand sesterces."

"The gods be praised! Not more? Seest thou these bracelets and this chain? They are well worth double that sum. I will give them thee if—"

"Tempt me not: I cannot release thee. Arbaces is a severe and awful master. Who knows but I might feed the fishes of the Sarnus? Alas! All the sesterces in the world would not buy me back into life. Better a live dog than a dead lion."

"Sosia, thy freedom! Think well! If thou wilt let me out, only for one little hour!—let me out at midnight—I will return ere tomorrow's dawn; nay, thou canst go with me."

"No," said Sosia, "a slave disobeyed Arbaces, and he was never more heard of."

"But the law gives a master no power over the life of a slave."

"The law is very obliging, but more polite than efficient. I know that Arbaces airways gets the law on his side. Besides, if I am once dead, what law can bring me to life again!"

Nydia wrung her hands. "Is there no hope, then?" said she, convulsively.

"None of escape, till Arbaces gives the word."

"Well, then," said Nydia, quickly, "thou wilt not at least, refuse to take a letter for me: thy master cannot kill thee for that."

"To whom?"

"The prætor."

"To a magistrate? No—not I. I should be made a witness in court, for what I know; and the way they cross-examine the slave is by the torture."

"Pardon: I meant not the prætor—it was a word that escaped me unawares; I meant quite another person—the gay Sallust."

"Oh! And what want you with him?"

"Glaucus was my master; he purchased me from a cruel lord. He alone has been kind to me. He is to die. I shall never live happily if I cannot, in his hour of trial and doom, let him know that one heart is grateful to him. Sallust is his friend; he will convey my message."

"I am sure he will do no such a thing. Glaucus will have enough to think of between this and tomorrow without troubling his head about a blind girl."

"Man," said Nydia, rising, "wilt thou become free? Thou hast the offer in thy power; tomorrow it will be too late. Never was freedom more cheaply purchased. Thou canst easily and unmissed leave home: less than half an hour will suffice for thine absence. And for such a trifle wilt thou refuse liberty?"

Sosia was greatly moved. It was true that the request was remarkably silly; but what was that to him? So much the better. He could lock the door on Nydia, and, if Arbaces should learn his absence, the offence was venial, and would merit but a reprimand. Yet, should Nydia's letter contain something more than what she had said—should it speak of her imprisonment, as he shrewdly conjectured it would do—what then? It need never be known to Arbaces that he had carried the letter. At the worst, the bribe was enormous—the risk light—the temptation irresistible. He hesitated no longer—he assented to the proposal.

"Give me the trinkets, and I will take the letter. Yet stay—thou art a slave—thou hast no right to these ornaments—they are thy master's."

"They were the gifts of Glaucus; he is my master. What chance hath he to claim them? Who else will know they are in my possession?"

"Enough—I will bring thee the papyrus."

"No, not papyrus—a tablet of wax and a stylus."

Nydia was born of gentle parents. They had done all to lighten her calamity, and her quick intellect seconded their assertions. Despite her blindness, she had therefore acquired in childhood, though imperfectly, the art to write with the sharp stylus upon waxen tablets, in which her exquisite sense of touch came to her aid. When the tablets were brought to her, she painfully traced some words in Greek, the language of her childhood, and which almost every Italian of the higher ranks was then supposed to know. She carefully wound round the epistle the protecting thread, and covered its knot with wax; and ere she placed it in the hands of Sosia, she thus addressed him:

"Sosia, I am blind and in prison. Thou mayst think to deceive me—thou mayst pretend only to take the letter to Sallust—thou mayst not fulfil thy charge: but here I solemnly dedicate thy head to vengeance, thy soul to the infernal powers, if thou wrongest thy trust; and I call upon thee to place thy right hand of faith in mine, and repeat after me these words: 'By the ground on which we stand—by Orcus, the all-avenging—by the Olympian Jupiter, the all-seeing—I swear that I will honestly discharge my trust, and faithfully deliver into the hands of Sallust this letter! And if I perjure myself in this oath, may the 'full curses of heaven and hell be wreaked upon me!' Enough!—I trust thee—take thy reward. It is already dark—depart at once."

"Thou art a strange girl, and thou hast frightened me terribly; but it is all very natural; and if Sallust is to be found, I will give him this letter as I have sworn. By my faith, I may have my little peccadilloes! But perjury—no! I leave *that* to my betters."

With this Sosia withdrew, carefully shooting the heavy bolt; and, hanging the key to his girdle, he retired to his own den, enveloped himself from head to foot in a huge disguising cloak, and slipped out by the back way undisturbed and unseen.

The streets were dim and empty. He soon gained the house of Sallust. The porter bade him leave his letter, and be gone; for Sallust was so grieved at the condemnation of Glaucus that he could not on any account be disturbed.

"Nevertheless, I have sworn to give this letter into his own hands—do so I must!" And Sosia, well knowing by experience that Cerberus loves a sop, thrust some half dozen sesterces into the hand of the porter.

"Well, well," said the latter, relenting, "you may enter if you will; but, to tell you the truth, Sallust is drinking himself out of his grief. It is his way when anything disturbs him. He orders a capital supper, the best wine, and does not give over till everything is out of his head—but the liquor."

"An excellent plan—excellent! Ah, what it is to be rich! If I were Sallust, I would have some grief or another every day. But just say a kind word for me with the atriensis—I see him coming."

Sallust was too sad to receive company; he was too sad, also, to drink alone; so, as was his wont, he admitted his favourite freedman to his entertainment, and a stranger banquet never was held. For, ever and anon, the kind-hearted epicure sighed, whimpered, wept outright, and then turned with double zest to some new dish or his refilled goblet.

"My good fellow," said he to his companion, "it was a most awful judgment—heigh ho!—it is not bad that kid, eh? Poor, dear Glaucus! What a jaw the lion has too! Ah, ah, ah!"

And Sallust sobbed loudly—the fit was stopped by a counteraction of hiccoughs.

"Take a cup of wine, said the freedman.

"A thought too cold; but then how cold Glaucus must be! Shut up the house tomorrow—not a slave shall stir forth—none of my people shall honour that cursed arena—No, no!"

"Taste the Falernian—your grief distracts you. By the gods it does—a piece of that cheesecake."

It was at this auspicious moment that Sosia was admitted to the presence of the disconsolate carouser.

"Ho!—who art thou?"

"Merely a messenger to Sallust. I give him this billet from a young female. There is no answer that I know of. May I withdraw?"

Thus said the discreet Sosia, keeping his face muffled in his cloak, and speaking with a feigned voice, so that he might not hereafter be recognized.

"By the gods—a pimp! Unfeeling wretch!—do you not see my sorrows? Go!—and the curses of Pandarus with you!"

Sosia lost not a moment in retiring.

"Will you read the letter, Sallust?" said the freedman.

"Letter!—*which* letter?" said the epicure, reeling, for he began to see double. "A curse on these wenches, say I. Am I a man to think of"—(*hiccough*)—"pleasure, when, when—my friend is going to be eaten up?"

"Eat another tartlet."

"No, no! My grief chokes me!"

"Take him to bed," said the freedman; and, Sallust's head now declining fairly on his breast, they bore him off to his cubiculum, still muttering lamentations for Glaucus, and imprecations on the unfeeling overtures of ladies of pleasure.

Meanwhile Sosia strode indignantly homeward. "Pimp, indeed!" quoth he to himself. "Pimp! a scurvy-tongued fellow that Sallust! Had I been called a knave or thief, I could have forgiven it; but pimp! Faugh! There is something in the word which the toughest stomach in the world would rise against. A knave is a knave for his own pleasure? And a thief for his own profit; and there is something honourable and philosophical in being a rascal for one's own sake: that is doing things upon principle—upon a grand scale. But a pimp is a thing that defies itself for another—a pipkin that is put on the fire for another man's pottage! a napkin, that every guest wipes his hands upon! And the scullion says, 'by your leave,' too. A pimp! I would rather he had called me parricide! But the man was drunk, and did not know what he said; and, besides, I disguised myself. Had he seen it had been Sosia who addressed him, it would have been 'honest Sosia!' and, 'worthy man!' I warrant. Nevertheless, the trinkets have been won easily—that's some comfort! And, O goddess Feronia! I shall be a freedman soon! And then I should like to see who'll call me pimp!—unless, indeed, he pay me pretty handsomely for it."

While Sosia was soliloquizing in this high-minded and generous vein, his path lay along a narrow lane that led towards the amphitheatre and its adjacent palaces. Suddenly, as he turned a sharp corner, he found himself in the midst of a considerable crowd. Men, women and children, all were hurrying on, laughing, talking, gesticulating; and, ere he was aware of it, the worthy Sosia was borne away with the noisy stream.

"What now?" he asked of his nearest neighbour, a young artificer; "what now? Where are all these good folk thronging? Does any rich patron give away alms or viands tonight?"

"Not so, man—better still," replied the artificer; "the noble Pansa—the people's friend—has granted the public leave to see the beasts in their *vivaria*. By Hercules! They will not be seen so safely by some persons tomorrow!"

"'Tis a pretty sight," said the slave, yielding to the throng that impelled him onward; "and since I may not go to the sports tomorrow, I may as well take a peep at the beasts tonight."

"You will do well," returned his new acquaintance; "a lion and a tiger are not to be seen at Pompeii every day."

The crowd had now entered a broken and wide space of ground, on which, as it was only lighted scantily and from a distance, the press became dangerous to those whose limbs and shoulders were not fitted for a mob. Nevertheless, the women especially—many of them with children in their arms, or even at the breast—were the more resolute in forcing their way; and their shrill exclamations of complaint or objurgation were heard loud above the more jovial masculine voices. Yet, amidst them was a young and girlish voice, that appeared to come from one too happy in her excitement to be alive to the inconvenience of the crowd.

"Aha!" cried the young woman, to some of her companions, "I always told you so; I always said we should have a man for the lion; and now we have one for the tiger too! I wish tomorrow were come!"

"A jolly girl!" said Sosia.

"Yes," replied the young artificer, a curly-headed, handsome youth. "Yes," replied he, enviously; "the women love a gladiator. If I had been a slave, I would have soon found my schoolmaster in the lanista!"

"Would you, indeed?" replied Sosia, with a sneer. "People's notions differ!"

The crowd had now arrived at the destination; but as the cell in which the wild beasts were confined was extremely small and narrow, tenfold more vehement than it hitherto had been was the rush of the aspirants to obtain admittance. Two of the officers of the amphitheatre, placed at the entrance, very wisely mitigated the evil by dispensing to the foremost only a limited number of tickets at a time, and admitting no new visitors till their predecessors had sated their curiosity. Sosia, who was a tolerably stout fellow, and not troubled with any remarkable scruples of diffidence or good-breeding, contrived to be among the first of the initiated.

Separated from his companion, Sosia found himself in a narrow cell of oppressive heat and atmosphere, and lighted by several rank and flaring torches.

The animals, usually kept in different vivaria, were now, for the greater entertainment of the visitors, placed in one, but divided from each other by strong cages.

There they were, the fell grim wanderers of jungle and desert. The lion, who, as being more gentle by nature than his fellow-beast, had been more incited to ferocity by hunger, stalked restlessly and fiercely his narrow confines; his eyes were lurid with rage and famine; and as he paused and glared around, the spectators fearfully pressed backward, and drew their breath more quickly. But the tiger lay quiet and extended at full length in his cage, and only by an occasional play of his tail, or a long impatient yawn, testified any emotion at his confinement, or at the crowd which honoured him with their presence.

"I have seen no fiercer beast than yon lion even in the amphitheatre of Rome," said a gigantic and sinewy fellow who stood at the right hand of Sosia.

"I feel humbled when I look at his limbs," replied, at the left of Sosia, a lighter and younger figure, with his arms folded on his breast.

The slave looked first at one, and then at the other. "*Virtus in medio!*—virtue is ever in the middle!" muttered he to himself; a goodly neighbourhood for thee, Sosia—a gladiator on each side!"

"That is well said, Lydon," returned the huger gladiator; "I feel the same."

"And to think," observed Lydon, in a tone of deep feeling, "to think that the noble Greek, he whom we saw but a day or two since before us, so full of youth, and health, and joyousness, is to feast yon monster!"

"Why not?" growled Niger savagely; "many an honest gladiator has been compelled to a like combat by the emperor—why not a wealthy murderer by the law?"

Lydon sighed, shrugged his shoulders, and remained silent. Meanwhile the common gazers listened with staring eyes and lips apart: the gladiators were objects of interest as well as the beasts—they were animals of the same species; so the crowd glanced from one to the other—the men and the brutes: whispering their comments and anticipating the morrow

"Well!" said Lydon, turning away, "I thank the gods that it is not the lion or the tiger I am to contend with; even you, Niger, are a gentler combatant than they."

"But equally dangerous," said the gladiator, with a fierce laugh; and the bystanders, admiring his vast limbs and ferocious countenance, laughed too.

"That is as it may be," answered Lydon, carelessly, as he pressed through the throng and quitted the den.

"I may as well take advantage of his shoulders," thought the prudent Sosia, hastening to follow him: "the crowd always give way to a gladiator, so I will keep close behind, and come in for a share of his consequence."

The son of Medon strode quickly through the mob, many of whom recognised his features and profession.

"That is young Lydon, a brave fellow; he fights tomorrow," said one.

"Ah! I have a bet on him," said another; "see how firmly he walks!"

"Good luck to thee, Lydon!" said a third.

"Lydon, you have my wishes," half whispered a fourth, smiling (a comely woman of the middle class)—"and if you win, why, you may hear more of me."

"A handsome man, by Venus!" cried a fifth, who was a girl scarcely in her teens. "Thank you," returned Sosia, gravely taking the compliment to himself.

However strong the purer motives of Lydon, and certain though it be that he would never have entered so bloodly a calling but from the hope of obtaining his father's freedom, he was not altogether unmoved by the notice he excited. He forgot that the voices now raised in commendation might, on the morrow, shout over his death-pangs. By nature fierce and reckless, as well as generous and warm-hearted, he was already imbued with the pride of a profession which he fancied he disdained, and affected by the influence of a companionship which in reality he loathed. He saw himself now a man of importance; his step grew yet lighter, and his mien more elate.

"Niger," said he, turning suddenly, as they had now threaded the crowd; "we have often quarrelled; we are not matched against each other, but one of us, at least, may reasonably expect to fall—give us thy hand."

"Most readily," said Sosia, extending his palm.

"Ha! What fool is this? Why, I thought Niger was at my heels!"

"I forgive the mistake," replied Sosia, condescendingly: "don't mention it; the error was easy—I and Niger are somewhat of the same build."

"Ha! Ha! That is excellent! Niger would have slit thy throat, had he heard thee!"

"You gentlemen of the arena have a most disagreeable mode of talking," said Sosia: "let us change the conversation."

"Vah! Vah!" said Lydon, impatiently; "I am in no humour to converse with thee!"

"Why, truly," returned the slave, you must have serious thoughts enough to occupy your mind: tomorrow is, I think, your first essay in the arena? Well, I am sure you will die bravely!"

"May thy words fall on thine own head!" said Lydon, superstitiously, for he by no means liked the blessing of Sosia, "*Die!* No—I trust my hour is not yet come."

"He who plays at dice with death must expect the dog's throw," replied Sosia, maliciously. "But you are a strong fellow, and I wish you all imaginable luck; and so, *vale!*"

With that the slave turned on his heel, and took his way homeward.

"I trust the rogue's words are not ominous," said Lydon, musingly. "In my zeal for my father's liberty, and my confidence in my own thews and sinews, I have not contemplated the possibility of death. My poor father!—if I were to fall—"

As the thought crossed him, the gladiator strode on with a more rapid and restless pace, when suddenly, in an opposite street, he beheld the very object of his thoughts. Leaning on his stick, his form bent by care and age, his eyes downcast, and his steps trembling, the gray-haired Medon slowly approached towards the gladiator. Lydon paused a moment: he divined at once the cause that brought forth the old man at that late hour.

"Be sure, it is I whom he seeks," thought he. "He is horror-struck at the condemnation of Olinthus—he more than ever esteems the arena criminal and hateful—he comes again to dissuade me from the contest. I must shun him—I cannot brook his prayers—his tears."

He turned abruptly in an opposite direction. He paused not till he found himself on the summit of a small acclivity which overlooked the most gay and splendid part of that miniature city; and as there he paused, and gazed along the tranquil streets glittering in the rays of the moon (which had just arisen, and brought partially and picturesquely into light the crowd around the amphitheatre, at a distance, murmuring, and swaying to and fro), the influence of the scene affected him, rude and unimaginative though his nature was. He sat down upon the steps of a deserted portico, and felt the calm of the quiet hour restore him. Opposite, and near at hand, the lights gleamed from a palace in which the master now held his revels. The doors were open for coolness, and the gladiator beheld a numerous festive group gathered round the table in the atrium; while behind them, closing the long vista of the illuminated rooms, the spray of the distant fountain sparkled in the moonbeams. There the garlands wreathed around the columns of the hall—there gleamed still and frequent the marble statue—there, amidst peals of jocund laughter, rose the music and the lay:

"Away with your stories of Hades,
Which the Flamen has forced to affright us—
We laugh at your three Maiden Ladies,
Your Fates—and your sullen Cocytus.

Poor Jove has a troublesome life, sir,
Could we credit your tales of his portals—
In shutting his ears on his wife, sir,
And opening his eyes upon mortals.

Oh, blest be the bright Epicurus!
Who taught us to laugh at such fables;
On Hades they wanted to moor us,
But his hand cut the terrible cables.

If, then, there's a Jove or a Juno,
They vex not their heads about us, man:
Besides, if they did, I and you know
'Tis the life of a god to live thus, man!

Content with the soft lips that love us,
This music, this wine, and this mirth, boys,
We care not for gods up above us—
We know there's no god for this earth, boys!"

While Lydon's piety (which, accommodating as it might be, was in no slight degree disturbed by these verses, which embodied the fashionable philosophy of the day) slowly recovered itself from the shock it had received, a small party of men, in plain garments and of the middle class, passed by his resting-place. They were in earnest conversation, and did not seem to notice or heed the gladiator as they moved on.

"O horror on horrors!" said one; "Olinthus is snatched from us! Our right arm is lopped away! When will Christ descend to protect his own?"

"Can human atrocity go farther?" said another; "to sentence an innocent man to the same arena as a murderer! But let us not despair; the thunder of Sinai may yet be heard, and the Lord preserve his saint. The fool has said in his heart, 'There is no God'."

At that moment out broke again, from the illumined palace, the burden of the revellers' song:

"We care not for gods up above us—
We know there's no god for this earth, boys!"

Ere the words died away, the Nazarenes, moved by sudden indignation, caught up the echo, and broke into one of their favourite hymns.

It was heard within, and brought silence to the startled hall of revel: the Christians swept on, and were soon hidden from the sight of the gladiator. Awed, he scarce knew why, by the mystic defiant hymn, Lydon, after a short pause, rose to pursue his way homeward.

Before him, how serenely slept the starlight on that lovely city! How breathlessly its pillared streets reposed in their security!—how softly rippled the dark green waves beyond!—how cloudless spread, aloft and blue, the dreaming Campanian skies! Yet this was the last night for the gay Pompeii! The colony of the hoar Chaldean! The fabled city of Hercules! The delight of the voluptuous Roman! Age after age had rolled, indestructive, unheeded over its head; and now the last ray quivered on the dial-plate of its doom! The gladiator heard some light steps behind—a group of females were wending homeward from their visit to the amphitheatre. As he turned, his eye was arrested by a strange and sudden apparition. From the summit of Vesuvius, darkly visible at the distance, there shot a pale, meteoric, livid light—it trembled an instant and was gone.

BOOK FIVE

45. The Dream of Arbaces

The awful night preceding the fierce joy of the amphitheatre rolled drearily away, and grayly broke forth the dawn of THE LAST DAY OF POMPEII! The air was uncommonly calm and sultry—a thin and dull mist gathered over the valleys and hollows of the broad Campanian fields. But yet it was remarked in surprise by the early fishermen, that, despite the exceeding stillness of the atmosphere, the waves of the sea were agitated, and seemed to run disturbedly back from the shore; while along the blue and stately Sarnus, whose ancient breadth of channel the traveller now vainly seeks to discover, there crept a hoarse and sullen murmur, as it glided by the laughing plains and the gaudy villas of the wealthy citizens. Clear above the low mist rose the time-worn towers of the immemorial town, the red-tiled roofs of the bright streets, the solemn columns of many temples, and the statue-crowned portals of the Forum and the Arch of Triumph. Far in the distance, the outline of the circling hills soared above the vapours, and mingled with the changeful hues of the morning sky. The cloud that had so long rested over the crest of Vesuvius had suddenly vanished, and its rugged and haughty brow looked without a frown on the beautiful scenes below.

Despite the earliness of the hour, the gates of the city were already opened. Horseman upon horseman, vehicle after vehicle, poured rapidly in; and the voices of numerous pedestrian groups, clad in holiday attire, rose high in joyous and excited merriment; the streets were crowded with citizens and strangers from the populous neighbourhood of Pompeii; and noisily—fast—confusedly swept the many streams of life towards the fatal show.

Despite the vast size of the amphitheatre, seemingly so disproportioned to the extent of the city, and formed to include nearly the whole population of Pompeii itself, so great, on extraordinary occasions, was the concourse of strangers from all parts of Campania, that the space before it was usually crowded, for several hours previous to the commencement of the sports, by such persons as were not entitled by their rank to appointed and special seats. And the intense curiosity which the trial and sentence of two criminals so remarkable had occasioned increased the crowd on this day to an extent wholly unprecedented.

While the common people, with the lively vehemence of their Campanian blood, were thus pushing, scrambling, hurrying on, yet, amidst all their eagerness, preserving, as is now the wont with Italians in such meetings, a wonderful order and unquarrelsome good-humour, a strange visitor to Arbaces was threading her way to his sequestered mansion. At the sight of her quaint and primæval garb—of her wild gait and gestures—the passengers she encountered touched each other and smiled; but as they caught a glimpse of her countenance, the mirth was hushed at once, for the face was as the face of the dead; and, what with the ghastly features and obsolete robes of the stranger, it seemed as if one long entombed had risen once more amongst the living. In silence and awe each group gave way as she passed along, and she soon gained the broad porch of the Egyptian's palace.

The black porter, like the rest of the world, astir at an unusual hour, started as he opened the door to her summons.

The sleep of the Egyptian had been unusually profound during the night; but, as the dawn approached, it was disturbed by strange and unquiet dreams, which impressed him the more as they were coloured by the peculiar philosophy he embraced.

He thought that he was transported to the bowels of the earth, and that he stood alone in a mighty cavern, supported by enormous columns of rough and primæval rock, lost, as they ascended, in the vastness of a shadow athwart whose eternal darkness no beam of day had ever glanced. And in the space between these columns were huge wheels, that whirled round and round unceasingly, and with a rushing and roaring noise. Only to the right and left extremities of the cavern, the space between the pillars was left bare, and the apertures stretched away into galleries—not wholly dark, but dimly lighted by wandering and erratic fires, that meteor-like, now crept (as the snake creeps) along the rugged and dark soil; and now leaped fiercely, darting across the vast gloom in wild gambols—suddenly disappearing, and as suddenly bursting into tenfold brilliancy and power. And while he gazed wonderingly upon the gallery to the left, thin, mist-like, ærial shapes passed slowly up; and when they had gained the hall they rose aloft, and vanished, as smoke vanishes, in the measureless ascent.

He turned in fear towards the opposite extremity—and behold! there came swiftly, from the gloom above, similar shadows, which swept hurriedly along the gallery to the right, as if borne involuntary adown the tide of some invisible stream; and the faces of these spectres were more distinct than those that emerged from the opposite passage; and on some was joy, and on others sorrow—some were vivid with expectation and hope, some unutterably dejected by awe and horror. And so they passed swiftly and constantly on, till the eyes of the gazer grew dizzy and blinded with the whirl of an ever-varying succession of things impelled by a power apparently not their own.

Arbaces turned away; and, in the recess of the hall, he saw the mighty form of a giantess seated upon a pile of skulls, and her hands were busy upon a pale and shadowy woof; and he saw that the woof communicated with the numberless wheels, as if it guided the machinery of their movements. He thought his feet, by some secret agency, were impelled towards the female, and that he was borne onwards till he stood before her, face to face. The countenance of the giantess was solemn and hushed, and beautifully serene. It was as the face of some colossal sculpture of his own ancestral sphinx. No passion—no human emotion, disturbed its brooding unwrinkled brow; there was neither sadness, nor joy, nor memory, nor hope; it was free from all with which the wild human heart can sympathize. The mystery of mysteries rested on its beauty—it awed, but terrified not; it was the Incarnation of the Sublime. And Arbaces felt his voice leave his lips, without an impulse of his own; and the voice asked:

"Who art thou, and what is thy task?"

"I am That which thou has acknowledged," answered, without desisting from its work, the mighty phantom. "My name is Nature, These are the wheels of the world, and my hand guides them for the life of all things."

"And what," said the voice of Arbaces, "are these galleries, that, strangely and fitfully illumined, stretch on either hand into the abyss of gloom?"

"That," answered the giant-mother, "which thou beholdest to the left, is the gallery of the Unborn. The shadows that flit onward and upward into the world are the souls that pass from the long eternity of being to their destined pilgrimage on earth. That which thou beholdest to thy right, wherein the shadows descending from above sweep on, equally unknown and dim, is the gallery of the dead!"

"And, wherefore," said the voice of Arbaces, "yon wandering lights that so wildly break the darkness; but only break, not reveal?"

"Dark fool of human science! Dreamer of the stars, and would-be decipherer of the heart and origin of things! Those lights are but the glimmerings of such knowledge as is vouchsafed to Nature to work her way, to trace enough of the past and future to give providence to her designs. Judge, then, puppet as thou art, what lights are reserved for thee!"

Arbaces felt himself tremble as he asked again: "Wherefore am I here?"

"It is the forecast of thy soul—the prescience of thy rushing doom—the shadow of thy fate lengthening into eternity as it declines from earth."

Ere he could answer, Arbaces felt a rushing wind sweep down the cavern, as the winds of a giant god. Borne aloft from the ground, and whirled on high as a leaf in the storms of autumn, he beheld himself in the midst of the spectres of the dead, and hurrying with them along the length of gloom. As in vain and impotent despair he struggled against the impelling power, he thought the wind grew into something like a shape—a spectral outline of the wings and talons of an eagle, with limbs floating far and indistinctly along the air, and eyes that, alone clearly and vividly seen, glared stonily and remorselessly on his own.

"What art thou?" again said the voice of the Egyptian.

"I am that which thou hast acknowledged," the spectre answered, laughing aloud, "and my name is *Necessity*."

"To what dost thou bear me?"

"To the unknown."

"To happiness or to woe?"

"As thou hast sown, so shalt thou reap."

"Dread thing, not so! If thou art the ruler of life, thine are my misdeeds, not mine."

"I am but the breath of God!" answered the mighty wind.

"Then is my wisdom vain!" groaned the dreamer.

"The husbandman accuses not fate, when, having sown thistles, he reaps not corn. Thou hast sown crime, accuse not fate if thou reapest not the harvest of virtue."

The scene suddenly changed. Arbaces was in a place of human bones; and lo! in the midst of them was a skull, and the skull, still retaining its fleshless hollows, assumed slowly, and in the mysterious confusion of a dream, the face of Apæcides; and forth from the grinning jaws there crept a small worm, and it crawled to the feet of Arbaces. He attempted to stamp on it and crush it; but it became longer and larger with that attempt. It swelled and bloated until it grew into a vast serpent: it coiled itself round his limbs; it crunched his bones; it raised its glaring eyes and poisonous jaws to his face. He writhed in vain; he withered—he gasped—beneath the influence of the blighting breath—he felt himself blasted to death. And then a voice came from the reptile, which still bore the face of Apæcides, and rang in his reeling ear: *"Thy victim is thy judge! The worm thou wouldst crush becomes the serpent that devours thee!"*

With a shriek of wrath and woe, and despairing resistance, Arbaces awoke—his hair on end—his brow bathed in dew—his eyes glazed and staring—his mighty frame quivering beneath the agony of that dream. He awoke he collected himself—he blessed the gods whom he disbelieved, that it was but a dream—he saw the dawning light break through his small but lofty window—he rejoiced—he smiled—his eyes fell, and opposite to him he beheld the ghastly features, the lifeless eye, the livid lip of the Hag of Vesuvius.

"Ha!" he cried, placing his hands before his eyes, as to shut out the grisly vision, "do I dream still?—Am I with the dead?"

"Mighty Hermes—no! Thou art with one death-like, but not dead. Recognize thy friend and slave."

There was a long silence. Slowly the shudders that passed over the limbs of the Egyptian chased each other away till he was himself again.

"It was a dream," said he. "Well—let me dream no more, or the day cannot compensate for the pangs of night. Woman, how comest thou here, and wherefore?"

"I came to warn thee," answered the sepulchral voice of the saga.

"Warn me! The dream lied not, then? Of what peril?"

"Listen to me. Some evil hangs over this fated city. Fly while it be time. Thou knowest that I hold my home on that mountain beneath which old tradition saith there yet burn the fires of the river of Phlegethon; and in my cavern is a vast abyss, and in that abyss I have of late marked a red and dull stream creep slowly, slowly on; and heard many and mighty sounds hissing and roaring through the gloom. But last night, as I looked thereon, behold the stream was no longer dull, but intensely and fiercely luminous; and while I gazed, the beast that lived with me, and was cowering at my side, uttered a shrill howl, and fell down and died, and slaver and froth were round his lips. I crept back to my lair; but I heard, all the night, the rock shake and tremble; and though the air was heavy and still, there were the hissings of pent winds, and the grinding as of wheels, beneath the ground. So, when I rose, I looked again down the abyss, and I saw vast fragments of stone borne on the lurid stream; and the stream itself was broader, fiercer, redder than before. Then I went forth, and ascended to the summit of the rock; and in that summit there appeared a vast hollow, which I had never perceived before, from which curled a dim smoke; and the vapour was deathly, and I gasped, and sickened, and nearly died. I returned home, I took my gold and my drugs, and left the habitation of many years; for I remembered the dark Etruscan prophecy which saith: 'When the mountain opens, the city shall fall—when the smoke crowns the Hill of the Parched Fields, there shall be woe and weeping in the hearths of the Children of the Sea.' Dread master, ere I leave these walls for some more distant dwelling, I come to thee. Be warned and fly!"

"Witch, I thank thee for thy care of one ungrateful. On yon table stands a cup of gold; take it, it is thine. I dreamt not that there lived one, out of the priesthood of Isis, who would have saved Arbaces from destruction. The signs thou hast seen in the bed of the extinct volcano surely tell of some coming danger to the city; perhaps another earthquake fiercer than the last. Be that as it may, there is a new reason for my hastening from these walls. After this day I will prepare my departure. Daughter of Etruria, whither wendest thou?"

"I shall cross over to Herculaneum, and, wandering thence along the coast, shall seek out a new home. I am friendless; my two companions, the fox and the snake, are dead. Great Hermes! Thou hast promised me twenty additional years of life!"

"Ay," said the Egyptian, "I have promised thee. But, woman," he added, lifting himself upon his arm, and gazing curiously on her face, "tell me, I pray thee, wherefore thou wishest to live? What sweets dost thou discover in existence?"

"It is not life that is sweet, but death that is awful," replied the hag, in a sharp, impressive tone, that struck forcibly upon the heart of the vain star-seer. He winced at the truth of the reply; and, no longer anxious to retain so uninviting a companion, he said: "Time wanes; I must prepare for the solemn spectacle of this day. Sister, farewell! Enjoy thyself as thou canst over the ashes of life."

The hag, who had placed the costly gift of Arbaces in the loose folds of her vest, now rose to depart. When she had gained the door she paused, turned back, and said: "This may be the last time we meet on earth; but whither flieth the flame when it leaves the ashes? Wandering to and fro, up and down, as an exhalation on the morass, it may be seen in the marshes of the lake below; and the Witch and the Magian, the pupil and the master, the great one and the accursed one, may meet again. Farewell!"

"Out, croaker!" muttered Arbaces, as the door closed on the hag's tattered robes; and, impatient of his own thoughts, not yet recovered from the dream, he hastily summoned his slaves.

It was the custom to attend the ceremonials of the amphitheatre in festive robes, and Arbaces arrayed himself that day with more than usual care. His tunic was of the most dazzling white, his many fibulæ were formed from the most precious stones; over his tunic flowed a loose eastern robe, half-gown, half-mantle, glowing in the richest hues of the Tyrian dye; and the sandals, that reached halfway up the knee; were studded with gems and inlaid with gold. In the quackeries that belonged to his priestly genius, Arbaces never neglected, on great occasions, the arts which dazzle and impose upon the vulgar; and on this day, that was forever to release him, by the sacrifice of Glaucus, from the fear of a rival and the chance of detection, he felt that he was arraying himself as for a triumph or a nuptial feast.

It was the custom for men of rank to be accompanied to the shows of the amphitheatre by a procession of their slaves and freedmen; and the long family of Arbaces were already arranged in order, to attend the litter of their lord.

Only, to their great chagrin, the slaves in attendance on Ione, and Sosia, as jailer to Nydia, were condemned to remain at home.

"Callias," said Arbaces, apart to his freedman, who was buckling on his girdle, "I am weary of Pompeii; I propose to quit it in three days, should the wind favour. Thou knowest the vessel that lies in the harbour which belonged to Narses of Alexandria; I have purchased it of him. The day after tomorrow, we shall begin to remove my stores."

"So soon! 'Tis well. Arbaces shall be obeyed—and his ward, Ione?"

"Accompanies me. Enough! Is the morning fair?"

"Dim and oppressive; it will probably be intensely hot in the forenoon."

"The poor gladiators, and more wretched criminals! Descend, and see that the slaves are marshalled."

Left alone, Arbaces stepped into his chamber of study, and thence upon the portico without. He saw the dense masses of men pouring fast into the amphitheatre, and heard the cry of the assistants, and the cracking of the cordage, as they were straining aloft the huge awning under which the citizens, molested by no discomforting rays, were to behold, at luxurious ease, the agonies of their fellow-creatures. Suddenly a wild strange sound went forth, and as suddenly died away—it was the roar of the lion. There was a silence in the distant crowd; but the silence was followed by joyous laughter—they were making merry at the hungry impatience of the royal beast.

"Brutes!" muttered the disdainful Arbaces, "are ye less homicides that I am? *I* slay but in self-defence—ye make murder a pastime."

He turned towards Vesuvius with restless and curious eyes. Beautifully glowed the green vineyards round its breast, and tranquil as eternity lay in the breathless skies the form of the mighty hill.

"We have time yet, if the earthquake be nursing," thought Arbaces; and he turned from the spot. He passed by the table which bore his mystic scrolls and Chaldean calculations.

"August art!" he thought, "I have not consulted thy decrees since I passed the danger and the crisis they fore-told. What matter?—I know that *henceforth* all in my path is bright and smooth. Have not events already proved it? Away, doubt—away, pity! Reflect, O my heart—reflect, for the future but two images—Empire and Ione!"

46. The Amphitheatre

Nydia, assured by the account of Sosia, and satisfied that her letter was in the hands of Sallust, gave herself up once more to hope. Sallust would surely lose no time in seeking the prætor—in coming to the house of the Egyptian—in releasing her—in breaking the prison of Calenus. That very night Glaucus would be free. Alas! The night passed—the dawn broke; she heard nothing but the hurried footsteps of the slaves along the hall and peristyle, and their voices in preparation for the show. By and by, the commanding voice of Arbaces broke on her ear—a flourish of music rang out cheerily; the long processions were sweeping to the amphitheatre to glut their eyes on the death-pangs of the Athenian!

The procession of Arbaces moved along slowly, and with much solemnity, till now, arriving at the place where it was necessary for such as came in litters or chariots to alight, he descended from his vehicle, and proceeded to the entrance by which the more distinguished spectators were admitted. His slaves, mingling with the humbler crowd, were stationed by the officers who received their tickets in places in the *popularia*—the seats apportioned to the vulgar. From the spot where Arbaces sat, his eyes scanned the mighty, impatient crowd that filled the stupendous theatre.

On the upper tier (but apart from the male spectators) sat the women, their gay dresses resembling some gaudy flower-bed; it is needless to add that they were the most talkative part of the assembly; and many were the looks directed up to them, especially from the benches appropriated to the young and unmarried men. On the lower seats round the arena sat the more high-born and wealthy visitors—the magistrates and those of senatorial or equestrian dignity: the passages which, by corridors at the right and left, gave access to these seats, at either end of the oval arena, were also the entrances for the combatants. Strong palings at these passages prevented any unwelcome eccentricity in the movements of the beasts, and confined them to their appointed prey. Around the parapet which was raised above the arena, and from which the seats gradually rose, were gladiatorial inscriptions, and paintings wrought in fresco, typical of the entertainments for which the place was designed. Throughout the whole building wound invisible pipes, from which, as the day advanced, cooling and fragrant showers were to be sprinkled over the spectators. The officers of the amphitheatre were still employed in the task of fixing the vast awning which covered the whole, and which luxurious invention the Campanians arrogated to themselves: it was woven of the whitest Apulian wool, and variegated with broad stripes of crimson. Owing either to some inexperience on the part of the workmen, or some defect in the machinery, the awning, however, was not arranged that day so happily as usual; indeed from the immense space of the circumference the task was always one of great difficulty and art—so much so, that it could seldom be adventured in rough or windy weather. But the present day was so remarkably still that there seemed to the spectators no excuse for the awkwardness of the artificers, and when a large gap in the back of the awning was still visible, from the obstinate refusal of one part of the *velaria* to ally itself with the rest, the murmurs of discontent were loud and general.

The ædile Pansa, at whose expense the exhibition was given, looked particularly annoyed at the defect, and vowed bitter vengeance on the head of the chief officer of the show, who fretting, puffing, perspiring, busied himself in idle orders and unavailing threats.

The hubbub ceased suddenly—the operators desisted—the crowd were stilled—the gap was forgotten—for now, with a loud and warlike flourish of trumpets, the gladiators, marshalled in ceremonious procession, entered the arena. They swept round the oval space very slowly and deliberately, in order to give the spectators full leisure to admire their stern serenity of feature—their brawny limbs and various arms, as well as to form such wagers as the excitement of the moment might suggest.

"Oh!" cried the widow Fulvia to the wife of Pansa, as they leaned down from their lofty bench, "do you see that gigantic gladiator? how drolly he is dressed!"

"Yes," said the ædile's wife with complacent importance, for she knew all the names and qualities of each combatant. "He is a *retiarius*; he is armed only, you see, with a three-pronged spear like a trident, and a net; he wears no armour, only the fillet and the tunic. He is a mighty man, and is to fight with Sporus, that thick-set gladiator, with the round shield and drawn sword, but without body armour; he has not his helmet on now, in order that you may see his face—how fearless it is—by and by he will fight with his visor down."

"But surely a net and a spear are poor arms against a shield and sword?"

"That shows how innocent you are, my dear Fulvia; the retiarius has generally the better of it."

"But who is yon handsome gladiator, nearly naked? By Venus! but his limbs are beautifully shaped!"

"It is Lydon, a young untried man! He has the rashness to fight the other gladiator similarly dressed, or rather undressed—Tetraides. They fight first in the Greek fashion, with the cestus; afterwards they put on armour, and use sword and shield."

"He is a proper man, this Lydon; and the women, I am surer, are on his side."

"So are not the experienced betters; Clodius offers three to one against him."

"Oh, Jove! how beautiful!" exclaimed the widow, as two gladiators, armed *cap-a-pié*, rode round the arena on light and prancing steeds. Resembling much the combatants in the tilts of the middle ages, they bore lances and round shields beautifully inlaid: their armour was woven intricately with bands of iron, but it covered only the thighs and the right arms; short cloaks, extending to the seat, gave a picturesque and graceful air to their costume; their legs were naked, with the exception of sandals fastened a little above the ankle. "Oh, beautiful! Who are these?" asked the widow.

"The one is named Berbix—he has conquered twelve times; the other assumes the arrogant name of Nobilior. They are both Gauls."

While thus conversing, the first formalities of the show were over. To these succeeded a feigned combat with wooden swords between the various gladiators matched against each other. Amongst these, the skill of two Roman gladiators, hired for the occasion, was the most admired; and next to them the most graceful combatant was Lydon. This sham contest did not last above an hour, nor did it attract any very lively interest, except among those connoisseurs of the arena to whom art was preferable to more coarse excitement; the body of the spectators were rejoiced when it was over; and when sympathy rose to terror.

The combatants were now arranged in pairs, as agreed beforehand; their weapons examined; and the grave sports of the day commenced amidst the deepest silence—broken only by an exciting and preliminary blast of warlike music.

It was often customary to begin the sports by the most cruel of all, and some bestiarius, or gladiator appointed to the beasts, was slain first, as an initiatory sacrifice. But, in the present instance, the experienced Pansa thought it better that the sanguinary drama should advance, not decrease in interest: and accordingly, the executions of Olinthus and Glaucus were reserved for the last. It was arranged that the two horsemen should first occupy the arena; that the foot gladiators, paired off, should then be loosed indiscriminately on the stage; that Glaucus and the lion should next perform their part in the bloody spectacle; and the tiger and the Nazarene be the grand finale. The spectacles of Pompeii could not, of course, equal the vast and wholesale exhibitions of magnificent slaughter with which a Nero or a Caligula regaled the inhabitants of the Imperial City. The Roman shows, which absorbed the more celebrated gladiators, and the chief proportion of foreign beasts, were indeed the very reason why, in the lesser towns of the empire, the sports of the amphitheatre were comparatively humane and rare; and in this, as in other respects, Pompeii was but the miniature, the microcosm of Rome. Still, it was an awful and imposing spectacle, with which modern times have, happily, nothing to compare—a vast theatre, rising row upon row, and swarming with human beings, from fifteen to eighteen thousand in number, intent upon no fictitious representation—no tragedy of the stage—but the actual victory or defeat, the exultant life or the bloody death, of all who entered the arena.

The two horsemen were now at either extremity of the lists; and, at a given signal from Pansa, the combatants started simultaneously as in full collision, each advancing his round buckler, each poising on high his light yet sturdy javelin; but just when within three paces of his opponent, the steed of Berbix suddenly halted, wheeled round, and, as Nobilior was borne rapidly by, his antagonist spurred upon him. The buckler of Nobilior, quickly and skilfully extended, received a blow which otherwise would have been fatal.

"Well done, Nobilior!" cried the praetor, giving the first vent to the popular excitement.

"Bravely struck, my Berbix!" answered Clodius from his seat.

And the wild murmur, swelled by many a shout, echoed from side to side.

The visors of both horsemen were completely closed, but the head was, nevertheless, the great point of assault; and Nobilior, now wheeling his charger with no less adroitness than his opponent, directed his spear full on the helmet of his foe. Berbix raised his buckler to shield himself, and his quick-eyed antagonist, suddenly lowering his weapon, pierced him through the breast. Berbix reeled and fell.

"Nobilior! Nobilior!" shouted the populace.

"I have lost ten sestertia," said Clodius, between his teeth.

"*Habet!*—he has it," said Pansa, deliberately.

The populace, not yet hardened into cruelty, made the signal of mercy; but as the attendants of the arena approached, they found the kindness came too late—the heart of the Gaul had been pierced, and his eyes were set in death. It was his life's blood that flowed so darkly over the sand and sawdust of the arena.

"It is a pity it was so soon over—there was little enough for one's trouble," said the widow Fulvia.

"Yes—I have no compassion for Berbix. Any one might have seen that Nobilior did but feint. Mark, they fix the fatal hook to the body—they drag him away to the spoliarium—they scatter new sand over the stage! Pansa regrets nothing more than that he is not rich enough to strew the arena with borax, and cinnabar, as Nero used to do."

"Well, if it has been a brief battle, it is quickly succeeded. See my handsome Lydon on the arena—ay, and the net-bearer, too, and the swordsmen! Oh, charming!"

There were now on the arena six combatants: Niger and his net, matched against Sporus with his shield and his short broadsword. Lydon and Tetraides, naked save for a cincture round the waist, each armed only with a heavy Greek cestus—and two gladiators from Rome, clad in complete steel, and evenly matched with immense bucklers and pointed swords.

The initiatory contest between Lydon and Tetraides being less deadly than that between the other combatants, no sooner had they advanced to the middle of the arena than, as by common consent, the rest held back, to see how that contest should be decided, and wait till fiercer weapons might replace the cestus, ere they themselves commenced hostilities. They stood leaning on their arms and apart from each other, gazing on the show, which, if not bloody enough thoroughly to please the populace, they were still inclined to admire, because its origin was of their ancestral Greece.

No person could, at first glance, have seemed less evenly matched than the two antagonists. Tetraides, though not taller than

Lydon, weighed considerably more, and the natural size of his muscles was increased, to the eyes of the vulgar, by masses of solid flesh; for, as it was a notion that the contest of the cestus fared easiest with him who was plumpest, Tetraides had encouraged to the utmost his hereditary predisposition to the portly. His shoulders were vast, and his lower limbs thick-set and slightly curved outward, in that formation which takes so much from beauty to give so largely to strength. But Lydon, except that he was slender even almost to meagreness, was beautifully and delicately proportioned; and the skilful might have perceived that, with much less compass of muscle than his foe, that which he had was more seasoned—iron and compact. In proportion, too, as he wanted flesh, he was likely to possess activity; and a haughty smile on his resolute face, which strongly contrasted the solid heaviness of his enemy's, gave assurance to those who beheld it, and united their hope to their pity; so that, despite the disparity of their seeming strength, the cry of the multitude was nearly as loud for Lydon as for Tetraides.

Whoever is acquainted with the modern prize-ring—whoever has witnessed the heavy and disabling strokes which the human fist, skilfully directed, has the power to bestow—may easily understand how much that facility would be increased by a band carried by throngs of leather round the arm as high as the elbow, and terribly strengthened about the knuckles by a plate of iron, and sometimes a plummet of lead. Yet this, which was meant to increase, perhaps rather diminished, the interest of the fray: for it necessarily shortened its duration. A very few blows, successfully and scientifically planted, might suffice to bring the contest to a close; and the battle did not, therefore, often allow full scope for the energy, fortitude and dogged perseverance which may win the day against superior science, and which heightens to so painful a delight the interest in the battle and the sympathy for the brave.

"Guard thyself!" growled Tetraides, moving nearer and nearer to his foe, who rather shifted round him than receded.

Lydon did not answer, save by a scornful glance of his quick, vigilant eyes. Tetraides struck—it was as the blow of a smith on a vice; Lydon sank suddenly on one knee—the blow passed over his head. Not so harmless was Lydon's retaliation; he quickly sprang to his feet, and aimed his cestus full on the broad breast of his antagonist. Tetraides reeled—the populace shouted.

"You are unlucky today," said Lepidus to Clodius; "you have lost one bet—you will lose another."

"By the gods! My bronzes go to the auctioneer if that is the case. I have no less than a hundred sestertia upon Tetraides. Ha, ha!

See how he rallies! That was a home stroke: he has cut open Lydon's shoulder. A Tetraides!—a Tetraides!"

"But Lydon is not disheartened. By Pollux! How well he keeps his temper! See how dexterously he avoids those hammer-like hands!—dodging now here, now there—circling round and round. Ah, poor Lydon! He has it again."

"Three to one still on Tetraides! What say you, Lepidus?"

"Well—nine sestertia to three—be it so! What! Again, Lydon. He stops—he gasps for breath. By the gods, he is down! No—he is again on his legs. Brave Lydon! Tetraides is encouraged—he laughs loud—he rushes on him."

"Fool—success blinds him—he should be cautious. Lydon's eye is like a lynx's!" said Clodius, between his teeth.

"Ha, Clodius! Saw you that? Your man totters! Another blow—he falls—he falls!"

"Earth revives him then. He is once more up; but the blood rolls down his face."

"By the thunderer! Lydon wins it. See how he presses on him! That blow on the temple would have crushed an ox! It has crushed Tetraides. He falls again—he cannot move—*habet!—habet!*"

"*Habet!*" repeated Pansa. "Take them out, give them the armour and swords."

"Noble editor," said the officers, "we fear that Tetraides will not recover in time; howbeit, we will try."

"Do so."

In a few minutes the officers, who had dragged off the stunned and insensible gladiator, returned with rueful countenances. They feared for his life; he was utterly incapacitated from re-entering the arena.

"In that case," said Pansa, "hold Lydon a *subdititius*; and the first gladiator that is vanquished, let Lydon supply his place with the victor."

The people shouted their applause at this sentence; then they again sank into deep silence. The trumpet sounded loudly. The four combatants stood each against each in prepared and stern array.

"Dost thou recognize the Romans, my Clodius; are they among the celebrated, or are they merely *ordinarii?*"

"Eumolpus is a good second-rate swordsman, my Lepidus. Nepimus, the lesser man, I have never seen before; but he is the son of one of the imperial fiscales, and brought up in a proper school; doubtless they will show sport, but I have no heart for the game; I cannot win back my money—I am undone. Curses on that Lydon! Who could have supposed he was so dexterous or so lucky?"

"Well, Clodius, shall I take compassion on you, and accept your own terms with these Romans?"

"An even ten sestertia on Eumolpus, then?"

"What! When Nepimus is untried? Nay, nay; that is too bad."

"Well—ten to eight?"

"Agreed."

While the contest in the amphitheatre had thus commenced, there was one in the loftier benches for whom it had assumed, indeed, a poignant—a stifling interest. The aged father of Lydon, despite his Christian horror of the spectacle, in his agonized anxiety for his son, had not been able to resist being the spectator of his fate. One amidst a fierce crowd of strangers—the lowest rabble of the populace—the old man saw, felt, nothing but the form—the presence of his brave son. Not a sound had escaped his lips when twice he had seen him fall to the earth—only he had turned paler, and his limbs trembled. But he had uttered one low cry when he saw him victorious; unconscious of the more fearful battle to which that victory was but a prelude.

"My gallant boy!" said he, and wiped his eyes.

"Is he thy son?" said a brawny fellow to the right of the Nazarene. "He has fought well: let us see how he does by and by. Hark! He is to fight the first victor. Now, old boy, pray the gods that the victor be neither of the Romans! Nor, next to them, the giant Niger."

The old man sat down again and covered his face. The fray for the moment was indifferent to him—Lydon was not one of the combatants. Yet—yet—the thought flashed across him—the fray was indeed of deadly interest—the first who fell was to make way for Lydon! He started, and bent forward, with straining eyes and clasped hands, to view the encounter.

The first interest was attracted towards the combat of Niger with Sporus; for this species of contest, from the fatal result which usually attended it, and from the great science it required in either antagonist, was always peculiarly inviting to the spectators.

They stood at a considerable distance from each other. The singular helmet which Sporus wore (the vizor of which was down) concealed his face: but the features of Niger attracted a fearful and universal interest from their compressed and vigilant ferocity. Thus they stood for some moments, each eyeing each, until Sporus began slowly, and with great caution, to advance, holding his sword pointed, like a modern fencer's, at the breast of his foe. Niger retreated as his antagonist advanced, gathering up his net with his right hand, and never taking his small glittering eyes from the movements of the swordsman. Suddenly, when Sporus had approached nearly to arm's length, the retiarius threw himself forward, and cast his net. A quick inflection of body saved the gladiator from the deadly snare. He uttered a sharp cry of joy and rage, and rushed upon Niger: but Niger had already drawn in his net, thrown it across his shoulders, and fled round the lists with a swiftness which the pursuer in vain endeavoured to equal. The people laughed and shouted to see the ineffectual efforts of the broad-shouldered gladiator to overtake the flying giant: when, at that moment, their attention was turned from these to the two Roman combatants.

They had placed themselves at the onset face to face, at the distance of modern fencers from each other; but the extreme caution which both evinced at first had prevented any warmth of engagement, and allowed the spectators full leisure to interest themselves in the battle between Sporus and his foe. But the Romans were now heated into full and fierce encounter: they pushed—returned—advanced on—retreated from—each other with all that careful yet scarcely perceptible caution which characterizes men well experienced and equally matched. But at this moment, Eumolpus, the elder gladiator, by that dexterous back-stroke which was considered in the arena most difficult to avoid, had wounded Nepimus in the side. The people shouted: Lepidus turned pale.

"Ho!" said Clodius, "the game is nearly over. If Eumolpus fights now the quiet fight, the other will gradually bleed himself away."

"But, thank the gods! He does not fight the backward fight. See! He presses hard upon Nepimus. By Mars! But Nepimus had him there! The helmet rang again!—Clodius, I shall win!"

"Why do I ever bet but at the dice?" groaned Clodius, to himself—"or why cannot one cog a gladiator?"

"A Sporus!—a Sporus!" shouted the populace, as Niger, now having suddenly paused, had again cast his net, and again unsuccessfully. He had not retreated this time with sufficient agility—the sword of Sporus had inflicted a severe wound upon his right leg; and, incapacitated to fly, he was pressed hard by the fierce swordsman. His great height and length of arm still continued, however, to give him no despicable advantages: and steadily keeping his trident at the front of his foe, he repelled him successfully for several minutes. Sporus now tried, by great rapidity of revolution, to get round his antagonist, who necessarily moved with pain and slowness. In so doing, he lost his caution—he advanced too near to the giant—raised his arm to strike, and received the three points of the fatal spear full in his breast. He sank on his knee. In a moment more, the deadly net was cast over him—he struggled against its meshes in vain; again—again—again—he writhed mutely beneath the fresh strokes of the trident—his blood flowed fast through the net and redly over the sand. He lowered his arms in acknowledgment of defeat.

The conquering retiarius withdrew his net, and, leaning on his spear, looked to the audience for their judgment. Slowly, too, at the same moment, the vanquished gladiator rolled his dim and despairing eyes round the theatre. From row to row, from bench to bench, there glared upon him but merciless and unpitying eyes.

Hushed was the roar—the murmur! The silence was dread, for in it was no sympathy; not a hand—no, not even a woman's hand— gave the signal of charity and life! Sporus had never been popular in the arena; and, lately, the interest of the combat had been excited on behalf of the wounded Niger. The people were warmed into blood— the mimic fight had ceased to charm; the interest had mounted up to the desire of sacrifice and the thirst of death.

The gladiator knew that his doom was sealed: he uttered no prayer—no groan. The people gave the signal of death! In dogged but agonized submission, he bent his neck to receive the fatal stroke. And now, as the spear of the retiarius was not a weapon to inflict instant and certain death, there stalked into the arena a grim and fatal form, brandishing a short, sharp sword, and with features utterly concealed beneath its vizor. With slow and measured steps, this dismal headsman approached the gladiator, still kneeling—laid the left hand on his neck—turned round to the assembly, lest, in the last moment, remorse should come upon them; the dread signal continued, the same: the blade glittered brightly in the air—fell—and the gladiator rolled upon the sand; his limbs quivered—were still, he was a corpse.

His body was dragged at once from the arena through the gate of death, and thrown into the gloomy spoliarium. And ere it had well reached that destination, the strife between the remaining combatants was decided. The sword of Eumolpus had inflicted a death wound upon the less experienced combatant. A new victim was added to the receptacle of the slain.

Throughout that mighty assembly there now ran a universal movement; the people breathed more freely, and resettled themselves in their seats. A grateful shower was cast over every row from the concealed conduits. In cool and luxurious pleasure they talked over the late spectacle of blood. Eumolpus removed his helmet, and wiped his brows; his close-curled hair and short beard, his noble Roman features and bright dark eyes, attracted general admiration. He was fresh, unwounded, unfatigued.

The editor paused, and proclaimed aloud that, as Niger's wound disabled him from again entering the arena, Lydon was to be the successor to the slaughtered Nepimus, and the new combatant of Eumolpus.

"Yet, Lydon," added he, "if thou wouldst decline the combat with one so brave and tried, thou mayst have full liberty to do so. Eumolpus is not the antagonist that was originally decreed for thee. Thou knowest best how far thou canst cope with him. If thou failest, thy doom is honourable death; if thou conquerest, out of my purse I will double the stipulated prize."

The people shouted applause. Lydon stood in the lists, he gazed around; high above he beheld the pale face, the straining eyes, of his father. He turned away irresolute for a moment. No! The conquest of the cestus was not sufficient—he had not yet won the prize of victory—his father was still a slave!

"Noble ædile!" he replied, in a firm and deep tone, "I shrink not from this combat. For the honour of Pompeii, I demand that one trained by its long-celebrated lanista shall do battle with this Roman."

The people shouted louder than before.

"Four to one against Lydon!" said Clodius, to Lepidus.

"I would not take twenty to one! Why, Eumolpus is a very Achilles, and this poor fellow is but a tyro!"

Eumolpus gazed hard on the face of Lydon; he smiled, yet the smile was followed by a slight and scarce audible sigh—a touch of compassionate emotion, which custom conquered the moment the heart acknowledged it.

And now, both clad in complete armour, the sword drawn, the vizor closed, the two last combatants of the arena (ere man would be matched with beast) stood opposite to each other.

It was just at this time that a letter was delivered to the prætor by one of the attendants of the arena; he removed the cincture—glanced over it for a moment   his countenance betrayed surprise and embarrassment. He re-read the letter, and then muttering: "Tush! it is impossible!—the man must be drunk, even in the morning, to dream of such follies!"—threw it carelessly aside and gravely settled himself one more in the attitude of attention to the sports.

The interest of the public was wound up very high. Eumolpus had at first won their favour; but the gallantry of Lydon, and his well-timed allusion to the honour of the Pompeian lanista, had afterwards given him the preference in their eyes.

"Holloa, old fellow!" said Medon's neighbour, to him. "Your son is hardly matched; but never fear, the editor will not permit him to be slain—no, nor the people neither; he has behaved too bravely for that. Ha! That was a home thrust!—well averted, by Pollux! At him again, Lydon! They stop to breathe! What art thou muttering, old boy?"

"Prayers!" answered Medon, with a more calm and hopeful mien than he had yet maintained.

"Prayers!—trifles! The time for gods to carry a man away in a cloud is gone now. Ha, Jupiter!—what a blow! Thy side—thy side! Take care of thy side, Lydon!"

There was a convulsive tremor throughout the assembly. A fierce blow from Eumolpus, full on the crest, had brought Lydon to his knee.

"*Habet!*—he has it!" cried a shrill female voice; "he has it!"

It was the voice of the girl who had so anxiously anticipated the sacrifice of some criminal to the beasts.

"Be silent, child!" said the wife of Pansa, haughtily. "*Non habet!*—he is not wounded!"

"I wish he were, if only to spite old surly Medon," muttered the girl.

Meanwhile Lydon, who had hitherto defended himself with great skill and valour, began to give way before the vigorous assaults of the practised Roman; his arms grew tired, his eyes dizzy, he breathed hard and painfully. The combatants paused again for breath.

"Young man," said Eumolpus, in a low voice; "desist; I will wound thee slightly—then lower thy arms; thou has propitiated the editor and the mob—thou wilt be honourably saved!"

"And my father still enslaved!" groaned Lydon to himself. "No! Death or his freedom."

At that thought, and seeing that, his strength not being equal to the endurance of the Roman, everything depended on a sudden and desperate effort, he threw himself fiercely on Eumolpus; the Roman warily retreated—Lydon thrust again—Eumolpus drew himself aside—the sword grazed his cuirass—Lydon's breast was exposed—the Roman plunged his sword through the joints of his armour, not meaning, however, to inflict a deep wound; Lydon, weak and exhausted, fell forward, fell right on the point: it passed through and through, even to the back. Eumolpus drew forth his blade; Lydon still made an effort to regain his balance—his sword left his grasp—he struck mechanically at the gladiator with his naked hand, and fell prostrate on the arena. With one accord, editor and assembly made the signal of mercy—the officers of the arena approached—they took off the helmet of the vanquished. He still breathed; his eyes rolled fiercely on his foe; the savageness he had acquired in his calling glared from his gaze, and lowered upon the brow darkened already with the shades of death; then, with a convulsive groan, with a half-start, he lifted his eyes above. They rested not on the face of the editor, nor on the pitying brows of his relenting judges. He saw them not; they were as if the vast space was desolate and bare; one pale agonizing face alone was all he recognized—one cry of a broken heart was all that, amidst the murmurs and shouts of the populace, reached his ears. The ferocity vanished from his brow: a soft and tender expression of sanctifying but despairing filial love played over his features—played—waned—darkened! His face suddenly became locked and rigid, resuming its former fierceness. He fell upon the earth.

"Look to him," said the ædile; "he has done his duty!"

"A true type of glory, and of its fate!" murmured Arbaces to himself, and his eyes, glancing round the amphitheatre, betrayed so much of disdain and scorn, that whoever encountered them felt his breath suddenly arrested, and his emotions frozen into one sensation of abasement and awe.

Again rich perfumes were wafted around the theatre; the attendants sprinkled fresh sand over the arena.

"Bring forth the lion, and Glaucus the Athenian," said the editor.

And a deep and breathless hush of overwrought interest, and intense (yet, strange to say not unpleasing) terror lay, like a mighty and awful dream, over the assembly.

47. Nydia's Letter

Thrice had Sallust awakened from his morning sleep, and thrice, recollecting that his friend was that day to perish, had he turned himself with a deep sigh once more to court oblivion. His sole object in life was to avoid pain; and where he could not avoid, at least to forget it.

At length, unable any longer to steep his consciousness in slumber, he raised himself from his incumbent posture, and discovered his favourite freedman sitting by his bed-side, as usual; for Sallust, who had a gentleman-like taste for the polite letters, was accustomed to be read to for an hour or so previous to rising in the morning.

"No books today! No more Tibullus! No more Pindar for me! Pindar! Alas, alas; the very name recalls those games to which our arena is the savage successor. Has it begun—the amphitheatre? Are its rites commenced?"

"Long since, O Sallust! Did you not hear the trumpets and the trampling feet?"

"Ay, ay; but, the gods be thanked, I was drowsy, and had only to turn round to fall asleep again."

"The gladiators must have been long in the ring."

"The wretches! None of my people have gone to the spectacle?"

"Assuredly not; your orders were too strict."

"That is well—would the day were over! What is that letter yonder on the table?"

"That! Oh, the letter brought to you last night, when you were too—too—"

"Drunk to read it, I suppose. No matter, it cannot be of much importance."

"Shall I open it for you, Sallust?"

"Do; anything to divert my thoughts. Poor Glaucus!"

The freedman opened the letter. "What! Greek?" said he; "some learned lady, I suppose." He glanced over the letter, and for some moments the irregular lines traced by the blind girl's hand puzzled him. Suddenly, however, his countenance exhibited emotion and surprise. "Good gods! Noble Sallust! What have we done not to attend to this before? Hear me read!"

"'Nydia, the slave, to Sallust, the friend of Glaucus! I am a prisoner in the house of Arbaces. Hasten to the prætor! Procure my release, and we shall yet save Glaucus from the lion. There is another prisoner within these walls, whose witness can exonerate the Athenian from the charge against him—one who saw the crime—who can prove the criminal is a villain hitherto unsuspected. Fly! Hasten! Bring with you armed men lest resistance be made—and a cunning and dexterous smith; for the dungeon of my fellow-prisoner is thick and strong. Oh! By thy right hand, and thy father's ashes, lose not a moment!'"

"Great Jove!" exclaimed Sallust, starting, "and this day—nay, within this hour, perhaps he dies. What is to be done? I will instantly to the prætor."

"Nay; not so. The prætor is the creature of the mob; and the mob will not hear of delay; they will not be balked in the very moment of expectation. Besides, the publicity of the appeal would forewarn the cunning Egyptian. It is evident that he has some interest in these concealments. No; fortunately thy slaves are in thy house."

"I seize thy meaning," interrupted Sallust. "Arm the slaves instantly. The streets are empty. We will ourselves hasten to the house of Arbaces, and release the prisoners. Quick! Quick! What ho! Davus there! My gown and sandals, the papyrus and a reed. I will write to the prætor, to beseech him to delay the sentence of Glaucus, for that, within an hour, we may yet prove him innocent. So, so; that is well. Hasten with this, Davus, to the prætor, at the amphitheatre. See it given to his own hand. Now then, O ye gods! Whose providence Epicurus denied, befriend me, and I will call Epicurus a liar!"

48. The Amphitheatre Once Again

Glaucus and Olinthus had been placed together in that gloomy and narrow cell in which the criminals of the arena awaited their last and fearful struggle. Their eyes, now accustomed to the darkness, scanned the faces of each other in this awful hour, and by that dim light, the paleness, which chased away the natural hues from either cheek, assumed a yet more ashy and ghastly whiteness. Yet they were erect and dauntless—their limbs did not tremble—their lips were compressed and rigid. The religion of the one, the pride of the other, the conscious innocence of both, and it may be the support derived from their mutual companionship, elevated the victim into the hero.

"Hark! Hearest thou that shout? They are growling over their human blood," said Olinthus.

"I hear; my heart grows sick; but the gods support me."

"The gods! O rash young man! in this hour recognize only the One God. Have I not taught thee in the dungeon, wept for thee, prayed for thee?—in my zeal and in my agony, have I not thought more of thy salvation than my own?"

"Brave friend!" answered Glaucus, solemnly, "I have listened to thee with awe, with wonder; and with a secret tendency towards conviction. Had our lives been spared, I might gradually have weaned myself from the tenets of my own faith, and inclined to thine; but, in this last hour, it were a craven thing and a base to yield to hasty terror what should only be the result of lengthened meditation. Were I to embrace thy creed, and cast down my father's gods, should I not be bribed by thy promise of heaven, or awed by thy threats of hell? Olinthus, no! Think we of each other with equal charity—I honouring thy sincerity—thou pitying my blindness. As have been my deeds, such will be my reward; and the Power or Powers above will not judge harshly of human error, when it is linked with honesty of purpose and truth of heart. Speak we no more of this. Hush! Dost thou not hear them drag yon heavy body through the passage? Such as that clay will be ours soon."

"O Heaven! O Christ! Already I behold ye!" cried the fervent Olinthus, lifting up his hands; "I tremble not—I rejoice that the prison-house shall soon be broken."

Glaucus bowed his head in silence. He felt the distinction between his fortitude and that of his fellow-sufferer. The heathen did not tremble; but the Christian exulted.

The door swung gratingly back—the gleam of spears shot along the walls.

"Glaucus the Athenian, thy time hath come," said a loud and clear voice; "the lion awaits thee."

"I am ready," said the Athenian. "Brother and co-mate, one last embrace! Bless me—and, farewell!"

The Christian opened his arms—he clasped the young heathen to his breast—he kissed his forehead and cheek—he sobbed aloud—his tears flowed fast and hot over the features of his new friend.

"Oh! Could I have converted thee, I had not wept. Oh! That I might say to thee: 'We two shall sup this night in Paradise!'"

"It may be so yet," answered the Greek with a tremulous voice. "They whom death parts now, may yet meet beyond the grave: on the earth—on the beautiful, the beloved earth, farewell forever!—Officer, I attend you."

Glaucus tore himself away; and when he came forth into the air, its breath, which, though sunless, was hot and arid, smote witheringly upon him. His frame, not yet restored from the effects of the deadly draught, shrank and trembled. The officers supported him.

"Courage," said one; "thou art young, active, well knit. They give thee a weapon. Despair not, and thou mayst yet conquer."

Glaucus did not reply; but, ashamed of his infirmity, he made a desperate and convulsive effort, and regained the firmness of his nerves. They anointed his body, completely naked save by a cincture round the loins, placed the stylus (vain weapon!) in his hand, and led into the arena.

And now when the Greek saw the eyes of thousands and tens of thousands upon him, he no longer felt that he was mortal. All evidence of fear—all fear itself—was gone. A red and haughty flush spread over the paleness of his features—he rose to the full of his glorious stature. In the elastic beauty of his limbs and form, in his intent but unfrowning brow, in the high disdain, and in the indomitable soul, which breathed visibly from his attitude, his lips, his eyes—he seemed the very incarnation, vivid and corporeal, of the valour of his land—of the divinity of its worship—at once a hero and a god!

The murmur of hatred and horror at his crime, which had greeted his entrance, died into the silence of involuntary admiration and half-compassionate respect; and, with a quick and convulsive sigh, that seemed to move the whole mass of life as if it were one body, the gaze of the spectators from the Athenian to a dark uncouth object in the centre of the arena. It was the grated den of the lion!

"By Venus, how warm it is!" said Fulvia, "yet there is no sun. Would that those stupid sailors could have fastened up that gap in the awning!"

"Oh, it is warm, indeed. I turn sick—I faint!" said the wife of Pansa; even her experienced stoicism giving way at the struggle about to take place.

The lion had been kept without food for twenty-four hours, and the animal had, during the whole morning, testified a singular and restless uneasiness, which the keeper had attributed to the pangs of hunger. Yet its bearing seemed rather that of fear than of rage; its roar was painful and distressed; it hung its head—snuffed the air through the bars—then lay down—started again—and again uttered its wild and far-resounding cries. And now, in its den, it lay utterly dumb and mute, with distending nostrils forced hard against the grating, and disturbing, with a heaving breath, the sand below on the arena.

The editor's lip quivered, and his cheek grew pale; he looked anxiously around—hesitated—delayed; the crowd became impatient. Slowly he gave the sign; the keeper, who was behind the den, cautiously removed the grating, and the lion leaped forth with a glad roar of release. The keeper hastily retreated through the grated passage leading from the arena, and left the lord of the forest—and his prey.

Glaucus had bent his limbs so as to give himself the firmest posture at the expected rush of the lion, with his small and shining weapon raised on high, in the faint hope that one well-directed thrust might penetrate through the eye to the brain of his grim foe.

But, to the astonishment of all, the beast seemed not even aware of the presence of the criminal.

At the first moment of its release it halted abruptly in the arena, raised itself to sniff the upward air with impatient sighs; then suddenly it sprang forward, but not on the Athenian. At half-speed it circled round and round the space, turning its vast head from side to side with an anxious and perturbed gaze, as if seeking only some avenue of escape; once or twice it endeavoured to leap up the parapet that divided it from the audience, and, on failing, uttered rather a baffled howl than its deep-toned and kingly roar. It evinced no sign either of wrath or hunger; its tail drooped along the sand, instead of lashing its gaunt sides; and its eyes, though they wandered at times to Glaucus, rolled again listlessly from him. At length, as if tired of attempting to escape, it crept with a moan into its cage, and once more laid itself down to rest.

The first surprise of the assembly at the apathy of the lion soon grew converted into resentment at its cowardice; and the populace already merged their pity for the fate of Glaucus into angry compassion for their own disappointment.

The editor called to the keeper:

"How is this? Take the goad, prick him forth, and then close the door of the den."

As the keeper, with some fear, but more astonishment, was preparing to obey, a loud cry was heard at one of the entrances of the arena; there was a confusion, a bustle—voices of remonstrance suddenly breaking forth, and suddenly silenced at the reply. All eyes turned in wonder at the interruption towards the quarter of the disturbance; the crowd gave way, and suddenly Sallust appeared on the senatorial benches, his hair dishevelled—breathless—heated—half-exhausted. He cast his eyes hastily round the ring. "Remove the Athenian!" he cried. "Haste—he is innocent! Arrest Arbaces, the Egyptian—HE is the murderer of Apæcides!"

"Art thou mad, O Sallust?" said the prætor, rising from his seat. "What means this raving?"

"Remove the Athenian!—Quick! Or his blood be on your head. Prætor, delay, and you answer with your own life to the emperor! I bring with me the eyewitness to the death of the priest Apæcides. Room there!—stand back!—give way! People of Pompeii, fix every eye upon Arbaces—there he sits! Room there for the priest Calenus!"

Pale, haggard, fresh from the jaws of famine and of death, his face fallen, his eyes dull as a vulture's, his broad frame gaunt as a skeleton—Calenus was supported into the very row in which Arbaces sat. His releasers had given him sparingly of food; but the chief sustenance that nerved his feeble limbs was revenge!

"The priest Calenus!—Calenus!" cried the mob. "Is it he? No—it is a dead man!"

"It *is* the priest Calenus," said the praetor, gravely. "What hast thou to say?"

"Arbaces of Egypt is the murderer of Apæcides, the priest of Isis; these eyes saw him deal the blow. It is from the dungeon into which he plunged me—it is from the darkness and horror of a death by famine—that the gods have raised me to proclaim his crime! Release the Athenian—he is innocent!"

"It is for this, then that the lion spared him. A miracle! A miracle!" cried Pansa.

"A miracle! A miracle!" shouted the people; "remove the Athenian—*Arbaces to the lion!*"

And that shout echoed from hill to vale—from coast to sea—*"Arbaces to the lion!"*

"Officers, remove the accused Glaucus—remove, but guard him yet," said the prætor. "The gods lavish their wonders upon this day."

As the prætor gave the word of release, there was a cry of joy—a female voice—a child's voice that rang through the heart of the assembly with electric force, and the populace echoed it back.

"Silence!" said the prætor—"who is there?"

"The blind girl—Nydia," answered Sallust. "It is her hand that has raised Calenus from the grave, and delivered Glaucus from the lion."

"Of this hereafter," said the praetor. "Calenus, priest of Isis, thou accusest Arbaces of the murder of Apæcides?"

"I do!"

"Thou didst behold the deed?"

"Prætor—with these eyes—"

"Enough at present—the details must be reserved for more suiting time and place. Arbaces of Egypt, thou hearest the charge against thee—thou hast not yet spoken—what hast thou to say?"

The gaze of the crowd had been long riveted on Arbaces: but not until the confusion which he had betrayed at the first charge of Sallust and the entrance of Calenus had subsided. At the shout: "Arbaces to the lion!" he had indeed trembled, and the dark bronze of his cheek had taken a paler hue. But he had soon recovered his haughtiness and self-control. Proudly he returned the angry glare of the countless eyes around him; and replying now to the question of the prætor, he said, in that accent so peculiarly tranquil and commanding, which characterized his tones: "Prætor, this charge is so mad that it scarcely deserves reply. My first accuser is the noble Sallust—the most intimate friend of Glaucus! My second is a priest; I revere his garb and calling—but, people of Pompeii! Ye know somewhat of the character of Calenus—he is griping and gold-thirsty to a proverb; the witness of such men is to be bought! Prætor, I am innocent."

"Sallust," said the magistrate, "where found you Calenus?"

"In the dungeons of Arbaces."

"Egyptian," said the prætor, frowning, "thou didst, then, dare to imprison a priest of the gods—and wherefore?"

"Hear me," answered Arbaces, rising calmly, but with agitation visible in his face. "This man came to threaten that he would make against me the charge he has now made, unless I would purchase his silence with half my fortune: I remonstrated—in vain. Peace there—let not the priest interrupt me! Noble prætor—and ye, O people! I was a stranger in the land—I knew myself innocent of crime—but the witness of a priest against me might yet destroy me. In my perplexity I decoyed him to the cell whence he has been released, on pretence that it was the coffer-house of my gold. I resolved to detain him there until the fate of the true criminal was sealed, and his threats could avail no longer; but I meant no worse. I may have erred—but who amongst us will not acknowledge the equity of self-preservation? Were I guilty, why was the witness of this priest silent at the trial?—then I had not detained or concealed him. Why did he not proclaim my guilt when I proclaimed that of Glaucus? Prætor, this needs an answer. For the rest, I throw myself on your laws. I demand their protection. Remove hence the accused and the accuser. I will willingly meet, and cheerfully abide by, the decision of the legitimate tribunal. This is no place for further parley."

"He says right," said the prætor. "Ho! Guards—remove Arbaces—guard Calenus! Sallust, we hold you responsible for your accusation. Let the sports be resumed."

"What!" cried Calenus, turning round to the people, "shall Isis be thus condemned? Shall the blood of Apæcides yet cry for vengeance? Shall justice be delayed now, that it may be frustrated hereafter? Shall the lion be cheated of his lawful prey? A god! A god!—I feel the god rush to my lips! *To the lion—to the lion with Arbaces!*"

His exhausted frame could support no longer the ferocious malice of the priest; he sank on the ground in strong convulsions—the foam gathered to his mouth—he was as a man, indeed, whom supernatural power had entered. The people saw, and shuddered.

"It is a god that inspires the holy man! *To the lion with the Egyptian!*"

With that cry up sprang—on moved—thousands upon thousands. They rushed from the heights—they poured down in the direction of the Egyptian. In vain did the ædile command—in vain did the prætor lift his voice and proclaim the law. The people had already been rendered savage by the exhibition of blood—they thirsted for more—their superstition was aided by their ferocity. Aroused—inflamed by the spectacle of their victims, they forgot the authority of their rulers. It was one of those popular convulsions common to crowds wholly ignorant, half free and half servile; and which the peculiar constitutions of the Roman provinces so frequently exhibited. The power of the praetor was as a reed beneath the whirlwind; still, at his word the guards had drawn themselves along the lower benches, on which the upper classes sat separate from the vulgar. They made but a feeble barrier—the waves of the human sea halted for a moment, to enable Arbaces to count the exact moment of his doom! In despair, and in a terror which beat down even pride, he glanced his eyes over the rolling and rushing crowd—when, right above them, through the wide chasm which had been left in the velaria, he beheld a strange and awful apparition—he beheld—and his craft restored his courage!

He stretched his hand on high; over his lofty brow and royal features there came an expression of unutterable solemnity and command.

"Behold!" he shouted with a voice of thunder, which stilled the roar of the crowd; "behold how the gods protect the guiltless! The fires of the avenging Orcus burst forth against the false witness of my accusers!"

The eyes of the crowd followed the gesture of the Egyptian, and beheld, with ineffable dismay, a vast vapour shooting from the summit of Vesuvius, in the form of a gigantic pine-tree; the trunk, blackness—the branches, fire!—a fire that shifted and wavered in its hues with every moment, now fiercely luminous, now of a dull and dying red, that again blazed terrifically forth, with intolerable glare.

There was a dead, heart-sunken silence—through which there suddenly broke the roar of the lion, which was echoed back from within the building by the sharper and fiercer yells of its fellow-beast. Dread seers were they of the Burden of the Atmosphere, and wild prophets of wrath to come!

Then there arose on high the universal shrieks of women; the men stared at each other, but were dumb. At that moment they felt the earth shake beneath their feet; the wells of the theatre trembled; and, in the distance, they heard the crash of falling roofs; an instant more and the mountain-cloud seemed to roll towards them, dark and rapid, like a torrent; at the same time it cast forth a shower of ashes mixed with vast fragments of burning stone! Over the crushed vines, over the desolate streets, over the amphitheatre itself—far and wide—with many a mighty splash in the agitated sea—fell that awful shower!

No longer thought the crowd of justice or of Arbaces; safety for themselves was their sole thought. Each turned to fly—each dashing, pressing, crushing, against the other. Trampling recklessly over the fallen—amidst groans and oaths and prayers and sudden shrieks, the enormous crowd vomited itself forth through the numerous passages. Whither should they fly? Some, anticipating a second earthquake, hastened to their homes to load themselves with their most costly goods, and escape while there was yet time; others, dreading the showers of ashes that now fell fast, torrent upon torrent, over the streets, rushed under the roofs of the nearest houses, or temples, or sheds—shelter of any kind—for protection from the terrors of the, open air. But darker, and larger, and mightier, spread the cloud above them.

49. One Who Would Not Fly

Stunned by his reprieve, doubting that he was awake, Glaucus had been led by the officers of the arena into a small cell within the walls of the theatre. They threw a loose robe over him, and crowded round in congratulation and wonder. There was an impatient and fretful cry without the cell; the throng gave way, and the blind girl, led by some gentler hand, flung herself at the feet of Glaucus.

"It is I who have saved thee," she sobbed; "now let me die!"

"Nydia, my child!—my preserver!"

"Oh, let me feel thy touch—thy breath! Yes, yes, thou livest! We are not too late! That dread door, methought it would never yield! And Calenus—oh! His voice was as the dying wind among tombs—we had to wait—gods! It seemed hours ere food and wine restored to him something of strength. But thou livest! Thou livest yet!" This affecting scene was soon interrupted by the event just described. "The mountain! The earthquake!" resounded from side to side. The officers fled with the rest; they left Glaucus and Nydia to save themselves as they might.

As the sense of the dangers around them flashed on the Athenian, his generous heart recurred to Olinthus. He, too, was reprieved from the tiger by the hands of the gods; should he be left to a no less fatal death in the neighbouring cell? Taking Nydia by the hand, he hurried across the passages; he gained the den of the Christian. He found Olinthus kneeling in prayer.

"Arise my friend!" he cried. "Save thyself, and fly! See! Nature is thy dread deliverer!" He led forth the bewildered Christian, and pointed to a cloud which advanced darker and darker, disgorging forth showers of ashes and pumice stones—and bade him hearken to the cries and trampling rush of the scattered crowd.

"This is the hand of God—God be praised!" said Olinthus, devoutly.

"Fly! Seek thy brethren! Concert with them thy escape. Farewell!"

Olinthus did not answer, neither did he mark the retreating form of his friend. High thoughts and solemn absorbed his soul; and, in the enthusiasm of his kindling heart, he exulted in the mercy of God rather than trembled at the evidence of His power.

At length he roused himself, and hurried on.

The open doors of a dark, desolate cell suddenly appeared on his path; through the gloom within there flared and flickered a single lamp; and by its light he saw three grim and naked forms stretched on the earth in death. His feet were suddenly arrested; for, amidst the terrors of that dread recess—the spoliarium of the arena—he heard a low voice calling on the name of Christ!

He could not resist that appeal; he entered the den, and his feet were dabbled in the slow streams of blood that gushed from the corpses over the sand.

"Who," said the Nazarene, "calls upon the Son of God?"

No answer came, and turning round, he beheld, by the light of the lamp, an old gray-headed man sitting on the floor, and supporting in his lap the head of one of the dead. The features of the dead man were firmly and rigidly locked in the last sleep; but over the lip there played a fierce smile—not the Christian's smile of hope, but the dark sneer of hatred and defiance.

Yet on the face still lingered the beautiful roundness of early youth. The hair curled thick and glossy over the unwrinkled brow; and the down of manhood but slightly shaded the marble of the hueless cheek. And over this face bent one of unutterable sadness—of yearning tenderness—of fond and deep despair! The tears of the old man fell fast and hot, but he did not feel them; and when his lips moved and he mechanically uttered the prayer of his benign and hopeful faith, neither his heart nor his sense responded to the words: it was but the involuntary emotion that broke from the lethargy of his mind. His boy was dead, and had died for him!—and the old man's heart was broken.

"Medon!" said Olinthus, pityingly, "arise and fly! God is forth upon the wings of the elements! The New Gomorrah is doomed!—Fly, ere the fires consume thee!"

"He was ever so full of life!—he *cannot* be dead! Come hither!—place your hand on his heart!—surely it beats yet?

"Brother, the soul has fled!—we will remember it in our prayers! Thou canst not reanimate the dumb clay! Come, come—

hark! While I speak, yon crashing walls!—hark! Yon agonizing cries! Not a moment is to be lost!—Come!"

"I hear nothing!" said Medon, shaking his gray hair. The poor boy, his love murdered him!"

"Come! Come! Forgive this friendly force."

"What! Who would sever the father from the son?" And Medon clasped the body tightly in his embrace, and covered it with passionate kisses. "Go!" said he, lifting up his face for one moment. "Go!—we must be alone!"

"Alas!" said the compassionate Nazarene. "Death hath severed ye already!"

The old man smiled very calmly. "No, no!" he muttered, his voice growing lower with each word. "Death has been more kind!"

With that his head drooped on his son's breast—his arms relaxed their grasp. Olinthus caught him by the hand—the pulse had ceased to beat. The last words of the father were the words of truth—*Death had been more kind!*

Meanwhile, Glaucus and Nydia were pacing swiftly up the perilous streets. The Athenian had learned from his preserver that Ione was yet in the house of Arbaces. The few slaves whom the Egyptian had left at his mansion when he had repaired in long procession to the amphitheatre, had been able to offer no resistance to the armed band of Sallust; and when afterwards the volcano broke forth they had huddled together, stunned and frightened, in the inmost recesses of the house. Even the tall Ethiopian had forsaken his post at the door; and Glaucus (who left Nydia without—poor Nydia, jealous once more, even in such an hour!) passed on through the vast hall without meeting one from whom to learn the chamber of Ione. Even as he passed, however, the darkness that covered the heavens increased so rapidly that it was with difficulty he could guide his steps. The flower-wreathed columns seemed to reel and tremble; and with every instant he heard the ashes fall crunchingly into the roofless peristyle. He ascended to the upper rooms—breathless he paced along, shouting out aloud the name of Ione; and at length he heard, at the end of a gallery, a voice—her voice, in wondering reply! To rush forward—to shatter the door, to seize her in his arms—to hurry from the mansion—seemed to him the work of an instant. Scarce had he gained the spot where Nydia was, than he heard steps advancing towards the house, and recognised the voice of Arbaces, who had returned to seek his wealth and Ione ere he fled from the doomed Pompeii. But so dense was already the reeking atmosphere that the foes saw not each other, though so near—save that, dimly in the gloom, Glaucus caught the moving outline of the snowy robes of the Egyptian.

They hastened onward—those three! Alas!—whither? They now saw not a step before them—the blackness became utter. They were encompassed with doubt and horror—and the death he had escaped seemed to Glaucus only to have changed its form and augmented its victims.

50. The Refuge of Diomed

The sudden catastrophe which had riven the very bonds of society, and left prisoner and jailer alike free, had soon rid Calenus of the guards to whose care the prætor had consigned him. And when the darkness and the crowd separated the priest from his attendants, he hastened with trembling steps towards the temple of his goddess. As he crept along, and ere the darkness was complete, he felt himself suddenly caught by the robe, and a voice muttered in his ear: "Hist!—Calenus!—an awful hour!"

"Ay! By my father's head! Who art thou?—thy face is dim, and thy voice is strange."

"Not know thy Burbo?—fie!"

"Gods!—how the darkness gathers. Ho, ho—by yon terrific mountain, what sudden blazes of lightning! How they dart and quiver! Hades is loosed on earth!"

"Tush!—thou believest not these things, Calenus! Now is the time to make our fortune!"

"Ha!"

"Listen! Thy temple is full of gold and precious mummeries!—let us load ourselves with them, and then hasten to the sea and embark! None will ever ask an account of the doings of this day."

"Burbo, thou art right! Hush! And follow me into the temple. Who cares now—who sees now—whether thou art a priest or not? Follow, and we will share."

In the precincts of the temple were many priests gathered around the altars, praying, weeping, grovelling in the dust. Impostors in safety, they were not the less superstitious in danger. Calenus passed them, and entered the chamber yet to be seen in the south side of the court. Burbo followed him—the priest struck a light. Wine and viands strewed the table; the remains of a sacrificial feast.

"A man who has hungered forty-eight hours," muttered Calenus, "has an appetite even in such a time." He seized food, and devoured it greedily.

"Wilt thou never have done?" said Burbo, impatiently; "thy face purples and thine eyes start already."

"It is not every day one has such a right to be hungry. O Jupiter! What sound is that?—the hissing of fiery water! What! Does the cloud give rain as well as flame? Ha!—what! Shrieks? And, Burbo, how silent all is now! Look forth!"

Amidst the other horrors, the mighty mountain now cast up columns of boiling water. Blent and kneaded with the burning ashes, the streams fell like seething mud over the streets at frequent intervals. And full, where the priests of Isis now cowered around the altar, on which they had vainly sought to kindle fires, and pour incense, one of the fiercest of those deadly torrents, mingled with immense fragments of scoria, poured its rage. Over the bended forms of the priests it clashed: that cry had been of death—that silence of eternity! The ashes—the pitchy stream—sprinkled the altars, covered the pavements, and half concealed the quivering corpses of the priests.

"They are dead," said Burbo, terrified for the first time, and hurrying back into the cell. "I thought not the danger was so near and fatal."

The two wretches stood staring at each other—you might have heard their hearts beat! Calenus, the less bold by nature, but the most griping, recovered first.

"We must to our task, and away!" he said, in a low whisper, frightened at his own voice. He stepped to the threshold, paused, crossed over the heated floor and his dead brethren to the sacred chapel, and called to Burbo to follow. But the gladiator quaked, and drew back.

"So much the better," thought Calenus, "the more will be the booty." Hastily he loaded himself with the more portable treasures of the temple; and thinking no more of his comrade, hurried from the sacred place. A sudden flash of lightning from the mount showed to Burbo, who stood motionless at the threshold, the flying and laden form of the priest. He took heart; he stepped forth to join him, when a tremendous shower of ashes fell right before his feet. The gladiator shrank back once more. Darkness closed him in. But the shower continued fast—fast; its heaps rose high and suffocatingly—deathly vapours steamed from them. The wretch gasped for breath—he sought in despair to fly—the ashes had blocked up the threshold—he shrieked as his feet shrank from the boiling fluid. How could he escape?—he could not climb to the open space; nay, were he able, he could not brave its horrors. It were best to remain in the cell, protected, at least, from the fatal air. He sat down and clenched his teeth. By degrees, the atmosphere from without—stifling and venomous—crept into the chamber. He could endure it no longer. His eyes, glaring round, rested on a sacrificial axe, which some priest had left in the chamber: he seized it. With the desperate strength of his gigantic arms, he attempted to hew his way through the wall.

Meanwhile, the streets were already thinned; the crowd had hastened to disperse itself under shelter; the ashes began to fill up the lower parts of the town; but here and there could be heard the steps of fugitives crunching them warily, or pale and haggard faces seen by the blue glare of the lightning, or the more unsteady flash of torches, by which they endeavoured to steer their steps. But, ever and anon, the boiling water, or the straggling ashes, mysterious and gusty winds, rising and dying in a breath, extinguished these wandering lights, and with them the last living hope of those who bore them.

In the street that leads to the gate of Herculaneum, Clodius now bent his perplexed and doubtful way. "If I can gain the open country," thought he, "doubtless there will be various vehicles beyond the gate, and Herculaneum is not far distant. Thank Mercury! I have little to lose, and that little is about me!"

"Holla!—help there—help!" cried a querulous, frightened voice. "I have fallen down—my torch has gone out—my slaves have deserted me. I am Diomed—the rich Diomed—ten thousand sesterces to him who helps me!"

At the same moment, Clodius felt himself caught by the feet. "Ill fortune to thee—let me go, fool!" said the gambler.

"Oh, help me up!—give me thy hand!"

"There—rise!"

"Is this Clodius? I know the voice! Whither fliest thou?"

"Towards Herculaneum."

"Blessed be the gods! Our way is the same, then, as far as the gate. Why not take refuge in my villa? Thou knowest the long range of subterranean cellars beneath the basement—that shelter, what shower can penetrate?"

"You speak well," said Clodius, musingly. "And by storing the cellar with food, we can remain there even some days, should these wondrous storms endure so long."

"Oh, blessed be he who invented gates to a city!" cried Diomed. "See! They have placed a light within yon arch: by that let us guide our steps."

The air was now still for a few minutes: the lamp from the gate streamed out far and clear: the fugitives hurried on—they gained the gate—they passed by the Roman sentry; the lightning flashed over his livid face and polished helmet, but his stern features were composed even in their awe. He remained erect and motionless at his post. That hour itself had not animated the machine of the ruthless majesty of Rome into the reasoning and self-acting man. There he stood amidst the crashing elements; he had not received the permission to desert his station and escape.

Diomed and his companion hurried on, when suddenly a female form rushed athwart their way. It was the girl whose ominous voice had been raised so often and so gladly in anticipation of "the merry show!"

"Oh, Diomed!" she cried, "shelter! Shelter! See"—pointing to an infant clasped to her breast—"see this little one!—it is mine! I have never owned it till this hour. But I remember I am a mother! I have plucked it from the cradle of its nurse. Who could think of the babe in such an hour but she who bore it?"

"Curse on thy shrill voice! Away, harlot!" muttered Clodius.

"Nay, girl," said the more humane Diomed. "Follow if thou wilt. This way—this way—to the vaults!"

They hurried on—they arrived at the house of Diomed—they laughed aloud as they crossed the threshold, for they deemed the danger over.

Diomed ordered his slaves to carry down into the subterranean gallery, before described, a profusion of food, and oil for lights, and there Julia, Clodius, the mother and her babe, the greater part of the slaves, and some frightened visitors and clients of the neighbourhood, sought their shelter.

51. The Progress of Destruction

The cloud, which had scattered so deep a murkiness over the day, had now settled into a solid impenetrable mass. It resembled less the thickest gloom of a night in the open air than the close and blind darkness of some narrow room. But in proportion as the blackness gathered, did the lightnings around Vesuvius increase in their vivid and scorching glare. Nor was their horrible beauty confined to the usual hues of fire; no rainbow ever rivalled their varying and prodigal dyes. Now brightly blue as the most azure depth of a southern sky—now of a livid and snake-like green, moving restlessly to and fro as the folds of an enormous serpent—now of a lurid intolerable crimson, gushing through the columns of smoke and lighting up the whole city from arch to arch—then suddenly dying into a sickly paleness, like the ghost of their own life!

In the pauses of the showers, could be heard the rumbling of the earth beneath, and the groaning waves of the tortured sea; or, lower still, and audible but to the watch of intensest fear, the grinding and hissing murmur of the escaping gases through the chasms of the distant mountain. Sometimes the cloud appeared to break from its solid mass, and, by the lightning, to assume quaint and vast mimicries of human or monster shapes, striding across the gloom, hurtling one upon the other, and vanishing swiftly into the turbulent abyss of shade: so that, to the eyes and fancies of the affrighted wanderers, the unsubstantial vapours were as the bodily forms of gigantic foes—the agents of terror and death.

The ashes in many places were already knee-deep; and the boiling showers which came from the steaming breath of the volcano forced their way into the houses, bearing with them a strong and suffocating vapour. In some places, immense fragments of rock, hurled upon the houses, bore down along the streets masses of confused ruin, which yet more and more, with every hour, obstructed the way; and, as the day advanced, the motion of the earth was more sensibly felt—nor could chariot or litter be kept steady, even on the most level ground.

Sometimes the huger stones, striking against each other as they fell, broke into fragments emitting sparks of fire, which caught whatever was combustible within their reach; and along the plains beyond the city the darkness was now terribly relieved; for several houses, and even vineyards, had been set on flame; and at various intervals, the fires rose sullenly and fiercely against the solid gloom. To add to this partial relief of the darkness, the citizens had in the more public places, such as the porticoes of temples and the entrances to the forum, endeavoured to place rows of torches; but these rarely continued long; the showers and the winds extinguished them, and the sudden darkness into which their fitful light was converted had something in it doubly terrible and doubly impressive, of the impotence of human hope, the lesser; of despair.

Frequently, by the momentary light of these torches, parties of fugitives encountered each other, some hurrying toward the sea, others flying back to the land; for the ocean had retreated rapidly from the shore—an utter darkness lay over it, and, upon its groaning and tossing waves, the storm of cinders and rocks fell without the protection which the streets and roofs afforded to the land. Wild—haggard—ghastly with supernatural fears, these groups encountered each other, but without the leisure to speak, to consult, to advise; for the showers fell now frequently, though not continuously, extinguishing lights, which showed to each band the death-like faces of the other, and hurrying all to seek refuge beneath the nearest shelter. The elements of civilizations were broken up. If, in the darkness, wife were separated from husband, or parent from child, vain was the hope of reunion. Each hurried blindly and confusedly on. Nothing in all the various and complicated machinery of social life was left save the primal law of self-preservation.

Through this awful scene did the Athenian wade his way, accompanied by Ione and the blind girl. Suddenly, a rush of hundreds, in their path to the sea, swept by them. Nydia was torn from the side of Glaucus, who, with Ione, was borne rapidly onward; and when the crowd (whose forms they saw not, so thick was the gloom) were gone, Nydia was still separated from their side. Glaucus shouted her name. No answer came. They retraced their steps—in vain: they could not discover her—it was evident she had been swept along in some opposite direction by the human current. Their friend, their preserver, was lost! And hitherto Nydia had been their guide. *Her blindness rendered the scene familiar to her alone.* Accustomed, through a perpetual night, to thread the windings of the city, she had led them unerringly towards the sea-shore, by which they had resolved to hazard an escape. Now, which way could they wend? All was rayless to them—a maze without a clue. Wearied, despondent, bewildered, they passed along, the ashes falling upon their heads, the fragmentary stones dashing up in sparkles before their feet.

"Alas!" murmured Ione, "I can go no farther; my steps sink among the scorching cinders. Fly, dearest!—beloved, fly! And leave me to my fate!"

"Hush, my betrothed! My bride! Death with thee is sweeter than life without thee! Yet, whither—oh! Whither, can we direct ourselves through the gloom? Already, it seems that we have made but a circle, and are at the very spot which we quitted an hour ago."

"O gods! Yon rock—see, it hath riven the roof before us! It is death to move through the streets!"

"Blessed lightning! See, Ione—see! The portico of the Temple of Fortune. Let us creep beneath it; it will protect us from the showers."

He caught his beloved in his arms, and with difficulty and labour gained the temple. He bore her to the remoter and more sheltered part of the portico, and leaned over her, that he might shield her, with his own form, from the lightning and the shower. For the unselfishness of love could hallow even that dismal time.

"Who is there?" said the trembling and hollow voice of one who had preceded them in their place of refuge. "Yet, what matters?—the crush of the ruined world forbids to us friends or foes."

Ione turned at the sound of the voice, and, with a faint cry, cowered again beneath the arms of Glaucus: and he, looking in the direction of the voice, beheld the cause of her alarm. Through the darkness glared forth two burning eyes—the lightning flashed and lingered athwart the temple—and Glaucus, with a shudder, perceived the lion to which he had been doomed couched beneath the pillars;—and, close beside it, unwitting of the vicinity, lay the giant form of him who had accosted them—the wounded gladiator, Niger.

That lightning had revealed to each other the form of beast and man; yet the instinct of both was quelled. Nay, the lion crept near and nearer to the gladiator as for companionship; and the gladiator did not recede or tremble. The revolution of Nature had dissolved her lighter terrors as well as her wonted ties.

While they were thus terribly protected, a group of men and women, bearing torches, passed by the temple. They were of the congregation of the Nazarenes, and a sublime and unearthly emotion had not, indeed, quelled their awe, but it had robbed them of fear. They had long believed, according to the error of the early Christians, that the Last Day was at hand; they imagined now that it had come.

"Woe! Woe!" cried, in a shrill and piercing voice, the elder at their head. "Behold! The Lord descendeth to judgment! He maketh fire come down from heaven in the sight of men! Woe! Woe! Ye strong and mighty! Woe to ye of the fasces and the purple! Woe to the idolater and the worshipper of the beast! Woe to ye who pour forth the blood of saints, and gloat over the death-pangs of the sons of God! Woe to the harlot of the sea!—woe! Woe!"

And with a loud and deep chorus, the troop chanted forth along the wild horrors of the air: "Woe to the harlot of the sea!—woe! Woe!"

The Nazarenes paced slowly on, their torches still flickering in the storm, their voices still raised in menace and solemn warning, till, as they were lost amid the winding of the streets, the darkness of the atmosphere and the silence of death again fell over the scene.

There was one of the frequent pauses in the showers, and Glaucus encouraged Ione once more to proceed. Just as they stood, hesitating, on the last step of the portico, an old man, with a bag in his right hand and leaning upon a youth, tottered by. The youth bore a torch. Glaucus recognized the two as father and son—miser and prodigal.

"Father," said the youth, "if you cannot move more swiftly, I must leave you, or we both perish!"

"Fly, boy, then, and leave thy sire!"

"But I cannot fly to starve; give me thy bag of gold!" And the youth snatched at it.

Striking the old man to the ground, he plucked the bag from a relaxing hand, and fled onward with a shrill yell.

"Ye gods!" cried Glaucus: "are ye blind, then, even in the dark? Such crimes may well confound the guiltless with the guilty in one common ruin. Ione, on!—on!"

52. Glaucus and Arbaces

Advancing, as men grope for escape in a dungeon. Ione and her lover continued their uncertain way. At the moments when the volcanic lightnings lingered over the streets, they were enabled by that awful light, to steer and guide their progress: yet little did the view it presented cheer or encourage their path. In parts, where the ashes lay dry and unmixed with the boiling torrents cast upwards from the mountain at capricious intervals, the surface of the earth presented a leprous and ghastly white. In other places, cinder and rock lay matted in heaps, from beneath which emerged the half-hid limbs of some crushed and mangled fugitive. The groans of the dying were broken by wild shrieks of women's terror—now near, now distant—which, when heard in the utter darkness, were rendered doubly appalling by the crushing sense of helplessness and the uncertainty of the perils around; and clear and distinct through all were the mighty and various noises from the Fatal Mountain; its rushing winds; its whirling torrents; and, from time to time, the burst and roar of some more fiery and fierce explosion. And ever as the winds swept howling along the street, they bore sharp streams of burning dust, and such sickening and poisonous vapours as took away, for the instant, breath and consciousness, followed by a rapid revulsion of the arrested blood, and a tingling sensation of agony trembling through every nerve and fibre of the frame.

"Oh, Glaucus! my beloved! My own! Take me to thy arms! One last embrace!—I can no more!"

"For my sake—for my life—courage, Ione—my life is linked with thine; and see—torches—this way! Lo! How they brave the wind! Ha! They live through the storm—doubtless, fugitives to the sea!—we will join them."

As if to aid and reanimate the lovers, the winds and showers came to a sudden pause; the atmosphere was profoundly still—the mountain seemed at rest, gathering, perhaps, fresh fury for its next burst: the torch-bearers moved quickly on. "We are nearing the sea," said, in a calm voice, the person at their head. "Liberty and wealth to each slave who survives this day. Courage! I tell you that the gods themselves have assured me of deliverance. On!"

Redly and steadily the torches flashed full on the eyes of Glaucus and Ione. Several slaves were bearing, by the light, panniers and coffers, heavily laden; in front of them—sword drawn in his hand—towered the lofty form of Arbaces.

"By my fathers!" cried the Egyptian, "Fate smiles upon me even through these horrors, and amidst the dreadest aspect of woe and death, bodes me happiness and love. Away, Greek! I claim my ward, Ione!"

"Traitor and murderer!" answered Glaucus, "Nemesis hath guided thee to my revenge!—a just sacrifice to the shades of Hades, that seem loosed on earth. Approach—touch but the hand of Ione, and thy weapon shall be as a reed—I will tear thee limb from limb!"

Suddenly, as he spoke, the place became lighted with an intense and lurid glow. Bright and gigantic through the darkness, which closed around it like the walls of hell, the mountain shone—a pile of fire! Its summit seemed riven in two; or rather, above its surface, there seemed to rise two monster shapes, each confronting each, as Demons contending for a World. These were of one deep blood-red hue of fire, which lighted up the whole atmosphere far and wide; but *below*, the nether part of the mountain was still dark and shrouded, save in three places adown which flowed, serpentine and irregular, rivers of molten lava. Darkly red through the profound gloom of their banks, they flowed slowly on towards the devoted city. Over the broadest there seemed to spring a cragged and stupendous arch, from which, as from the jaws of hell, gushed the sources of the sudden Phlegethon. And through the stilled air was heard the rattling of fragments of rock, hurtling one upon another as they were borne down the fiery cataracts—darkening for one instant the spot where they fell, and suffused the next in the burnished hues of the flood along which they floated!

The slaves shrieked aloud, and, cowering, hid their faces. The Egyptian himself stood transfixed to the spot, the glow lighting up his commanding features and jewelled robes. High behind him rose a tall column that supported the bronze statue of Augustus; and the imperial image seemed changed to a shape of fire.

With his left hand round Ione—with his right raised in menace, and grasping the stylus which was to have been his weapon in the arena, with his brow knit, his lips apart, the wrath and menace of human passions arrested as by a charm upon his features, Glaucus fronted the Egyptian.

Arbaces turned his eyes from the mountain—they rested on the form of Glaucus. He paused a moment: "Why," he muttered, "should I hesitate? Did not the stars foretell the only crisis of imminent peril to which I was subjected? Is not that peril past?"

"The soul," cried he aloud, "can brave the wreck of worlds and the wrath of imaginary gods! By that soul will I conquer to the last! Advance, slaves! Athenian, resist me, and thy blood are on thine own head! Thus I regain Ione!"

He advanced one step—it was his last on earth. The ground shook beneath him with a convulsion that cast all around upon its surface. A simultaneous crash resounded through the city, as down toppled many a roof and pillar—the lightning, as if caught by the metal, lingered an instant on the Imperial Statue—then shivered bronze and column. Down fell the ruin, echoing along the street, and riving the solid pavement where it crashed. The prophecy of the stars was fulfilled!

The sound—the shock, stunned the Athenian for several moments. When he recovered, the light still illumined the scene—the earth still slid and trembled beneath. Ione lay senseless on the ground; but he saw her not yet—his eyes were fixed upon a ghastly face that seemed to emerge, without limbs or trunk, from the huge fragments of the shattered column—a face of unutterable pain, agony, and despair. The eyes shut and opened rapidly, as if sense were not yet fled; the lips quivered and grinned—then sudden stillness and darkness fell over the features, yet retaining an aspect of horror never to be forgotten.

So perished the wise Magician—the great Arbaces—the Hermes of the Burning Belt—the last of the royalty of Egypt!

53. Despair

Glaucus turned, caught Ione once more in his arms, and fled along the street, that was yet intensely luminous. But suddenly a duller shade fell over the air. Instinctively he turned to the mountain, and behold! one of the two gigantic crests, into which the summit had been divided, rocked and wavered; and then, with a sound, the mightiness of which no language can describe, it fell from its burning base, and rushed, an avalanche of fire, down the side of the mountain! At the same instant gushed forth a volume of blackest smoke—rolling on, over air, sea, and earth.

Another—and another—and another shower of ashes, far more profuse than before, scattered fresh desolation along the streets. Darkness once more wrapped them as a veil; and Glaucus, his bold heart at last quelled and despairing, sank beneath the cover of an arch, and, clasping Ione to his heart—a bride on that couch of ruin—resigned himself to die.

Meanwhile Nydia, when separated by the throng from Glaucus and Ione, had in vain endeavoured to regain them. In vain she raised that plaintive cry peculiar to the blind; it was lost amid a thousand shrieks of more selfish terror. Again and again she returned to the spot where they had been divided—to find her companions gone, to seize every fugitive—to inquire of Glaucus—to be dashed aside in the impatience of distraction. Who in that hour spared one thought to his neighbour? At length it occurred to Nydia, that as it had been resolved to seek the sea-shore for escape, her most probable chance of rejoining her companions would be to persevere in that direction. Guiding her steps by the staff which she always carried, she continued, with incredible dexterity, to avoid the masses of ruin that encumbered the path—to thread the streets—and unerringly (so blessed now was that accustomed darkness, so afflicting in ordinary life) to take the nearest direction to the sea-side.

Fate seemed to favour one so helpless. The boiling torrents touched her not, save by the general rain which accompanied them; the huge fragments of scoria shivered the pavement before and beside her, but spared that frail form: and when the lesser ashes fell over her, she shook them away with a slight tremor, and dauntlessly resumed her course.

Weak, exposed, yet fearless, supported but by one wish, she was a very emblem of Psyche in her wanderings; of Hope walking through the Valley of the Shadow; of the Soul itself—lone but undaunted, amidst the dangers and snares of life!

Her path was, however, constantly impeded by the crowds that now groped amidst the gloom, now fled in the temporary glare of the lightnings across the scene; and, at length, a group of torch-bearers rushing full against her, she was thrown down with some violence.

"What!" said the voice of one of the party, "is this the brave blind girl? By Bacchus, she must not be left here to die! Up! My Thessalian! So—so. Are you hurt? That's well! Come along with us! we are for the shore!"

"O Sallust! It is thy voice! The gods be thanked! Glaucus! Glaucus! Have ye seen him?

"Not I. He is doubtless out of the city by this time. The gods who saved him from the lion will save him from the burning mountain."

As the kindly epicure thus encouraged Nydia, he drew her along with him towards the sea, heeding not her passionate entreaties that he would linger yet awhile to search for Glaucus; and still, in the accent of despair, she continued to shriek out that beloved name, which, amidst all the roar of the convulsed elements, kept alive a music at her heart.

The sudden illumination, the burst of the floods of lava, and the earthquake, which we have already described, chanced when Sallust and his party had just gained the direct path leading from the city to the port; and here they were arrested by an immense crowd, more than half the population of the city. They spread along the field without the walls, thousands upon thousands, uncertain whither to fly. The sea had retired far from the shore; and they who had fled to it had been so terrified by the agitation and preternatural shrinking of the element, the gasping forms of the uncouth sea things which the waves had left upon the sand, and the sound of the huge stones cast from the mountain into the deep, that they had returned again to the land, as presenting the less frightful aspect of the two. Thus the two streams of human beings, the one seaward, the other from the sea, had met together, feeling a sad comfort in numbers; arrested in despair and doubt.

"The world is to be destroyed by fire," said an old man in long loose robes, a philosopher of the Stoic school: "Stoic and Epicurean wisdom have alike agreed in this prediction; and the hour is come!"

"Yea; the hour is come!" cried a loud voice, solemn but not fearful.

Those around turned in dismay. The voice came from above them. It was the voice of Olinthus, who, surrounded by his Christian friends, stood upon an abrupt eminence on which the old Greek colonists had raised a temple to Apollo, now time-worn and half in ruin.

As he spoke, there came that sudden illumination which had heralded the death of Arbaces, and glowing over the mighty multitude, awed, crouching, breathless—never had meeting of mortal beings been so stamped with the horror and sublimity of dread. And above those the form of Olinthus, with outstretched arm and prophet brow, girt with the living fires. And the crowd knew the face of him they had doomed to the fangs of the beast—*then their victim—now* their warner; and through the stillness again came his ominous voice:

"The hour is come!"

The Christians repeated the cry. It was caught up—it was echoed from side to side—woman and man, childhood and old age repeated, not aloud, but in a smothered and dreary murmur:

"*The hour is come!*"

At that moment, a wild yell burst though the air—and, thinking only of escape, whither it knew not, the terrible tiger of the desert leaped amongst the throng, and hurried through its parted streams. And so came the earthquake—and darkness once more fell over the earth.

New fugitives arrived. Grasping the treasures no longer destined for their lord, the slaves of Arbaces joined the throng. One of all their torches yet flickered on. It was borne by Sosia; and its light falling on the face of Nydia, he recognized the Thessalian.

"What avails thy liberty now, blind girl?" said the slave.

"Who art thou? Canst thou tell me of Glaucus?"

"Ay; I saw him but a few minutes since."

"Blessed be thy head! Where?"

"Couched beneath the arch of the forum—dead or dying!— gone to rejoin Arbaces, who is no more."

Nydia uttered no word. She slid from the side of Sallust; silently she glided through those behind her, and retraced her steps to the city. She gained the forum—the arch; she stooped down—she felt around—she called on the name of Glaucus.

A weak voice answered: "Who calls on me? Is it the voice of the Shades? Lo! I am prepared!"

"Arise! Follow me! Take my hand! Glaucus, thou shalt be saved!"

In wonder and sudden hope, Glaucus arose: "Nydia still? Ah! Thou, then, art safe!"

The tender joy of his voice pierced the heart of the poor Thessalian, and she blessed him for his thought of her.

Half leading, half carrying Ione, Glaucus followed his guide. With admirable discretion, she avoided the path which led to the crowd she had quitted, and, by another route, sought the shore.

After many pauses and incredible perseverance, they gained the sea, and joined a group, who, bolder than the rest, resolved to hazard any peril rather than continue in such a scene. In darkness they put forth to sea; but, as they cleared the land and caught new aspects of the mountain, its channels of molten fire threw a partial redness over the waves.

Utterly exhausted and worn out, Ione slept on the breast of Glaucus, and Nydia lay at his feet. Meanwhile the showers of dust and ashes, still borne aloft, fell into the waves, and scattered over the deck. Far and wide, borne by the winds those showers descended upon the remotest climes, starting even the swarthy African, and whirled along the antique soil of Syria and of Egypt.

54. The Fate of Nydia

Weekly, softly, beautifully dawned the light over the trembling deep—the winds were sinking to rest—the foam died from the glowing azure of that delicious sea. Around the east, thin mists caught gradually the rosy hues that heralded the morning; Light was about to resume her reign. Yet, still, dark and massive in the distance, lay the broken fragments of the destroying cloud, from which red streaks, burning dimlier and more dim, betrayed the yet rolling fires of the mountain. The white walls and gleaming columns that had adorned the lovely coasts were no more. Sullen and dull were the shores so lately crested by the cities of Herculaneum and Pompeii. The darlings of the Deep were snatched from her embrace. Century after century shall the mighty Mother stretch her azure arms, and know them not—moaning round the sepulchres of the Lost!

There was no shout from the mariners at the dawning light—it had come too gradually, and they were too wearied for sudden bursts of joy—but there was a low deep murmur of thankfulness amidst those watchers of the long nights. They looked at each other and smiled—they took heart—they felt once more that there was a world around, and a God above them. And in the feeling that the worst was past, the over-wearied ones turned round, and fell placidly to sleep. In the growing light of the skies there came the silence which night had wanted: and the bark drifted calmly onward to its port. A few other vessels bearing similar fugitives might be seen in the expanse, apparently motionless, yet also gliding on. There was a sense of security, of companionship and of hope, in the sight of their slender masts and white sails. What beloved friends, lost and missed in the gloom, might they not bear to safety and shelter?

In the silence of the general sleep, Nydia rose gently. She bent over the face of Glaucus—she inhaled the deep breath of his heavy slumber—timidly and sadly she kissed his brow—his lips; she felt for his hand—it was locked in that of Ione; she sighed deeply, and her face darkened. Again she kissed his brow, and with her hair wiped from it the damps of night. "May the gods bless you, Athenian!" she murmured, "may you be happy with your beloved one!—may you sometimes remember Nydia! Alas! She is of no further use on earth!"

With these words, she turned away. Slowly she crept along by the platform to the further side of the vessel, and, pausing, bent low over the deep; the cool spray dashed upward on her feverish brow. "It is the kiss of death," she said. "It is welcome." The balmy air played through her waving tresses—she put them from her face, and raised those eyes—so tender, though so lightless—to the sky, whose soft face she had never seen.

"No, no!" she said, half aloud, and in a musing and thoughtful tone, "I cannot endure it; this jealous, exacting love—it shatters my whole soul in madness! I might harm him again—wretch that I was! I have saved him—twice saved him—happy, happy thought!—why not die happy?—it is the last glad thought I can ever know. Oh, sacred Sea! I hear thy voice invitingly—it hath a freshening and joyous call. They say that in thy embrace is dishonour—that thy victims cross not the fatal Styx—be it so!—I would not meet him in the Shades, for I should meet him still with *her!* Rest—rest—rest!—there is no other Elysium for a heart like mine!"

A sailor, half dozing on the deck, heard a slight splash on the waters. Drowsily he looked up, and behind, as the vessel merrily bounded on, he fancied he saw something white above the waves; but it vanished in an instant. He turned round again, and dreamed of his home and children.

When the lovers awoke, their first thought was of each other—their next of Nydia. She was not to be found—none had seen her since the night. Every crevice of the vessel was searched—there was no trace of her. Mysterious from first to last, the blind Thessalian had vanished forever from the living world. They guessed her fate in silence: and Glaucus and Ione, while they drew nearer to each other (feeling each other the world itself) forgot their deliverance, and wept as for a departed sister.

55. Wherein All Things Cease

Letter from Glaucus to Sallust, ten years after the destruction of Pompeii.

Athens

Glaucus to his beloved Sallust—greeting and health!—

"You request me to visit you at Rome—no, Sallust, come rather to me at Athens!—I have forsworn the Imperial City, its mighty tumult and hollow joys. In my own land henceforth I dwell forever. The ghost of our departed greatness is dearer to me than the gaudy life of your loud prosperity. There is a charm to me which no other spot can supply, in the porticoes hallowed still by holy and venerable shades. In the olive-groves of Ilyssus I still hear the voice of poetry—on the heights of Phyle, the clouds of twilight seem yet the shrouds of departed freedom—the heralds of the morrow that shall come! You smile at my enthusiasm. Sallust!—better be hopeful in chains then resigned to their glitter. You tell me you are sure that I cannot enjoy life in these melancholy haunts of fallen majesty. You dwell with rapture on the Roman splendours and the luxuries of the Imperial court. My Sallust—*non sum qualis eram*—I am not what I was. The events of my life have sobered the blood of youth. My health has never quite recovered its wonted elasticity ere it felt the pangs of disease, and languished in the damps of a criminal's dungeon. My mind has never shaken off the dark shadow of the Last Day of Pompeii—the horror and the desolation of that awful ruin! Our beloved, our remembered Nydia! I have reared a tomb to her shade, and I see it every day from the window of my study. It keeps alive in me a tender recollection—a not unpleasing sadness—which are but a fitting homage to her fidelity, and the mysteriousness of her early death. Ione gathers the flowers, but my own hand wreathes them around this tomb. She was worthy of a tomb in Athens!

"You speak of the growing sect of the Christians in Rome. Sallust, to you I may confide my secret; I have pondered much over that faith—I have adopted it. After the destruction of Pompeii, I met once more with Olinthus—saved, alas! Only for a day, and falling afterwards a martyr to the indomitable energy of his zeal. In my preservation from the lion and the earthquake he taught me to behold the hand of the unknown God! I listened—believed—adored. My own, my more than ever beloved Ione, has also embraced the creed!—a creed Sallust which, shedding light over this world, gathers its concentrated glory, like a sunset, over the next. And as the earth from the sun, so immortality drinks happiness from virtue, which is the smile upon the face of God! Visit me, then, Sallust; bring with you the learned scrolls of Epicurus, Pythagoras, Diogenes; arm yourself for defeat; and let us, amidst the groves of Academus, dispute, under a surer guide than any granted to our fathers, on the mighty problems of the true ends of life and the nature of the soul.

"Ione is by my side as I write: I lift my eyes, and meet her smile. The sunlight quivers over Hymettus: and along my garden I hear the hum of the summer bees. Am I happy, ask you? Oh, what can Rome give me equal to what I possess at Athens! Here, everything awakens the soul and inspires the affections— the trees, the waters, the hills, the skies, are those of Athens—fair, though mourning—mother of the Poetry and the Wisdom of the World. In my hall I see the marble faces of my ancestors. In the Ceramicus, I survey their tombs. In the streets I behold the hand of Phidias and the soul of Pericles. If anything can make me forget that I am an Athenian and not free, it is partly the soothing—the love—watchful, vivid, sleepless—of Ione—a love that has taken a new sentiment in our new creed. This is the time type of the dark fable of our Grecian Eros and Psyche—it is, in truth, the soul asleep in the arms of love. And if this, our love, supports me partly against the fever of the desire for freedom, my religion supports me more; for whenever I would grasp the sword and sound the shell, and rush to a new Marathon (but Marathon without victory) I feel my despair at the chilling thought of my country's impotence—the crushing weight of the Roman yoke, comforted, at least, by the thought that earth is but the beginning of life—that the glory of a few years matters little in the vast space of eternity—that there is no perfect freedom till the chains of clay fall from the soul, and all space, all time, become its heritage and domain. Yet, Sallust, some mixture of the soft Greek blood still mingles with my faith. I can share not the zeal of those who see crime and eternal wrath in men who cannot believe as they. I shudder not at the creeds of others. I dare not curse them—I pray the Great Father to convert. This lukewarmness exposes me to some suspicion among the Christians: but I forgive it; and, not offending openly the prejudices of the crowd, I am thus enabled to protect my brethren from the danger of the law, and the consequences of their own zeal. If moderation seem to me the natural creature of benevolence, it gives also the greatest scope to beneficence.

"Such, then, O Sallust, is my life—such are my opinions. In this manner I greet existence and await death. And thou, glad-hearted and kindly pupil of Epicurus, thou—But come hither, and see what enjoyments, what hopes are ours—and not the splendour of imperial banquets, nor the shouts of the crowded circus, nor the noisy forum, nor the glittering theatre, nor the luxuriant gardens, nor the voluptuous baths of Rome—shall seem to thee to constitute a life of more vivid and uninterrupted happiness than that which thou so unreasonably pitiest as the career of Glaucus the Athenian!—Farewell!"

* * * * * * *

Nearly seventeen centuries had rolled away when the city of Pompeii was disinterred from its silent tomb, all vivid with undimmed hues; its walls fresh as if painted yesterday—not a colour faded on the rich mosaic of its floors—in its forum the half-finished columns as left by the workman's hand—in its gardens the sacrificial tripod—in its halls the chest of treasure—in its baths the strigil—in its theatres the counter of admission—in its saloons the furniture and the lamp—in its triclinia the fragments of the late feast—in its cubicula the perfumes and the rouge of faded beauty—and everywhere the skeletons of those who once moved the springs of that minute yet gorgeous machine of luxury and of life!

In the house of Diomed, in the subterranean vaults, twenty skeletons (one of a babe) were discovered in one spot by the door, covered by a fine ashen dust, that had evidently been wafted slowly through the apertures, until it had filled the whole space. There were jewels and coins, candelabra for unavailing light, and wine hardened in the amphoræ for a prolongation of agonized life. The sand, consolidated by damp, had taken the forms of the skeletons as in a cast; and the traveller may yet see the impression of a female neck and bosom of young and round proportions—the trace of the fated Julia! It seems to the inquirer as if the air had been gradually changed into a sulphurous vapour; the inmates of the vaults had rushed to the door, to find it closed and blocked up by the scoria without, and, in their attempts to force it, had been suffocated by the invading atmosphere.

In the garden was found a skeleton with a key by its bony hand, and near it a bag of coins. This is believed to have been the master of the house—the unfortunate Diomed, who had sought to escape by the garden, and been destroyed either by the vapours or some fragment of stone. Beside some other vases lay another skeleton, probably of a slave.

The houses of Sallust and of Pansa, the Temple of Isis, with the juggling concealments behind the statues—the lurking-place of its holy oracles—are now bared to the gaze of the curious. In one of the chambers of that temple was found a huge skeleton with an axe beside it: two walls had been pierced by the axe—the victim could penetrate no farther. In the midst of the city was found another skeleton, by the side of which was a heap of coins, and many of the mystic ornaments of the fane of Isis. Death had fallen upon him in his avarice, and Calenus perished simultaneously with Burbo. As the excavators cleared on through the mass of ruin, they found the skeleton of a man literally severed in two by a prostrate column; the skull was of so striking a conformation, so boldly marked in its intellectual, as well as its worse physical developments, that it has excited the constant speculation of every itinerant believer in the theories of Spurzheim, who has gazed upon that ruined palace of the mind. Still, after the lapse of ages, the traveller may survey that airy hall within whose cunning galleries and elaborate chambers once thought, reasoned, dreamed, and sinned, the soul of Arbaces the Egyptian.

Viewing the various witnesses of a social system which has passed from the world forever—a stranger, from that remote and barbarian Isle which the imperial Roman shivered when he named, paused amidst the delights of the soft Campania and composed this history.

ABOUT THE AUTHOR

SYDNEY FOWLER WRIGHT (1874-1965) penned over seventy volumes of science fiction, fantasy, classic mysteries, historical novels, poetry, and non-fiction, many of them being published by the Borgo Press Imprint of Wildside Press.

www.ingramcontent.com/pod-product-compliance
Lightning Source LLC
Chambersburg PA
CBHW020437270626
47155CB00022B/614